THE HANGWOMAN

THE
HANGWOMAN

Pavel Kohout

Translated from the Czech
by Káča Poláčkova-Henley

G. P. Putnam's Sons
New York

Original Czech title: *Katyně*
German language edition © 1978 by Reich Verlag, Lucerne
English translation © 1981 by G. P. Putnam's Sons and the Hutchinson
Publishing Group, Ltd.
Published simultaneously in Canada
by Academic Press Canada Limited,
Toronto.

Library of Congress Cataloging in Publication Data

Kohout, Pavel.
  The hangwoman.

  Translation of Katyně.
  I. Title.
PG5038.K64K313 1981   891.8′635   80-22407
ISBN 0-399-12416-0

PRINTED IN THE UNITED STATES OF AMERICA

*For Jürgen and Liza
who urged me for so long
to write this book
that it has finally been written!*
PK

THE HANGWOMAN

I

It was on Maundy Thursday that Lizinka Tachezy learned she had failed her entrance examination for the Drama Conservatory.

The chairman of the examination committee, a famous actor, informed her mother with unfeigned regret that the jury had made its decision only after a stormy session, following repeated auditions which showed that her daughter's shyness would make a career as a physician, scholar, or writer much more suitable for her.

On Good Friday they learned that Lizinka had failed to pass the high school entrance examination, which had been the alternate choice on her application for a secondary school education.

The principal, an eminent pedagogue, told her mother with genuine sorrow that the faculty had arrived at its conclusion only after a fierce debate following further tests which confirmed that, given her good looks, Lizinka would do far better as a model, a stewardess, or

1

an actress.

When Emil Tachezy, PhD, returned from work, he found only his daughter, sitting in a corner of the living room opposite the television, pressing buttons on the remote control. When she pressed one button, two men appeared on the screen, punching each other violently. When she pressed another, a children's chorus appeared, singing folk songs. When she pressed the two simultaneously, the screen went blank and began to buzz.

"How did it go?" asked Doctor Tachezy.

Lizinka shrugged her shoulders.

"Where is your mother?"

Lizinka nodded toward the bedroom.

Doctor Tachezy went out into the hall and gently turned the bedroom doorknob. The door was locked. After hesitating for a moment, he knocked. Not a sound. After a longer pause, he asked his wife through the closed door whether she didn't want a cup of tea or something.

At that, Lucie Tachezy stormed out of the bedroom, screaming that what she wanted most of all was not to live with a man who couldn't even arrange a proper education for his one and only daughter. Weeping, she locked herself in the bathroom.

Doctor Tachezy fried for his one and only daughter the one and only remaining egg—the rest of them had already been dyed for Easter—and sent her to bed. Then he started knocking on the bathroom door, while speaking gentle words of consolation to his wife. He was becoming increasingly worried by the silence. He didn't know where to turn off the gas heater, and he was sure there were razor blades and pills in the bathroom. He crossed to the telephone and began frenziedly to flip through the pages of the directory. He had lost contact with his family, he had no friends, and he was afraid of the police; in desperation he dialed the Crisis Line.

The psychiatrist on duty listened while he babbled his message, then asked, "Has she been in there long?"

"About two hours."

"Does she do this often?"

"No," said Doctor Tachezy. "Usually she locks herself in the bedroom."

"Where do you sleep when she does this?"

"Usually in the bathroom."

"Then sleep in the bedroom tonight. Make the most of it."

"Excuse me, but I have reason to fear that—"

"Excuse *me*, but this is my third nightshift in a row. Do you think she'd come to the phone?"

"I don't think so. I was wondering . . . that is, couldn't you come over . . .?"

10

"Hardly," said the psychiatrist. "I have to stay by the phone. We get lots of parents climbing the walls this time of year. Have you got a chisel?"

"What's *that?*"

"You're a philosopher?"

"A philologist."

"I see. How about telling her that the school inspector is on the line and wants to talk to her."

"Excuse me," said Doctor Tachezy, "but I never lie. It's a matter of principle."

"Doctor," said the psychiatrist, "someone may be trying to reach me at this very moment, someone I can really help. If you can still afford to have principles, your situation is far from hopeless."

Doctor Tachezy slowly replaced the receiver. Just then, his wife strode out of the bathroom. Her hair was freshly done and her face made up as if she were going to a ball. Without so much as glancing at her husband, she took a fancy little notebook from her purse, went to the telephone, dialed a number and waited, tapping her heel. Then she asked, in bell-like tones, "Oscar?"

"Yes," said Oscar. "Who's calling?"

"Lucie."

"Which Lucie?"

"Lucie Alexander."

Doctor Tachezy, standing by the bathroom door, swallowed hard at the use of her maiden name.

"Lucie Alexander!" said Oscar. "Well, this is fantastic! Lucie!"

"What are you up to, Ossi? Still single?"

"Well, you know how it is. What about you? Still married?"

"Well, you know how it is. I thought I might stop by for a drink."

From the bathroom door, Doctor Tachezy said, "Lucie—"

"Well, that'd be fantastic," said Oscar. "Except—"

"You're not alone."

"Well, you know how it is."

"I'd be happy to make it some other time," said Lucie. "Actually today I'm more in need of some advice."

"You need a car?" asked Oscar. "Or an apartment?"

"Neither. I have a daughter."

"Congratulations. You need a nursery school?"

"I've had her for fifteen years."

"Hm? Oh, sorry. You mean it's been fifteen— Well, that's incredible!"

"She was turned down by all the high schools she applied to. They thought she was either too pretty or too smart."

11

"So what does she need high school for?"

"I want her to make something of herself. I don't want her to wind up like I did."

"Lucie—" said Doctor Tachezy from the bathroom door.

"High school," said Oscar. "Dammit, who could . . . who can I . . . wait a minute, there's a commission or something for that . . . just a moment, sweetie—"

"You haven't called me that for a long time."

"Hm? Oh, sorry, I wasn't talking to you."

"More's the pity."

"Can it wait a week? Till I get back from the mountains? So we could take care of everything at once?"

"Could you at least remember the name of that commission?"

"I remember it now," said Oscar. "The Municipal Career Selection Advisory Commission. I can't recall the chairman's name, but feel free to mention mine. I was the one who got him a good deal on his houseboat."

"Thanks," said Lucie. "And, Ossi, run along now so you don't catch cold."

"How did you know?"

"Well, I know how it is. Tell sweetie that it was your aunt on the phone. And Happy Easter, Ossi."

She hung up and wiped away her glowing smile.

From the bathroom door, Doctor Tachezy said, "Who was that, Lucie?"

"Someone," said Mrs. Tachezy, "who once wanted to marry me. Do you mind?"

Her husband moved aside, clearing the way to the bathroom for her.

"Why did you phone him?"

"Because," said his wife, "if I hadn't been so stupid sixteen years ago, Lizinka's father would have been

2

him!"

"That's quite possible. Yes. Indeed, it is in fact probable," the chairman of the Municipal Career Selection Advisory Commission said dryly, "and it was doubtless the same houseboat that was the reason my predecessor had to resign."

This was what finally convinced Mrs. Tachezy that Lizinka's cause had not been blessed by a lucky star. Experience and habit had forced her to consider very carefully what she and Lizinka should wear. The conventions called for the suppression of all natural charms on such an occasion, especially when the official in charge was a woman. But this time the official was a man and, moreover—as Mrs. Tachezy knew only too well—the friend of another man who cultivated an almost pathological susceptibility to the charms of the fairer sex. And so she had decided against the usual and had put her money on the best cards she had.

She was wearing a couturier model from Paris, in a colorful *imprimé* design which emphasized her tiny waist, her full bosom, and her long neck. For Lizinka, she had selected a white sleeveless minidress, the color of snow just before dawn.

But she now realized with dismay that they would have done better had they worn nuns' habits.

The new chairman of the commission was a man who over the years had adapted to his thankless tasks the way medieval knights had grown used to wearing suits of armor. His head, with its prominent chin, rested on a rotund body without the benefit of a neck, which gave him an air of invulnerability. His immaculate fingers told Mrs. Tachezy that he was a nonsmoker, the slightly musty smell of his clothes that he was a bachelor. She could tell that he was entirely devoid of passion, that he had no use for bribes, and that he was afraid of women.

With him was his secretary, an elderly, bony woman who examined them sharply, turned her eyes away with revulsion, and proceeded to scribble a row of crosses in her notebook. The conclusion that Mrs. Tachezy drew was that the woman worked at the commission to compensate for her own failures in life through the failures of others, to which she contributed in no small degree.

The chairman never looked up. Having buried his predecessor with a single sentence, he indicated the vacant chairs with the back of his hand, opened Lizinka's file, and began to shake his head.

"Conservatory, of course . . . lyceum, of course, of course," he said with something akin to disgust, "simply a diploma at any cost, whether she has what it takes or not. Well, to be brief, dear lady: the only secondary school we have left that awards its graduates diplomas is the High School of Music for the Visually Handicapped, which, as I see here from the medical report, she unfortunately is not. So kiss a diploma goodbye and be glad of it! If you are truly fond of her, you'll see to it she learns a trade while she still has time. There's always money to be earned in a trade. But you must realize that getting into the conservatory, dear lady, is child's play compared to getting into the most popular trade schools, the ones for stewardesses or hairdressers. So that you can simply forget about those, too, and be glad of it! Why should a young and healthy girl like this," continued the commission chairman without raising his eyes, "wish to drown her years in permanent waves, or spend her life in airplanes when there are vocational establishments like the Gardening

School that can offer her solid ground under her feet and fresh air the whole year around? What do you say to that?"

"But she . . . can't stand the cold," said Mrs. Tachezy, coming up with the only excuse she could think of.

"Of course," said the chairman indulgently, "and what of it? There are more interesting careers than planting and hoeing potatoes in the rain and the mud. If she prefers warm temperatures, I can think of nothing better than the Bakers' Vocational Training School. Well?"

"She can't stand heat either," said Mrs. Tachezy, profoundly depressed.

"Of course, of course," said the chairman amiably, because he was approaching his target. "No problem! And why should she have to be up at three in the morning, come summer, come winter, for a measly pittance, when the Vocational Training School for Agriculture, Automatic Feeding Specialty, can offer her automated work in an equalized climate?"

"Good Lord!" said Mrs. Tachezy, feeling she was about to faint, "would you have *her* waiting on pigs?"

If she had shouted, or threatened or wept, he wouldn't have paid any attention, but because she whispered it in a strange, choked voice, as if the Good Lord were sitting with them in the office, the chairman unwittingly raised his head . . . and caught sight of Lizinka. As he gazed at her delicate elbows and knees, her still childish and almost translucent little face, deluged by a flood of long golden hair, he suddenly felt a strong blast of emotion and memory which propelled him back to a land of primal innocence. He could hear a voice he thought was gone from him forever. "Madonna!" his mother said in front of the cathedral one day. "Get down on your knees, my son—that's the Holy Virgin!"

He put down the questionnaire he had been holding and turned to the secretary.

"Give me," he said, "the Top Secret file!"

The bony woman shifted her gaze from her notebook to take another look at Lizinka, this time a worried one. She knew her boss and failed to understand what could have brought on such an unusual reversal. Reluctantly, she put down the pencil, walked over to the safe, and handed the chairman a folder with the inscription TOP SECRET. it contained a list of special fields for which requirements had been issued by several central institutions. Each was followed by a brief but precise definition of what was required of a prospective applicant.

An honorable man who had betrayed his conscience only once (when he had been obliged to deny his God so that he might serve his state), the chairman did not now intend to do anything contrary to his duty. Leafing through the various fields of study open to boys and girls, he scrupulously rejected all those for which Lizinka was not qualified by nature, education, or class origin, such as diplomatic courier, ambassador, or member of parliament. He paused at counterespionage, which had openings for three students. Another memory flitted through his mind: that of the young Greta Garbo in the role of Mata Hari. The image dissolved before his eyes when he realized that he had passed on to the section labeled SEX:M. He turned back a page. His glance fell on the final entry, the last in the SEX: F. section, the last one of all:

SPEC. FD. HUM. W/DIPL.: 9 YRS. ELEM (F)—

INSP. CONF. — OUTSTG. PUBL. COMPORTMENT—

PHLEGM NATURE—VERY PLEAS. APPCE.

Appended to the description was a parenthetical comment, the only one of its kind in the entire file: (THE KIND YOU'D LIKE TO ENCOUNTER AT THE DENTIST'S)

The chairman looked up again. No one could deny that Lizinka fulfilled the requirements in every respect. Indeed, he had never encountered a face that he would rather look up to from a dentist's chair, where he had suffered such unspeakable horrors. As soon as he was convinced that he was really acting in the public interest he was quick to make up his mind.

"Miss"—he turned directly to Lizinka—"wouldn't you like to be an executor?"

"What's that?" asked Mrs. Tachezy, reviving rapidly.

The chairman of the Career Selection Advisory Commission again buried his face in the papers.

"A special field of the humanities, with a diploma upon graduation," he said, after a brief look.

"And what sort of field?" the mother asked, quite blandly, so as not to extinguish the tiny flame of new hope.

Only then did he notice that there was a note attached to the announcement: APPL. CALL FOR APPT. PROF. WOLF, 61460.

"The applicant," he continued, "is to call Professor Wolf for an appointment. He will give you all the necessary details. Of course, I have to know whether you are at all interested, so that I can write you a referral slip. Well, now"—the chairman concluded impatiently—"gardener, baker, pig feeder, or—"

"Definitely!" exclaimed Mrs. Tachezy. "Definitely

3

executor!"

"What's that?" asked Doctor Emil Tachezy, when his wife finished her report of the interview.

They were sitting in the living room over their soup. Lizinka was observing her face reflected in the surface. When she submerged the spoon, the face wrinkled and puckered, when she took it out again, the face rippled out to the rim of the bowl.

"What do you mean, what is it? It's a field of the humanities that gives a diploma upon graduation."

"And roughly what sort of field?" asked Doctor Tachezy mildly, so as not to kindle the flame of a new conflict. He rose, stepped over to the bookcase, and began to turn the pages of the dictionary.

"It doesn't say much," he said. "'Executor . . . executor of a will . . .' But that's not a job. Cross reference to 'operate, to perform a labor or a function.'"

"A functionary," said Mrs. Tachezy. "All the better."

"It could as well be a call girl for all we know," said Doctor Tachezy.

"Lizinka," said Mrs. Tachezy, "finish your dinner, sweetheart, and go to bed. You need your beauty sleep."

No sooner had the daughter kissed them goodnight and closed the door behind her than the mother spoke, this time without raising her voice or shedding tears, which made the speech all the more momentous.

"The only thing you have ever done for your daughter," she said, "was to take advantage of my trust sixteen years ago. I had no idea that a man with a university degree would get me pregnant, and then I was convinced that he would at least be able to take care of the child. But you," she continued, with increasing matter-of-factness, making Doctor Tachezy realize how very critical the situation was, "are ashamed to even speak up when a bus driver shortchanges you, let alone offer a petty bribe so that your daughter can pass an exam. The only thing you offered me when her future was collapsing was a cup of tea. And when I go in your place and find one last chance for her, so she won't be reduced to herding cows, you tell me I'm making a whore out of her. I—"

She raised her voice a little, as if to challenge an objection that Doctor Tachezy hadn't even begun to contemplate.

"—don't know what an executor is, and I don't have to know—I'm satisfied that she'll have a diploma and that she'll be able to do whatever she wants with it. And if you want her to keep calling you Daddy, you'll phone that man Wolf tomorrow and make an appointment with him. And you'll do as any decent father would do and bring him a bottle of cognac. If he seems hesitant over the phone, you'll bring two bottles. And if," added Mrs. Tachezy, as a smile spread over her face, "you find yourself unable to do this, *I* will, and instead of cognac, I'll offer him everything a mother and a woman

16

can."

Friday morning, as soon as he had taken his place at his desk at the Language Center of the Academy of Sciences, Doctor Tachezy dialed 61460.

"Yes," said a voice at the other end.

"Hello," said Doctor Tachezy. "Would you be so kind as to connect me with Professor Wolf?"

"Who's calling?" asked the voice.

"Doctor Tachezy."

"I don't think I know you," said the voice.

Doctor Tachezy could feel his face getting hot. His usual reaction to people with powerful voices was to allow them to push ahead of him in lines or to bring him pork liver instead of goose liver, and he would pay without hesitation for the piece of pipe they'd wrap up for him instead of the fresh pike he'd asked for. He was about to stutter an apology and hang up when he realized that it was to this voice that he might be surrendering his beloved wife. With uncharacteristic boldness, he said, "Pardon me, but I'm calling about my daughter."

"Your daughter?" asked the voice.

"My daughter Lizinka," continued Doctor Tachezy and shut his eyes, feeling as if he were hurling himself over a cliff. "She and her mother went before the commission yesterday and they were given this number to call."

"Your number, please?" asked the voice.

"27 14 25," said Doctor Tachezy obediently. "Extension fifteen."

"Hang up," said the voice. "I'll call you back."

A click announced that he had hung up. Doctor Tachezy did the same and stayed at his desk, paralyzed by his own audacity. Then he realized that he had not only failed to achieve anything, but that he hadn't even asked when his call would be returned, so that in spite of his courageous effort he had nothing to report at home. The telephone did not ring again for some time. There was nothing for him to do but call again, a feat beyond his strength. But his dry scholarly mind, accustomed only to processing facts, suddenly projected an image. He saw his wife, larger than life, naked and desirable, sinking once again onto the grass, this time under the weight of a stranger's masterful body. He reached for the telephone. Just at that moment, it rang.

"This is Professor Wolf," said the familiar voice; it sounded pleasant now, almost friendly. "Forgive me, I had to verify what you told me. So you say you have a daughter. Would you say that she inspires confidence?"

"I think so," said Doctor Tachezy. "Every Christmas she collects for charity."

"Would you say she has excellent comportment in public?"

"I think she has. She was a most graceful Sleeping Beauty in her school play."

"May I assume then that her appearance is pleasant?"

"I think it is."

"And that her nature is on the phlegmatic side?"

"I'd say so."

"And would you say, Doctor," asked Professor Wolf, "that she is the kind of girl you would welcome encountering in an unpleasant situation? Say, at the dentist's?"

"I don't know," said Doctor Tachezy truthfully.

"You think not?" asked Professor Wolf, disturbed.

"I can't say, as I've never been to the dentist."

"Congratulations," said Professor Wolf, laughing with relief. "Dentists are worse than murderers. Except for mine, fortunately. But you don't deny the possibility that your daughter might have a calming influence on patients in a dentist's office?"

"I certainly wouldn't deny that possibility."

"Well, that's splendid. Splendid!"

"Of course," said Doctor Tachezy, "it isn't entirely clear to my wife and me just what field we're really talking about. That is why my wife asked me to arrange a meeting with you."

"The most important thing is to meet with the young lady," said Professor Wolf, "in order to test her."

"Might I ask in what area? So that she might prepare for your exams—"

"Not necessary. It's just a psychotechnical examination."

"Where should we bring her, then?"

"Have you got a bathroom?"

"I think so," said Doctor Tachezy, startled by the question. But he corrected himself immediately. "Yes, of course we have."

"We'll come to you, then. She'll feel more at ease in her own home, and we can talk in peace. Say tomorrow at half past two?"

"Tomorrow is Saturday."

"We work mainly on Saturdays," said Professor Wolf. "Please convey my kindest regards to your wife, and tell your daughter to have a good night's sleep. If she is a normal, healthy youngster, she'll succeed with one hand tied behind her

18

back."

"And what if there are two of them?" asked Mrs. Tachezy. "How are you going to cut the bottle in half?"

"Then they can drink it together here," suggested her husband.

"You certainly have some incredible ideas about bribery."

They were sitting in the living room with nothing to do but wait. Mrs. Tachezy smoked nervously, occasionally sprinkling some sugar on the marble cake. Doctor Tachezy examined his stamp albums, stopping every so often to clean his magnifying glass. Lizinka was watching a fly on the windowpane. When she closed her right eye, the fly seemed to be climbing a telephone pole. When she closed her left eye, the fly was creeping along a path in the grass. Opening both eyes and looking in a certain way, she could see two flies, while both the pole and the path dissolved.

"If somebody said to me, 'We'll come,' then I'd ask, 'Who?'" said Mrs. Tachezy.

"I understood it as the royal we," said her husband.

"For God's sake," said his wife, "why don't you put away those stupid stamps of yours?"

After her experience on Thursday, she was wearing a loose gray dress which concealed her waist, her bosom, and her neck.

"I'm sorry," said her husband in surprise. "I didn't know they bothered you."

He, in turn, was wearing a tailored suit, inherited from his father and altered. He had worn it for years for Saturday afternoon tea.

"They've only bothered me for about the last fifteen years," said his wife. "Lizinka, stop crossing your eyes!"

Lizinka abruptly stopped crossing her eyes. She was wearing a long skirt the color of her hair and a white blouse that lifted touchingly over her delicate little breasts.

Mrs. Tachezy sugared the cake again and lit another cigarette.

"Shouldn't you smoke a little less?" asked Doctor Tachezy with concern.

"It's the only luxury your wife can afford," said Mrs. Tachezy.

"I only thought that, what if he happens to be a nonsmoker?"

"You think so?" Startled, she stubbed out her cigarette, opened both windows, and waved the smoke out with both her hands. She glanced at her watch.

"It's one minute past half past," she said uneasily.

"It's a minute to," he reassured her.

A time signal sounded from somewhere, and at the same moment, so did their doorbell. Mrs. Tachezy picked up the ashtray and dumped it out the window.

Three men were standing in the hallway. They wore almost identical black overcoats, black hats, and white gloves. The first carried a bouquet of red roses. The second, a gift-wrapped cylinder. The third, a milk can and a massive suitcase.

"I am Professor Wolf," said the first, removing his hat and gloves. "Allow me, dear lady, to kiss your hand and present you with this small token of our respect."

He was a vigorous-looking man in his sixties, with deep-set eyes, his black mane and bushy eyebrows showing just a touch of gray. He evoked memories of enlightened country doctors from noble families that had come upon hard times.

"I'm pleased to make your acquaintance," said Mrs. Tachezy with the same charming voice she had used long ago when she had first met Doctor Tachezy. She sniffed the roses and regretted that she had not put on Thursday's dress. Without realizing it, she began to envy Lizinka.

"Allow me to present my assistant, Associate Professor Simsa."

"Simsa," said the latter, bowing and handing Doctor Tachezy the brown-wrapped cylinder. "We assumed you would like a good cognac."

He was Mrs. Tachezy's contemporary, shorter than she but athletically built, with close-cropped hair. Crow's-feet fanned out in the corners of his eyes, implying that he enjoyed a good laugh.

"That wasn't necessary," stammered Doctor Tachezy, extremely embarrassed. He began to be jealous of the assistant. In order to conceal it, he set down the bottle and hurried to help relieve the third man of his luggage.

"Allow me," he said, "to give you a hand, Mr.— Mr.—"

The stranger was a plump fellow of indeterminate age. His eyes were almost buried in his meaty face, from which only his broken nose protruded. The overall impression was one of an abandoned battlefield.

"That is Karli," said Professor Wolf, "our helper and chauffeur. Would you be good enough to show him the bathroom?"

"Yes," said Doctor Tachezy, "certainly, of course, naturally—"

He opened the door to the hall bathroom and switched on the light. Karli waited respectfully until the doctor stepped back and then set his load down beside the bathtub. He too removed his hat, and his shaven pate glistened. He bent over and, picking up the bottle, handed it to Doctor Tachezy.

20

"Karli," said Professor Wolf, "if we aren't out in fifteen minutes, take everything back, run along home, and pick us up at five sharp!"

"Thanks, chief," said Karli gratefully and turned to the others. "Good afternoon, goodbye, ma'am."

He replaced his hat and saluted. His immense hand flapped like an elephant's ear.

"May we take off our coats?" asked Professor Wolf.

"Heavens, Emil," said Mrs. Tachezy. "Help the gentlemen, won't you?"

Doctor Tachezy again put down the bottle but the professor and his assistant were too quick for him. Under their raglans they wore identical crimson jackets. The state insignia was embroidered on the left side of the chest. They looked like captains of the Olympic team, which reassured Mrs. Tachezy.

"You must forgive us, madame," said Professor Wolf, "we've come directly from work. But where is the young lady we've come to meet?"

"She's waiting in the living room," she said with an apologetic smile. "She's nervous, you see. No wonder, after all, she's still a child."

"If she takes after you, madame," said Professor Wolf as they entered the living room, "then there's nothing in life she need fear. Would you be so kind as to allow us to make her acquaintance?"

"Lizinka!" called Mrs. Tachezy.

The door opened. Lizinka stood framed in the doorway like a lovely portrait.

"This is our Lizinka," said Mrs. Tachezy with happy pride. "Lizinka, this is Professor Wolf and his assistant, Mr. Simsa."

Lizinka bent her knees a trifle in a polite curtsy. Professor Wolf and Mr. Simsa exchanged glances of unconcealed excitement, a bit like talent scouts. Doctor Tachezy felt quite uneasy.

"Emil," said Mrs. Tachezy, "ask the gentlemen to sit down!"

"No, no," said Professor Wolf, "first, would you kindly allow us to take the young lady to the

6

bathroom?"

"What are they doing to her in there?" Doctor Tachezy asked for the third time.

"For God's sake, calm down," said his wife for the third time. "Didn't you say she has to pass an exam?"

"In the *bathroom?*"

"Well, without the parents being present, at any rate."

"We could have gone into the kitchen, then," said Doctor Tachezy.

"They didn't want to put us out. That professor has something of the English lord about him."

"Whereas his assistant looks like a Casanova."

"That's just what you looked like when I met you."

"I might have looked a bit like him, but that's all."

"More's the pity," said Mrs. Tachezy.

From the bathroom, the sound of running water became audible through the two doors.

"They're running water in the tub," said Doctor Tachezy.

"Some sort of experiment," said his wife.

"In the bathtub?"

"Didn't you have to learn that Law? The one about the weight of water being equal to the weight of the body?"

"We didn't learn it in the bathtub."

"You mean you think they're giving her a bath in there or something?"

"It wouldn't surprise me."

"It may be too much for you to take in," said Mrs. Tachezy, "but there are some men left in the world who don't jump into bed with a girl the first time they meet."

"I'd like to remind you, once again, that I asked you first, quite formally."

Dull thuds were audible from the bathroom.

"What's all that pounding?" asked Doctor Tachezy.

"They must have dropped something," said his wife.

"Those were blows."

"Well, then, they're hammering something into the wall."

"Have you ever hammered something into the wall in somebody else's bathroom?"

From the bathroom came an inhuman screech.

"And what was *that?*" asked Doctor Tachezy.

"Somebody laughing," said his wife.

"Somebody screaming!" said her husband. "I'm going in there."

"For God's sake, don't make an ass of yourself!"

The sound grew louder.

"Why, that's a chicken!" exclaimed Doctor Tachezy.

"Now you've really lost your mind!" said his wife.

The sound stopped suddenly.

"I don't care what you say," said Doctor Tachezy, "that was a chicken."

"For God's sake, what would a chicken be doing in our bathroom?"

22

"That's exactly what I want to know!"

"Emil, please, go back to your stamps! Lizinka's future is at stake here and you're letting it get on your nerves."

"If you say so," said her husband. "But if she loses that—future—in our own bathroom, you've only yourself to blame! I wash my hands of the whole thing."

"That's what you've always done, as long as I've known you. Next to you, Pontius Pilate was a mere amateur!"

Just then came the sound of the bathroom door opening, followed by the sound of men's voices. Then the door to the living room opened too. Professor Wolf and Mr. Simsa stood in the doorway. In the bathroom, the shower was running.

"Gentlemen," said Doctor Tachezy, "it's high time you told us what this is all about!"

"There's a problem . . ." said Professor Wolf.

Mrs. Tachezy turned pale.

"The problem is that we neglected to bring any champagne to celebrate," grinned Mr. Simsa.

Mrs. Tachezy broke into a smile too. Professor Wolf stepped over to the parents and solemnly shook their hands.

"Congratulations. Congratulations. Your Lizinka has passed with flying colors. We shall have to toast her success with cognac."

Mr. Simsa had already torn the wrapping paper from the bottle.

"I knew it," said Mrs. Tachezy, controlling her emotions. "Emil, I told you so!"

"Gentlemen," repeated Doctor Tachezy in a burst of impatience, "are we finally going to find out—"

"Precisely why we are here, Doctor," said the Professor, placing a friendly hand on his shoulder. "But wouldn't it be better if we waited for Lizinka?"

"And where is she?" asked Doctor Tachezy.

"She's washing out the bathtub," said Professor Wolf. "But I suppose there's no harm in our having a drink without her, after all."

Meanwhile, Mrs. Tachezy had taken her best crystal goblets out of the china cabinet, and Mr. Simsa had filled them with the Courvoisier. Professor Wolf raised his glass with a hand so steady that the surface didn't even ripple.

"Life," he said, "has denied me your good fortune, Doctor. I have no children. But my work has given me the opportunity to observe a great deal. That is why I'm able to empathize with the feelings of parents whose only daughter is standing at the most decisive crossroads of her life. Here's to her success along the path on which she has taken her first step today!"

Both the Professor and his assistant stood at attention, nodded their heads, and emptied their glasses. Mrs. Tachezy joined them spontaneously. Doctor Tachezy did the same, although he never drank that way.

"Excuse me, madame," said Professor Wolf, "would you mind if we sat down? We've been on our feet since half past four this morning."

Mrs. Tachezy was horrified.

"Good God!" she said. "Emil, offer the gentlemen a chair. Tell me, have you had anything to eat?"

"Thank you for your kindness," said the Professor, sitting down at the table. "We have had plenty to eat, but twice as much work as usual. The same old story—staff shortages."

"But you really told them off," his assistant said admiringly.

"I told them," said the Professor, "that it's the same as asking someone to play Hamlet and at the same time build the stage sets."

"And do makeup too!" added his assistant.

"Yes," said the Professor with disgust. "I'm horrified when I realize how easy it would be for a few foolish bureaucrats to snatch from mankind one of its oldest traditions. It was high time"—he motioned to his assistant to refill the glasses—"for some decent and influential people to grasp that fact. By the time Lizinka completes her studies, though, all this will be no more than an embarrassing footnote in the textbooks."

"You mean," asked Mrs. Tachezy, "you had some sort of rehearsal?"

"A rehearsal, a premiere, and a closing all in one," said Mr. Simsa.

"Is that worth the effort?"

"It all depends on your point of view," said Mr. Simsa, grinning. "For three of us it was, and for the other two it wasn't. Here's to them!" He laughed heartily. Professor Wolf and Mrs. Tachezy laughed too. Before Doctor Tachezy realized he was holding an empty glass, Mr. Simsa had refilled it.

"Gentlemen," he said for the third time; he had every intention of speaking out categorically, but only a whisper emerged.

"You have a lovely apartment," said the Professor, stepping over to the window. "The neighborhood is not very pleasant, though."

One window gave a view only of the windows of the houses opposite, the other of a field beyond the housing project, with a corner of the garbage dump.

"I'm forever telling my husband that," said Mrs. Tachezy, not removing her admiring glance from the Professor. "When Lizinka was still a child this place had its advantages, but now that she's grown up, it's quite dangerous."

"A woman can defend herself better than a man, though," said Mr.

24

Simsa. "Men are cowards. It sometimes takes four men to overcome a woman."

"But what if there are actually four?"

"Then she can only pray," Mr. Simsa said with a smile.

"Personally," said Mrs. Tachezy, "I'd skin them alive."

Professor Wolf turned to her with an irritated look. "Now, now," he said primly, "why would you skin them alive?"

"Well," she said, confused, "does a mother bring into the world and raise a daughter, only to have her assaulted by four hooligans who are going to get off scot free?"

"Oh, I see," said the Professor, relaxing. "I didn't realize to whom you were referring. Of course, you are right. And skinning alive, or flaying, was used officially in the sixteenth century under King Vladislav."

"Here's to King Vladislav, then," said Mrs. Tachezy, grateful that the momentary discord was dissipated.

"To King Vladislav!" repeated Professor Wolf, and rose to toast her and her husband.

Doctor Tachezy downed his drink in one gulp and Mr. Simsa refilled it immediately with a mischievous wink.

"King Vladislav," continued the Professor, "was actually a very interesting man. In the year 1509, he condemned one criminal to be shot from a cannon. Unfortunately neither skinning alive nor shooting criminals from cannons became standard forms of punishment here."

"Personally," said Mrs. Tachezy with conviction, "I would reinstitute them, for criminals like that."

As unaccustomed to drinking as her husband, she was beginning to think that it really was too bad. Alcohol multiplied her joy at her daughter's success, while the presence of these two interesting men allowed her to voice thoughts which usually went unexpressed.

"I," she continued, "I'd skin them alive with my own two hands, and every daughter's mother would kiss the hands that skinned them. It's a pity I'm not a man."

Her husband raised a languid hand in protest. It happened to be the hand holding the goblet. The Professor immediately raised his own in response, and glass clinked against glass.

"Precisely, Doctor!" he said admiringly. "We cannot but drink to your wife!"

Doctor Tachezy rose, emptied his glass, and sat down abruptly. The others remained standing.

"Madame," said Professor Wolf, "what you have just voiced must express the innermost thoughts of all women, but it is the rare exception who dares to say it aloud. Wasn't it women who comprised the largest audience to the executions at the guillotine? But even the French Revolution, which raised the act of execution to a civic ceremony, failed to eliminate the greatest injustice of all. Equality of rights still did not apply to one human activity, the very one that makes a human being most human. It took another two hundred years, until—"

continued Professor Wolf, gradually losing his cool restraint and beginning to take on the air of a romantic poet,

"—this very day. Before today, the privilege of legal retribution was, most illogically, reserved to men. A woman not only was prevented from applying her cold-bloodedness and wit to the administration of justice, even when sentenced to death herself, she could not receive the ultimate penalty from the hand of another woman. Such injustice and such backwardness, at a time when women are piloting spaceships and leading nations into wars! All the greater, then, is our joy that we four can be the first to greet the true culmination of our modern age. Thanks to enlightened souls who have dedicated their entire lives to this idea—"

"Thanks to *you,* Professor!" Mr. Simsa interrupted.

"No, no, my friend," said Professor Wolf, moved but firm. "We are only the deckhands to captains long since dead; they determined the course, it is we who have the joy of first exclaiming from the crow's nest: *Land ahoy!* For the first time in history, a dignified institution has been established in our field in which future practitioners can be educated. Today's date will enter history as the day when the sexual equality of executioners was established. And here she is—"

The door opened, and Lizinka entered, her usually pale skin rosy from exertion.

"—here she is, *the world's*

7

first hangwoman."

Mrs. Tachezy did not hear those last few words. Overcome by the occasion, she stepped up to her daughter and pressed the delicate face to her full breasts.

"My sweet Lizinka!" she said in tears. "My darling girl, you don't know how happy I am!"

Professor Wolf motioned to Mr. Simsa to refill the glasses.

"Indeed, Doctor," he said, "this is reason enough for a toast!"

Doctor Tachezy began to laugh.

"Oh, well done!" he said. "You really did do this well, didn't you!"

26

He laughed harder and harder until he began to hiccup. Although the expression on his face remained unchanged, it seemed as though he had begun to weep.

Mr. Simsa moved over to him, obviously intending to slap his back, but the Professor was quicker. He grabbed Simsa's hand and said, "You'd better not—"

Simsa nodded apologetically as he glanced at his open hand, its sharp edges indicating training in karate. Doctor Tachezy continued to hiccup and weep with laughter simultaneously. When he realized that he might choke, he scrambled up from his chair. After pausing a moment to allow the spinning room to settle down, he concentrated on finding his way through the narrow passage leading to the hallway and the bathroom.

For a moment he was startled to find himself in a winter landscape among a crowd of tobogganing children. Then he became aware of the fact that he was resting his forehead against a picture frame. He shut his eyes and shifted his head until it was touching the wall of the hallway, which led him like a train track safely to the bathroom.

There he removed his jacket and hung it meticulously right next to the hook. Then he carefully turned his tie around to his back so he wouldn't get it wet, leaned over the tub and, fumbling, turned on the shower. When the stream of cold water hit the back of his neck, he opened his eyes. His gaze was directed to another picture, this one a still-life, with chicken and carp. As the water flowed along his necktie, down the back of his trousers, he strained to decide who had painted it and how it came to be in the bathtub. Finally it dawned on him that it was not a painting at all, but in fact

8

a dead carp and a freshly slaughtered chicken.

"Out!" exclaimed Doctor Tachezy, reappearing in the doorway to the living room. Water was dripping from his hair, his shirt and trousers, but except for that, he looked surprisingly sober. Lizinka sat decorously in her mother's chair, while Mrs. Tachezy, who had set the table with the good china, was slicing the marble cake.

"For God's sake, Emil!" said Mrs. Tachezy, horrified. "What are you . . . and what have you got in your hand?"

"A chicken," said her husband. "Now shut up! You," he asked Wolf, "are you a professor?"

"Certainly, Doctor."

"Professor of what?"

"I am Professor of Executionary Sciences Wolf, and this is my assistant, Associate Professor of Executionary Sciences Simsa."

"You're hangmen!" said Doctor Tachezy furiously.

"Our diplomas, sir," said Professor Wolf with dignity, "are just as valid as yours."

"You're *hangmen*," exclaimed Doctor Tachezy, "and you're on your way from work!"

"Emil, get hold of yourself!" exclaimed his wife.

"Be quiet!" her husband barked at her. "And you two have the audacity to propose that my daughter go out and murder people?"

Professor Wolf rose. He no longer resembled a country doctor or a romantic poet. The very color of his jacket was like that of warm blood. He was on the verge of exploding, and the state insignia on his jacket lent his wrath a suprapersonal dimension.

Doctor Tachezy, however, was not intimidated. At that critical moment, he had finally attained full paternal stature and the defense of one's offspring is a source of greater strength than the interests of the state. Although he had never in his life struck anyone, he was ready now to strike down Wolf, with the dead chicken.

Wolf was too good a psychologist not to realize this. He avoided a confrontation by crossing the room to the bookshelf.

"Do you mind?" he asked, and without waiting for a reply, reached for the second volume of eight identically bound books.

"I could quote a number of experts in my field," he said, "but I will select one of those whom you yourself will recognize, Doctor Tachezy. You would certainly not accuse Alexander Dumas of being after your daughter's soul. So let's have a look at what he says on page 543 of *The Three Musketeers*: 'On reaching the bank of the river, the executioner approached Milady and tied her hands and feet. Then she broke her silence and cried, "You are cowards, you are wretched assassins, you need ten to murder one single woman."—"You are not a woman," said Athos coldly. "You do not belong to the human race, you are a demon, escaped from the hell to which you are about to return."—"Ah, my virtuous gentlemen," said Milady, "remember that he who so much as touches a hair on my head is in his turn an assassin!"—"An executioner may kill, madame, without being an assassin," said the man in the red cloak. "He is merely the last judge."'"

concluded Professor Wolf, snapping the book shut and replacing it on the shelf. "However, you are a theoretician, Doctor," he continued, "and you might raise the objection that a character in a novel simply reflects the opinion of the author. But set aside your emotions for a moment and follow me into the field of scholarship. You used the term hangman to give vent to your contempt. The very origins of the word in many languages would prove above all to you, a linguist, that the executioner entered our history as a messenger from ancient cultures. The modern-day genesis of the profession is best illuminated by the document *On the Origins of Executioners* by Rudolf Rauscher, published in 1930 in Lwow by Pierwsa Drukarnia, which says, and I quote: 'The origin of executioners in our lands dates back to the thirteenth century. Executioners were the *accusatores publici,* established by Otakar II, drawn exclusively from the old families of the nobility, who in time became judges and executioners as well.' I am certain, Doctor, that it did not escape you that, in this trinity form, executioners constitute all of jurisprudence, a full one hundred years before the first doctor of law received his education from the first European university. Nonetheless, to you, as to the Milady in the book, an executioner remains simply a murderer. How diametrically opposed to your viewpoint is that of your colleague, Joseph de Maistre, when in his *Soireés de Saint Petersbourg* he wrote his famous study of the executioner in 1821. I'll quote a fragment of it: 'A Consequence of This Prerogative,'"

The Professor turned to clarify this for Lizinka,

"a prerogative is any exclusive or special right or privilege of the ruler in which the common people have no share, for example, the punishment of criminals. All right, then, its consequence, and I quote, 'is the essential existence of an individual who will punish crime with penalties determined by human laws; and this individual does in fact emerge everywhere, without our being able to explain how; for reason can find no motivation in the nature of man which could force him to opt for this pursuit. What sort of an inexplicable being is it who before every other pleasant, profitable, honest, even honorable calling, gives preference to one that tortures and puts to death his neighbors? Is such a mind, such a heart, created like ours? Is there not something strange in it, something alien to our nature? As for me, I have no doubt about it; he is born as we are; but he is an exceptional being, for whom there must be a special designation in the family of man. He was created the way the world was created.' End quote. I apologize for any minor inaccuracies, which could be only in terms of syntax, since this was the subject of my dissertation, and before long I should be lecturing on it to your—"

the Professor turned to Mrs. Tachezy—

"—daughter. A particularly beautiful passage speaks of the relationship of an executioner to his work, and I quote: 'He arrives on the public square, filled with an immense crowd. He is brought a poisoner, a parricide or a heretic: he grasps him, stretches him out, binds him to the horizontal cross, raises his arm: suddenly there is a terrible silence, nothing can be heard but the sound of bones shattering and the screams of the victim. . . . He is finished: his heart is pounding, but with joy; he applauds himself, saying in his heart, no one breaks on the wheel better than—' "

continued Professor Wolf,

" '—I do.' After this illuminating description, de Maistre formulates his world-famous apotheosis, which should become the life's credo of every executioner, and which at examination time I will insist that every pupil know—"

Professor Wolf turned to Lizinka,

"—by heart, and I quote: 'All greatness, all power, all subordination in the world rests in the executioner; he is both the terror and the bond of the community of man. Remove this incomprehensible element from the world, and order becomes chaos, thrones collapse, society vanishes. God, who is the creator of sovereignty, is also the creator of punishment: he has established our earth on those two poles and about them he causes the world to rotate.' You, sir—"

Professor Wolf turned to Doctor Tachezy without the slightest hint of reproach or ridicule,

"—will certainly, in keeping with your nature, be a proponent of the thesis of Jean Jacques Rousseau's 'Man is born good, it is society that demoralizes him,' which is the basis of all so-called European humanism. It is no coincidence that in 1764, a mere two years after the publication of Rousseau's *Contrat social,* the infamous pamphlet by Cesare Beccaria entitled *Dei deliti e delle pene,* or—"

Professor Wolf turned to Mrs. Tachezy and translated,

"—*On Crime and Penalties,* was published in Monaco, attempting by means of a forced logical structure to prove that human life is not a property of which society may dispose, and suggesting, first of all, the abolition of capital punishment. But, as Goethe said,

Professor Wolf turned to Lizinka,

" 'Gray is all theory, but green the golden tree of life.' The French Revolution, putting into effect Rousseau's theory of a new society, in time could get by without Marat, without Danton, and Robespierre, yes, even without Rousseau. It could not, however, get by without the man who in three years practically eliminated a centuries-old society, citizen Charles-Henri Sanson, Executioner to revolutionary Paris. He is the hero of the well-known *Memoires pour servir à l'histoire de la révolution française,* which was published under his name, although it was discovered later that he let his name be used by a struggling young novelist named Honoré—"

Professor Wolf did not so much as give a dramatic pause,

"—de Balzac. That was the first in a splendid gallery of portraits of executioners. Contributors to which include masters like Sir Walter Scott as well as the Czech poet and writer Karel Macha, whose novella

30

Executioner even presents the hero as the last descendant of the royal family of the Premyslids. 'He was tall, slender,' writes Macha, 'his black curly hair covered his forehead down to his thick brows, under which sparkled two blazing eyes; the rest of his face was hidden by a black beard. A red cloak billowed over his black garb, and attached diagonally across his back was a broad—'"

Professor Wolf was quoting from the classic, and it seemed to Mrs. Tachezy that he was describing his own photograph as a student,

"'—sword with a long handle.' Incidentally, I believe that Krejci is mistaken in his study *The Symbol of the Executioner and His Victim in the Work of Macha,* when he views the separation of the functions of king and executioner as a sign of the disruption of the social order. On the contrary: the double-edged oxymoron with which they address each other, 'Royal Executioner!' and 'Executioner King!', resounds once again with the de Maistre polarity of these two fundamental social functions. Such is the approach of responsible artists, culminating in the great works of Kafka and Pär Lagerkvist, who quite deservedly was the recipient of a Nobel Prize. Such is the true portrait of the executioner. And even if some individuals were unworthy of it, this does not give you the right as a scholar to denigrate everything that thousands of honest executioners gave to their country and to mankind over the generations. For that matter, Doctor—"

Professor Wolf turned to Doctor Tachezy, and for the first time a delicate irony tinged his voice,

"—be perfectly frank: does every graduate of the philosophical faculty become a Schopenhauer? Some of them, indeed, have wound up justly in the hands of the executioner, who, on the other hand, is mentioned by every decent encyclopedia. Let me quote a representative German one, *Meyers Lexikon,* Leipzig 1964. Executioner: 'A professional person who carries out the death penalty imposed by a court in the manner prescribed by law.' That and only that is what your daughter is to do. In short, then, it is not a matter of her—"

Professor Wolf was addressing Doctor Tachezy, and for the first time, a mild touch of reproof tinged his voice,

"—murdering people, but rather that she be introduced to an area of human endeavor, certainly a most popular one, inestimably older than medicine, the law, not to mention philosophy. I, and my colleague here—"

Professor Wolf turned to Simsa,

"—and other pedagogues intend to turn over to her a wealth of knowledge which, as my short discourse has indicated, belongs among the keystones of civilization. Moreover, we want to impart to her our own wealth of practical experience, so that Capital Punishment does not become a livelihood for dilettantes, but rather again the domain of the best sons, and now the best daughters, of our age. Because—"

and Professor Wolf again spoke to Doctor Tachezy,

"—if you are a true humanist, you cannot close your eyes to the fact that in the course of any military campaign, be it a local revolution or a world war, many individuals are executed by people to whom hanging means literally that and no more. But believe me, there is a considerable difference between a noose breaking your neck instantaneously, or over a fifteen-minute period strangling you so slowly that you come near to flapping yourself to death. Today, for example, my assistant Mr. Simsa worked so adroitly that the attending physician was able to declare his patient dead in twenty-eight seconds."

"You were better by three seconds!" said Mr. Simsa admiringly.

"For that matter," Professor Wolf quickly brushed off the compliment, "it is stated nowhere that she will have to execute people. Perhaps after graduation she will specialize in theory. But even if she were to become an active executioner, no one could ask her to draw and quarter someone or break them on the wheel. She would carry out only those penalties legalized in today's civilized world. With the exception of the firing squad, which has by tradition become exclusively a military matter, these include in Europe only the garotte, the guillotine, and the noose. America reached out to the potential female executioner when it introduced executions by electricity and gas, to which women—"

Professor Wolf turned to Mrs. Tachezy,

"—are accustomed by the modern kitchen. It could be argued that an executioner today takes his work clothes to the cleaners less frequently than a laborer washes his overalls. And that—"

Professor Wolf turned back to Doctor Tachezy,

"—is all I have to say regarding your objections, and now—"

glancing at his watch, which showed five minutes to five,

"—we shall leave. No, no, madame—"

the Professor turned to Mrs. Tachezy, who, he had noticed, was taking a deep breath preparing to support him,

"—your good husband has every right to consider my arguments at his leisure, and find them either so inconsequential as not to be worth further discussion, or on the other hand so important as to encourage him to submit a written request that his daughter be accepted at our school. We, on the other hand, Doctor, have every right to select from the swarm of applicants those who will have a supportive background. Many meritorious executioners would give I don't know what to have us educate their offspring. But if we want to do away with the outdated tradition of keeping trades in the family, and if we are willing to give a chance to children of scholars in the field of philology, we must be certain that we can justify our innovation with good results. We certainly can't risk that the world's first hangwoman would suffer from a lack of understanding on the part of her own father. If she were to have such an obstacle to face on top of the demands of her profession, she would receive no thanks from the condemned. So you will forgive us if we now—"

Professor Wolf kissed Mrs. Tachezy's hand and flashed Lizinka an encouraging smile,

"—take our leave."

Professor Wolf offered a friendly hand to Doctor Tachezy. "Oh, sorry," he said, taking the dead chicken from the doctor's right hand and passing it to Mrs. Tachezy. "After all this excitement, a hearty meal will not come amiss. You will find the first course in the bathtub."

"Oh, you mustn't," said Mrs. Tachezy, her voice trembling, "put yourself to such an expense for us!"

"What expense," said Professor Wolf, "dear lady? There is a grand old tradition that the condemned order their last meal from the executioner. In exchange, we have the right to all the leftovers."

"And their eyes are generally bigger than their stomachs," added Mr. Simsa merrily. "Because it's free, they order everything they can think of—but then they lose their appetites. Do you mind if I get our equipment from the bathroom?"

Doctor Tachezy looked on weakly as his wife helped Professor Wolf into his overcoat. Mr. Simsa declined any assistance and put on his own coat. The two guests overlooked the awkwardness of their host with understanding smiles. The Professor gave a solemn bow.

Lizinka gave a polite little curtsy.

"Oh," said Mr. Simsa, "just a moment."

He knelt beside the trunk and opened it. Among the spikes, mallets, and thongs lay a coil of rope. He took out his pocket knife, sliced off an arm's length of hemp, and handed it to the girl as if it were a flower.

"That's for good luck, miss," he said in a courtly tone. "It's still warm."

Then the guests touched white gloves to black hats and departed.

Even before the sound of their footsteps had faded on the stairs, Mrs. Tachezy, still holding the chicken, marched into the bedroom, slammed the door, and turned the key. Doctor Tachezy was left alone with his daughter.

Now he had her entirely under his intellectual influence. But the rage that so recently had enabled him to fight, physically if necessary, had evaporated. However, he found the strength for one last effort. He raised Lizinka's chin so that her childlike eyes looked into his.

"Lizinka," he whispered with feeling, "we've always been friends and we've never lied to each other. Now tell me, in all honesty: would you really be able to kill people?"

In all honesty, Lizinka shrugged her delicate shoulders.

"Lizinka," said her father, shattered, "you mean that you, my own daughter, would prefer to be a hangwoman rather than, say, a respectable baker or gardener?"

In all honesty, Lizinka

9

nodded her lovely head.

II

At a quarter to eight on the morning of September 1, Doctor Tachezy, in the front seat, shut his eyes and tried to convince himself that the gateway the taxi was approaching was that of the Philosophy Department.

In the back seat, Mrs. Tachezy was recalling her first day at the High School for Girls. She could see herself as she had been then, her hair permanently waved, wearing high heels, a narrow plaid skirt, and a tight red sweater which even then emphasized her ripening womanhood. She had to admit, however, that, although there was little if any resemblance between them, her daughter was no less lovely. She tried to think herself into the girl's mind, and battled a flood of emotion.

Lizinka

10

was observing the cabdriver. Whenever he turned left, he would turn his right hand all the way over to the left on the steering wheel. Whenever he turned to the right, he would reach his left hand all the way over to the right and pull with both. When he was driving straight ahead, he held his right hand on the top edge and his left hand on the bottom edge of the steering wheel.

It was a dry, fragrant, and sunny September day. The pleasant scent of summer still clung to everything. But the building with the barred windows, the steel doors that opened like an accordion, introduced a jarring element. During the entire trip, the driver did not take his eyes off the rearview mirror; at one point he turned on the headlights, because of an uncanny feeling that he was chauffeuring a princess. When they stopped in front of the prison, he asked, confused, "Who have you got inside?"

"We're taking our daughter here," said Mrs. Tachezy with pride.

The man looked at Lizinka again and asked in amazement, "For how long?"

"One year," said Mrs. Tachezy proudly.

"The swine!" said the cabdriver. "She isn't more than a child!"

Whereupon, startled at his own courage, he drove off.

The guard studied Lizinka's identification and her gate pass for quite a while. Then he said, "What about you two?"

"We're her parents," said Doctor Tachezy, "and we thought—"

"That's a bad habit to get into," said the guard, but the words were more the expression of long years of routine than of personal disapproval. "Move on now!"

Then he pressed the buzzer, drumming his fingers on the butt of his pistol. Doctor Tachezy thought to himself that he ought to grab Lizinka and run as fast as he could with her to the bus stop. Then he remembered his signature on her application and hung his head in resignation.

"Lizinka," said Mrs. Tachezy solemnly, "go ahead, sweetheart, study hard and make us proud of you."

She recalled the parting scene with her own mother at the gate to the High School for Girls, and she made the sign of the cross on Lizinka's forehead with her forefinger. Lizinka turned her cheek to her father, and Doctor Tachezy gave it a weary kiss.

"God

11

damn,"

said the handsome but strangely pallid boy. He jumped down from the window ledge and stared at Lizinka with admiration and astonishment.

"You," he asked, "are the girl who's supposed to be in our class?"
Lizinka nodded.

"I'll be damned!" he said, still gaping. Then he crossed the corridor, opened a door, and exclaimed, "Hey you guys! She's here!"

In a big room containing a blackboard, seven desks, a human skeleton, and some display cases—only the bars on the windows differentiated it from an ordinary science classroom—five boys were playing a game called Meat. Four of them were taking turns snapping two-finger flicks at the behind of a fifth boy, who was squatting on his haunches, elbows on his knees, and trying, at this point still unsuccessfully, to guess who had just struck him so that he might take his turn. The introductions took place as they usually do among peers.

"Hi," said a pleasant-looking fat boy; the waistband and the crotch of his jeans were patched with some sort of flowered material. "My name is Frantisek."

"Hi," said two boys in unison. "We're Peter and Pavel."

They were twins, identical in appearance and dress, except for the sides on which their straight black hair was parted.

"Hi," said a fourth. "I'm Albert."

His splendid shoulder-length chestnut hair and his large doelike eyes usually made people, on first acquaintance, overlook his handicap: he was a hunchback.

The fifth boy was still squatting with his back to them. He was breathing heavily in anticipation of the next blow and was not paying any attention to the conversation.

"Come on, you jerks," he said impatiently, "get on with it!"

"Simon," said Frantisek, "you're sticking your ass out at a lady. Anyway, she's seeing your best side."

The boy turned around. He was a hulk of a youth with a ridiculously tiny head; shaved bare, it looked like a tennis ball, just a bit over regulation size. When he saw Lizinka, his eyes bulged and his mouth dropped open.

"Say your prayers, Simon!" Albert said in a voice that was unexpectedly deep. "The Angel of the Lord has come to punish you for all the cats you've strangled!"

The husky boy dropped to his knees with a thud and covered his face with hands larger than his head.

"Mercy . . . !" he exclaimed, his adolescent voice squeaking.

Youthful laughter burst from five throats in reply.

"You really are an asshole!" said Peter and Pavel.

The boy spread his fingers over his face and peered suspiciously at Lizinka with wet eyes.

"And me, I'm Richard," said the boy who had brought her into the room. "Hi!"

At that moment, Associate Professor Simsa opened the door and then stepped aside so that Professor Wolf could enter first.

Their association went back to the day when Wolf, having hanged the first three prisoners himself (in the order of their former importance) found himself

12

faced with a weak-willed criminal who seemed determined to put up a fight. Wolf had four assistants, led by a man called Karli, and they all had to hold the fourth prisoner down. Even so it took three tries before the old one-two jerk paid off. True, no one would have held it against him if he had simply tripped the man and let him strangle to death as best he could. But Wolf had already begun to study his subject systematically and had filled entire copybooks with his notes. It was his destiny to be the perfect hangman.

While they were rolling number four into the mortuary, and wheeling number one back into the hanging room following the medical examination, Wolf spoke to his youngest helper. The youth had already shown himself to be as skillful as Karli, if not more so. In addition, his sparkling humor never seemed to wane, a rarity among executioners. Just a moment earlier, when number four had been trying with almost superhuman strength to release his adam's apple for a second time from the noose, this young hangman gave the client's head a yank and said in his ear, "Hey, Jojo, act right!"

Wolf was close enough to see the mortal terror in the victim's eyes turn for a split second into childish amazement; that made him relax his neck muscles just long enough for Wolf's deft fingers to find the right spot and to exert the pressure to which number four responded with nothing more than a relaxation of his anal sphincter. Wolf had to admit that the youth had shown a better sense of psychology than he, who considered himself to be on a par with the greatest hangmen in civilized history. Perhaps it was as a gesture of appreciation that he turned to the lad as the prison commander was calling out number five, with the question:

"You want to do him yourself?"

A flash of mistrust flitted across those good-humored eyes, but it was immediately replaced by gratitude and joy. He struck his left biceps with his right hand. "Don't I, though!" he said in a clear voice. "But can I tie the noose myself, sir?"

"Wouldn't it be better to jerk him?" asked Wolf dubiously. He was on the verge of withdrawing his offer.

"That wouldn't be fair to him," said the lad to his surprise, "because

38

nobody has a better one-two jerk than you do, sir. But I guarantee my schnoose."

"Your what?" asked Wolf.

"My schnoose—Simsa's noose," said the youth, grinning. "That's my name—Simsa."

"I don't think we can do any experimenting today," said Wolf sternly. "This is an important one, and if he should happen to slip out of the noose, the authorities could get good and mad."

"Sir," Simsa insisted, "I tested it next door on the dead ones, and it went like clockwork."

His frankness carried conviction, and besides, number five, who was just then being carried rather than escorted in, was obviously in a state of shock. Wolf, without realizing it, had crossed his Rubicon and taken on the stature of a real master: he had become a pedagogue. So it followed that he would use a classical expression when he addressed Simsa:

"Do your duty!" he said.

He watched as the young man deftly measured the height of number five's top vertebra and then, in a flash, tied an unusual noose with an eccentric knot out of the hemp rope.

"Up with him," Simsa instructed the helpers. Before they could lift him on to the three-legged stool, young Simsa had already tossed the noose over his head in a single motion, pulling it to where the knot stood behind the left ear like a big fat bow.

"Here we go!" he added, kicking the stool out of the way. The air rang with a crack like that of a ruler snapping. Number five only broke wind noisily, and as the hold of his vertebrae relaxed, he stretched almost to the ground; then, without so much as a quiver, he dangled lightly on the gently revolving rope.

A sparse round of applause came from the group of witnesses. From the corner of his eye, Wolf noted that the Doctor was applauding too. For the first time, Wolf tasted the bitter flavor of envy, and he realized immediately that this young man's talent must remain by his side forever, so that it might never be in a position to act against him. . . .

Suddenly, he was aroused by an intense burning pain in his groin and as soon as he was aware of what was causing it, it was all he could do to keep from

13

killing the bitch who was responsible. God knows where they found the girls they brought to these *soirées*. Every time there were new and eager faces, and he more than most—heaven knows what dark intuition told them what his occupation was!—excited them to near madness. The more he rejected and ignored them (he knew that his monogamy was near-pathological, but he couldn't help it) the more they pursued him. This one had not hesitated to break into his own room in her attempt to get him, and he felt certain that if he were to beat her up, he would excite her to even higher levels of bliss. He simply threw her out, and then glanced at the rococo night stand, where the alarm clock flanked his wife's photograph. It was barely half past one, but he knew he wouldn't be able to get back to sleep. He got up and went out on the balcony of the hunting lodge. The meadow sloped down to the banks of the lake, where a fire was still blazing. Voices carried up to the balcony. He tried to guess whose they were.

Executions had once been scheduled on a random basis. It had been Wolf's idea to concentrate them on one or two days a week, and to intersperse them with relaxation, not only for the executioner, but also for the judges, prosecutors, *ex officio* defense attorneys, and other personalities whose job descriptions stipulated attendance at executions. He received effective support for this innovative program from many prominent individuals, including the Doctor, even though the Doctor never seemed to show up at the worksites. (Wolf attributed that to his other obligations.) Soon a suitable site was found, formerly an exclusive hunting lodge, actually a small mansion confiscated from one of the first perpetrators of high treason. It had a splendid location: close to the city and yet inside a patrolled military zone. By means of "Action Mansion," Wolf proved to himself that he possessed not only a God-given organizational talent, but a diplomatic one as well.

Now that the first serious competitor had appeared on the horizon, he decided to do something he had been too tired to attend to earlier. He strode across the moonlit meadow, feeling like a gambler holding a royal flush. The August air was relatively cool, but he—in his forties at the time and at the height of his intellectual and physical powers—was hot. That is why he was barefoot, enjoying the feel of the dew, and naked except for the towel he had wrapped around his loins—not out of prudishness but because he knew that total nudity deprives even the most impressive personage of his last shred of dignity. He had been very disappointed when he was unable, even in such a relatively enlightened time, to get the authorities to deliver to him prisoners unclothed. Some idiot from the Institute of Law wrote an encyclical, supported by old chronicles and engravings, in which he stated that the thin line between barbarism and civilization rested in the bit of rag which covered the criminal's genitals during the execution. He remembered wanting to exclaim at the time, "Too bad there's also the thin line between the real men and the milksops who don't mind sending even petty offenders to the noose, but pass out if a condemned man farts on the scaffold . . .!" Of course Wolf never actually said it, he had long since arrived at the philosophical conclusion that it is more useful to an executioner to be enraged and to hang than to enrage and be hanged. So he continued to put them in the noose in the traditional linen shifts, but he never got over the unpleasant feeling that, clothed, they resembled human beings far more than they should have. At least he succeeded in having the condemned announced by number rather than by name. All the same he would always go immediately for the neck, so that he need not perceive them as real people with feelings. It gave him the reputation of being an ace hangman, but he himself knew very well that he had an Achilles' heel. And when he saw the youthful Simsa tying a complex noose while examining his client from head to foot, like a butcher appreciatively examining a hog, he realized that here was his Paris, notching the arrow. As he contemplated Simsa, his splendid brain simultaneously went to work on the plan he was now on his way to execute. His guess had been right. They were there, sitting side by side on lawn chairs, holding hands, the two people most admired by the contemporary public at large, the State Prosecutor and the Defense Attorney. They were the leading figures in the great criminal trials which were helping the epoch carve its niche in history. But these two iron-principled men had a weakness, one that made them more human. They were lovers. So deep was their passion for each other that the Defense Attorney, reading the verdict in his mate's eyes, had on two separate occasions suggested the death penalty even before the Prosecutor.

That evening, as always, they had left the lovely young ladies to others. Wolf's presence did not disturb them. On the contrary, they felt respect for this athletic man who crowned their work with such precision, and who kept surprising them with his intellect. Although their first encounter with him had been under extremely unfavorable circumstances, they had been the first to discover his talents. Ever since, they had felt more than a mere liking for him. Indeed they had once tried to proselytize him to their mode of sexuality. Wolf, monogamous male to the marrow of his bones, was naturally too clever to turn them down flat. In a feigned confession that smacked of some titillating secret, he explained that he, like many executioners, had his own particular sexual deviation. However, for social reasons, he was obliged to conceal it. He could only say that he needed neither man nor woman in order to gratify his desire. Each execution was for him a sexual act, for (as they could have seen for themselves were it not for those stupid nightshirts), death by hanging mobilizes the victims' sexual apparatus for the last time, and the victim's orgasm, he added discreetly, became his own.

They were very taken by his perversion and had called him by his first name ever since. They had never again propositioned him. Furthermore, they were always pleased to see him, for he was the only one for whom they didn't have to pretend.

"Hello, Frederick," said the Prosecutor. "Lovely night, isn't it?"

"Will you have some cognac with us?" The Defense Attorney moved to pour him a glass.

"Don't let me disturb you," said Wolf, knowing that they would be grateful to him even for such a small courtesy. He leaned down for the cognac bottle and tipped the bottle to his lips to take a drink. Then he proceeded to discuss his interests.

"Soon," he said, "I am going to need an extra room here. Could that be arranged?"

"Are you thinking of bringing your old lady?" smiled the Defense Attorney.

"Not quite. I am thinking of bringing that young man," said Wolf.

At that, they almost exploded.

"You've g-got—" stuttered the Defense Attorney.

"You want to b-bring—" stuttered the Prosecutor.

"Who is *that young man?*" both asked urgently.

"The one with the fancy knot," said Wolf. "I believe you rather liked him, too."

Although he had expected that they would respond negatively, he was surprised at the violence of their reaction.

"The one with a head like a chicken?" the Defense Attorney asked.

"Did you see his complexion?" asked the Prosecutor.

"Have you taken up cradle-snatching?" exclaimed the two of them.

"No, you have it all wrong, my friends," said Wolf with a pleasant smile. "I want that Simsa fellow for business, not for pleasure."

The atmosphere grew more relaxed, but there was still tension in the air.

"You said you want to bring him here," said the Defense Attorney.

"Yes," said Wolf, "and I have my reasons. Tell me, friends, do you think that criminal activity is winding down and that soon society won't need us anymore?"

"What are you talking about?" The Prosecutor was amazed. "Every day brings new opportunities. If I didn't despise clichés I would say that every neck you break gives birth to nine new heads. I don't know what you think, Mirda—"

the Prosecutor turned to the Defense Attorney,

"—but I'm convinced that the criminal conspiracies against the peaceful efforts of our people are only the tip of the iceberg, barely a tenth is visible, and we are far from finished with that small percentage, which—"

and the Prosecutor turned back to Wolf,

42

"—logically implies that we are only at the beginning, so that you, Beda, will be lucky if you ever get to retire. I see that Mirda here agrees with me, and if Willi—"

the Prosecutor indicated the brightly lit window which echoed with the amatory sighs of the Judge, and he grasped the Defense Attorney's hand a bit more tightly,

"—were not under some compulsion to prove that he can still hump every one of those perspiring nymphets, and if he were to give preference, like ourselves, to the gentle play of the senses and the intellect, he would agree, too!"

During this entire conversation, Wolf had been twirling the cognac bottle in his hands. Flashes of the amber liquid glowed in the green glass. A smile flickered across the corners of his lips.

"And what," he asked then, "if, by chance, I get the flu?"

"You?" exclaimed the Defense Attorney. "You're joking!"

"I'm serious," he said.

"Serious?" asked the Prosecutor. "Then I'll give you a serious answer. We'll just wait until you get better. Your clients will forgive us. I've never seen anyone yet who was in any rush for you to get on with your job."

"I do hope," said Wolf, "that you won't consider me immodest if I recall a certain event. In the fall of 1899, the heart of a Viennese citizen named Selinger suddenly stopped beating. History would have passed over this event were it not for one alarming fact: that little clot of blood blocking his coronary artery eliminated in what was then the most powerful state in Europe—"

said Wolf, gazing meaningfully at the Prosecutor,

"—an executioner. The loss was all the more tragic in that several delinquents had just received the death penalty. According to the pseudohumanitarian laws of the time, allowing the execution date to pass would have meant commutation to life imprisonment. For that matter, it was no secret that it was the senile monarch Franz Joseph's frequent last-minute pardons that had finally broken Selinger's health. The most pressing execution at hand, that of child murderess Juliana Hummel, was scheduled for New Year's Day of 1900, and the most qualified candidate for the vacated post was called in to perform it, Prague's executioner, Wohlschläger. Thanks to him, however, the newborn century, which promised to return to the executioner's office the authority of the state and the sympathy of the popular masses, was doomed—"

continued Wolf, gazing meaningfully at the Defense Attorney,

"—to begin with a shocking scandal. Wohlschläger brought with him a complex harness system of his own devising, into which the Hummel woman was literally strapped. To quote a witness of the period, 'She was bound up like a sacrificial animal, and the sight alone was an unprecedented insult to the dignity of justice.' The vain Wohlschläger, in order to prove the economy of his invention, dispatched her himself. Her exit was supposed to occur by the momentum of her own weight, but she wasn't heavy enough. There ensued an incredible situation wherein the open trapdoor prevented the use of the one-two jerk or even the completion of the operation by a leg-pull. To quote from the press of the day, 'Juliana Hummel, in terrible pain and with inhuman sounds issuing from her throat, took forty-five minutes to choke to death, so that many official witnesses fainted. It was not an execution that we witnessed,' exclaims the author, 'but a judicial butchery.' Wohlschläger was obliged to leave town by the first train. It was on that day that the supreme penalty experienced its most difficult hour to date when even the censors allowed publication of articles calling for its immediate abolition. Luckily—"

continued Wolf, now gazing meaningfully at the two of them,

"—fortune was on the side of the just at that fateful moment, for Josef Lang, Vienna coffeehouse owner, turned up. In 1868, Lang's father, a very enlightened man, had taken him to the last public execution in Vienna. The beautiful day, the crowds of spectators in their Sunday best, the sausage vendors, the organ grinders, the solemnity of the ceremony and above all the execution of murderer and thief Ratkay, hanged by the classical method of kicking from a high ladder, left an indelible impression on the thirteen-year-old lad. He felt that he was predestined for the noble calling of hangman. When on February 27, 1900, as a mature man, he received the decree by which he was named Imperial Executioner for the entire Austro-Hungarian Empire, he felt a burden of responsibility equal to that of the Imperial ruler himself. When on March 3, 1900, he approached his first execution, that of the gypsy Held, he thought above all of the commission of experts present, headed by Professor Haberda, whose face was still twitching from recollections of the Hummel woman's agonies. 'I want him,' he had told Lang the previous evening, 'to have it over within less than a minute!' Literature is full of descriptions of the last nights of condemned men. Every writer sheds a tear for society's castoffs, but where—"

continued Wolf, gazing straight ahead,

"—is there a new Shakespeare who would describe the *first night* of the executioner? How tirelessly he rehearses various holds with his henchmen, how painfully he recalls all previous infamous blunders, as, for example, the *faux-pas,* once again from the annals of Prague, when they dropped a certain Vaclav Slepicka through the trap without putting his head in the noose. The result was that he broke both legs and couldn't be hanged until they mended. There are no such authors, and so the executioner himself must step in, as did Lang himself, who later wrote, and I quote from Dorfler and Zettel, these wise words: 'I once saw a book

44

in which a man was depicted as a translucent but very colorful show of muscles on one side, and on the other side, gray organs—stomach, gullet, breathing pipes and so forth. In this diagram, one can observe what a work of art a human being is, and how wise nature is to have something so complex and beautiful actually function. And I had to stop and say to myself, you see, Pepi, you have the power to put this wonder of nature out of operation!' Then came the morning. A dismal one for Held the gypsy, but a brilliant one for Josef Lang. He was able to stand up before Professor Haberda and declare that the death penalty had been carried out, and to add modestly, 'In forty-five seconds.' The stern Professor Haberda patted him on the shoulder and said, 'Bravo, Lang!' And to think that Josef Lang was soon to execute the quadruple murderer Grossrubatscher in forty-two seconds, and shortly thereafter, in Lvov, Theodore Bibierski in an even forty. For a long time this remained the continental record, until—"

and Wolf's tone dropped to a modest pitch,

"—a new generation of executioners broke it. But there is no surpassing the memory of this man who had a copper plate engraved with the insignia of his honorable profession by his door. The reason I have related this story to you, my friends, is to remind you—"

continued Wolf, now gazing directly overhead, where the blue-black map of the summer sky was slowly but surely traveling from east to west,

"—that not even executioners are immune to heart attacks. And if one day I should be stricken, what would be left of your splendid plans?"

"There's always Karli . . ." said the Prosecutor uncertainly.

"Karli," said Wolf, with more compassion than contempt, "was born five centuries too late. At best, I could picture him as a rural henchman who ends up beating the client to death while trying to decapitate him. No, no, you can't—"

said Wolf, rising to give his words greater emphasis,

"—wipe our problem out that way. I'm not even considering the possibility that the iceberg may surface all at once. Then things may get out of hand. Regional and district courts will clamor for their share, and who is going to cope with all the hangings? Or would you put classified ads for hangmen in the newspapers? How capable would such executioners be? And what would they say about it abroad?"

The ensuing silence was interrupted only by the hooting of an owl and the recurring squeals of the Judge's concubines feigning orgasms. Wolf knew, with the certainty of a pharmacist, that even one syllable more at that moment would weaken his argument. He took another long swig of cognac and then spoke only two words: "Good night."

"Wait!" called the Prosecutor, just as Wolf had anticipated. "If you say 'A,' you've got to say 'B'! If something happens to you, that Simsa lad of yours won't save the day. I'd hate to be around if he had to handle it all by himself!"

"It isn't just scholars," said Wolf, with precise irony, "who must be educated. Executioners also have to be schooled. Trying to teach Karli even the most primitive concepts of, say, physiology, not to mention psychology, would be like casting pearls before a swine. Whereas Simsa—"

said Wolf, pointing a finger across the lake, where the glow of the city hung over the woods like a faint mist,

"—that young man fully deserves an experienced teacher, so that he need not grope in the dark the way we did."

"If memory serves me," giggled the Defense Attorney, "your first attempt was from a lamppost!"

The last flame had gone out, the fire had become no more than a flicker, and the moon, rising from the mansion park, resembled the scimitar the Turks employed to cut off people's heads. Even in the poor light, Wolf's sudden flinch was visible.

"Mirda, love," said the Prosecutor quickly, digging his fingernails into his lover's palm, "this is no time for jokes. Now, tell me, Beda—"

continued the Prosecutor, turning back to Wolf,

"—what exactly did you have in mind?"

The ability to turn the other cheek is one of the prerequisite qualities for one who has decided to improve the world. Were it not for the infinite patience of an unknown Spanish monk, an ordinary French physician, and a famous American inventor, the world would have neither the garotte, the guillotine, nor the electric chair. Wolf had full command of that ability. The flash of his lethal rage remained as invisible to his companions as did the rush of blood into his cheeks. He anticipated, with icy bliss, that one day the capricious Dame History would present him with these two fat creeps, two nicely wrapped packages, exuding instead of the fragrance of expensive cologne, the smell that fear raises on the human body. Then who could reproach him, an executioner of world renown, for neglecting—for experimental reasons—to use his merciful one-two jerk or Simsa's extra-fast fancy knot? Instead, he would allow the two of them to bob gently and lightly, like ornaments on a Christmas tree. That way they could take advantage of the endless seconds when they would be turning slowly at the end of their ropes (their eyes bulging, their tongues swelling to block the sound, but still permitting the passage of air) to recall, *con sordino,* this cozy fireside chat and the jibe about the lamppost.

"Exactly what I had in mind," Wolf said as pleasantly as before, "was that we stop calling him in twice a week as needed but that we employ him full-time."

46

"And have you any idea," asked the Prosecutor, "what he'd be doing the rest of the week?"

"You remind me," replied Wolf, dispensing venom with the meticulousness of a pharmacist, "of the people who ask an actor what he does by day. Three years ago it seemed perfectly all right for the state's chief executioner to be listed on payrolls as a chauffeur and to be remunerated under the heading of 'mileage' until, finally, I was given the status of an independent specialist with special bonuses, called capital commissions. Of course, no bureaucratic rank could change the fact that I am and shall always remain a hangman, and my so-called secretary, Karli, is and will stay my helper, or my henchman, if you will, because only a janitor calls himself a superintendent, whereas we have no intention of making fools of ourselves for anyone's benefit. So now it is your turn to say 'B,' and to allow me the apprentice that every executioner has always had, because my field is not a trade, but rather a *science*. It has its own laws and subcategories, its classics and its inventors and, last but not least, its own literature."

"You mean like *Secrets of an Executioner* by Henri Sanson?" asked the Defense Attorney. "I've read that too."

"The memoirs of our French colleagues," replied Wolf indulgently, "like the Czech memoir of the Mydlar Family of executioners are items that I would be as ashamed to offer Simsa as I would be to offer a primer to a student of philosophy. Simsa's curriculum, in the field—"

said Wolf, now in full command of the situation,

"—of literature alone, since for the present I am setting aside fields like the judiciary, medicine, etcetera, would begin with the encyclopedic works, from Cesare Beccaria's fundamental work of the late eighteenth century entitled *On Crimes and Penalties,* to von Henting's two-volume *Die Strafe,* which is the bible of the contemporary generation. It would continue with a series of thematic studies like Siegmund Stiassny's *Execution by Impalement,* Kershaw's *Guillotine* or Rolph's *Hanged by the Neck,* and it would culminate with writings that are purely scholarly and hence essential, for example, Shlabov's *Arkheologicheskove obsledovanive dvukh trupov iz balot.* A special line of study would consist of the critical analysis of books which I refer to ironically as *'libri anti-executi,'* by morally defective graphomaniacs like Camus and others, who are opposed to capital punishment. As one example of many, suffice it to open Mr. Stefan Zweig's *Mary Stuart* and a text will spill out that is amoral, bathetic, cynical, dissolute, in a word—"

Wolf squinted his eyes to enable his photographic memory to project the quoted passage for him,

"—Judaic: 'On no one (however much the books and reports may lie

47

about the matter) can the execution of a human being produce a romantic and touching impression. Always death by the executioner's ax must be a horrible spectacle of slaughter. The first blow fell awry, striking the back of the head instead of severing the neck. A hollow groan escaped the mouth of the victim. At the second stroke, the ax sank deep into the neck and the blood spurted out copiously. Not until a third blow had been given was the head detached from the trunk. Now came a further touch of horror. When the executioner wished to lift the head by the hair and show it to those assembled, he gripped only the wig, and the head dropped to the ground. It rolled like a ball across the scaffold; and when the executioner stooped once more to seize it, the onlookers could discern that it was that of an old woman with close-cropped and grizzled hair. . . . For nigh onto a quarter of an hour the lips continued to twitch convulsively. . . . Then, while amid a paralyzed silence some underlings were carrying away the gruesome burden, a trifling incident relieved the general consternation. As the executioner and his assistant were raising the decapitated trunk, to take it into a neighboring room to be embalmed, something stirred beneath the clothing. Unnoticed, Mary's Skye terrier had crept beneath her petticoat. Now the little beast sprang forth "embued in her blood." Afterwards, "it would not leave the corpse, but came and lay between her absent head and—"'"

as he finished the quotation, Wolf opened his eyes,

"'"shoulders."' My pupil would study propaganda like that, obtained by the purging of public libraries and confiscation of books from private collections, confute it on a scholarly basis, and subsequently—"

as he spoke, Wolf could feel his enthusiasm carrying over to his audience,

"—he would burn it, which is a task that has always been a part of the job of executioners; thus theory would be carried over painlessly to practice. Nor would the curriculum be lacking in recreational fiction, as long as the author treats the pertinent subject authoritatively. For example, there is the Bible, which describes a wide range of classical executions. So that—"

for the first time in years Wolf had to strain to keep his steely voice from trembling with emotion,

"—the demeaning portrait of executioners would be overcome. Moreover we would finally take a field of endeavor which the Dark Ages in an uncivilized manner cast out beyond the city gates, a field that even here is not allowed to receive the publicity that any clown gets on the stage, and finally return it to its rightful position, into the family of the humanities."

"Good gracious, Beda," said the Prosecutor almost in a whisper. "What you're proposing here is actually a university for hangmen!"

At that moment, one of the Perseids, also known as the Tears of St.

48

Lawrence, spent by its flight through space, broke away, and expired in a long, dazzling streak. It dawned on Wolf, in the same dazzling manner, that this horrible little flit had verbalized Wolf's own dream, and that it was going to come true.

Wolf lifted his right foot and transferred his weight across the threshold

14

of the classroom. In that split second, it was as if time had stopped and in midstep he was drawn into the *tableau vivant* of which Lizinka was the focus. As yet unobserved, his glance moved from one face to the next, while he recalled the names, biographies, and personality traits of his pupils.

Frantisek (15), as good-natured as he was fat, IQ near the lower limit of average; healthy in spite of his obesity; hobby: weight-lifting; father: a well-liked prison guard because of whom recidivists looked forward to returning to jail. He had accompanied a number of clients to Wolf's execution room, and had personally requested his son's admission to the school, inspired surprisingly by Wolf's own idea, that it is a field like any other, calling for the requisite education. The boy's acceptance was also in part a reward for his father's moral idealism, furthering the interests of his child and those of society as well.

The twins (15), identical, differing only by the side on which their hair was parted (a concession to teachers at the elementary school); IQ at the midpoint of the curve; hobbies: mountain climbing and sailing, i.e., work with ropes and knots; fathers: the District Judge at K *(de jure)* and the District Prosecutor at L *(de facto)*. Pavel and Peter, originally discovered by Simsa through some family connections, approached their entrance exam, the vivisection of a squirming dog, with a lack of precision, but with such enthusiasm that Wolf was hard put to reject them.

Albert (16), however, was his favorite. Father: a sadistic murderer whom Wolf executed a month before the boy was born; mother: the man's only victim to survive the rape; as a simple farm girl, she refused to abort the pregnancy but when the child was born hunchbacked, she saw it as God's punishment and slashed her wrists in the cow barn. Wolf had made a rule of not interfering in the life of a client for more than the few seconds he needed to deprive him of it, but here he had made an exception that confirmed his pedagogical talent. From a distance, he had watched the boy bravely fighting his destiny in a series of children's institutions. In an effort to repair nature's evil caprice, he devoted himself to physical training; the hump on his back did not diminish in size, but soon no one dared laugh at him: the underset hunchback developed muscles of steel. When Wolf checked his IQ (110) and his hobbies (fencing and history), he conceived a plan and accepted Albert practically without an entrance exam.

Those four were roughly the same age as Lizinka. The remaining two were older.

Simon (19) had failed in his sixth, seventh, and eighth grades (IQ 71). He was finally allowed to pass in the ninth as a result of interventions and protests. The protests were from teachers, who, as a revenge for failing grades, had been rewarded with strangled cats hung from their doorknobs. The interventions, however, came from influential people in the fields of jurisprudence as well as historiography, for Simon came from a long line of executioners.

The last of the boys was Richard (17), who had lost two years in a sanatorium, but was now in the best of health. He had all the prerequisites—a decent IQ, many-sided interests, a tall, slender and muscular build, and besides, he was the son of a butcher! And yet, the reason he was accepted was solely and exclusively

15

Lizinka Tachezy.

Coincidence, the director of history and destinies, had also written an account of an incident that had taken place a number of years after the flames by the lake at the hunting lodge died down. The clients dispatched by Wolf on the eve of that night had long since been found innocent and granted a posthumous pardon. If later he had any hopes of dispatching those responsible for the error, he was painfully disappointed; they simply vanished and no one—except perhaps their heirs—took much trouble to find out what happened to them. The press reports from abroad increasingly confirmed that the world was becoming exceedingly narrow-minded. Capital Punishment was referred to in the same tone as Venereal Disease; a person would have had to flay his wife and children to death, or to have incited a workers' uprising in his district, for the powers-that-be, still reluctantly, to order a hempen necktie for him. Wolf and Simsa, along with Karli, often didn't get to carry out their calling except maybe once a quarter, and they only remained on the payroll thanks to the support of secret sympathizers in the justice and police departments. But how much longer could this continue? They had before their eyes the recent abdication of Albert Pierrepoint who, many years ago, at the age of twenty-four, following in the footsteps of his father Henry and his uncle Tom, had been named the Royal Executioner of Great Britain. Although he had four hundred and thirty-three males and seventeen females to his credit—including the twenty-seven war criminals in a single day—he was obliged to resign, in order to avoid the humiliating suspension that would have followed the abolition of the death penalty. How depressing to read that this giant in his field, this "smiling gentleman" who laid aside his cigar only when he was performing an execution, who had broken the neck of eightfold "acid murderer" John Haigh, had been heard to declare, "The death penalty is a deterrent to no one!" He had also said, "The inner voice which once ordered me to do this work now tells me—enough!"

These were the thoughts going through Wolf's mind as he sat in the bus on his way to a meeting with one of his truest friends. He knew neither the man's profession nor his real name, but the fact that for years he had been showing up at hangings with a special permit and no specific mission was an indication of his friend's importance and durability. Wolf made a rule not to inquire into matters meant to be kept secret; he had squeezed lifeless many a throat because its owner had said too much. Personally, Wolf was convinced that "the Doctor," as he was called by everyone, was secretary to an important personage, all the more important because, at that time, the turnover of personages was considerable, and yet the Doctor remained. Many of those who obtained permission to attend hangings through influence or bribes could be described as potential necrophiliacs. But the Doctor had seemed different to Wolf from the moment he had first approached him.

"You know, maestro," he had said to Wolf, "I am all for progress, and so what I look for is a nice, clean strangulation. As far as I am concerned, Simsa's noose has the same elementary significance as the steam engine had for transportation. But your one-two jerk, that is as brilliant and simple as the invention of the wheel!"

Wolf obviously was responsive to such statements. Whenever the Doctor appeared, clients could be sure that Wolf would be the one to see them off, and that they would be done before they knew it. The Doctor was not stingy with his praise, and the relationship between the two men deepened. Simsa, a born athlete, fortunately realized that at the gallows—as on the playing field—there is no shame in sitting on the bench. Wolf had been officially charged with Simsa's continuing education, and the diligent youth soon outgrew the psychology of a primitive executioner. He realized that almost anyone is capable of hanging someone by the neck until he is dead. The art is in hanging him in a manner that reflects the

51

entire cultural history of mankind, up to the present technoscientific revolution. Otherwise a client would have every right to ask why they don't simply punish him by roasting and making a meal of him.

It soon became apparent that the Doctor's knowledge was as extensive and well-founded as Wolf's. True, he lacked Wolf's immense experience, but he compensated for that with his knowledge of penological statistics and a memory for them that even a computer would have been proud of. Wolf, who had to repeat out loud every date in order to memorize it, admired and sincerely envied the bravado with which the Doctor, fountain pen in hand, rattled off numbers and percentages like a teletype machine.

"In France," he spoke as he wrote, one day when they were discussing how often the demand for executioners surpasses the supply (a situation often taken advantage of by amateurs), "in 1944 alone, 10,519 persons were executed for collaboration, 8,348 of them without a trial. Data from a statement by Minister of Justice Martinaud-Delplas."

"Horrible," Wolf had replied at the time, "but of course a need like that often awakens talents that otherwise would never have emerged . . ."

"In the United States," the Doctor said, when they were discussing how, in contrast, a sufficiency of executioners fortified national discipline, "as recently as the first decade of this century, lynching comprised 92.5 percent of all executions. It was only afterward that the trend began to drop. And yet, continuing data indicate that between 1900 and 1944, the number of people executed by professionals in accordance with the law exceeded the number lynched by only a few individuals. Data from Henting's book, *The Criminal and His Victim,* New Haven, 1948."

"Revolting," Wolf had said at the time, "particularly when you realize that all those 'professionals' had to do was pull a switch. I'd like to see how they'd cope if the power were switched off!"

"Certainly," the Doctor had said animatedly. "What kind of professionalism is it when Elliot of New York checks the voltage before an execution by roasting a hunk of beef on the chair? See page forty-two of his Memoirs!"

If there was an area where the erudition of the two men was balanced, it was in the field of penological fiction. Later on, when Simsa was permitted to take part in their sessions, he always regretted not to have available a tape recorder. Those verbal duels would have been wonderful on television.

"'Here is,'" the Doctor quoted from memory, "'the scaffold. His legs have grown weak and wooden, and he felt sick. There were crowds of people, there was noise and shouting; ten thousand faces, twenty thousand eyes—all that he has had to bear, and, worst of all, the thought: "They are ten thousand, but not one of them is being executed, and I am to be executed."' Author, book, narrator?"

"How," replied Wolf with a smile, "could one not recognize an author who had the devilish good fortune to experience a similar scene personally, if not to the very end. Dostoyevsky, *The Idiot,* Prince Myshkin."

"*Touché!*" exclaimed the Doctor.

"But," said Wolf, "which winner of the Nobel Prize in Literature recorded in verse the story of a public execution in India?"

"'They are 'anging,'" recited the Doctor with a smile, "'Danny Deever, they are marchin' of 'im round, they 'ave 'alted Danny Deever by 'is coffin on the ground!' Who doesn't know the 1907 Nobel Laureate, author of *Jungle Book,* Rudyard Kipling?"

"*Touché!*" exclaimed Wolf.

Sometimes the questions were so clever, and the replies so precise that young Simsa would ask himself t same question as did a drama student after watching Laurence Olivier: shouldn't I rather get a job with the post office?

"What," asked Wolf slyly, "is a Swedish tipple?"

"I might," said the Doctor with a smile, "refute your question by noting that the forays of the troops of Swedish General Baner in Europe in 1638 do not fall within the scope of the executionary sciences. But because later, during the witch trials, the Swedish tipple was included in the rite of torture, I will cite the record: 'They would take—'"

quoted the Doctor, writing with his finger in the air,

"'—the wretches whose concealed gold pieces they were bent on confiscating, and bind them; placing them supine on the ground; they would take a funnel and through it pour excrement water down their throats until many a man choked and suffered a death most terrible.'"

"*Touché!*" exclaimed Wolf.

"*Exempla,*" the Doctor modestly added a marginal comment, "*trahunt:* In the sentences of the municipality of Nymburk, we can read under 1606 of an incredible penalty 'suffered by the man Jan Spicka because he "approached a mare,"' which is not further clarified. As punishment, he was 'disemboweled as he watched, beaten about the head with his privates, and afterward his innards were bound in his shirt and all of it was hanged from the gallows.' A simple reader might applaud, but a scholar must wonder where such imagination came from in a backwoods place like Nymburk. Then he reads Volume Two of Janssen's *History of the German People,* page 506, and discovers that two years earlier, the same punishment was meted out in Braunschweig, to an attorney accused of consorting with the devil. Some smart-aleck from Nymburk was apparently passing by and when he got home, sold the idea as his own. But—"

asked the Doctor cunningly,

"—where in the classics do we find the oddest last request of a client before the execution?"

"Plutarch, in his *Sulla,* writes of the Roman general Carbo, sentenced by Pompey to be beheaded. The executioner was already raising his sword when Carbo asked that he be permitted to urinate."

It was on these elevating reminiscences that, as he rode to see the Doctor, Wolf concentrated his thoughts in order to dispel his annoyance. He was annoyed to be spending a summer Sunday in the steamy city, since they had recently transformed the hunting lodge into a children's camp, then into an exclusive retreat for government use. He was annoyed to be suffocating in a bus. And so the only thing that improved his frame of mind was the fact that he had once again, after a long time, been invited by the Doctor to join him at the Animated Film Company screening room, which—apparently thanks to his position—the Doctor occasionally borrowed on Sundays.

When Wolf suddenly felt a tap on his shoulder, he realized that he had forgotten to pay his fare. That was the last straw, and he was overcome by depression. To his surprise, the person standing behind him was a bald, toothless old man in a sweaty shirt, resembling no one less than a Department of Transportation inspector.

"Ekfcuve me, funny," he asked with a strange lisp, "aren't you Beda?"

"Yes," replied Wolf, confused, "I am."

He came to his senses in a moment and started to object to the familiarity, but the old fogey didn't give him a chance.

"Beda, my boy!" he exclaimed and threw his arms around Wolf in a violent embrace. "Fo good to fee you."

The other passengers, half dead with the heat, paid little attention to them, but Wolf still felt as if he had been dragged up on a stage into the spotlight. Besides, he was perplexed by his inability to identify the man. A former classmate? An army buddy?

"Fun of a gun, wuf new wiv you?" asked the man, and he had to repeat it several times before Wolf figured out that he used "f" and "v" to replace sounds like "s," "sh," "th."

"Fine thanks," replied Wolf carefully. "And what about you?"

"On penfun, retired," the man answered. "Aren't you?"

"Unfortunately not," Wolf said. "I haven't racked up enough years."

"How come?" the man asked, surprised. "Don't vey count your yearv double? Or did the fwine ftrike vat codifil, too?"

"You know how it goes," replied Wolf vaguely. It was obvious, now, that the fellow must know him from work. A guard? He would have remembered him, he thought. Maybe a coffin-man; he never paid much attention to those.

"How's the wife?" he asked, to escape the thin ice.

"Vat old bitf?" said the man. "I toffed her out on her aff. But Fuvan turned out to be a fip off the old block."

"Who?" asked Wolf.

54

"My girl, of courf," the old man lisped proudly. "It took fum doing, but fe finally got into univerfity."

"Where?" asked Wolf.

"Law fchool," the man lisped gleefully as the bus ground to a clattering halt. "Fe's got herfelf a courtroom too now, maybe fe'll be better off, eh? How do you fee fingv working out?"

"Unfortunately," said Wolf, deciding suddenly to walk the last two stops, "this is my stop."

"Vat'f a pity," said the man petulantly, "Did you ever get vat fchool?"

"School?" asked Wolf, the light beginning to dawn.

"Fchool for hangmen!" the man called after him as the bus pulled away.

At that moment, the eye in Wolf's mind visualized dark greasy hair growing out of the bald head, the sunken cheeks swelled with a mouthful of shark's teeth, and from between the lips, sensuous as he had once known them, issued the sharp blade of a tongue that had once distributed, with equal generosity, both love and death.

"Willi!" shouted Wolf, but the former judge could no longer hear him.

"Quidquid agis, prudenter agas," said the Doctor, pouring the Black

16

Label over the loudly crackling ice cubes in Wolf's glass, "or, whatever you do, do with prudence. Of course, those boys went a bit too far, and many of our problems today are on their conscience. Who made them dish out nooses like so many hot-cross buns? Here too, it pays to show restraint."

The athletic Simsa had jogged from his cottage; it was only an hour away, and his breath and pulse were already back to normal.

"When I recall," Simsa said timidly, for he could never help feeling a bit ill at ease with the two of them, "what a dapper gentleman Willi used to be, it makes me sad. Why didn't they just do away with him too? What's the good of leaving him to wander around like a broken-down wreck? Will the younger generation be willing to carry the torch when they see how the world rewards their predecessors?"

"A toothless judge," said the Doctor, as he poured grapefruit juice over the softly crackling shaved ice in Simsa's glass, "is better than a headless one. Should he and the others be spared in the interest of the state, in spite of general indignation, as confirmation that *ius regit aut errant,* or that justice rules, even—"

55

said the Doctor, mixing clear tequila and red sangria together in his own glass,

"—when it errs, then care must be taken that they not wind up hanging from the nearest available lamppost, no allusions—"

added the Doctor quickly with an apologetic glance to Wolf,

"—intended."

"But," Simsa objected hesitantly, "won't the daughter, having observed what happened to her father, fall prey to laxity? And isn't that the very reason that there's hardly any work for us now?"

"The young lady," replied the Doctor, "can go right ahead and pass judgment like a kindergarten teacher now, because thanks to an international situation that calls for certain considerations—that's all anyone is asking of her. When she is told, she'll start handing out long sentences and nooses until her daddy bursts his cummerbund with pride, if not—"

the Doctor added, passing around a box of Winston Churchill cigars, which Wolf accepted with thanks and Simsa turned down with thanks,

"—with envy."

"And what if," said Simsa, leaping to his feet to utilize the cigarette lighter he had purchased for that very purpose, and lighting first the Doctor's and then Wolf's cigar, "she refuses? Young people today keep jabbering about conscience, and how it is immoral to use force even for a good cause! How are they to be taught?"

"A certain Russian writer," said the Doctor, "a Nobel Prize-winner but such a militant opponent of Capital Punishment that, out of anger, his name escapes me, once made an observation that ought to become a basic precept for every modern state: 'They used to torture us with hot irons, now they—'"

quoted the Doctor, gesticulating as if he were burning the words into the air with the glowing tip of his cigar,

"'—do it with cold cash.' If the older generation acted severely, either out of conviction or out of the fear that he who doesn't grind will himself be ground up, their sons and daughters, who neither believe nor fear, will do the same for higher salaries or lower taxes. The important thing is that, through all democratizations and liberalizations, a farsighted leadership hold on to one solid point—even if the attention of the public need not be drawn to it—and that point is—"

smiled the Doctor,

"—the gallows. . . . But I don't want to bore you with lectures, now that we have finally obtained two unique reels (and the very fact of our being able to receive them again, after a long hiatus, is symptomatic), films that will certainly—"

added the Doctor, snapping his fingers, which was the signal to the projectionist to start rolling the film,

56

"—interest you as experts."

The darkness was broken by a cone of light from the projection room, and the silence by the hum of the motor drawing the curtain back from the screen. A pleasant suspense came over Wolf, and since the alcohol had just reached his nerve centers, he felt the bitterness of the past few months give way to a sort of hope. In the past, they had come here to see many a select *PF*—they used that abbreviation (employed in Europe on New Year's greetings to indicate the words *"Pour féliciter")* to label "Penological Films." The Doctor must have had access to archives, and he submitted for their consumption anything that either might have some practical significance for them or might inspire theoretical considerations. The films were of a wide range of quality, both penologically and cinematically. For the most part, the cameramen were amateurs obliged to do their filming on the sly, from a briefcase or through a buttonhole, so that often the film was under- or overexposed, out of focus, and of course, silent. An old reel from China—or was it Japan?—of a half-naked man with a pigtail skillfully decapitating some soldiers or coolies who were placed before him like logs on a wooden sawhorse, was filmed at such a slow speed that the participants moved ridiculously quickly, and they had watched it several times as a comedy short.

It was really depressing, however, when the amateurs stood before the camera instead. How to forget the Congolese film in which some nice-guy type was cutting off his countrymen's heads, not only with a repulsive lethargy, but also with a half-toothless saw, totally disregarding what the ones holding the clients would look like? That was when Wolf had realized how much the developing countries needed help in this sphere. But the variable quality of the films did not alter the fact that the screenings provided a great deal of inspiration. They could admire the clean and precise, perhaps almost too pedantical work of their colleagues among the Allies in films labeled TS/NT (Top Secret—Nuremberg Trials). They had to down a couple of stiff drinks to drown the "oeuvre" of an anonymous dilettante from the foot of the Pyrenees: he stood with a silly smile on his face behind his client, turning the screw of the garotte millimeter by millimeter so that he could be on camera longer, while the fellow in the foreground already had his tongue hanging down to his belly like a necktie. They saw the supremely controversial electrocution of Alice Ferris, who survived until they shot 25,000 volts through her, when in a flash, she turned from white to black. They got to view the famous public strangulation of Pfitzner, the German mayor of wartime Prague, with thousands of Czechs lifting their children to their shoulders so that they might see the rebirth of humanism with their own two little eyes. And now they were sitting back, in expectation of what new surprise their well-wisher would present for their enjoyment.

The screen darkened to show the logo of *Die Deutsche Wochenschau,* the German weekly newsreel.

"This," said the Doctor, with the pride of a pioneer, "is a silent copy, which does nothing to diminish its tremendous value. The original had a soundtrack, probably with a commentary by *Reichsfilmintendant* Hans Hinkel, who had the film made on the direct orders of the Führer himself."

After the initial title, the screen showed a shot of a little table with a bottle of cognac and several goblets.

"The time," continued the Doctor, with the joy of a narrator, "is August 1944. The scene appears at first glance to be a booth in a pleasant little tavern and—"

continued the Doctor as the camera panned to a ceiling track with movable hooks,

"—then the corner of a meat processing plant, but in fact it is the central executions room at Berlin's Plötzensee prison."

The shot of the hooks gave way to a view of a small doorway, with a group of men in robes, uniforms, and mufti walking through, turning toward the camera, raising their right arms and shouting something.

"Heil Hitler!" exclaimed the Doctor with the enthusiasm of the men he was dubbing, who then poured themselves some cognac, clicked their heels together, and drank it down—*"Heil Hitler"* was the only thing they could have been exclaiming under the circumstances, these men selected to put an end to the assassination attempt of July 20, fully aware that the Führer would be appreciating their efforts that selfsame evening in his private screening room. After all, it had been his own creative idea, expressed *(Ein Drama des Gewissens,* Herder Bücherei, Volume 96) in the instruction to the executioner: 'I want them to hang like cattle!"

All at once, the men on the screen looked away. A prompt swing of the camera turned to the door in time to catch a naked middle-aged man, his arms wired to his sides, stumbling through the doorway, driven by a guard.

"The lack of a commentary," the Doctor reverted back to a matter-of-fact tone, "unfortunately precludes our determining the name of this hero—"

he was referring to the civilian who was taking the naked man in a grip that revealed him to be an experienced executioner,

"—but his effort here is a memorial to him more permanent than bronze."

From the initial footage, Wolf and Simsa could tell that they indeed had the honor of observing a true artist, one they would hate to have to compete with. With the skill of a magician, he wove the rope into the top hook-loop and the bottom noose-loop; with the skill of an orchestra

58

conductor, he directed his helpers to raise Number One onto the stool and to catch the loops simultaneously on the first hook and the first neck, and finally with the skill of a sculptor, he began to model the death mask by tipping the stool away millimeter by millimeter, in order that the rope take over the weight of the body gram by gram, and the unclothed client, without so much as a shroud, was obliged to show the prominent spectator of this film his demise from A to Z, including the pertinent physiological responses which made it possible for the naked eye to determine the exact moment of the end. At that point, the executioner leaned his full weight against the finished client and sent him swinging along the track, hook and all, to the other end of the room. Then he pursed his lips—the Doctor gave an explanatory whistle—and they ran the naked Number Two through the door. With the sensitivity of a television news reporter, who knows when to help the viewer with commentary and when to allow the picture to speak for itself, the Doctor fell silent. The buzz of the projector was the only background sound for the spectacle that followed, filmed in one long, suggestive, uninterrupted shot. Because they also had on two occasions been obliged to do ten at a time, Wolf and Simsa had to give this trio credit for the perfection of their efforts. With indomitable humor— what a pity that the lack of a soundtrack made it impossible for them to appreciate the wit that made even the witnesses smile!—the chief took care that face after face went through all the stages of strangulation in equal, rhythmic intervals. Penis after penis rose for a final salvo to life, and as each drooped to announce the *exitus,* its owner was rolled along the track like a mine cart, to come to rest against his predecessor, without the slightest change in rhythm or deterioration of style. No wonder, then, that not only Wolf and Simsa, but also the Doctor, who was familiar with the film, experienced the sensation common to those attending a truly great concert: it seemed to them that it couldn't all be over yet, even though the final shot of eight dangling pieces of human cattle (swiftly turned sideways to the camera by the helpers, in order that the Führer not see them sticking out their flaccid tongues at him, or—what would be even worse— their soiled behinds) had long since faded, and the screen before them was just a flickering white space.

"Eight," the Doctor said finally, holding up his stopwatch for them to see, "men hanged, and they all fit on a single reel. Which proves that each number lasted not the thirty minutes average that one might expect, but thirty seconds. If we are aware of the fact that the orders for this spectacle were for a brutal and protracted slaughter, the 'slow hanging' method utilized by the executioner-in-chief strikes me as being a daring game, and all the attendant obscenities to be an integral part of it; that man was as much on the side of his clients as your old favorite Mydlar the Executioner used to be. And if the central archives will not release his name, he deserves to enter the textbooks, after the fashion of the great painters as an Unknown—"

said the Doctor quickly, noting that the letters I.R.T.C. had appeared on the screen,

"—Master. But let us leave the appraisal for later, because the videotape from Baghdad is going to be a sad letdown from what we have just seen."

The title gave way to a shot of three chairs, each one of a different age, origin, and purpose.

"The time," said the Doctor, and his voice rang with the intensity of a scholar, "is the winter of 1963. The scene would appear to be a stage set for Ionesco's play *The Chairs,* or—"

continued the Doctor, as the camera panned to a number of music stands, and on them a number of machine guns, each one of a different caliber and manufacture,

"—some other work by some other Absurdist playwright, but in fact it is the music studio of the Iraqi Radio Television Corporation."

The camera panned from the shot of the music stands to a group of men in military uniforms making their way through piles of musical instruments, stumbling over coils of cables, stopping directly in front of the camera, clicking their heels, and issuing what appeared to be an exclamation.

"Victory!" translated the Doctor, while all the men marched out of the picture but one, who began to read something nervously into the camera in an incomprehensible guttural language. "'Victory!' was the only thing they could have been exclaiming under the circumstances, the leaders of the recent revolution, selected to put an end to the leaders of the last revolution, fully aware that their heroism would be simultaneously appreciated by the entire nation thanks to the miracle of television."

The man on the screen finished speaking and glanced to one side. The camera followed his glance and focused on the chairs: in the meantime, three puffy men in ragged uniforms had been bound to them with electrician's wire; their eyes, sunken like mountain lakes among the bruises, were wide open, but they appeared to be staring beyond this world.

"The sentence that was just read," continued the Doctor, and he reverted once again to the sobriety of the historian, "permits us to identify who is who, so that we may join the viewers of the live action report in enjoying the comparison between the manner in which the end is approached by the Great and Sole Leader of the Iraqi Revolution, Abd-el Karim Kasim, by his famous fellow-revolutionary and Chairman of the Supreme Military Tribunal, Colonel Mahdavi, and by the outstanding soldier and patriot and Commander of the Executions Section, Sheik Taha. But man proposes and some damned fool disposes!"

The soundtrack gave off a rattle like a New Year's noisemaker. The three men dropped their chins to their collarbones. If it had not been for a belated shot that whipped through Taha's skull, so that a stream of blood welled out, not even Wolf and Simsa would have realized what had happened.

"Imagine having such a historical opportunity and," the Doctor exclaimed with the indignation of a disappointed fan, "screwing it up that way! Doing them all at once, without so much as a command or at least a comment by an announcer, the director neglecting even a cue to the execution squad; imagine dreaming up such an attractive setting and then tying them down so they don't even twitch, wrecking the sound by misplacing the microphones, not taking advantage of the trick that is used even for the dumbest soccer game between the Backwoods Skunks and the Legless Riders, the slow-motion—"

as he spoke, the Doctor raised his right palm vertically into the cone of light and crossed it horizontally with his left, indicating dismissal to the projectionist by means of the resultant shadow cross on the screen,

"—instant replay, all of that is a scandalous underestimation of the medium of television, and of the executionary sciences. Why be surprised, then, that this creative experiment was never repeated, although television stations throughout the world spend horrendous sums of money on various pseudoartistic *ersatz* scenes? And so—"

continued the Doctor, pouring Wolf another drink,

"—we arrive at the paradoxical situation where a splendid UFA film, which could chalk up box office records and walk off with a stack of Oscars, is stashed away behind seven locks, while this amateurish bungle does the rounds of the world via Eurovision. And isn't that grist for the mill of those who are forever poisoning the air with exclamations about the ineffectiveness of Capital Punishment, opening the floodgates to the basest of instincts which often lead to its abolition, which—"

continued the Doctor, pouring Simsa another glass of juice,

"—may infuriate us, but mustn't depress us, if we understand that along with errors, something else is coming into existence, something entirely new, something that one day will evoke in us the same nostalgia as the first automobile or the first gramophone!"

The silence was broken only by the hum of the motor that furled the curtain back over the screen. But the Doctor was still staring straight ahead, as if captivated by a sight that remained unrevealed to the others.

"But," Wolf objected, "what can a handful of isolated partisans do against the specter of humanism that is stalking Europe? What can the enlightened but isolated elite achieve when not a year passes without another government retreating before the moral blackmail of writers and other base elements, and abolishing the supreme penalty, although it is the very motive force of progress, and without it even the most developed nations would still be swinging in the trees with the apes?"

"We mustn't"—the Doctor came to, and the meditating philosopher was replaced by the fiery debater and the tireless organizer—"lose our awareness of the context, nor our faith in the revitalizing force of unspoiled communities! What if a few degenerate governments do retire their executioners prematurely, when at the same time a new government in a less developed but obviously progressive land dares to execute its predecessors on TV? When another government in an even less developed but obviously even more progressive archipelago has a million of its culpable citizens done at once, although the method, it is true, is the rather primitive one of 'kill as kill can'? *Ex oriente lux,* from the east comes the light, to penetrate the darkness of Europe. And so we are duty bound to do everything we can today to cultivate them for tomorrow's campaigns, thanks to our experience!"

"How," asked Wolf, uncomprehending, "when we ourselves are on our last legs, how are we to improve conditions on the other side of the world?"

"Beer," started the Doctor with a knowing smile.

Wolf and Simsa looked at him with unconcealed apprehension.

"Beer," repeated the Doctor in a level voice, "has for years been the traditional product of two European regions. If today it is a beverage enjoyed by Hottentots and Eskimos alike, then it is not thanks to the efforts of governments or the United Nations, but of a number of Bohemian and Bavarian brewmasters who placed their love of beer, their talent, and their ability at the service of a thirsty mankind. All right, today you men have a shortage of customers. But you have all the more time and energy! Well, then, apply them to the task of enlightenment! We boast of compatriots who have made our glass and our cheeses famous throughout the world. But our land is above all the cradle of pedagogues. Why then should not our own people, trained professionally and ideologically, and their know-how, be in demand by the leaders of the black, the yellow, and for all I know the polka-dotted revolutions of all continents? Who thinks of us as a nation of musicians in this day and age when music festivals are held in every, if you'll excuse the expression, asshole of the world? But why shouldn't they call us the nation of the best educated, most adroit and humane executioners?"

"But for that," Wolf whispered, and for the first time in years he had to take care that his steely voice would not falter in his excitement, "we would have to open a school . . ."

62

"Well," said the Doctor, as if he were already handing them the keys to the school building, "and why

17

not?"

"God," Simsa said suddenly, "God, look at that!"

"God," Wolf agreed, "I must be dreaming."

The brunette who was walking toward them was of that extraordinary southern provenance which makes it hard to tell if she is fifteen or thirty. Although the last snow had just finished thawing, and the sun was still having trouble coaxing the first buds out of the trees, she was wearing a summer dress, a cotton print that revealed everything it could: the long, strong, bare legs, the tanned arms, and above all, the splendidly curved breasts; the clinging fabric even allowed her dark triangle to show through. A flock of screaming birds circled in her wake and it seemed that what was approaching was the personification of Spring.

It was early in the afternoon, but Wolf and Simsa had already been sitting at their favorite table at the Café Sparta for nearly three hours. And almost three years had passed since that summer evening in the stuffy screening room when the Doctor had formulated his momentous question. His prophecy, based, of course, on reliable information, was gradually becoming reality. True, the golden age of mass executions had not yet returned, still hampered by the prudish revulsion against political trials, but the crisis was over, and the stabilization was becoming evident in a stricter attitude toward criminal acts. Responsible elements finally realized—and in the change Wolf and Simsa detected the Doctor's diligent efforts at enlightenment—that executions have a healthy effect on the population: the common citizen feels the firm hand of the government, as well as the value of his own probity; the political opposition, no matter how legal, is intelligent enough to know that as long as capital punishment has its roots in the law, the decision about how it is to be used is in the hands of those in power, who use it to dictate the price of loyalty.

The revival in their field brought with it numerous other advantages. With the increasing number of clients, there was a decrease in petty disputes over fringe benefits like bonuses, official cars, leftovers from last suppers, and even the traditional right to sell the rope used for the execution. It would have been only natural, after so many lean years, for Wolf and Simsa to have sat back and devoted themselves to the joys of living. Ninety-nine out of a hundred of their colleagues would certainly have done just that. But not these two! Wolf's genuine relationship to his chosen field had been crystallizing for almost a quarter of a century; it had brought him to the highest peaks of professionalism and the most profound depths of philosophy. And although Simsa was a much younger man, he wasn't Wolf's pupil for nothing.

Wolf was childless. The only woman he had ever loved and with whom he yearned to have children had miscarried when, in response to her disclosure of her sweetest innermost secret, he had reciprocated with his own; from that moment, Margaret had been sterile. So it is small wonder that Wolf soon transferred his unconsummated paternal affection to Simsa. And small wonder that the orphaned Simsa, who had known only the impersonal attention doled out in children's homes, school dormitories, and military barracks, returned that affection with a relationship that was in no way inferior to filial love—all the more intense for the lack of those repulsive exchanges common in families, and for Simsa's profound admiration of Wolf's art and aim.

That aim, having germinated years before with the fall of one of the Perseids in the sky above the hunting lodge, and having temporarily faded with it too, was now being revived. Such a tremendous opportunity, however, bore with it responsibilities that were no less tremendous. Wolf had always held to the heretical opinion that the much-touted guillotine had in fact damaged his field considerably; that an overgrown cheesecutter like that could be operated by any primitive, and that primitives certainly took advantage of it. Was it not symptomatic that the French had failed to disseminate this patent of theirs any further than their own Devil's Island? That even the Nazis in the fairy-tale Reich, where citizens were divided into executioners and their clients, gave preference to the ax and the block, until they ran short of qualified personnel? How much greater a contribution to the field than a dead mechanical device was the establishment of a living school, not an apprenticeship training course that cranks out assembly-line copies of mechanical operators, but a genuine *alma mater poprawczonorum,* to borrow a phrase from *Majestas Carolinas.* Its graduates would be exposed to every benefit that mankind had gained from the field of executionary sciences, in all epochs and on all continents, and further, they would learn to develop their own individuality! That, according to Wolf, was the only obstacle that the field must overcome to bring it into line both with its own great traditions and with the expanding needs of the times.

The basic decision was made quite early on. Late in the fall, the Doctor had come to his friends with news that had the same epochal significance for them as the go-ahead for the production of the A-Bomb had for American physicists. They were smart enough not to ask where it had come from, all the more so since they could easily figure out who had the authority, the finances, and also who could keep the new institution a secret both from the bottom up and the top down; such secrecy had been the first condition which the wise Wolf had insisted upon and of which he had convinced the ambitious Simsa as well.

That same evening, Wolf had first invited Simsa to his home, where he normally didn't bring anyone in an effort to keep out the tumult of the world. He regretted the one time in the past he had been inconsistent: if he had not been, he would now be observing the miraculous metamorphosis of his little girl—the embryo had been mature enough to be classified as to sex—into a young woman. Wolf's wife, still attractive in spite of the marks of time and the nostalgia of unfulfilled motherhood on her face, had prepared a little *soirée* for them. They danced a little, drank a lot, and they felt good together; Wolf even offered Simsa the privilege of calling him by his first name, in private, of course.

High days are followed by low days. They were all the sadder when qualification gave their original plan a nasty shock. The unknown decision-maker—they referred to him in conversations with the Doctor as the Investor—had strictly vetoed the status of a university-level school, insisting instead that the complete course of study must take a single academic year. For several days Wolf experienced a crisis, and he had almost decided to opt for a lovely dream rather than a crippled reality; it was, surprisingly, Simsa who helped him to overcome it. Had not his own education, he argued, taken less than three years, in spite of the fact that everything had been done at odd moments and with no teaching aids except for a few books, and then nothing but clients? All they would need, he calculated in the air with a pencil in his hand, as he had learned from the Doctor, would be to eliminate Saturdays off and organize intensive instruction from beginning September to end June, from morning till evening, but above all from one bell to the next, in order to triple the effectiveness of their school as compared to that of other institutions.

"You're right!" Wolf finally admitted, and at that moment all his doubts deserted him, to be replaced by the familiar self-confidence. Messages by means of which the Investor strove to make up for the initial restrictions contributed to this state of mind. Prime among them was the promise that the faculty would get the requisite means for salaries, scholarships, and teaching aids, and what's more, a decent roof over its head, attached to some other major faculty, so that, as the Doctor said, they would get lost in the shuffle. And then came a promise of no lesser importance, that in spite of the one-year study program, successful graduates who passed their masters exams would not only receive their masters certificates, but high school matriculation diplomas as well.

By early spring, the Doctor was able to inform the Investor that his conditions had been accepted, and to bring back from him yet one more:

that by the end of the winter they submit a precise plan for the trial year, and proposals for faculty systemization, class composition, and budget. That was why they found themselves now, as they had every day but Sunday for months, seated behind the panoramatic plate glass window at the Café Sparta. Surrounded by stacks of books and notes, armed with a ruler, an eraser, and pencils in a rainbow of colors, the two men hunched over the sheets on which they were assembling the curriculum that they knew would some day become educational history.

They decided to build their structure on four main pillars. The first of these was to be Classical Executions, for it was Wolf's conviction that without a theoretical but firm foundation in the classics, no executioner could achieve the requisite professional or human dimensions. It was understood that the lecturer in this field would be himself. It was to be supplemented by Modern Executions, with lectures by Simsa, also mainly on the theoretical side, comprising contemporary executions, but in other geographical regions. It promised a solid background to those graduates who, the Doctor hoped, would export their talents in cultural exchanges. Two major areas of study would be Torture and Hanging. In these, the students would undergo a multilateral course of study, so that they would be prepared to fulfill the most challenging tasks that society might demand of them. Because of his greater experience, Wolf decided to lecture on Hanging himself. Surprisingly, Simsa asked to lecture on Torture. They decided, in the interest of maximum quality at the lectern, that Wolf would lecture on the Specifics of the Right to Torture in Simsa's course, and Simsa would take the rostrum in Wolf's on the Specifics of Strangulation, i.e., each would lecture on his own specialties in the other man's classroom.

On the afternoon of New Year's Eve, the Outline Plan for the Year's Curriculum saw the light of day. From the pigeonholes representing the months of the school year, the ideological spine of the entire project emerged as if illuminated by X rays. Wolf decided early on to lead an attack on overspecialization, which may have had its place in the dungeons of the past, when it prevented amateurs from entering the field, but had long since become a byword for conservatives: the loudest objections to modern educated executioners came from dilettantes who had never learned even to break a neck properly. Wolf, and Simsa too, wanted their pupils to know that even if they could recite the collected works of von Henting (*Die Strafe, Henkersmahlzeit, Der Gangster*) by heart, it wasn't going to help them unless they could bring off a flawless hanging at the snap of a finger. But on the other hand, they also wanted them to be aware of the fact that, given an equally good performance in practice, a better grade in Hanging and hence a better job placement chit would go to the student who could rattle off the collected works of von Henting like the multiplication tables. And so the four basic subjects—

OP/YC	Classical Executions	Modern Executions	Torture	Hanging	ANATOMY	PSYCHOLOGY	KNOT-TYING	LITERATURE	LANGUAGE	SPORTS	CULTURE	STUDY TRIPS	OTHER TOPICS
Sept.	Burial, water & fire	Garotte	Interrog. torture I (history)	Theory of hanging									
Oct.	Stoning, stake & cross	Guillotine	Operative torture (punitive)	Knots & necks									
Nov.	Rope, cable & wire	Firing squad	Preventive torture (pressing)	Preparing hanging team									
Dec.	The wheel	Electric chair	Interrog. torture II (police)	Preparing hanging apparatus									
Jan.	Sword & ax	Gas chamber I (individual)	Corrective torture (prison)	Preparing client	All determined on the basis of covered subject matter and detailed in monthly, weekly, and daily curriculum plans								
Feb.	Special Executions I	Gas chamber II (mass)	Repressive torture (wartime)	The one-two jerk									
Mar.	Special Executions II (exotica, anomalies)	In the Third World	Torture in the Third World	Strangulation									
Apr.	Hist. duties, rights & remuneration of executioners	Mod. duties, rights & remuneration of executioners	Legal aspects of torture	Regulations & customs at home and abroad									
May	Supplementary material & review (to be determined as required)			Possible live seminar									
June	Matriculation and Masters Exams												

OP/YC = Outline Plan for the Year's Curriculum

December OP/MC	Week 17 — Dec. 24-29 (at home)	Week 16 — Dec. 17-22	Week 15 — Dec. 10-15	Week 14 — Dec. 3-8
CURCLASEX	Practice with meatgrinder & carrot scraper (at home)	Binding onto wheel and off (w/ practice on dummies)	Divers techniques with wheel (w/ practice on dummies)	Intro. to wheel; hist. origins and devt., literature & documents (w/ slides)
CURMODEX	Work with electric stove	Computing voltage (by both methods) and practice w/ simulator	Basics of high-voltage power; practice on elect. chairs (w/ slides)	Basic electricity; intro. to hist. of electrocution; problematics
GENTO	Kill lobster by removal from water, observe responses	Most effective forms of police torture (w/ practice on dummies)	Effective forms of police torture (w/ practice on classmates)	Development & importance of police torture; examples (w/ films)
HAN	Attach ornaments to Christmas tree (difficult knots)	Disassembly, storage & maintenance of hanging apparatus (at practice sites)	Installation and check of hanging apparatus (at practice execution sites)	Assembly &/or building of divers hanging apparatus (w/models, blueprints)
ANAT	Breaking bones of poultry	Anatomy of the chest	Anatomy of knee, elbow	Anatomy of wrist, ankle
PSYCH	Prep. parents for matriculation	Torture at Christmastime	Gaining confidence of client	Importance of humor
KNOTS	Tying Christmas presents		Sailor's knots (cont.)	
LIT	Executions in Grimms' tales	Executions in Poe's tales	Meister Franntzn Schmidt: recollections	
LANG	elective	German	English	Russian
SPORTS	elective	Soccer & volleyball	Bowling & swimming	Weights & boxing
CULT	elective	Christmas party w/ gifts	Torture & executions in Gothic art	Theater: *Macbeth*
TRIPS	elective	Sat. free: Christmas shopping	Medieval torture chamber	Crematory
OTHER	elective	Rehearse carols	Flail practice	Basics of carpentry & elect.

LANG (Week 16 / Week 15 / Week 14): Terminology of the executioner: German / English / Russian

Dec. 30: Recommended conditioning exercises and review of material covered to date (at home)

Dec. 30, 6:00 a.m., depart for excursion w/other secondary school (under designation High School for Educ. in Nutritional Sciences); skiing lessons; joint New Year's party (rent costumes); return Jan. 2, resume instruction Jan. 3

OP/MC = Outline Plan for Monthly Curriculum

Classical Executions, Modern Executions, Torture, and Hanging—were supplemented by eight ancillary ones, so that the spine of the curriculum, supplemented by systems nervous and gastric, became a living organism.

The plan for the year's curriculum, although it was the most difficult one to put together, was also the briefest. What proved to be the most complex were the Outline Plans for Monthly Curricula, ten in all, which they took on right after the New Year, when they could feel the ax hanging heavy over their heads. Now it was no longer sufficient to simply fill the box labeled MARCH/CLASSICAL EX. with the words SPECIAL EXECUTIONS II—EXOTICA. No, the topic had to be broken down into a minimum of four blocks, to permit a further, weekly breakdown. A decision had to be made, for example, as to whether "Exotica" would comprise executions in all other cultural regions or whether it would be used merely to apply to the problematics of underdeveloped countries.

"If we accept the first alternative," mused Wolf at the time, while at a neighboring table a group of girls from the Academy of Theater Arts held a pre-exam discussion as to which of the examining instructors was most likely to be seducible, "then we shall have to include in the Culture category the most primitive forms of execution, for instance the execution by means of the so-called execution tree, the *upas* tree mentioned in his book on gardening by Petrzilka in 1907: 'If an individual—'"

quoted Wolf from memory, while at the neighboring table some pensioners ordered glasses of water so they could read the newspapers free,

"'—is sentenced to die, the judge turns to him and inquires whether he would prefer to die at the hand of the executioner or to collect some gum from the upas tree instead. Generally the sentenced man chooses the latter, sensing in it a certain hope for his life. Try as they might, however, nine out of ten men, upon laying a finger on a leaf, fall from the tree—'"

continued Wolf while the headwaiter shooed the pensioners away, so that he might make room for members of the faculty of the Academy of Theater Arts.

"'—dead.' For a civilized person, a choice between an experienced executioner and a repulsive bit of flora is no choice at all. But on the other hand—"

continued Wolf while at the neighboring table, Theater Arts Academy professors discussed which of the girls about to be examined was most likely to be available,

"—alternative number two would deprive our student body of what is in fact truly exotic in more developed civilizations, which devoted as much loving attention to refinements in our field as they did to the field of gastronomy. Naming an example at random, there is the famous Chinese Imperial water torture, in which drops fall at regular intervals onto the client's fixed nape. Or for another—"

continued Wolf while a couple of old women at the neighboring table ordered glasses of water, so that they might discuss their ailments for nothing,

"—there is the well-known mass execution of the Incas, in which Spaniards were lined up before the altar, where each in turn was sliced open with a stone knife and his beating heart cut out. Or for yet another—"

continued Wolf while the old women were being chased off by the headwaiter, who wanted to seat a mixed company from the Academy of Theater Arts,

"—in our own century, showing the use of the benefits of the industrial revolution, the favored Japanese execution by steam locomotive, in which the boiler is fueled by shovelsful of coal, alternating with an occasional—"

Wolf drew his discourse to a close, while the chairs were being piled upside-down on the neighboring tables and faculty and students were departing by twos, to confirm the correctness of their guesses,

"—Bolshevik."

But neither Wolf nor Simsa was primarily a talker. True, their every dispute—which in fact constituted the basis for future textbooks—would overflow its banks like a river during a monsoon, to cover all aspects of the question, but then it would return obediently to flow between the banks laid down in the plan. In this spirit, the dilemma concerning the exotica, for example, was resolved before the waiter arrived with the check. To mark a distinct line between developmental levels, the first three weeks in March would be devoted to truly exotic methods in other civilized regions, while during the last week, they would consider Anomalies. It seemed to Wolf a clever way to avoid use of the word "primitive," and it would allow the students to learn, for instance, about the delicate Asian process of flaying alive with the skin remaining whole, and the relatively basic African executions by elephant, by termites, or by a leaping palm tree or a collapsing bamboo.

Going into this kind of detail, Wolf and Simsa needed a number of days to put together each individual monthly plan, and even the slightest delay would have meant that they could be delayed by an entire school year. And so they were truly desperate when late in January they received notice of not one but two clients to be done. That was the first time that Wolf used the secret phone number to call the Doctor late at night In spite of the hour, a severe-sounding female secretary took the call, and Wolf had to identify himself by the code name of Chairman before she put the Doctor on. If he would arrange for those two to wait, Wolf told him, until the plans were finished, he and Simsa would be willing to pay for their clients' extended stay in the death cell out of their own pockets. The Doctor couldn't turn down such a generous offer, and so they were able to complete the monthly plans even earlier than they had expected, by February 20.

On the other hand, their *Outline Plan for Weekly Curricula*—which had worried them the most—was no problem. That of course was owing to the care and precision they had devoted to scheduling the topics in the preceding stages. The fundamental idea and the working methods of the school acted like a monolithic structure, from which it was possible to hang panels of various sizes and weights without the risk of its collapse. Forty-two sheets of paper gradually filled up. The remaining one, bearing the number 17, was labeled by the generous Wolf as Christmas Vacation, after Simsa convinced him that it would only benefit their cause if the kids (as they were already calling them, even without knowing just who they would be) were allowed to enjoy the beautiful celebration of the Crucifixion like their peers. He even talked Wolf into scheduling an excursion to the mountains for the entire student body and faculty, preferably along with some ordinary school. Would it not be wise to rid the kids of that feeling of superiority which the students from, say, the Academy of Theater Arts seemed to radiate? Was it not important to cultivate in them a feeling of belonging to their generation, to give them a better understanding of their clients-to-be?

Wolf liked Simsa's enthusiasm. It revealed that, mentally, he was still close to being one of them. He didn't mind going along with him, because the way the planning had gone had dispelled all his doubts, and had even revealed considerable reserves of time. And so it was Wolf himself who amazed Simsa with the proposal that they build the summarizing and repetition of each week's work into the schedule for Fridays and save Saturdays for excursions. Study trips, he qualified when he saw that Simsa was about to faint, and then he elaborated: the class would travel to one or another of the many localities in their homeland that had some connection with the subject matter at hand—be it a famous historical Hanging Hill or the modern execution room in the district penitentiary or some other place of interest. On the way, the kids could get some exercise, and the faculty would have the opportunity of getting to know them from a vantage point other than that of the lectern and the classroom. Simsa was delighted, and his feelings toward Wolf grew even warmer, without overstepping the bounds dictated by respect and by his subordinate position.

Those days in late February were happy and productive ones. The two men were impervious to the world around them: they had long since moved into the universe that was to be born of their scribblings. They made plans for excursions. They discussed equipment required for the various topical collections. They invented cultural and recreational events. They debated the question of lunch breaks, and hence the matter of meals; they resolved a hundred and one problems. The forty-second sheet was entitled *Matriculation and Masters Examinations.* They initialed that sheet on March the first.

Whereupon they immediately dived into the Outline Plan of Daily Curricula. Even after they subtracted excursions, Sundays, Christmas, and exams, there remained 205 school days, and exactly ten times as many classroom periods. Each one had to be filled with a precisely predetermined content, and its pedagogical success ensured. It meant replying 2,050 times to questions that would have better suited a detective: what, and how, who and where, whence and whither, and also with what. It was a mechanical task, in a way, requiring—as Wolf so cleverly put it—a good behind more than a good head, but a task all the more complex in that the first unknowns had to enter upon the scene: off-campus collaborators.

Earlier, the Doctor had accepted and convinced the Investor of the validity of their proposal that some special peripheral fields should be studied by the pupils elsewhere. That ensured that the circle of those informed about the specific purpose of the school would not have to be expanded, since the faculty members of the relevant vocational schools would lecture in their own schools in their free time, moonlighting by teaching their regular subjects for an extra remuneration, without having any idea of the context in which they were doing it. It had been agreed that a condition for acceptance at the High School for Executionary Sciences—as the school was to be called—would be a written oath of silence on the part of students and their parents, with a severe penalty for the violation of that oath. Organizational conditions, however, had to be established for total secrecy—oversights could be as dangerous as indiscretions. For that reason, the name of the school was selected in such a way that the acronym HIENS could equally well be applied to the cover appellation of High School for Education in the Nutritional Sciences. This cover was to be used when pupils would attend other schools for lessons in peripheral subjects, and in conversations with relatives and friends. The vigilant Doctor realized that sooner or later they might be called upon to cook something, and so he made sure that in his plans, Wolf included a culinary minimum under Other Activities.

Another problem raised its head. If Wolf and Simsa were to bear the brunt of the ideological, legal, and material responsibility for the entire institution, and if they each had to teach two main subjects and if in addition they each had to keep their hand in as executioners (so as not to wind up like many scholars and theoreticians who lose contact with the real world), they could not be expected to do jobs like moving equipment from storage to the classrooms, locking the building, and so on. That is why the daily teaching schedules would have to be entrusted to the janitor and assistant, and later on, to qualified help. It followed that they had to

72

OP/DC
Mon.
Dec. 10
Day 85

Time	Subject	Material	Instructor	Location	Teaching Aids
8:00 8:30 9:00	CURCLASEX (Special prelims for study of the wheel)	The flail as antecedent of rack and wheel	NEXICOL (guest instructor)	STAMMP	Flails from STAMMP inventory
9:30	Recess and transportation from STAMMP to HIENS				
10:30 11:00 11:30	CURCLASEX	The wheel: breaking "from the top down"	PROW	CLASEX	Wheels, crowbars, dummies, slide projector
12:00 12:30	CURCLASEX (Seminar)	and PRAYING	JANT (O/T)	CLASEX	As above
1:00 1:30	Lunch breaks (meals at GRECAN) and transportation from HIENS to SVELTS				
2:00 2:30 3:00 3:30	CURMODEX	Introduction to high-voltage electricity	NEXICOL (guest instructor,)	SVELTS	Bring notebooks!
4:00	Recess and transportation from SVELTS to HIENS				
4:30 5:00 5:30	KNOT-TYING	3rd-generation sailor's knots	ASP	MODEX	Ropes to be issued for executions
6:00	Weekly Class Meeting (plan extracurricular activities, review filling of study commitments)				

OP/DC = Outline Plan of Daily Curriculum

73

SUPERCLASSIFIED

Group	Symbol	Definition	Computer Code
I	HIENS	High School for Executionary Sciences (FOR INTERNAL USE ONLY!)	0001
		High School for Education in Nutritional Sciences (COVER DESIGNATION)	0002
II	NESTOR	"Investor"	1001
	DOOR	"Doctor"	1002
III	PROW	Professor Wolf	2001
	ASP	Associate Professor Simsa	2002
	JANT	Janitor and Assistant	2003
	EXICOL	Expert Informed Collaborators	2004 ff
IV	NEXICOL	Expert Uninformed Collaborators	3001 ff
V	CLASEX	Classical Executions Room	4001
	MODEX	Modern Executions Room	4002
	AUPROR	Audiovisual Projection Room	4003
	GRECAN	Guards' Restaurant and Canteen	4004
	GRECREAR	Guards' Recreation Room	4005
	CENTEX	Central Executions Site	4006
	CRAFHEX	Central Repository, Aids for Hanging Executions	4007
	CRUDFE	Central Repository, Unspecified DEVICES for Executions	4008 ff
VI	LAGS	Language School	5001
	SSHIT	Secondary School for Health Instruction and Training	5002
	SVELTS	Secondary Vocational Electronics Training School	5003
	PISS	Pedagogical Instruction Secondary School	5004
	OCOFINS	Other Cooperating Functional Institutions	5005 ff

74

VII	STAMMP	State Military Museum Property	6001
	CRIMP	Criminology Museum Property	6002
	MOCET	Museum of Classical Executions and Torture	6003
	UTYRARY	University Library	6004
	URP	Unspecified Research Properties	6005 ff
VIII	CURCLASEX	Curriculum in Classical Executions	7001
	CURMODEX	Curriculum in Modern Executions	7002
	HAN	Hanging	7003
	GENTO	General Torture	7004
	TOWAT	Torture: Water	7005
	TRACK	Torture: Rack	7006
	TOSCREW	Torture: Thumbscrew	7007
	EXITS	Examinations and Tests	7008
	PRAYING	Practical Utilization and Training	7009
	EXSIN	External Study and Instruction (off HIENS campus)	7010
	UNSTOP	Unspecified Study Topics	7011 ff
IX	HANAP	Hanging Apparatus	8001
	TINA	Guillotine	8002
	ROTTE	Garotte	8003
	HOTSIE	Electric Chair (familiarly known as hot seat)	8004
	GACHA	Gas Chamber	8005
	EXSCASH	Execution Scaffold, short	8006
	EXSCAT	Execution Scaffold, tall	8007
X	CRAAP	Central Reserves, Additional Appellations (to be designated by Nestor or Doctor)	9001 ff

75

consider the possible danger of inadvertent disclosure by the loss of such plans, or by coincidence, or by act of God. The only way around it was the use of code names and code words. When they sat down to work out the first, a code name for the Doctor, Simsa picked up a pencil and tried a variety of acronyms; the first, DORC, he discarded right away and came up with DOOR. The reaction was spontaneous, after so many weeks of serious intellectual work: they both burst out laughing at the aptness of it. From that moment on, it was as if they had finished a long, exhausting hike and the rest was just a matter of letting themselves be borne on the wings of their success. Amid giggles and gales of laughter, they completed the list of code symbols, many of them as apropos as they were clever, and turned their attention to the schedules of classes. Although it meant bearing in mind the complex interplay of subject matter, locations, and teaching aids, they found themselves doing as many as thirty days in a single day's work, so that by noon of March 20, they had before them a timetable worthy of a railroad, which guaranteed that both they and their pupils would be everywhere on the minute, and that they would arrive at the terminus on the dot.

Like a couple of athletes who, in spite of fatigue, do an extra round of the track out of the sheer exuberance of victory, they immediately turned to the final question: *whom* would they be teaching, and *how* would they find them. They sensed that they were having one of those days when the painter refuses to lay down his paintbrush, the poet his pen, for fear of insulting God. They had decided earlier that the school should not turn out a bunch of assembly-line robots, but individuals, personalities, with a variety of profiles. They decided now that there would be seven of them. That number, not too small and not too large, a number endowed with a certain magical power, represented a manageable group, and promised at least a usable quintet. The selection was made from either end—using as their departure point both ideal types and specific individuals.

The first of the latter was Albert. Wolf argued that one of the future executioners should be able to frighten fractious clients by his very appearance. Deep down, however, he hoped that Albert would be the one to take over after him, perhaps, to occupy the University Chair in Classical Executionary Sciences. Simsa knew of Wolf's feelings for Albert, indeed, he was secretly jealous of the youth. But once again he reminded himself of his superiority, and he agreed to the lad's selection all the more fervently in the knowledge that it would make it easier when he came to suggest his own candidates. Two of them.

"It is truly inhumane," Simsa began, "when two are to be executed for the same deed, for one or another of the clients to be at a disadvantage, either by being done first—which limits his chances of being pardoned—or later—which increases his anxiety, as Truman Capote writes in his book

76

In Cold Blood. Why couldn't both of them be done simultaneously by twin executioners?"

The idea captivated Wolf, but he still had his doubts: the frequent appearance of classified ads for twins indicated how difficult it was to find capable identical twins for something even as undemanding as a movie extra! Whereupon Simsa tossed out his trump card: he knew a couple of clever kids like that, and he had even touched on the topic successfully with their mother. He did not go into any detail, because the sphere of emotions was the only area in which he and Wolf, epicure versus moralist, did not have any common ground. It would have been difficult indeed to discuss with Wolf his long-standing and consuming desire for the lovely brunette who stood fast in the face of his pleas and remained true to both husband and lover.

The fourth name surfaced in Wolf's memory when they decided that they both had an affinity for intellectual types as executioners. But if the main requirement stated by both DOOR and NESTOR (as they always referred to them now) were to be fulfilled, they would have to respect the requirements of the market for export to regions with a high execution rate. They labeled one slot for a "robust unemotional type with a subaverage IQ, capable of uninterrupted periods of work." There was no candidate at first, but they knew they had at their disposal a reservoir of talent in reform schools. That was when it occurred to Wolf to seek out the last descendant of the famous Karl Hus.

For the sake of variety, they labeled the fifth slot as "an executioner with a happy and friendly disposition, for clients suffering severe anxiety symptoms." They had no one specific in mind here either, but were firm in their belief that they would find what they needed if they asked around among the sons of men in the juridical or corrections system or in related fields.

Their sixth description proved that they had not approached their task with pedantic narrow-mindedness, but rather as progressive technocrats. With an eye to the trends of civilization, they decided to accept at least one pupil with a preliminary education in the field of chemistry (gases) and physics (high voltage electricity). They had no contacts in these areas, and so they decided to go through DOOR to the Career Selection Advisory Commission. They formulated the text that would evoke the necessary interest without giving anything away: SPEC. FD. HUM. W/DIPL.: 9 YRS ELEM. CHEM-PHYS (M)—RELIABLE & ENERG.—OUTSTG. PUBL. COMPORTMENT—HLTHY. NERV. SYSTEM.

They appended a parenthetical comment: (MUST LIKE THE SMELL OF ALMONDS AND BURNED ROAST).

At that point, it seemed as if the wellspring of inspiration that had nourished them for months suddenly dried up. They had arrived at number seven. They realized that the holiday was over and that they were once again experiencing one of those innumerable ordinary days when painters break their brushes and poets their pens, because God has deserted them. Then when Simsa raised his eyes again in desperation from the tabletop of the Café Sparta and glanced out the window, seeking an idea as a drowning man might seek air, he stiffened.

"God," he said, "God, look at that!"

"God," Wolf agreed, "I must be dreaming."

They forgot their codes and symbols, their plans; they felt neither the joy nor the tortures of creation; all they perceived was the dark hair of a southern provenance, the bare legs, the tanned arms, the uplifted breasts and above all the little triangle, provocative even through the printed fabric. With the smile of a Mona Lisa but the stride of a hungry lioness, what was crossing the street and approaching them was Spring herself, ripping from them the shell of their intellectuality and uncovering their sheer joyful masculinity, which they had been sublimating into the solution of problems. Their long period of celibacy had done its work:

"Hangwoman!" Wolf muttered absently; for the first time in his long marriage he yearned to surrender to a woman other than his wife.

"Number seven!" Simsa involuntarily murmured what was foremost in his mind; for the first time in months of work he felt a yearning for all the brunettes he had ever wanted to embrace.

"What?" exclaimed the two in unison, when they simultaneously realized the significance of what they had said.

They stared at each other penetratingly yet absently, victorious and yet confused, like men who had just discovered an old painting or a new comet and were afraid to believe it.

"But that would be," Simsa said softly, and this time it was he who had to take care that his youthful voice did not betray him, "the first in the whole world . . ."

"Well, and why," asked Wolf solemnly, as if he were already presenting her with her diploma and certificate, "not?"

He shifted his center of gravity, putting the rest of his weight on his right foot, and finally he was standing in the

18

classroom. He could feel Simsa's impatient breath on his neck, but he didn't want to spoil the charm of the moment. He looked at them as they still stared at Lizinka, moved, excited, or at least confused, like everyone who saw her for the first time.

Frantisek was experiencing his shapelessness in a way that was actually physical, and he was ashamed of the patches on his jeans, which in the past had been a source of pride. The twins realized all of a sudden that being identical isn't always an advantage, that it can be a handicap depriving both of their individuality. For the first time in years, Albert sank under the weight of his hunched back; he became aware that muscles could gain him respect, but never love. Simon was gifted with neither intelligence nor sensitivity, but his animal instinct told him that if he hadn't just met an angel, what he was experiencing was something extraordinary anyway. And Richard, aware that he was blushing, knew that he had just fallen in love.

Then Simsa cleared his throat and everyone, even the girl, looked at the doorway. They saw the majestic Professor and his sinewy associate—they had both dressed in their crimson jackets, so that the state emblem could stress the solemnity of the occasion—and behind them, Karli in the blue smock of the JANT, carrying the neatly covered Class Record Book. The future pupils curiously observed their future instructors, whom they had for the most part only seen during entrance exams, and their eyes, those of the cautious ones and the trusting ones alike, were clearly legible: "What are you? What will you be like? What will you do with us?"

Wolf, a pedant and a perfectionist, had naturally not left this moment to chance. Not only had he written his opening address, he had learned it by heart, to demonstrate the emphasis he intended to place on independent and spontaneous thinking. Because Simsa was to follow him with details about the plan, the code symbols, and the election of a class leader, he could concentrate on matters of consequence. He intended to start with several telling sentences that in their depth surpassed parallel passages by de Maistre, by tracing a general portrait of the executioner ("from whose rib," the text joked in an aside that was to have been addressed to Lizinka, "woman has been formed this very day"), entering the history of mankind from the dark depths of prehistory, irrespective of his often debasing position, to rise to become the one who rules (and the text gave a clever threeway pun on the etymological relationship between the words "executor," "executive," and "executioner") ultimately over human life, being the only one permitted by law to relieve anyone of it. Then he intended to move to the field of endeavor itself. To prove that it is art more than craft, and that an imaginatively carried out execution could even win the appreciation of the client, he included verbatim the fascinating narrative from the family memoirs of the Sansons concerning François Robert Damiens, who was done on March 28, 1757, on the Place de Grève, for an attempt on the life of Louis XV:

His hand was firmly bound to a pole, so that its palm hung over the log. Gabriel Sanson moved the pan closer, with its burning sulfur mixed in with flaming coals. When Damiens felt the bluish flame devouring his flesh, he emitted a horrible scream and writhed in his bonds. When the first swell of pain passed, he raised his head and watched his hand burn. The only evidence he gave of his suffering was a loud gnashing of his teeth. This first part of the execution lasted three minutes. Then the executioner's man, André Legris, took up the pincers and began to tear away the flesh of his arms, his chest, and his thighs. Each move of those awful iron jaws ripped off a piece of flesh, and Legris poured boiling oil alternating with boiling pitch, melted sulfur and lead into the open wounds. It was a scene the human tongue cannot describe, that reason has difficulty comprehending, something without equal except perhaps in hell. With his eyes bulging dreadfully, his hair standing on end, his lips twisted, Damiens urged his torturers on, defying them and calling for new and more formidable tortures. As his flesh sizzled at the touch of the burning fluids, it blended with the repulsive croak of his voice—lacking the least vestige of anything human—screaming "More! More! More!" And that was only the preliminary to the execution. They removed Damiens from the log and placed him on a set of beams that was in the form of the Cross of Saint Andrew. Then they bound his limbs to ropes attached to four horses. One helper held each of the horses by the reins and a second stood behind the horse, holding a whip. Charles Henri Sanson stood on the execution ground and directed his men. At his signal, the double team burst forward. It must have been a terrible force, as one of the horses stumbled and fell. Yet the muscles and nerves of the human body withstood the shock. Three times the horses burst forward, urged on by shouts and blows of the whips, and three times they fell back as a result of the resistance. All that happened was that Damiens' arms and legs grew visibly longer. But he remained alive and his breathing was audible, as penetrating as the wheezing of a blacksmith's bellows. The executioner's crew was sincerely overwhelmed. The priest from Saint Paul's fell into a faint. The court scribe covered his eyes with his robe and the crowd quivered with the murmur of discontent that generally presages a storm. At that point the physician, Monsieur Boyer, went running to the Town Hall to announce to the judges that no quartering would come to pass unless the horses were assisted by cuts to Damiens' sinews. He obtained the permission. There was no knife on hand. André Legris used an ax. The horses broke into a wild run. One leg ripped off, then the second, then one arm. Damiens was still breathing. Finally, when the horses were pulling at the second arm, his eyelids fell open, his eyes turned to the sky, and the helpless torso died.

In his commentary, Wolf called upon his students to take note of the difficulty and the challenge presented by the execution described, and never to neglect the physical condition of the client under the false assumption that executions in this day and age are fully mechanized. Society, he explained in his text, does not begrudge the means to allow executioners to utilize the fruits of technology, but even the best-quality rope, the most solidly constructed hanging apparatus, changes nothing of the fact that the client generally doesn't want to go. (In the text, the lapidary formulation read: "The hangman triumphs, but it takes some doing!")

Wolf then considered the position of the world's executioners in general and in our society in particular. He noted that society looks after its executioners both in their productive periods (secrecy, capital commissions—spoken of lightly as "bonus per neck," recreational holidays, accident insurance) and in their old age (official change of name and special retirement pension computed on the basis of cumulative lifetime total of capital commissions). In conclusion, Wolf wanted to urge his pupils to be aware that by swearing their professional oath (a pendant to that of Hippocrates) by means of which they pledge themselves to do each and every client delivered unto them regardless of race, color, creed, conviction, or social position, they would become guardians of the best traditions of their profession and obliged to expand on it and enrich it with their own creative impulses.

And with the exhortation never to forget that they would be a new breed of executioner, with an obligation to give a bright perspective to a world still divided, the text concluded.

It was a wise, clever, penetrating, effective address. And yet it was never presented.

Wolf stood before them incapable of speech; it was as if he were suddenly overcome with the fatigue of the endless path that had begun, yes, to himself he could admit it, had begun so long ago, under that lamppost with the sizzling body, and then he—he, who hadn't even been moved when breaking the necks of weeping beauties—now found himself moved almost to tears at seeing them all together, no longer seven unknown and insignificant creatures with a variety of banal destinies, now his *own school,* finally a deed which would survive him, since the prime witnesses to all his other deeds (that was the ungrateful side of his profession) were prevented by his own hand from doing so. And now Wolf, ignoring Simsa's amazement, nodded that they be seated.

"There," he said with exceptional amiability, almost with tenderness, indicating to Simsa that he should begin at once with organizational matters, "there now—"

and Wolf had to clear his throat, to conceal from all of them the fact that the change in schedule was the result of his own emotion,

"—kids, let's get right down

19

—to it!"

III

On Friday, December 21, winter arrived astride Capricorn. The previous morning it had still seemed that the exceptionally muddy, foggy, and murky autumn would never end. But by evening it had stopped raining, by nightfall the mercury had dropped two points below freezing, and morning arrived to the tune of the sirens of ambulances bearing the first fractures. By eleven it began to snow, first powder, then down and finally goose feathers.

On the way back from dining at GRECAN—the class had had the traditional Christmas goose and each student was given half a braided Christmas cake to take along—there was enough snow for a snowball fight. They had to deny themselves the pleasure, though, because they had Wolf for their two o'clock class, and he insisted on punctuality. He didn't do anything right away, but the latecomer could be sure that when they would be reviewing the rack, the Spanish boot, or torture by alternating current—since the Algerian war called *le téléphone*—he would be the one chosen as subject, and that he'd be certain to get one turn, one wedge, or twenty volts over the school norm. So they had to make do with sliding along the icy concrete, raising the soft snow in geysers like spray in the wake of a ship.

Before class, Lizinka stood at a window in the CLASEX, nibbling at the

Christmas cake she was holding absently to her lips like a lollypop. This was how

20

Richard found her. Although he had last seen her a few moments before, sliding through the whirling snow by his side, looking like a slender pageboy, her hair tucked inside her woolen stocking cap, now he felt his heart twitching painfully and his recently regenerated lungs gasping for air. He experienced each encounter with her with such intensity that he tried not to let her out of his sight more than necessary. Mornings at the bus stop, he would await her arrival concealed in a passageway so that he might experience his attacks of tachycardia and hyperventilation in private. He would follow her through the guard post at the gate and down the warden's corridor only close enough not to lose sight of her, and he would catch up with her on the staircase, somewhere between the third and fourth floors, high enough to be able to attribute his condition to physical exertion.

"Hi!" he would say, and when she would reply with a timid smile, then and only then would his day begin to live; from then on, he would just try to keep her in sight, so as not to have to go through it all again. This morning, however, Simsa had been doing practical exams in TOWAT, and Richard had drawn the job of subject. When Simon was being examined, he had overdone it, pouring an unholy quantity of water down Richard's throat; on the way back from lunch, Richard had to relieve himself, and now caught sight of Lizinka again.

She was watching some prisoners during their exercise period. The guard was leading them in calisthenics: when he did "Arms forward," they had to do "Arms up." When he did "Arms out" they had to do "Arms down." When he did "Arms up," they had to do "Arms forward." When he did "Arms down," they had to do "Arms out." When someone made a mistake he had to put his hands behind his head and do kneebends while the others amused themselves by kicking his backside.

The vision of her chaste countenance, which had been taking his breath away and devouring his heart for almost four months now, forcing the blood to his cheeks and robbing him of his voice, suddenly, for reasons as mysterious as love itself, had a different effect entirely. Although all their classmates were present—class leader Albert was checking the teaching aids for the day's class on a practice scaffold and the rest of the boys were playing Meat (their teachers put up with it because it had elements of

84

karate)—he walked right up to her with an uncharacteristic boldness and put his right arm around her shoulders. That touch, which she didn't even register in her fascination with the scene outside, affected him like an electrical shock. He glanced around in panic and was about to jump away; but then he realized how amazingly easy it had been. He saw that actually no one, not even she, could take it as anything more than a spontaneous gesture of camaraderie, and decided to prolong that blissful moment, and intensify it. He leaned over toward her and took a bite of her cake from the other side. That was how Wolf found them.

Although it was the ninety-fifth day of classes, the Professor caught himself responding to the sight of Lizinka the same way he had the very first time: surprised that such beauty could exist, touched that he had been allowed to experience it, and frightened that she was his responsibility.

At first, both DOOR and NESTOR had been shocked by the suggestion that a girl be accepted at the school, but that was all. They were among those invisible and yet decisive apostles of progress who may never invent the wheel, the lightning rod, the funnel, or ice cream, yet carry a lion's share of the responsibility for these inventions in that they didn't ban them. Their silence indicated their blessing, and the difficult problem of selection ensued.

Neither Wolf nor Simsa intended to introduce the first female into the profession simply by virtue of her femininity. "The culmination of a century of emancipation"—that would someday be a catchy phrase for textbooks, but now they were after something more significant. As masters of their profession, justifiably proud of how far it had progressed to date, they had gazed with awe and envy in the screening room with DOOR at their more fortunate colleagues who were able to work in front of the cameras. They felt it as a gross injustice that, in a civilization which televises photographs of the other side of the moon, they shared the fate of famous fin-de-siècle actors: they would never be properly appreciated, because their work was not documented. They would have given a month's salary apiece had they been invited by the motion picture or the television people to demonstrate something of their art. But as intelligent and critical individuals, who—as Wolf liked to assert—"do not love themselves in their work, but rather the work in themselves," they were quite aware of the fact that the prejudice sown during various periods of crisis could not be eradicated by two professionals who, however charming they might be, could not conceal that they had heard a death rattle far too often. How much easier it would be for a woman!

So the day that the door to the living room opened and into its frame stepped the pastel portrait that was Lizinka, they knew right away: this girl could stand before a camera and do anything, even bury people alive, and viewers' hearts would bleed at the thought that she might get a blister.

Though Wolf had since encountered his lovely student many times, on each occasion he was overcome by a feeling that he could not define. He only knew that in some way it determined their relationship. Now, when he walked into the CLASEX—he had spent the noon break with his wife buying a Christmas tree and he could already hear the silvery tinkle of the decorations—he had decided to review the principles of secrecy for the New Year's excursion with the kids and then send them home—and found Richard with his arm intimately draped around Lizinka's fragile neck, he stopped dead in his tracks. It was as if the door to a thirteenth chamber in his soul had fallen open, a chamber where he had never been before. He examined it now with a sensation that baffled even his mighty intellect: by a freak of destiny this miraculous creature, born to crown his life's work, was the child of a weakling philologist. The birth certificate, indeed the very seed—unearthed, without doubt, by the efforts of that energetic woman—could not alter his conviction that her real father, the one who would shape her to his own image, her Pygmalion, would be he, Frederick Wolf.

At that moment she rose in his scale of priorities, taking her place right beside his wife, far and away above Albert and even Simsa. At that moment, he also experienced the bitterness and the burning chill of conflicting emotions known only to the fathers of beautiful adolescent girls: pride that she has appeal and fury at the one to whom she appeals. . . .

"All right, Masin," said Professor Wolf icily, "light into 'er!"

Richard ripped the clothes off her, tripped both her legs and tightly bound her so that her limbs lay on the wooden base, with gaps in the places where her bones were to be broken. Then he picked up a heavy, metal-sheathed, twelve-spoked wheel, raised it to the height of his forehead and released it with such precision that it struck her chest exactly between the breasts. His classmates gave off an admiring rumble, and Richard was about to raise the wheel to begin to break her left leg.

"Wrong!" said Professor Wolf dryly, "sit down, I'm marking you—

21

—unsatisfactory."

The class rumbled again, this time with surprise.

"Albert," Wolf turned to his favorite, placing his pencil between the pages of the Class Record Book, "where did Masin make his mistake?"

"His mistake," repeated the cripple immediately, "was that he struck the first blow on the chest, in spite of the fact that the verdict you read him did not specify the order in which she was to be broken. In that case the *Codex Carolinas* automatically applies, which considers the first blow to the chest to be a moderation of the penalty, and states that unless the verdict specifies breaking 'from the top down' it is prohibited. So that Masin should have broken her 'from the bottom up,' which means: legs below the knee, arms below the elbow, legs above the knee, arms above the elbow, and only then, with the ninth blow, the chest or the neck—that is left up to the executioner."

"Which would you choose?" asked Professor Wolf.

"The chest, sir," said Albert, while Richard stood on the scaffold with the wheel in his hand like a memento of failure, "because a blow to the neck is a hundred per cent fatal and if the penalty is to have any deterrent effect, the client should get as much out of it as possible. Besides, it gives her a fair chance, because according to the law of custom, and I quote, 'If one broken on the wheel survives the rise of three suns, he may be removed and treated.'"

"Has it ever happened?" asked Professor Wolf.

"Yes, sir," said Albert. "In 1777 in Bordeaux, when the client was treated by the local physician, who had stolen the allegedly dead body for the study of anatomy. The revived scoundrel confirmed his wickedness by turning his rescuer in, since the stealing of corpses by scholars had become so common that there was a reward given for the culprits. 'The authorities, horrified at such loathsome ingratitude,'" the boy quoted, "'ordered the miracle-worker to leave town; the accursed informer was sentenced to a second execution.'"

"Fine, Albert," said Professor Wolf, opening the Class Record Book again. "I'm giving you an Excellent. Yes, Masin—"

He turned to Richard, who had put down the wheel and, blushing this time with shame, was untying the wooden mannequin designed especially for practice in this particular manner of execution, like other mannequins of both sexes designed for practice in impalement and crucifixion, drowning, burning at the stake, decapitation, hanging and torturing, the second generation of which were to be so sophisticated that they would respond to fire, water, or a blow with weeping, wailing and inhuman screeching,

"—yes," repeated Wolf, closing the book to show that the testing was over, "if I were you, I would devote my Christmas holidays to reviewing the material in which you are so sadly lacking, rather than to your other interests, in which you apparently excel. Because here it is no longer a question of a hog, which can take a lot, but rather, in case this escaped you, a question of live—"

Professor Wolf made no effort to conceal the threat implicit in his tone,

"—human beings!"

Through the newly discovered prism of his paternal feelings, he watched Richard descend abjectly from the scaffold, and for the first time wondered whether he and Simsa hadn't been mistaken.

"Take off your clothes!" ordered Associate Professor Simsa.

Richard removed his jacket, his shirt, trousers and socks, and hung everything neatly over the back of a chair.

"Shorts too!" said Professor Wolf.

His hesitation indicated to them that he was shy. Still, he obeyed at once. With his briefs in his hand, Richard seemed afraid that by setting them down, he would also be setting aside his dignity; he stood before them naked in the cone of light cast by the setting sun through the open window.

It was late in

22

the summer, shortly before the prisoner-carpenters were due to march into this room, which was to become the CLASEX, to construct one of the several school execution facilities, according to designs by a NEX-ICOL from the Drama Academy (under the title of "a stage for passion plays"). The sound of pneumatic hammers was already audible from what was to become MODEX across the hall; according to designs by other NEXICOLs, they were completing the construction of a gas chamber (under the title of "a high-pressure chamber for training deep sea divers"), an electrocution chamber (under the title of a "dentist's chair for a spaceship") and, most important of all, a structure that used to be called a gallows, now officially known as a hanging apparatus, coded by Wolf under the gentle symbol HANAP (under the titles "a post with arm for hanging a giant lantern" and "a theatrical trap on the principle of the lever"). But now the only things in the CLASEX room were a few chairs and the lectern from behind which Wolf and Simsa were conducting the last of the entrance examinations.

The Saturday that Karli had driven them away from the Tachezys' flat, their imaginations worked overtime. Lizinka's nature—they had no doubt, knowing Mrs. Tachezy, that Doctor Tachezy would end up submitting the written application—forced them to think the matter through to the end. Letting her graduate, throwing the diploma and certificate to her, and then tossing her into the water like some schoolteacher or nurse, to swim or sink, would have been irresponsible and unwise. Even experienced old hands like they sometimes had trouble handling themselves at some of the district execution grounds, where many helpers were still recruited from the ranks of the *déclassé;* it was easy to imagine what it would do to an inexperienced young girl. They could of course help her with their own presence, but at what cost? The word would get around that HIENS turns out graduates whom professors have to lead by the hand to the very foot of the scaffold!

They found the solution easily. It was based on Simsa's idea of "double-hangmen." The problem was whom to give Lizinka as a partner. The hunchbacked Albert, the mongoloid Simon, the obese Frantisek—none of these seemed suitable. Wolf, connoisseur of the theater, expressed it graphically: with Albert, the image was one of old-fashioned romanticism on the lines of *The Hunchback of Notre Dame;* with Simon a poetic allegory like *The Beauty and the Beast,* and with Frantisek, a comical cabaret. They didn't want to split up the twins, and adding Lizinka to the duo, thought Wolf, would result in something like a trio of circus acrobats minus the sequins. Finally they decided to do away with the gas-and-electric slot, and, as Wolf said, to find a Romeo for their Juliet. Coincidence, that rare sister of success, favored them once again.

Early in June, when practical preparations were going forward at full speed, so that they were able to see to the final details at excursion sites, they were doing a village postman for pushing a widow off a cliff. In vain did the fellow plead that she used to write herself postcards every day to make him climb up to her isolated cabin to deliver them, so she could try to seduce him. And that she had jumped off the cliff herself, to get even with him for rejecting her. They heard the story from the prison warden, one of those talkative fellows for whom they felt only contempt, but with whom they had to stay on good terms, more now than ever when their graduates would be dependent on such men for their livelihoods. But soon it turned out that his talkativeness had an ulterior motive, to wheedle himself into their good graces, and ask them a favor: they were famous for being fast workers, couldn't they possibly do the postman in the morning instead of the afternoon?

"It won't kill him to be done early," he said, "and I'm due at my brother-in-law's for a hog-slaughtering." He proceeded to urge the two of them to join him there. "All my folks are dying to meet you."

They agreed, but soon regretted it. Because there was not enough time to weigh the postman beforehand and calculate the length and thickness of rope required, they took as their basis the nationwide norm, and were unpleasantly surprised when they walked into the death cell and found a scrawny, desiccated fellow. They knew that he wouldn't be able to help himself by his own weight, and because the one-two jerk was out of the question too since he had no neck to speak of, they had to use an old-fashioned trick: they simply grabbed his feet and pulled. Even so, he gurgled and defecated for more than a minute, which was enough to spoil their mood—even though there was no one to reproach them, as both judge and prosecutor had also been invited to the pig feast.

The warden himself drove them there; fortunately, he babbled all the time about the right way to make head cheese, but they were morose and silent and when they arrived, they viewed it as God's punishment that instead of the fragrance of bubbling pork cracklings, they were welcomed by a live pig, snorting and rooting around a tub filled with boiling water.

"Toni!" the brother-in-law called to the warden, running to meet them as they got out of the car, "we're screwed—the butcher didn't show!"

"Where is," said the warden, turning pale, "that shit? Give me his address and Ludva here—"

the warden turned to the prosecutor,

"—will fry his butt for him!"

"But the asshole is in the hospital!" the brother-in-law explained apologetically.

The realization that no power on earth could set things right depressed them to the point of total silence. And into that silence, a small voice spoke from behind the fence that separated the courtyard from the neighboring garden.

"Excuse me, but I," said a slender and very pale youth dressed in faded jeans, "could take a crack at it for you . . ."

"You?" said the brother-in-law suspiciously. "You're a butcher?"

"No," replied the man with a mustache standing behind him, apparently the neighbor, "not him, but his father, my brother. The kid don't look like much, but he's pretty smart."

"But we don't have what with," said the brother-in-law desperately.

"If you hold it for me," said the lad, "I could stick it. Or else—"

the boy was blushing at all the attention he was calling to himself,

"—if you've got a mallet, I could really take a crack at it, like I said."

Without waiting for a reply, he leaned on a fence picket with one hand and swung both legs over the fence. By then he had aroused Wolf and Simsa's interest: all he lacked for Romeo was the Renaissance costume. And then, when they stood him in the middle of the courtyard with a mallet in his hand, and when he stunned the hog unassisted with a single blow between the eyes as it ran past, he interested them even more. Simsa felt a chill go up his spine, so much did it remind him of his own past. Then the lad dropped the mallet, pulled out a long knife, and stuck the hog so deftly that not a drop of blood fell.

Two hours later, rivers of pork fat were flowing in the farmhouse and the company, sparked by parallel rivers of homebrewed spirits, was singing bawdy folk songs. Wolf responded to all the usual questions, like

90

"Are men braver than women?" or "Does it hurt worse than a toothache?" and "Is it true they always piss their pants?", he signed kiddies' autograph books, and, leaving Simsa to entertain the ladies, approached Richard, who was stuffing pieces of gut with a liver sausage mixture.

"Have you," he asked him, "got your diploma?"

The reaction was an unexpected one: the boy dropped the half-stuffed sausage into the spiced liver mixture and leaned on the table with both hands so as to hide his trembling. The red spots that appeared on his cheeks gave him away.

"I know," he said pleadingly, "but what was I supposed to do, let everybody down?"

Soon everything was explained. Richard, the only child of the butcher, had shown a singular talent for his father's trade since early childhood. His favorite playthings had been veal bones, at ten he could tell from the tissue of the meat which animal and indeed which muscle it had been cut from. It was a foregone conclusion that he was developing into a master butcher, until a banal germ—which according to the press had long since been wiped out—turned all his plans upside down. At the lung sanatorium he was overtaken by puberty, which affected him strangely. His favorite pastimes became sculpture and reading, and soon he could tell from a rhyme what author and indeed what collection it had been culled from. Two years later, he came home certified healthy as a horse, but also— what a contradiction—forbidden to work in any field involving the handling of foodstuffs. Thanks to his new interests, he survived that crisis successfully, in spite of the fact that it was exacerbated by his first—and unrequited—love affair. This he overcame with the help of physical training. Now he had come to his uncle's place in the mountain village to decide what to do with his life. Without realizing it, he had just passed a preliminary entrance exam for HIENS; soon thereafter, he received a summons for an interview which would decide whether he would become Lizinka Tachezy's partner.

Now, as he stood before them in what was to become the CLASEX, clutching his white briefs in his left fist, with the pale, delicate face of a consumptive and the tanned, smooth body of a Greek god, Wolf and Simsa both felt that rather than selecting a pupil, they were purchasing a work of art. Wolf, the aesthete, had a vision of this Apollo Masin alongside Aphrodite Tachezy, both nude and anointed with oil, as a young and beautiful couple beside a HANAP in Van Gogh gold against a background in Modigliani pink. Rapidly and without any particular interest, they exhausted the obligatory questions as to origin, life history, opinions, and hobbies, to arrive at the ones which, in this case, interested them most.

"Have you ever had a woman?" asked Professor Wolf.

"No, sir," replied Richard.

"And why not?" asked Professor Wolf.

"Sir, because I'm single."

Wolf and Simsa exchanged somewhat rattled glances.

"Have you ever copulated?" asked Professor Wolf.

"I . . . sir . . . I don't know, sir . . ." replied Richard uncertainly.

"What do you mean, you don't know?" asked Professor Wolf.

"I . . . sir . . . I don't know what that is."

"Have you ever screwed?" Associate Professor Simsa asked.

The boy was obviously embarrassed.

"Don't you know what that is either?"

"Yes, sir, I do."

"So you haven't screwed!"

"No, sir."

"No you haven't screwed or no you have screwed?" Simsa asked impatiently.

"But I told you," said Richard, "that I'm single—"

Wolf and Simsa exchanged surprised glances.

"You've never loved a woman?" asked Wolf, who was decidedly old-fashioned in these matters.

"Yes, sir, I have," replied Richard.

"And yet you never humped her?" asked Simsa.

"No, sir."

"It doesn't turn you on?" asked Wolf with a suspicion.

"Yes, sir," replied Richard.

"Yes it doesn't or yes it does?" demanded Associate Professor Simsa with irritation.

"Yes it does, sir."

"Then why didn't you take her?" asked Professor Wolf.

"Because she wouldn't have me," replied Richard, "for a husband."

The two men exchanged embarrassed glances.

"Who was she?" Wolf finally asked, to move the questioning forward.

"Sister Mary."

"You wanted to marry," Wolf asked, amazed, "your own sister?"

"No, sir, she was a nurse in the sanatorium—they called them sisters. I said I'd do it if she married me, but all she wanted was just to do it."

This revelation seemed to exhaust him. He hung his head and stared at the floor.

"Are you religious?" asked Wolf with a ray of hope.

"No, sir," replied Richard.

The two teachers were at their wits' end. Then something else occurred to Wolf.

92

"Do you like poetry?"

"Oh, yes, sir!" replied Richard, and for the first time his reply sounded enthusiastic.

"Do you by any chance write poetry yourself?" asked Wolf, hot on the trail like a bloodhound. "Or am I mistaken?"

"Yes, sir."

"Yes I'm mistaken or yes you write poetry?" asked Wolf urgently.

"Yes I write poetry," replied Richard, standing a bit taller.

"Then surely you know one of your poems by heart," said Wolf.

"Yes, sir, I do," replied Richard, so softly that they almost had to read the answer from his lips.

"Splendid!" said Professor Wolf triumphantly. "Recite it for us, then."

The naked god nodded obediently, stood at attention, gave a stiff little bow and began to recite:

> Love of my heart, my sweet one, I fear
> I've something I must say tonight:
> You cannot entice me, try as you might.
> I cannot lie with you, my dear.

His voice quivered and his cheeks were aflame. But he continued.

> I turn to the moon in sheer despair
> to speak for me in the dusky dark:
> Love is not merely lust in the park,
> Love also is a commitment rare.

He had overcome the crisis, his breathing became more regular, and his voice gained in volume.

> Oh, let us be married, love, if you care.
> Before the world, we'll be man and wife,
> to lie together the rest of our life.
> *Then let them judge us, if they dare . . .*

He stressed the final line with a sweep of the hand holding his white briefs. Then he bowed again and fell silent. The pallor was gradually returning to his face.

"You may go," said Wolf after a long moment. "We'll write and let you know."

The boy bowed again and left the room.

"I think—" began Wolf, but he was interrupted by a timid knock at the door.

"What is it?" called Simsa, annoyed.

The door opened and Richard peeked in.

"What do you want?" exclaimed Wolf. "Didn't you hear that we'll write you our decision?"

"Yes, sir," said Richard, "but I just wanted to get my clothes . . ."

They had to exercise a great deal of control to hold off until he ran in, picked up his things, and left. Only then did they burst out laughing.

"I think so too," said Simsa. "We can put him with her, he's certain not to knock her up!"

Although in this they were not mistaken, they did commit a miscalculation that was to have fatal results. . . .

Richard's mother walked in with a steaming tureen. With energetic movements—there had been a time when she could stun a calf with a single punch—she poured soup in both men's bowls.

"Fish soup?" asked the elder. "Why not shit soup?"

"Up yours!" said the mother and sat down to the

23

Christmas meal. Richard bent his head over his plate and tried to ignore the crudities with which his mother was responding to his father. Good lord, he thought, it's always the same.

His parents were not bad people, and they idolized him, their only child, but their gross manners made it impossible for him ever to feel what song and story had led him to believe was "home, sweet home." His gentility, or at least so it was boasted in the family, was of Armenian origin, dating back to an Armenian aristocrat who was sent from a prisoner of war camp to help his grandmother out during the First World War. Coded in that nobleman's genes—which did not surface until the birth of the grandson—were in all probability both Richard's susceptibility to his disease and his love of poetry.

Richard was showered with luxury—the butcher occupies a privileged position in crisis or wartime, and is pampered even during times of peace—and his teachers and physicians alone consumed a herd of swine. Night after night he swore to himself that he would show his gratitude by exhibiting a loving interest in his parents' doings, but come morning, all it took was the first "Shit" with which they greeted each other to force him back into his shell.

Now, as he sipped his fish soup, his mind was elsewhere. He was picturing a room lacking these fancy rococo sideboards displaying gilded glass, gilded china, maybe even gilded gold, but all the more majestic in that it breathed the quiet gentility with which She surrounded herself. I wonder if She found my . . . he thought to himself breathlessly; it had only been two hours since he had run across town, as the buses had begun to pull into the terminals and the first Christmas candles were being lit, to hang his gift on the knob of Her front door.

"What are you gawking at?" asked his mother. "Feed your face, love, or it'll be cold as dog piss!"

He knew that her words were her way of showing maternal concern, but all the same, they revolted him. Surrounded by his closest family, at a table overflowing with bounty, beside a tree decorated with his mother's jewels instead of glass ornaments, "so they'd get some fucking air at least once a fucking year," and beneath the tree a mountain of costly gifts—a Swiss watch, a Russian cap of Persian lamb, and a portable American electric shock-inducer developed by psychiatrists but used mainly by the Green Berets, in this setting he realized that this would never be his home, and if he were not to go mad, he would soon have to think very seriously about setting up one of his own. He had tried to do so in the sanatorium, but had fixed his hungry soul on a nurse who unfortunately was only another version of his mother: his mother collected material things for their own sake; the nurse collected lovers. And if he hadn't rebelled, the nurse would still be inviting him over now and then, "so he'd get some fucking air." He had learned a lesson, though: that the gentility of his aristocratic Armenian forebears which he had inherited could only be entrusted to hands that had not yet grown coarse with dozens of lovings. And it was that kind of hands that might at this very moment be unwrappig his Christmas . . .

That was when the chair he sat in was suddenly transformed into an electric chair, and he knew what it felt like when thousands of volts of power jolt through a body: *what if someone stole it?* Lizinka

24

observed the flickering of the candles on the Christmas tree, bearing witness to otherwise invisible air currents. The flames of the uppermost candles inclined from the hall toward the windows. The flames of the candles on the middle branches burned straight up and down.

Doctor Tachezy finished reading, and his wife sang the carol about the kings bearing gifts to Bethlehem. Then it was time for the presents.

Doctor Tachezy unwrapped the package from his wife, and this year as every year, he found in it handkerchiefs, gloves, and a scarf, items to replace the ones he had lost during the year. In the package from Lizinka, he found a cigarette box, cigarettes, and matches, which surprised him.

Mrs. Tachezy unwrapped the package from her husband, and found the traditional colognes and creams to replace the ones she had used up in the course of the year. In the package from Lizinka, she found a pair of tweezers, a magnifying glass and a stamp catalogue, which startled her.

It turned out that Lizinka had inadvertently switched the names on the packages, and they all had a big laugh over it.

In the huge package from her father, Lizinka found Mauger's five-volume *Cours de langue et de civilisation Française,* three volumes of the *Etymologichesky slovar ruskogo yazika, English Idioms* in two volumes, and a rare German edition of Goethe's *Faust* published in 1840. On the card, her father expressed the hope that after reading these works, Lizinka would come to appreciate the joys of philology, and that her mother would not stand in her way.

In the tiny package from her mother, Lizinka found the lovely Baroque cross and chain she had admired not long before in the window of an antique shop. On the sales slip, her mother expressed the hope that Lizinka would wear it for her graduation, and that her father would buy her a dress, shoes, a purse, and a coat to go with it.

One present remained under the tree, beside the carved crêche, and it had an odd history: before dinner, a neighbor had rung at their door to say that the doorknob had broken off. It had apparently done so under the weight of a box that leaned against it. Lucie replaced the doorknob; her husband dragged the box to the tree. There was no label on it.

It occurred to Doctor Tachezy, a wild hope, that as a reconciliation present, his father-in-law was sending him the *Etymologicum Gudianum* (the 1819 edition, published by Sturz in Leipzig) that Mr. Alexander had inherited sixteen years before, and put up for sale in a classified newspaper ad, but when the honest Doctor Tachezy had turned up in reply to the ad and had offered him double the asking price, the man had fallen victim to the delusion that he owned an object of infinite value, and gave the prospective buyer his daughter instead.

It occurred to Mrs. Tachezy, a sensual fancy, that, as a reconciliation present, Oscar was sending her the rocks that she had thrown at him sixteen years earlier, when, after dazzling her, confusing her, and finally deflowering her, he had allowed her to find him making love to two of her classmates at once—so that out of spite she had seduced Tachezy.

Nothing occurred to Lizenka, because she was just counting windows on the house opposite. Forty-one windows were glowing pink with the reflection of Christmas candles, twenty-eight were glowing blue with the reflection of TV screens. One window was glowing a clear red and behind it the family was spraying a burning Christmas tree with a fire extinguisher.

Doctor Tachezy began meticulously to unknot the string, but his wife went for the carving knife. When she ripped off the lid, a deluge of heavy, foil-wrapped packages tipped out, followed by a much lighter one wrapped in Christmas paper. Mrs. Tachezy unwrapped package after package and her amazement knew no end. She found: one beef tenderloin; six pork chops; one veal tenderloin; one smoked pork loin; one leg of lamb; a slab of beef liver, one of pork liver, and one of calves' liver; a large Hungarian salami; and a smoked ham. The last package contained a sculpture made of white modeling clay. It depicted a youth, supine on a Cross of Saint Andrew and a girl in a Grecian tunic, standing over him holding a wheel above his chest. The proportions were not all perfect, but there could be no doubt that the girl's face was Lizinka's.

Mrs. Tachezy stepped closer to the tree and examined the face of the youth by the light of the candles: his expression, in spite of the threatening situation, was one of ecstasy. A soft tinkling sounded, over and over— Lucie had installed a special door chime due to her frequent migraines— and she went to the front door.

When she opened it, they both were startled. Convinced that it wasn't working, Richard was caressing the doorbell that Her hand had touched, and the mother saw a replica of the sculpted youth. Although he blushed and his mouth opened and closed comically, he was a handsome lad and his gifts indicated good intentions and possibilities.

"Good evening," said Mrs. Tachezy amiably. "You've come to see Lizinka, haven't you."

Richard made a noise that was meant to be an apology and a goodbye.

"Come on in—she'll be pleased—right this way," said Mrs. Tachezy in a motherly tone. She had, over the years, visualized many pictures of the first young man who would come to see her daughter: this handsome and elegant Adonis in a black suit—purchased by his parents when his fate was far from certain—who first sent them, as a calling card, food for body and spirit, who had arrived, from the look of his clothes, by taxicab, and who was even blushing, seemed near perfection. She took his arm and led him into the living room.

"This," she told Richard, indicating Doctor Tachezy, who only now was examining in detail the face of the boy on the cross, "is my husband, *Doctor*—"

she stressed the title as the only thing of value that he had brought into their marriage,

"—Tachezy, and this, Emil, is Mr.—"

"Masin . . ." mumbled Richard and bowed.

Doctor Tachezy bowed too, not taking his incredulous eyes from the enlarged original of that face.

"I guess I don't have to introduce you to Lizinka," said Mrs. Tachezy with a knowing smile.

"Hi," whispered Richard and made a feeble attempt at a smile.

Lizinka smiled back.

Doctor Tachezy was certain he was not the fool his wife took him for. True, he was more interested in the soft sign in the Cyrillic alphabet, which happened to be the current subject of his research, but whenever something concerned his daughter, a reliable kind of radar clicked into operation in his head. Now it told him that the boy had come neither to see him nor his wife, but to call on Lizinka. He examined him from this point of view and saw a minimum of defects in his appearance and bearing. He resembled the students of literature that came to his office at the Academy—except that they wore ragged jeans. A year ago he would probably have gone crazy if a strange man had appeared in the proximity of his child. But now, when her destiny had been wrenched from his grasp, he allowed himself to reach even for this straw. Mrs. Tachezy would have been astounded if she could read his matchmaking thoughts. A clever, decent, and good-looking youth, said his logical mind, and he decided to encourage the relationship. But first he had to make sure that he was betting on the right horse.

"What do you do?" he asked Richard, who was still trying with all his might to adjust to the sudden encounter with Lizinka.

"Aren't you going to offer Mr. Masin a chair?" asked Mrs. Tachezy.

"Forgive me," said Doctor Tachezy. "Take a seat."

Richard sat down and began to feel a bit better.

"What do you do?" repeated Doctor Tachezy.

"Won't you have a cup of coffee?" asked Mrs. Tachezy.

"No, thank you," said Richard. "I don't drink coffee."

"What do you do?" asked Doctor Tachezy for the third time.

"A little wine perhaps?" asked Mrs. Tachezy.

"No, thank you," said Richard. "I don't drink."

"What do you do?"

"I'm a student."

"Cigarette?" asked Mrs. Tachezy. "Lizinka's just given me a sweet little cigarette box. Offer Mr. Masin one, Lizinka."

98

"No, thank you," said Richard. "I don't smoke."

"Medicine?" asked Doctor Tachezy urgently, giving his wife a look that shut her mouth. "Or law? Or perhaps philosophy?"

"No, thank you," replied Richard automatically, but then added, as he had been drilled in school daily until it had become so much a part of him that even in his classmate's home, nothing else occurred to him: "I'm studying nutrition."

"Nutrition," said Doctor Tachezy, "is of course an important field too. It would upset me no end, Mr. Masin, if you were to believe that I am one of those fanatics who think that philology is the navel—"

continued Doctor Tachezy, observing Richard and taking a fancy to him with the realization that students of literature all smoke and many smell of rum, while this lad seemed almost ascetic,

"—of the world. I know perfectly well that nutrition is essential, today more than ever, when the world is in the throes of a population explosion which exceeds the production of foodstuffs, nutrition shares first place with philology among the world's problems. We've tried to resolve the question of communications with artificial languages like Esperanto—how are you making out with synthetic foods?"

"I don't know about that," Mrs. Tachezy broke in hurriedly, "but you certainly know your way around meat! Such choice cuts could only have been selected by someone who has both access to and knowledge of meat."

"The meat is from Mr. Masin?" asked Doctor Tachezy in amazement.

"Of course," said Mrs. Tachezy, implying her superiority. "Of course it's from Mr. Masin—who else would it be from? My husband," she told Richard apologetically, "is well versed in syntactical relationships, but sometimes relationships between people and things tend to escape him."

"The fact is," said Richard, uncomfortable at being the cause of their disagreement, "that it's from my dad—"

"Dear me," said Mrs. Tachezy, "isn't that sweet of him. You must give him our sincere thanks."

"Thanks?" exclaimed Doctor Tachezy, hurrying to the bookshelf. "That would be sheer ingratitude. I think that we can reciprocate with something that would please him. I have a splendid article here about the dual function of the tongue as an instrument of language and of the sense of taste. Does your good father read—"

asked Doctor Tachezy, returning from the bookshelf carrying a thin booklet,

"—Italian?"

"No, sir," replied Richard, embarrassed.

"No matter!" exclaimed Doctor Tachezy, realizing his tactlessness, and he returned to the bookshelf, where he exchanged the booklet for another. "Your father is certain to know German," he said.

"No, sir," replied Richard, abashed.

"No matter, no matter," said Doctor Tachezy, returning to the table without any more books, realizing his rudeness. "I'm sure we can think of something else. What is your father's area in the field of meats? A scientist? A researcher? An exporter, perhaps?"

"A butcher," said Richard, his voice breaking; not until now, face to face with this enlightened intellectual, the man who had given life and a home to his chosen one, did he realize that a few drops of blue blood are not enough to remove the stink of meat and bones from his family tree.

Mrs. Tachezy put out her cigarette and clapped her hands together. "A butcher?" she exclaimed enthusiastically. "Emil, did you hear that? His daddy is a butcher!"

She was overdoing it a little, intentionally, but the father's trade really impressed her, perceiving it as she did not with her nose but with her ears: it rang with the jingle of coins.

A butcher, Doctor Tachezy said to himself. And why not? His own father and grandfather had both contributed to that golden treasury of the nation, its language, and what had it brought them? Whenever in their lives they encountered a crisis, they had to meet it with empty pockets. He glanced at Richard and guessed what was going through the lad's mind. He felt guilty at having contributed to his discomfort, and he was overwhelmed with a complex that impractical intellectuals sometimes have when faced with men who work with their hands. A butcher, he repeated to himself, and see?—he has a decent son who is applying himself to problems of the nourishment of a hungry mankind, while his own Lizinka, the daughter of a doctor of philosophy . . .

"A butcher," he said aloud, "has a very important profession, and I'd like you to know, Mr. Masin, that I am one of those members of the intelligentsia with his roots in the soil. My own grandfather was a common miller, and I believe that if mankind were to select three professions capable of establishing a new civilization, they would be a miller, a butcher, and a philologist, so—"

continued Doctor Tachezy, rising and returning to the bookshelf while Richard perked up like a garden after a rain,

"—please feel all the more welcome in our home. Take your good father these handsome Mongolian stamps—"

continued Doctor Tachezy, coming back to the table with a sheet of rare postage stamps,

"—showing motifs of cattle, with my greetings, and tell me what I might do to please you."

100

"A wise kettle marrow," said Richard, in the excitement of the opportunity that had fallen in his lap.

"A wise kettle of marrow?" repeated Doctor Tachezy, startled.

"Mr. Masin," explained Mrs. Tachezy mildly, "is asking you if he might go ice skating tomorrow with Lizinka."

"Ho ho likewise!" continued Richard, emboldened by her assistance.

"Mr. Masin," continued Mrs. Tachezy, "knows how much Lizinka likes to skate."

Doctor Tachezy stared from one to the other in silence.

"Frog my lettuce!" Richard added, overcome by his own courage.

"Mr. Masin," added Mrs. Tachezy, "is afraid that the frost might let us down."

Doctor Tachezy pulled himself together. "Is that it?" he asked Richard with disbelief. "How did you know?" he asked his wife in wonder.

His wife gave him an indulgent smile. It did not surprise her that he had forgotten how years ago she had had to play a similar role of interpreter for him when he was asking her father for her hand. Richard just nodded exhaustedly.

"And you," said Doctor Tachezy, turning to his daughter, "you want to?"

Lizinka was eating cherry compote, and inadvertently swallowed a cherrystone. To her father it looked as if she had nodded.

"Go," he said solemnly, "and skate! One day the time must come when a young person has to make his way alone on the ice of life, and the parents can only stand by and watch. I am pleased that at such a time, my daughter finds in you the support of a peer who will not allow her to fall, and I would be even happier should you see fit to accompany her to libraries, art galleries, and museums, so that she might discover that the world has more than one aspect, and that man faces constant—"

continued Doctor Tachezy urgently,

"—choice, and I would be happiest of all should you, as the gifted son of a simple man, see fit to explain to her how much more the daughter of a scholar owes the world. And in return, you must always consider our—"

he added, rising as he talked, and mechanically illustrating his point by opening the door to the hall,

"—door open to you!"

Mrs. Tachezy guessed his plan and decided that he was an even bigger fool than she thought. True, she knew he had a certain radar that would click into operation when something concerned his daughter, but his study of the soft sign in the Cyrillic alphabet and other topics of his research over the years had diverted it, the way a magnet diverts a compass needle. She decided that the proper moment had arrived for her to strike home.

101

"Yes, my dear Mr. Masin," she said, and, interrupting herself, she asked, "what is your Christian name?"

"Richard," replied Richard hoarsely.

"Yes, my dear Richard," she continued, taking his arm and guiding him amiably past Doctor Tachezy, who stood with his hand still on the doorknob, "I am also very grateful, and I join my husband in his thanks, his wishes and his promises, and I would like to invite you, in his name as well as my own, to join us for lunch tomorrow, before you and Lizinka go ice skating. Meanwhile let me wish you a good evening, and let me tell you how pleased we both are that Lizinka has such a pleasant and decent—"

she concluded, opening the door to the staircase and giving him her hand to kiss,

"—classmate."

"Bye," said Richard, by now entirely unhinged; he kissed her hand and stumbled out.

Mrs. Tachezy locked the door behind him, walked back past her husband, gave her daughter a conspiratorial wink, and began to clear the dinner table.

"Wait!" exclaimed Doctor Tachezy and dashed to the front door. After a few seconds of rattling it, he realized that it was locked and ran back into the living room.

"Where's the key?" he shouted at his wife.

"What key?" she asked, carefully stacking the dinner plates, soup plates, and dessert plates with the blue onion pattern.

"The key to the door!" shouted her husband.

"Isn't it in the door?"

"No, it isn't!"

"Did you take a good look?"

"Of course I did!"

"Then look again," said his wife, carefully carrying the good china into the kitchen.

"Not there!" he shouted at her when he returned.

"Who?"

"The key!"

"Didn't it fall out of the keyhole?"

"No, it didn't!"

"Did you look carefully?"

"Of course I did!"

"Then turn on the light and look again," said Mrs. Tachezy, carefully placing the good china in the sink.

"It isn't there!" he shouted at her when he returned again.

102

"What isn't?"

"They key! The key to the door—the key to the front door!"

"Oh, *that* key!" said Mrs. Tachezy, listening to the sound of a car stopping in front of the house and then starting up again. "And isn't it by any chance on the dinner table?"

"What would it be doing on the dinner table?"

Mrs. Tachezy walked into the room and pointed at the table in silence. The only thing on it was the statuette that Doctor Tachezy had put there earlier.

"You see," he shouted, "it isn't here!"

Mrs. Tachezy picked up the sculpture. Under it lay a key.

"If a person wants to find something," she said icily, "he has to use his eyes and not his belly button."

It took him a while before his quivering fingers found the keyhole and unlocked the door. When he ran out of the house, there wasn't a living soul in the street. Snow glistened on the sidewalk and in the road. Long rows of illuminated windows blended with the bright stars. From somewhere came the sweet sound of a Christmas carol. Doctor Tachezy suddenly trembled with the chill and sneezed. He ran back inside the house. His wrath gave him the energy to take the stairs two by two. "Classmate, classmate!" he intoned to himself. "I'll show you a classmate!" He knew that his indignation would not last long, and so he was determined to put his family to rights now, once and for all, at any cost.

When he got to the door of his apartment, he found that he had left the key in the lock on the inside. He pressed the doorbell. Nothing happened. He cursed the day he had ever let himself be talked into buying those stupid chimes instead of a proper doorbell. He knocked on the door. Nothing happened. He beat on the door. No response. In a fit of rage, he began to pound on the door with both fists.

Almost at once, the other doors on the floor opened and the neighbors and their children appeared in the doorways. They watched in amazement as the doctor of philosophy drummed on his own apartment door, wheezing and gasping. At that moment, Mrs. Tachezy opened the door too.

"You might at least," she said reproachfully, "have spent Christmas Eve with your family. Oh—"

she continued, apparently just noticing the gathering in the corridor,

"—good evening. My husband just went out for a breath of fresh air . . ."

Doctor Tachezy looked around. In the eyes of the children he could see a vivid interest, in the eyes of the men, surprise and envy. He tried to laugh, to minimize the situation. But a sneeze welled up at the same moment, and the two sounds blended into a braying sound. He tried at least to make an apologetic gesture with his hand, but another sneeze knocked him off balance and he stumbled into the apartment.

"I'm *so* sorry," Mrs. Tachezy said to her neighbors, affecting a noble dignity, and she added, "Merry Christmas!" as she closed the door.

The eyes of the other women conveyed sympathy.

Doctor Tachezy stood in the front room. At first glance, nothing had changed. The candles were flickering silently on the tree. The unwrapped Christmas presents were piled picturesquely under it. The table was set with plates with colored stripes, and among them stood the white statuette. He finally comprehended the scene it depicted and caught his second wind. Indignation, revulsion, and humiliation all merged inside him into a critical mass on the verge of exploding.

"Now," said Doctor Tachezy softly, but his nostrils were quivering, "that's enough of that! The meat gets sent back, the lunch gets called off, the ice skates get locked up, and the girl—"

his voice grew louder and the veins on his throat began to swell,

"—doesn't set foot outside the house! Maybe I allowed myself to be temporarily distracted to let her study at that monstrous school—and I intend to take a closer look at that too—but under no circumstances will I for a single second allow her to go out with a hangman's—"

yelled Doctor Tachezy, and his eyes bulged,

"—henchman!"

He picked up the statuette and flung it to the floor so hard that it bounced, broke two of the ornaments on the tree, and landed in the crèche, where it overturned a pair of oxen and an ass. The sculpture itself remained unscathed, and, in its new context, gained in significance: the girl was now aiming the wheel at the baby in the manger, and the boy's feet were sticking out from under the manger like a garage mechanic's.

"Lizinka"—Mrs. Tachezy turned to her daughter—"wash up and go to bed—you're going skating tomorrow."

With her goodnight kiss, Tachezy's daughter released the pent-up pressure inside him. Before it could build up again, his wife took the floor.

"A man," she said, emphatically but with a certain diffidence, "who has nasty names for decent boys who invite girls skating, in spite of the fact that he himself violated their mothers in the first—"

as she spoke, she stacked the striped dinner plates, soup plates, and dessert plates with a clatter,

"—clover patch he could find, made them a baby to force them to marry him so he could wheedle rare books out of their fathers-in-law, a man who can't get his daughter into a decent school because he refuses to dirty his hands with a bottle of cognac, but who makes a scene in front of the whole—"

104

she spoke quickly, assuming that in his absentmindedness, he would not ask why the china was back on the table or why it wasn't the good china with the blue onion pattern,

"—neighborhood, someone who cares more about a stupid soft sign than about his home and family, hasn't got the moral—"

continued Mrs. Tachezy, checking one last time to make sure that what she held in her hands was in fact the cheap china set she had bought for just such a purpose at a discount store,

"—right to break anything in that home, not so much as—"

added Mrs. Tachezy, raising her voice and her hands with the dishes,

"—a toothpick!"

With those words, she threw the stack of plates at his feet and ran past him to lock herself in the bedroom. Doctor Tachezy stood up to his ankles in shards, listening to the Christmas carols that had been turned up to maximum volume in the neighboring apartments, so that the idyllic phrases about Bethlehem might drown out the sounds of real life from the Tachezys'. Euphoria was giving way to depression. The critical mind of the scholar, accustomed to relentlessly exposing truth and rejecting error, now turned against him. Let us disregard inaccuracies born of her emotionality, he told himself . . .

Relevant or not, was it not the truth that sixteen years ago he had sought the acquaintance of a girl on account of the Sturz rare edition?

Was it not the truth that—be it in the clover or elsewhere, with or without her assent—he had made that girl a woman and later his wife?

Was it not the truth that he had failed—albeit for a cause as noble as that of the Cyrillic soft sign—to be to that wife what perhaps other men might have been to her?

Was it not the truth that—albeit for reasons as virtuous as adherence to principle—he had failed to obtain access to an education for his daughter?

Was it not the truth that—albeit for motives as human as anger and feelings of injustice—he had caused his family to become the object of public obloquy, insulted a young man who appealed to him, and spoiled Christmas Eve for his wife and daughter?

And was it not the truth that for that reason alone, his wife had just smashed her favorite set of china?

Doctor Tachezy stepped carefully over the pile of shards, picked them up, and wrapped them individually in Christmas paper, so that they could be put together and glued. He blew out the candles, scraped the wax off the rug, gathered up the broken decorations, and straightened the crêche. He put the packages of meat in the refrigerator. He hesitated over the statuette, but ended up placing it on the dining table. Then he spent a long time knocking on the bedroom door, speaking words of consolation.

Around midnight he took the pillows from the armchairs for a mattress, the dirty tablecloth for a cover, and, dejected, went to lie down

25

in the bathtub. . . .

He leaned his head back and shut his eyes. The blood began to hum in his ears. In that precarious position, with the entire weight of his body supported only by the muscles of his arms tensed behind his back while his feet on the slippery skis carried him down the steep slope, he stood immobile. He grasped the loops of his ski poles even more firmly, to stabilize the skis and to use the time remaining for a reassessment of the love that was approaching consummation.

Richard had inherited a basically sound constitution and a firm will from his butcher forebears. He resembled Albert in the Spartan way he had overcome his indispositions. Albert, however, had been unable to erase his hump, and so he hoarded his strength against the world. Richard had been able to overcome his illness, and so he was almost prodigally generous with the strength he had regained. If his uncle's neighbor's pig-slaughterer had not fallen ill, he would probably have wound up lavishing it all on the fields as a farmer or as a teacher on his pupils. Instead, he was now concentrating it all on Her. But the sensitivity his one aristocratic ancestor had bequeathed him brought him to the same state as the driver of a car going the wrong way down a one-way street. The result was the inner schism common to bastard children. He was too much an aristocrat to douse his gentle feelings with beer or, even more simply, with an orgasm. And yet he was too much a butcher to be able to demonstrate his feelings to his love in a refined manner. His brain swam with rhymes and his heart with tenderness, but his face could only blush and grin and his lips could barely stutter a greeting.

No one had ever taught him how to converse with a girl, what to say after he said hello, how to say goodbye and invite her to meet him again, what else to talk about when all the basics—their names, what they do—is known and after everything else—what they like to read, what they hate to eat—has been said, how to profess his love and how to make it. The nurse in the sanatorium had done all the seducing, she had directed the play herself, and dropped the curtain herself, too—that experience was worthless to him now. While in his imagination he had not only spoken with Lizinka, covered her from head to toe with kisses, taken her as his wife and spent a thousand and one nights of love with her, in reality he had done no more than place his arm around her neck and taken a silent bite of her Christmas cake.

When he dropped the spoon in his fish soup and walked out of the house without so much as a goodbye, he was sure that he was leaving for good. As he rode in the taxi through the deserted streets with Christmas trees lit behind every window, he realized bitterly that tonight everyone belonged to someone, that Christmas was a beginning, whereas he, alone and superfluous, was approaching his end. And when he gave the driver all his money at the door to Her building, and was rewarded by a flood of the season's good wishes, he foresaw his own destiny to the very last breath:

He would mount the stairs to Her door one more time, approach Her door and touch the handle Her hand had touched. Then he would walk out into the field behind Her house, which the snow had transformed into a huge white featherbed. He would lie down in it and gaze up at Her window, which he had located that afternoon, until the snowflakes buried him. Not until weeks later, when they would long since have stopped searching for him, would the spring sun melt the lid of his snowy coffin, only then would She look out of her window and see his face, embalmed by the frost: it would be handsome, peaceful, and full of love.

He climbed the stairs slowly, in time with the funeral march that his imagination was playing in his head. Nothing was leaning against the door. The music stopped and he was shaken by a terrible fury at the rotten thief who was gross enough to lay a hand on Her present. Then a flash of common sense told him that it might just as well be She who was holding his work—his shyness had grown to the point where he could no longer even write: good thing that he still knew the language of shapes—in Her merciful hands. And what if She finally sensed in it the tenderness to which he had never been able to give voice? What if She were just now yearning to see his face in the living flesh, while all She would get was a sculpted replica and then a death mask? He was overwhelmed by uncertainty. What to do? Leave and die? Live and ring the bell? And what then? Walk past her parents, whom he didn't know, and take their daughter away? And where? That was when his finger, fondling the pushbutton which responded to the lightest touch, brought Mrs. Tachezy to the door. Richard underwent the process of growing up—which, unless they go through it on a battlefield or over a coffin, takes some people years—in half an hour fragrant with evergreen and burning candles. He was a boy when he entered the flat, but a man when he left.

It was a man who walked out into the thoroughfare and blocked the path of a taxicab, its driver hurrying to get home to his family: it was a man who climbed out on the other side of town and showed the driver an empty wallet, with the words, "Come for it tomorrow!" Even the taxi driver was aware of it and he drove off, pleased that the young thug hadn't made him turn over his day's takings. It was a man who awakened his parents with the question of whether or not there was any grub in that fucking pigsty of a kitchen. And it was a man who at lunch the next day enlightened Doctor Tachezy on the principle of the wheel and the rack with such authority that Lizinka's father—although he did not finish his meal—did not even try to interrupt him.

Unfortunately, no sooner did he find himself alone with the daughter than Richard became a boy again.

The old problem—when, where, how and about what to talk with a girl—emerged before him with even greater urgency than before. When they were crossing the street, he called out apprehensively, "Look out, a car!"

Lizinka nodded. He was grateful to the car for having chosen that street and this particular moment. When a lady who had almost missed her stop pushed her way roughly past them in the bus, he asked solicitously, "She hurt you?"

Lizinka shook her head. He was obliged to the lady for having selected her, of all people, to jostle. When they arrived at the ticket window at the skating rink, he said desperately, "All these people!"

Richard was so depressed that he asked for two children's tickets, and then it was all he could do to get them let in. Finally, in a group that resembled a flock of giant waddling ducks, they started out on their skates along the concrete walk from the dressing rooms to the ice, where his opportunity finally arrived.

Richard raised an inviting elbow to the girl. First he led her slowly, but with gradually increasing bravado, experiencing a twofold bliss: that he could hold her hand in public, and that he was not required to speak. After several rounds of the rink, he turned and, skating backward, faced her, grasped her other hand, and led her, adding another facet to his bliss, for now he could gaze into her eyes. The effect was so hypnotic that after another couple of rounds, the girl began to follow him in variations on simple steps, and then in simple figures. The other skaters made way for them; spontaneously, they cleared the center of the rink; in short, the whole stadium fell victim to the charm of the pair, which seemed to personify the beauty and talent of the human race. What a shame that Wolf and Simsa were not there to confirm how right they had been! Then came a moment when, in the cabin that hung like a bird's nest under the vault of the stadium roof, even the sound technician succumbed to the sight. He replaced the tape of a sprightly brass band with a waltz.

A joyful quiver went through the skating mass as even the clumsiest of them felt the beat of the waltz suffuse their limbs. Richard, on the other hand, jumped as if he had received an electric shock; he lost the beat and

108

stopped in horror. When he came to his senses, he gave Lizinka's hand a squeeze that made her flinch, and skated her swiftly toward the dressing rooms. In his own moral code, dancing was vice number one. It was revolting to him, he hated it murderously.

Even a beginner in the field of psychology could have explained to him the cause of his problem, upon a cursory examination of his sexual history. Richard's furious antipathy to social dancing was founded in his painful memory of the way his nurse in the sanatorium had determined who would be her next lover: by dancing with them. But Richard hadn't the foggiest notion that he might need a psychologist, and so the destructive explosive of hatred accumulated inside him, even now, when it was he who was preventing himself from embracing his own love.

That was how he spent the five days of his Christmas holiday—going from the heights of bliss to the depths of despair and back. He never gave a thought to school. Every afternoon, he and Lizinka excelled on skating rinks. If they hadn't alternated rinks and if some observant sports official had noticed them, who knows what their destinies would have been. But they were stopped only by one wild-eyed old man who claimed he wanted to write a newspaper feature about them. On the ice, they got along fine, but Richard went through purgatory twice a day during the trips to and from the rink. Then he would spend the sleepless nights torturing himself trying to think up conversational gambits to impress her with his intellect. He was suffering some sort of impotence of the mind, and at the end of the fifth day, he fell into a state of utter hopelessness.

Tomorrow, he said to himself, contemplating the New Year's excursion, they will all come between us, the professors, the guys, and some jerks from PSS. What will I do with them around, he asked himself, when I've lost the five days that I had her all to myself? In the din of the bus, he watched her captivating profile, reminiscent of the still surface of a lake that conceals the secret flow of currents in its depths. And what, he asked himself glumly, can I offer her if I ask her to spend the rest of her life by my side? Who am I, that I dare? A bastard with a drop of blue blood for every barrel of pig's blood! His crisis reached its peak. He decided to give up the vain struggle, apologize to his parents, and spend the rest of his life, loveless but in his place, among those who, regrettably, were his equals. That was the moment that Lizinka gave him the first indication of her favor.

A drunken man with a rose in his buttonhole, who had pushed them aside as they boarded the bus so that he might be the first to reach the seat reserved for invalids, had been observing them. Standing over him, Lizinka was seeing if she could play a game with herself. Reading, letter by letter, the Department of Transportation Regulations posted over the window, she would give her right hand a point every time she came to an "i," and her left hand a point every time she came to an "e." She was two words from the end and her left hand was ahead, 74:73.

Both Richard, who didn't know how to think any other way, and Lizinka, who didn't know how to read any other way, were soundlessly moving their lips. When the man noticed what they were doing, he was so ashamed that he stood up and offered them the seat.

"I'm awfully sorry," he said loudly, enunciating exaggeratedly so that they might read his lips, "I had no idea you were deaf-mutes. I wish you better luck in the new year."

He took the rose from his buttonhole, gave it to Lizinka, and stumbled out of the bus. Lizinka was just finishing her game, and she decided she'd give the rose to the winner. The last word but one was "traffic," and her right hand tied the score 74:74. The last word was "regulations," and first her left hand made a point and then the right, and the final score was a tie. So Lizinka gave the flower to Richard.

He couldn't remember walking her home, he couldn't recall how he had made it back to his own little room. He placed the rose on a bed of moistened cotton and started to write. Shame, bitterness, hatred—all slipped away like layer upon layer of petals, until his liberated soul opened out like a blossom, offering him an inexhaustible supply of ideas and words. It was all he could do to organize them into structured formation, for Her to review.

"Theosebud that you gave to me . . ." proclaimed the parade's first rank at twilight.

". . . puts the blazing stars to shame . . ." declared the sixth rank, to the sound of the clock striking midnight.

". . . stands for the youth we share!" was the oath the rear guard swore when the glare of the desk lamp faded with the encroaching daylight.

Richard switched it off and lay down on the bare floor, exhausted as only an artist can be. The psychological perspective that he had gained, along with his victorious battle over words, flanked on one side by explosions of poetic phrase, on the other by salvos of rhyme, were such that he was able to consider his future relationship with Lizinka like a born strategist.

By six o'clock he had the entire operation planned for the next forty-two hours. Within two hours, in the bus—where they would naturally sit together—he would tell her how he had averted dependence on an artificial lung and a surrogate love, so that he might be healthy and pure when he found her. He had no doubt whatever that this time, he would not be at a loss for words; they champed at the bit in his brain like thoroughbreds at the starting gate.

On the trip up the mountain—where they would naturally share one of the double seats on the ski lift—he would use the receding landscape to

110

illustrate how they were both leaving the past behind them and heading toward a life as unblemished as the white plains ahead. They would spend the afternoon modestly with all the others, who would be stumbling around on the training slope; he wanted to surprise her all the more with his skiing prowess when the time came. In the dining room, of course, he would again sit beside her. The twins would be gabbling about sports, Frantisek would crack a crude joke or two, smartaleck Albert would undoubtedly take on the protective coloring of a student of nutrition, rattling off memorized texts about the baking of bread, and Simon would perform his whole repertoire of slurping and belching. Then Richard would ask her softly to come outside after the meal when the others would be sneaking out for a smoke, and to meet him at the first grove of pines above the chalet. Beneath them, they would have the flickering butts of cigarettes, above them the nocturnal lights of the eternal heavenly bodies. The girl would be waiting breathlessly for their first kiss, but he would surprise her afresh. Against the splendid backdrop of the stage of nature, framed by the massive mountain peaks, he would recite to her his lines sweet with the redolence of the rose.

"The rosebud that you gave to me . . ."

After he finished his recitation, he would just shake her hand and walk down to the cottage, to give her time to assimilate the meaning of his poetic communication. And while the dining room would be quaking with the heehaw of jackasses' laughter, he would go down to the ski storage area, carrying the case with his portable electrical apparatus. He would be equipped, in addition to the electrical-shock instrument, with a set of battery-operated needles, so that besides psychiatrists and Green Berets, it could also be used by dermatologists to remove subcutaneous fat globules—and he would engrave his poem on the underside of her skis, as an engagement present. . . .

In the morning, he didn't go on the planned ski tour with the others, so that he might set out for the peak above the chalet as soon as possible after lunch. For an hour he herringboned, for an hour he traversed, and for an hour he climbed on foot, skis on his shoulders. Finally he was at the top. He buckled on his skis and turned to look down. Although he had expected a steep incline, it made him wobble: it was a terrain more for pilots than for skiers. But then he saw far beneath him the school excursion group approaching the chalet along the footpath. He tried to picture what had happened when they took off their skis at the rest stop and stuck them vertically in the snow. Had she been the first to see his poem? Or had it been someone else? What effect did that unconcealed message of love have on the hangmen-to-be? How did they react? With envy? Derision? Or profound admiration? The latter would be his objective when he unsheathed his secret weapon. He waited another few moments, calculating the exact moment to start so that he might enter their field of vision at just the right spot. Then, like a prehistoric hunter, he gave a wild yell and pushed off. They spied him when an overhang in the middle of the slope catapulted him into an enormous leap, from the shadow into the sunlight. His orange windbreaker glowed like a flying torch and then they recognized him. Now it was their turn to yell, but they fell into an awed silence as he vanished in a dip, and they imagined the sound of bones shattering against the stumps. But then he swung up in another jump, over a strip of low evergreens, to land in a beautiful telemark and sideslip to an abrupt stop. It raised a spray of snow which slowly dissipated and floated to the ground, revealing Richard.

"Darling!" exclaimed Lizinka, throwing herself into his arms and shamelessly covering his face with kisses. Before midnight, Professor Wolf himself had ordered a bottle of champagne and waited for the clock to strike midnight, so he could wish them good fortune in the name of the whole class. The chime struck only once. Richard raised his head in surprise and looked at the clock. It was half

26

past seven in the morning. He jumped up from the floor like a madman, stuffed whatever was at hand into his knapsack, ripped the orange windbreaker from the hanger, and plunged down the stairs. The bus was full to overflowing; he couldn't squeeze on but he didn't dare risk waiting for the next one. He ran along the gutter, waving at every vehicle that passed, but with his half-open knapsack and his loose skis he looked like a dangerous lunatic. So he ran across half the city on foot, and when he arrived at the rendezvous, he was almost unconscious. They were waiting just for him.

"Of course," said Associate Professor Simsa sarcastically, "Mr. Masin!"

Simsa waved to the driver to start. Richard's vision blurred; he looked around for his love. He wasn't holding on, the minibus started forward, and Richard fell. Laughter burst out of youthful throats. When he succeeded in regaining his feet, he looked around again. He saw Lizinka, right up in front. Beside her sat Professor Wolf.

Never had the minutes seemed so endless. The only thing that helped Richard survive was the knowledge that soon he would be mounting to the pinnacles of love by her side. When the minibus stopped, he jumped off so eagerly that he forgot his skis and knapsack inside, so he had to wait until the others got out with all their paraphernalia. When he got back in, the automatic door locked shut behind him, and he spent several minutes pounding on the window until he caught the attention of the driver, who was drinking some coffee at a nearby stand. Richard had to sprint after the group, and when he arrived, bathed in sweat, it was the Professor who was waiting for him.

"Of course," said Professor Wolf icily. "Mr. Masin again!"

Richard and the Professor mounted the ski lift and swung out over the trees. The landscape began to recede, as he had imagined it, but under different circumstances. All he could see was the annoyed Professor. Not until they swung up over the mast of the first pylon did he catch sight of the little halo of Lizinka's hair, far ahead and way up. Beside her sat Associate Professor Simsa.

And the black day wasn't over yet. When the gong sounded and the dining room filled up with the noisy voices of the young teachers-to-be who had arrived earlier, along with the young executioners-to-be, representing themselves of course as students of the nutritional sciences, Richard hurried to reserve two seats. Then the world swam before his eyes. The leaders of the two scholastic groups had decided to take the head table, and to have one girl and one boy representing each school join them. For HIENS, the two were Albert and Lizinka.

Richard barely touched his soup and only toyed with his meat. He did not take his eyes off the head table. Lizinka was eating in silence, and when she bent her head over her plate, her hair formed a golden canopy that protected her from intrusive glances. Richard was all the more grateful to her for that when he saw the frequent and curious looks she was getting from the PISS student seated beside the lady principal of his institute. His tortoise-shell glasses, his sloping shoulders, his thin hair (the kind that falls out early) and his obvious inclination to obesity, all this reassured Richard. Just before lunch was over—he gave his rum cake to Simon—he finally caught Lizinka's eye. He could have sworn that she gave him a tiny smile. His good humor was rapidly returning. He couldn't wait until he could lead with his trump.

In the afternoon, he did not go out on the downhill slope with the advanced skiers, but remained instead with the majority as he had planned, on the practice slope. He did not pretend to be a nonskier, but he did not show his cards, either. Occasionally he flinched, when Lizinka fell, but more often, he felt a certain satisfaction when that bespectacled ass who had had lunch with her took a tumble. When they were putting away their skis, he succeeded with the most important part of his plan. He was able to speak with her in private.

113

"Right after dinner," he whispered with urgency, "at the first pines on the right, up over the chalet—be sure to come, I've got something for you!"

He was the first to leave the dining room, he ran down the stairs to the ski storage area and left by the side door, opposite the right slope. As he climbed the slope, he repeated, in time with his steps, "The rosebud that you gave to me . . ."

He was the first to arrive at the pines. In a while, he saw the flicker of cigarette butts beneath him. Overhead, the lights of supersuns. The moon had also risen and illuminated the splendid stage of nature, framed by mountain peaks.

". . . fills the world . . ." he continued reciting his poem, and was stunned at how precisely he had captured the atmosphere of the moment in the intimacy of his room.

Then he realized that the area in front of the chalet was silent and empty. He looked around. No one was coming. He listened. There was no sound of squeaking snow. He ran several steps down the hill, to see if she hadn't just emerged from the chalet. A weak lightbulb lit the empty hallway beyond the front door. He looked past the chalet to the slope opposite, where there was also a grove of pines and froze. He had said on the right, but that depends on which side you're looking from. He ran down to the chalet, no longer stopping to go around back, sprinted across the icy front walk, through the light from the dining room, and started up the opposite slope. It was steeper, with a number of terraces where the snow had piled up; he fell into it up to his knees several times and was miserable because he had forced her to make this climb.

When he reached his destination, she wasn't there. Wasn't and hadn't been. Looking back, all he could see was snow, disturbed only by his own tracks. He realized that she must have been delayed and was waiting on the opposite slope. He turned around and, for the third time that day, broke into a run. It was even worse going down; he tumbled and dug his way out like a puppy. Past the chalet again. Up the slope once more. He was drenched with sweat and soaked with snow. The pines. No one. He was breathing hard; he couldn't understand. Then he realized that while he had been climbing the opposite slope like an idiot, she had had enough time to come here, not find him, and go back. In the chalet, they had turned on the hi-fi and the screeching decibels bit into the silence of the mountain night like a pneumatic hammer. He pictured her, sitting miserably in a corner, in the smoke and noise, not understanding what had happened. He stumbled down the slope.

When he opened the door to the dining room, he couldn't tell at first what kind of game they were playing. The tables were stacked up against the walls, and in the middle of the floor, a wild combat of mixed singles

114

was going on. Richard saw Lizinka. That bespectacled fat ass was holding her around the waist and trying to trip her up backward. He was about to jump him, when at the last instant it dawned on him:

They were dancing. Richard

27

passed out.

"Mornin'," said Albert; he was sitting on the other bed under the slope of the ceiling, nibbling at an apple and studying Plutarch.

"What . . . ?" said Richard weakly. "Where . . . ? How . . . ?"

"The fresh air last night must have knocked you on your ass," said Albert, who in spite of his education used the language of the street, having realized that the common touch was the one appropriate to the epoch, whereas to be an intellectual exposed one to serious risks. "The local croaker gave you a downer and you've been flat-out all day."

Reflexively, Richard sprang out of bed to the chair where his clothes were, but that was as far as he got. Between the residue of sleep and the residue of the barbiturate, the boy felt as if he were in free-fall. His movements were a step behind his intentions, and objects that he reached for seemed to recede.

"Don't fart around like that," said Albert, putting down his book. "You want some eats—I'm your man!"

From the very outset he had hated Richard's good looks, and the reason he came on like a bosom buddy was that he wanted to show him up when the moment arrived. But there was one area in which he couldn't: not even his illness had deprived Richard of his masculine good looks; in fact it had given them a spiritual cast and thus diminished Albert's advantage over him. With the sixth sense of born schemers, Albert was the only one who had realized last night that Richard's indisposition had been a condition of the mind rather than of the body. He wanted to know more, should he need some compromising information in case of a facedown with Richard.

In the middle of his fumblings, Richard stopped short. His memory was beginning to come back.

"Is"— He started urgently, but corrected himself with the vigilance that was returning along with memory. "Are they still out skiing?"

"Well, ASP and the PISS-ass gym teacher," said Albert, combining his wit and his assiduous adherence to the secrecy code, "have got them out on the training slope because the boobtube said *baaad* weather. Good thing PROW told me to hang in there, so you can re–lax. The wingding's at seven."

Richard obeyed. He hadn't liked the hunchback from the time he first set eyes on him, and he exaggerated his attention to his appearance above all to show him up. But there was one area in which Richard could never equal him: not even Albert's hump diminished the boy's steelly self-confidence. In fact he carried the hump as if it were the very thing that ensured him a privileged position. Richard's sudden acquiescence was nothing more than an effort to turn Albert's weapon against him—that of guile. With the heightened perception of a cornered man, he realized that Albert was the greatest threat to his plans, but also the best source of the information he wanted.

"Who," he asked as nonchalantly as he could, "is the guy?"

"Which one?" asked Albert.

"The one that eats with you," said Richard, half-closing his eyes in mock exhaustion, the better to observe him.

"Don't you know," said Albert, with a flash of respect in his eye, "Michael Dujka?"

"Why," asked Richard, with as much contempt as he could muster, "should I know him?"

"Man," said Albert, "even PROW knows him! He's a poet, he's even supposed to have published a book."

"A poet!" exclaimed Richard. "I never heard of him!"

"So what's the hassle?" Albert sensed something of interest here.

"He reminded me of somebody, with that bald head and that paunch of his," Richard said quickly, and added in Albert's own idiom, "Well, aren't you going to hustle me some eats?"

As soon as the door had fallen shut behind the hunchback, Richard got out of bed again and took a few steps. He was all right now. He carefully gathered up his ski suit, took the little locked case out of his knapsack, felt for the key on a string around his neck, and ran across the hall to the bathroom. The shower in the ancient chalet worked more like a sieve, but its nine icy trickles had the effect of a cat-o'-nine-tails. Richard's brain was once again capable of seeing clearly, into both the past and the future.

She was dancing, he said to himself. So what? Was it her fault that he hadn't been there? She could have objected, it wouldn't have done her any good. He evoked the last image that had burned itself on his retina: fatso ecstatically scatting the melody, clapping his sweaty hands together, while she spun before him like a marionette, her face concealed in the shadows. Dujka, Dujka, he repeated. And they permit an animal like that to write poetry? His poetry must smell of his grossness for miles. For the first time in his life, a wild and specifically aimed hatred arose in Richard,

116

and it was reined in only by the whip of the icy water. Invisible hooves pawed the air closer and closer to Dujka's head. . . .

Richard did not go back into the room, he didn't want to chance it. Dressed, he ran down into the ski storage area with his little case. If her skis had been there, he might have gone ahead and engraved them as he had planned, and that would have let off some of the excess steam. But they weren't, and that settled it. He would recite his poem to her in person, until she would embrace and kiss him before God and everybody as a reward for his talent. He laughed. In that concrete windowless bunker, with skihooks on one wall, and on the floor opposite, cartwheels, chains, and other summer harvest paraphernalia in a jumble rather like a medieval torture chamber, his laughter sounded almost mad.

From the ski room, he turned behind the chalet, so they couldn't see him from the training slope. From there, he took the shortest possible route to the peak. Effortlessly, he cut the planned time in half. He was rested and, above all, impatient. For half an hour he herringboned, for half an hour he traversed, and for half an hour he climbed on foot, his skis on his shoulders. When he reached the top, he buckled on his skis and looked down. He was rewarded by an aerial view of the landscape. The sun, which in spite of the forecast was blocked neither by an apron of fog nor by a curtain of clouds, illuminated the surrounding area—the stage of his life, the region where he had been born, reared, where he had sought and today would finally find his fortune, where he would marry, make a hangman's honest living, rear his children, pass the torch on to them, and, one day, die in the knowledge that he had lived a full and useful life. He pushed off.

During the first half of his descent, he was unable to perceive anything but his near free-fall. Not until an overhang in the middle of the slope catapulted him into a long, graceful leap, from the shadow into the light, did he register some confused movement down by the chalet. It stopped short immediately afterwards: they had apparently recognized his wind-breaker. They disappeared when he slid into a dip. He had to concentrate to avoid the brush and the trees, and above all to push off again in time at the second overhang. The emergence of the immense silhouette of the chalet before him frightened him, but by then he was already turning the tips of his skis to the ground. He landed with a crackle of his skis in an exemplary telemark and sideslipped to an abrupt stop while the spray of snow he had raised slowly dissipated and floated to the ground. He had done it. A single glance at them assured him that he had won.

Although the murky lava of the clouds had arrived at the scrub pines, and the muted howl announced the coming of the fierce snowstorm, the silence on the plain before the chalet was that of a *tableau vivant*. Against the snow and upstairs in the dining room windows, he could see faces reflecting revulsion, reverence, relief, and respect.

Then he heard a giggle. A giggle he didn't recognize because he had never heard it before. He turned.

From the grove of pines, which had waited in vain last night for the sound of his verses, ran Lizinka, her cheeks aflame and her cap in her hand, pursued by Dujka. Dujka was throwing snowballs at her. Lizinka was

28

giggling.

As New Year's parties go, it seemed a happy, successful one in spite of the storm raging outside—a storm the likes of which not even the manager of the chalet could recall. It had torn down the power lines, but nobody seemed to care. An abundance of heat, candles, music, and above all wine—the faculties of both schools agreed that for tonight they would look the other way—made for an excellent frame of mind. All that was missing was Richard.

He had vanished as soon as he arrived. They had looked for him but they couldn't find him. Because it was a costume party—theme: an old-time school and an old-time bakery—they assumed that he was among them, incognito.

Wolf sat at the head table in the costume of a master baker, sewn for him by his wife from some shrouds never used by a pardoned client. Around him danced baker's apprentices and oven slaveys, schoolmasters, students, and dunces from down the ages, and he appreciated the kids' inventiveness. But his glance fell the most frequently, and with the greatest appreciation, on the delicately powdered miller's wife, Mrs. Tachezy having sewn Lizinka a replica of the costume of *Die Schöne Müllerin* out of her own old wedding dress. It had not escaped him that the girl had spent most of the evening dancing with a slightly paunchy Florentine scholar, who kept adjusting his nonperiod spectacles. But Wolf kept reminding himself that the poet's verse showed an ardent inclination toward revolution and an icy revulsion toward sex, so he was not really concerned. Still, he was quite pleased when the manager bent over him, shouting to drown out the joyful noise, to ask if one of his students wasn't named Dujka, because someone outside needed him urgently. Wolf

118

indicated the Florentine, and when the manager led Dujka off the improvised dance floor, Wolf even toyed with the thought that it would be nice if the miller's wife were to ask him to dance. But the PISS gym teacher took her arm instead, and he had to come to grips with two conflicting sensations: one of mild irritation, and one of self-satisfaction that he had retained a proper distance.

Shortly before midnight, champagne corks began popping, and that was when something happened that made Wolf's blood freeze in his veins. Into the room full of merrymakers came a tall figure wrapped in a red cloak. In order that no one should mistake the person he represented, he carried a wheel dripping with mock blood, as red, thought the Professor, as only raspberry jam can be. To a loud round of applause, the "Executioner" walked over to the head table and placed the wheel on Dujka's empty chair. Then he bowed and vanished.

A cold sweat broke out on Wolf's brow. He wondered, confused, who it was and what he wanted. Had someone from HIENS got crazy drunk? He would kick him out of school, but what a catastrophe nonetheless . . . if someone from PISS had caught on? . . . He took advantage of the bedlam that had just broken out in honor of the arrival of the New Year to leap to the other side of the table. He wanted at least to remove the damned wheel before he decided what other steps to take. He grasped it and shoved it under the table. He got some of the raspberry jam on his right hand. His handkerchief was in his right-hand pocket, so he licked his hand. It was blood.

"Professor!" Albert whispered hoarsely in his ear, "Downstairs!"

The hunchback looked as if he had floured his face for the increased credibility of his costume, but that was just how pale he was. He had no time to say more than that, because the scream that sounded from outside the door silenced everyone. The manager's wife stood holding a flashlight in the doorway to the dining room, gasping for breath and pointing downstairs. Then she dropped the flashlight.

Wolf was the first to arrive in the ski storage room, but he didn't have time to lock the door to keep the others out. For that matter, he knew immediately that not even God could help him here, perhaps only his own highly placed protectors might—that is of course if they decided that they still wanted to.

Bound by chains to a Saint Andrew's cross constructed from skis lay Dujka, stark naked. Wolf, the expert, realized immediately that before he had been broken "from the top down"—and it had been a fine job, worth a grade of Excellent—he had undergone intense torture by electrical shock. He immediately covered the corpse with an orange windbreaker he found on the floor nearby, so that even this time Lizinka was prevented from acquainting herself with the verses that the unfortunate Richard had burned with the finest of needles on Dujka's broad chest and fat belly:

> The rosebud that you gave to me
> Stands for the youth we share
> For all the jealous world to see.
> Our friendship, gentle, fair.
> It puts the blazing stars to shame,
> That friendship pure and clean.
> It outshines God's own sunny flame.
> And fills the world, unseen.
> Yes, is it not a blessing grand
> That we've a love so rare.
> The rosebud from your own sweet hand
> Stands for the youth we share.
> RICHARD MASIN

They did not find the author until the thaw in mid-March. He lay in his shirtsleeves under the first pine on the right above the chalet. His face, embalmed by the frost, was

29

monstrous, frightening, and full of hate.

IV

On the evening of Friday, March 21, on the eve of a new spring, Simsa's telephone rang. The first ring escaped him entirely. Between the first and the fifth, he emerged very slowly—his entire organism objecting—from his dreaming. By the seventh ring, he felt displeasure, by the eighth, irritation, by the ninth anger, and by the tenth he was overcome by a distinctly physical revulsion for the sound that embodied the impersonal forces that had always manipulated his life. By the eleventh ring, he swore to himself that he would never again listen to another authority except his own heart; he mobilized his will and returned to the fantasies from which he had been so brutally ripped. By the nineteenth ring, the battlefield inside him fell under the control of his eternal enemy, which—as he realized for the first time—had always triumphed over his other, free, self: drill. In the middle of the twentieth, he picked

30

up the receiver.

"ASP here," he said tersely, as he had learned irrevocably in his many years in closely guarded buildings, using his code name, the one that had engraved itself ineradicably on his mind in the past few months as a part of the strictly guarded secret that was the school.

"This is Margaret Wolf," said a soft voice at the other end.

"Good evening," he said, as pleasantly as he could, so as not to sound formal to the only woman who had ever had his respect.

"Good evening," said Mrs. Wolf. "Were you asleep, Paul?"

"No," he lied, as convincingly as he was able, so as not to upset the only woman who had ever displayed unselfish concern about him. "I'd just finished dinner."

"What a shame," said Mrs. Wolf merrily. "When you turned down the invitation for Sunday dinner, I hoped that you'd fallen in love."

"No!" he lied as emphatically as possible, "I am still alone and I'll stay alone until you get a divorce."

"But Paul!" she said with feigned indignation, obviously flattered. "You wouldn't wish anything like that on Frederick! You could have ten women for every finger on your hands, but where would my hero find a single one to massage his back? Frederick is sick in bed."

"Sick?" repeated Simsa incredulously. "Frederick?"

That had never happened, as long as he had known him.

"Lumbago. I can't understand why you let him," said Mrs. Wolf reproachfully, although Wolf himself had insisted on replacing Richard on the team, "play volleyball. He isn't as young as he used to be. But at least I'll get to spend the weekend with him. He asked me to tell you to call off tomorrow."

"Shouldn't I take it for him?" asked Simsa, more out of politeness than anything else. He heard Mrs. Wolf repeat his question to Professor Wolf, and he knew the reply in advance. The next day's excursion was to have been to the out-of-town depository of the Oriental Museum, with its collection of exotic torture devices. It had been established by an enlightened aristocrat to inspire the imagination of domestic executioners. But they proved to be a bunch of obscurantists, incapable of tearing themselves away from rusty thumbscrews, bulky racks, and other antiquities that would sooner elicit a man's life than his confession. It was Wolf, then still nothing but a selfmade man with neither name nor patron, who gave back to mankind the fruit of a millennia of inventiveness. It happened during a critical stage of the mass trials, when interrogations were stymied because the ones being questioned were professional revolutionaries, unmoved by common European tortures. It was Wolf's first triumph. Later, when torture was no longer part of his job, he might have had a personal interest in having the unpopular traces vanish in the mire of ancient moats. Nevertheless, he arranged with the Doctor's help for all the equipment to find a home in closed collections. Therefore,

122

Simsa understood that for sentiment's sake Wolf would like to show them to the kids himself.

"Paul"—Mrs. Wolf returned to the phone—"Frederick would like to show it to the kids himself."

"I thought he might," said Simsa politely. Materials that were still classified top secret had prevented him from admitting to his mentor that he, Simsa, could teach Wolf a thing or two about torture himself. In fact, he had good cause to consider these relics junk, and to view work with them as ineffective piddling; but he remained silent.

"You're to call them and tell them to do some revising; Frederick wants to give them a test on Monday. He also asks that you handle the preparations for Monday's execution yourself—take one of the kids who hasn't taken his practical midterms yet."

When her warm voice rang off, Simsa did not hang up the receiver. Instead, he dialed the number of the dormitory for Third World students, where the HIENS students from out of town also stayed. The choice of the dorm was circumspect and expedient: foreign students had no visitors, and if they were to glance at the HIENS textbooks or notes, there was no danger of exposure, since they were still struggling with an unknown language.

The dorm administrator reminded him that it was Friday. It was the only free evening they had, and the boys had taken off, each after his own pursuits. Albert went to see a historical film, the twins were off playing basketball and then to a disco, and Frantisek had gone out for a beer. So the administrator called Simon Hus, who was in bed asleep. Because Simon's sleepy voice did not inspire confidence, Simsa dictated the message to him word by word, instructing him to deliver it that night, unless he wanted to risk that someone might have to get up unnecessarily early and then feel the need to get even with him. The kids had long since adopted Wolf's method of settling accounts in torture classes.

Then Simsa dialed again, listening to the ringing at the other end, still concentrating on the message he was to convey.

"Hello!" said a high-strung female voice. "Mrs. Tachezy speaking!"

Simsa was struck by a sudden idea.

"Who's there?" the female voice asked irritably.

Simsa sat immobile on the bed, but the idea was already bearing him through the night.

"Who is calling?"

The idea carried Simsa to the threshold of the next morning, and sat him behind the wheel of his sports car.

"Paul?" asked the female voice, a bit choked.

The thought drew Simsa through the sparse Saturday-morning traffic across town to the slaughterhouse. At the foot of the statue of a butcher poising a mallet aimed at a calf, their usual meeting place for outings, he saw a figure looking out in vain for her schoolmates. The golden glow of her hair blinded him.

"Paul!" whispered the female voice passionately. "I'm not ang—"

Associate Professor Simsa hung

31

his skis on the hook of the ski lift and swung up into the seat instead of Wolf, who wanted to wait for Masin. He waited for the pleasurable lurch when the lift swung him up off the ground. He felt that he was being pulled away from all his obligations, his destiny, from the very force of gravity itself, and that he was floating forward to the land of dreams.

He hadn't always responded like that. When the state had picked him out of the ashcan where his unfeeling mother had tossed him, it did what it could for him. It placed him, like a chunk of raw material to be processed at length into a useful product, in one of its orphanages. Then it went on to enroll him, for final assembly, in a military school, which was supposed to issue him at the end in the stiff uniform of a professional noncommissioned officer. Like an animal rescued from cold and hunger and given a full dish near a warm stove, every bite he took confirmed him in his love and respect for the kindly if severe master reminiscent of God. Like God, the state was neither visible nor addressable but equally omniscient and omnipotent. Like God, the state manifested itself only through its priests, who were granted various ranks and titles, but equal power to punish. Simsa became as accustomed to drill as an Eskimo to ice; he submitted to it devotedly, indeed with pleasure, because he had never known anything else. The state had saved his life, and he offered it up daily, so that his existence was uncomplicated and his career followed a constant, upward course.

Then, while carrying out a certain military task in the execution of which he had to spend a few weeks at a luxury mountain hotel, a change began imperceptibly to set in. Later on, as Wolf's assistant, he began to spend his time off here in the mountains instead of at the hunting lodge, and the cult of the state was gradually eroded in him, to be replaced by the cult of nature and sex. With the passage of years, he grew increasingly pleased to feel the world retreating from him—a world full of screaming nurses, house fathers, commanders, and finally of clients—pleased that he would arrive at the top and step out onto the snow, unviolated by civilization. He would travel across it against the current of history, where all technology was represented by a man's muscle, and all culture, including poetry, was supplanted by his penis.

He couldn't count how many times he had waited on top, when the ski lift would bulldoze up from the valley like a giant bucket excavator, dumping at his feet an endless line of women, how many times he had waited for a girl whose eyes would show an equally strong desire to spend the day with him on the white hillsides and the night between the white sheets. Rarely did he encounter the same girl twice, but it was possible that he just didn't recognize her, there were too many of them and they were too much alike: he went for big-busted brunettes, because he soon decided that these could equal him in passion and staying power. Under the influence of the ascetic Wolf, at first he was frightened of the explosion of unbridled lust. It sometimes went so far that after achieving a climax, he would flee from his partners or even chase them out. In time, of course, he came to realize that it was Wolf and not he who was abnormal, that the state had nothing against sex—at least not where it aids its employees to be more amenable to taking orders. But the period during which he had considered his vitality to be a vice, when he had been ashamed of it and concealed it, had left a permanent mark on him. His relationships with women had been reduced to animal pleasure, unblessed by the grace of emotion. He had never known love, but so far he had missed it about as much as an Eskimo misses a rose.

Now he felt that pleasurable sensation again; it was the first time he had come here since the birth of HIENS. He did not doubt that this time, as always, he would find a brunette beauty, either among the students of the other school or among the chalet's employees, who would be pleased to give herself to him. He felt as if any moment he would float up over the sparkling hilltops, and in a surplus of good humor, he turned to the one who was sharing the lift with him.

"Well, Miss Tachezy," he said, "isn't it great?"

Lizinka was playing a new game. When a blue seat passed them in the opposite direction, she gave a point to her left hand. When it was a red one, she gave it to the right. When it was a green one, a point went to the one that happened to be behind. The left hand was leading by a single point, the score was 15:14, and Lizinka had to pay attention so as not to make a mistake.

Observing that the girl was moving her lips, but that he could not hear a sound, Simsa attributed it to the change in altitude and shook his head hard to clear his ears.

"What was that, Miss Tachezy?" He addressed his pupil as formally as he was accustomed to doing in the classroom.

Now her right hand was ahead, 16:15, and Lizinka was concentrating so as not to cheat either out of a point.

125

Simsa realized that he could hear the metallic ring of the cable, and that the fault was not necessarily in his hearing. He had no idea that the girl was counting and it occurred to him that she might be praying. This fragile being by his side, holding her knitted cap in her folded hands while the wind fluttered through her golden hair, appeared in the unearthly space above the retreating cones of snowy fir trees to resemble nothing so much as a saint experiencing her assumption.

When he had set eyes on her that first day in the apartment, she had reminded him of a picture, but pictures didn't have anything to say to him. The nurses in children's homes, the house fathers and the commanders, had led him along paths that avoided art and emotion like lepers. By the time the more cultivated Wolf and his wife entered his life, it was too late for him to catch up. Moreover, Lizinka lacked the heavy breasts, the sensuous lips and, above all, the nocturnal coloring that could attract him to her as a woman. He had appreciated her, however, as a pupil from the time of the initial exam, when she did the carp in two blows and the chicken in a single slash. And then the grave and delicate girl proceeded to progress so well in school that soon she was ahead of all but Albert. He and Wolf gradually became accustomed to her reticence; it was enough for them that she was consistently well-prepared for written tests and practical exams. She made up for any lack of physical strength by an adroitness and feeling for each and every situation that belongs only to women. Only once did she hesitate, and that was when he first became aware that she was . . .

It was on the afternoon of December 13 and Simsa was lecturing on the crushing of testicles, when toward the end of the period, the time had arrived for a demonstration. The usual procedure was for students to alternate regularly as clients and as executioners, so that there not be any delays. Being executioner fell to Lizinka this time, while Simon acted the client. Simsa was pressed for time: he was annoyed that testicle-crushing had gotten the worst of it when they had set up the plan. Next year, he thought, they would have to give it more, possibly to the detriment of nipple-burning with cigarettes, which they had got through in a jiffy. In order to save time, he had Simon set up while he was finishing his lecture at the blackboard. Tying him with leather thongs to the adapted cot, which the school had scrounged from the prison gynecological section, was a mechanical task that the twins were able to manage while listening to Simsa. So it happened that when Lizinka had picked up the ballbreaker—an instrument developed by Simsa years earlier, and so well that in spite of the advancing technological revolution, it had remained up-to-date—and approached Simon, she stopped in embarrassment.

"Come on, Tachezy," said Simsa with some irritation, because it was only ten minutes short of the bell, "mangle his nuts for him!"

126

It was the intention of the faculty that the kids learn the language of the worksites. All the instruments used as instructional aids were adapted the way a stage dagger is. The ballbreaker exerted only a certain pressure, unpleasant but not painful, then it blocked itself.

Lizinka did not move, and it was only then that Simsa noticed that Simon was wearing green cotton boxer shorts, with his obese white paunch lifting out of the elastic waistband. No one had bothered to remove them, because so far the students had never gone below the belt. Simsa did not intend to lose any time.

"Fleischer"—he turned to Albert, taking a sharp antique flayer out of the cabinet—"slice those drawers off—at least he'll have to buy something classier."

Deftly, Albert cut the fabric with a single slash and removed the shorts to reveal Simon's underbelly: beneath a comically tiny penis lay a scrotum of monstrous dimensions. A tremendous roar went up, the only ones not to laugh were Lizinka and Richard.

"It's not the size," called Simsa into the merriment, aware that a good laugh could only help the lesson along, "that marks the prize—and you couldn't ask for a better pair for breaking than Hus here has—so, Tachezy, get on with it!"

Simon gave her a friendly wink. Then he shut his eyes and began to wheeze, as was his habit. But Lizinka still hesitated. What have we here? Simsa asked himself in surprise. Could it be that the young lady hasn't been paying attention? For the past three and a half months, he had been unstinting with his praise. His instinct as a teacher told him that he finally had an opportunity to rebuke her, so that success should not go to her head. He opened his mouth to speak when he noticed her eyes. What he saw in them was not indecision. They were directed at Simon's crotch and they reflected sheer astonishment. Simsa closed his mouth, but all the louder did he reproach himself in his mind: *You jackass!*

He was witnessing his pupil's first view of a man's penis.

He handled it perfectly, of course. He pretended to see a fault in the blocking mechanism of the ballbreaker and interrupted the lesson with a clever commentary, saying that he'd hate to have them damage the very parts of Simon's anatomy that he was going to need the most, if only, he added to the general merriment with an intentional crudity aimed at concealing his own embarrassment, to play pool with. With characteristic perspicacity, he handed Lizinka a tangerine, which, like the pupils, he had received as dessert for lunch. He was struck dumb a second time when she squashed it with such a verve that it splashed everyone with its sticky juice. The blocking mechanism had indeed failed, and Simon had been saved from mutilation by a miracle. . . .

A miracle? Simsa glanced again at the girl by his side. Her lips were still moving and her eyes were fixed on the return cable moving opposite them, as if she were reading from it some mysterious message. Even then he did not see her as a woman, but she didn't seem like a student to him either. Who was she, really? What was going on inside her? And why had she captivated him like this, all of a sudden?

His thoughts lasted only until they had passed the last pylon, beyond which lay terra firma. There, Simsa, the experienced sportsman, took over, and he had to see to a number of things. First he had to arrange for a single room for Wolf, so that he himself might have solo quarters. Wolf, the moralist, did not demand the same rigid monasticism of others, but why irritate him unnecessarily? As usual, fortune was on his side. The manager's wife got the lady principal of PISS out of the only first-class single room by telling her that there was a rat in it. For Simsa, she got the watchman's room behind the ski storage area; because she had full breasts and raven hair, he was all set. Lizinka once again blended in with the rest of the student body. He had no way of knowing that soon she would distinguish herself in such a way that he wouldn't forget her till the day he died.

On the other hand, he did not fail to notice the interest she aroused among the men who saw her first. As for Dujka, he didn't take him seriously; Dujka was an adolescent and a poet to boot, and he had always suspected poets of being impotent. But the PISS gym teacher cum ski coach was his own contemporary, and a man with interests parallel to his own. They discovered that when they were classifying the students into beginners and advanced skiers.

"Fantastic," said Simsa, enviously staring to the left, where PISS was lining up and giggling, "all those nice pussies you've got there!"

"I'd trade them all," said his colleague, hungrily staring to the right, where HIENS was noisily lining up, "for that angel of yours!"

Simsa had just enough time to ponder that remark, whereupon he spent the next thirty-three hours fascinated by the soft allure of the snow and of the manager's wife. She was one of those Class A catches that even an angler of his talent and experience rarely pulled in. He was more than pleased to accept her invitation that he slip down to his little room right after midnight, so that they might ring in the New Year with a salvo of the senses. Leaning against the bar, sipping a Coke, he was just waiting for the moment when he could wish Wolf and the kids a happy New Year, when an urgent voice disturbed him.

"Say," the ski coach was hissing in his ear, with a glance to the table where the lady principal was beckoning to him, "that old bitch is calling me—can I tell her that this is your girl, so I don't land in the shit?"

And he placed Lizinka, dressed in the costume of *Die Schöne Müllerin*, in Simsa's arms. Simsa recognized her right off and wanted to lead her to

128

her table, because the vision of the hot cavern that would soon be welcoming his plunge of relief made the thought of dancing with this underdeveloped Lolita seem very tame indeed. But a teacher's obligation to be polite made him dance at least a few steps with her. The ski coach had been in such a hurry that he had literally leaned the girl against him. She was waiting like a mannequin for someone to breathe life into her again. He placed his hand on her waist and took her hand to dance. Then he felt something extraordinary.

She hadn't squeezed his hand, or pressed close to him, or used any of the other tricks women employ to show their attraction to a man, but he had the intense sensation that she had penetrated him totally.

It is amazing that Lucie Tachezy, who believed in the golden lode of her daughter's talent and represented her as a genius to coaches of winter and summer sports, as well as directors of the stage and screen, had not recognized the true genius with which nature had endowed the girl. Were it not for a complex of coincidences by which Lizinka had aroused the disfavor of examination commissions, it would never have come out that, unlike women whose mission is to give life, she was born to take it. And were it not for another casual series, beginning with the beckoning of the aging lady principal, jealous of her subordinate lover, no one would have found out that Lizinka was also a born dancer. Had it been someone more interested in dance than Associate Professor Simsa who discovered it, her entire life might have taken a different course. For Simsa, dancing was just a kind of exercise, and in some cases, amorous foreplay. He was incapable of relishing the aesthetic uniqueness of Lizinka's dancing, but he understood something that was far more important to him: the fact that he was dancing with—a woman.

From that moment forward, he couldn't tell if he was leading her or if she was leading him, but one thing he could tell for certain: he had never experienced anything like this before. Suddenly he thought of that day years ago—he hadn't been any older than Lizinka—when a voluptuous gypsy had let him go all the way. Both his hands had been too small to cover a single one of her breasts. And it wasn't until she had threatened to take him to court that he had discovered to his horror that she was thirteen. Had he set out on the wrong track? What if it was the bodies of fragile blondes, so different from his ideal, that concealed a volcano he never dreamed of?

His self-control disappeared. In spite of the fact that he was not only deviating from his erotic taste, but also violating Wolf's first commandment (Thou shalt keep away from women at work) he took advantage of the merciful halflight and pressed so close to Lizinka that he could feel her breasts against his chest. Because sex was his hobby, one that took the place of art or travel, he had at his command every minute nuance of physicality, including the ability to read from a fleeting touch a woman's entire anatomy and her sexual psyche. What he read surpassed in its intensity anything he had ever encountered.

It was as if someone had taken an immense eraser and rubbed out what the past decades had written on his soul; he was spinning not only on the dance floor, but in some sort of capricious sexual circle. There was only one way out of it, as he realized, amazed, when he was almost jolted away from her by a magnificent erection. And that way was suicidal: to have her, soon, so that she would lose her aura of uniqueness and he could begin on another long line of brunettes . . . That was when he heard the scream and the crash of the flashlight dropped by the manager's wife, his most recent bed companion. . . .

The erection did not let up. The pressure in his groin was such that he had to do something. He kicked off his bedroom slippers, removed his beige corduroy slacks and his red cotton briefs. It helped his body, but his soul was still in pain. He realized that it had been more than twenty years since he had held a night watch like this, alone with his manhood erect. He had given up masturbation when he found the gypsy; he didn't want to waste the powers that he needed for his sexual forays. How malicious had been his pity for his peers, when he used to listen to their ersatz moans in darkened dormitories, deprived by nature of sex appeal and, by the tight-fistedness of the state, of money for whores. Now, in his comfortable studio apartment, furnished like his cottage with all the luxury a bachelor lover could want, he felt himself to be even more pathetic than they.

Moreover, the idea that had made him hang up the phone without delivering the Professor's message to the girl was so risky, indeed so mad, that he strove to put it out of his mind as quickly as possible.

He had had more than one virgin in his life. When he still kept an erotic diary, he had recorded "puncturing"—as they used to say in the orphanage—half a dozen of them. Since then, although he had always preferred "secondhand models"—as they used to say in the home—another healthy gross. In spite of his experience, though, he now felt as though she had the upper hand—he, Paul Simsa, whose potency was related by aging woman to their nubile daughters! He, Associate Professor of Executionary Sciences, in spite of his youth an executioner of note who had woven himself a rope ladder of schnooses right into the history books! He, to whom strangulation and defloration was what the alphabet is to writers, he was at his wits' end.

How to win a girl like her? By means of a frontal assault? That was the way, as they said in the barracks, he often managed to "dip the wick"—with women whom Lizinka resembled as much as fire resembles snow. Even if he weren't allergic to poetry, he was put off by the fate of Dujka and Masin. Only the military precept that in any contest between armor

130

and artillery, the latter eventually emerges victorious, buttressed his conviction that not even Lizinka was invulnerable.

And how would a girl like her respond, once conquered? With a flood of liberated lewdness? He dismissed that idea. That kind of "snatch"—as his sex-maniac clients used to say—was again typical only of the women of his fancy, whom Lizinka resembled as much as a nightingale resembles a nanny goat. With tears? Not for her, with that stoical calm of hers. By turning him in? And what if this time he didn't get off with just support payments? He thought of his signature on a certain old document and shivered. Then the phone rang again, and he grabbed the receiver as if it might be the answer to all his tortured questions.

"Simsa here," he said piteously, the ineradicable eradicating itself from his mind.

"Paul," said a female voice with a woeful tremor, "are you angry with me?"

Simsa was silent.

"What have I done," asked the female voice, with a self-righteous tremor, "to you, that you torture me like this, seventy-seven evenings. Yes, Paul, I've just been waiting for you to call me, and then you hang up—no, don't deny it. I recognized you—"

continued the female voice with a humiliated tremor,

"—by your breathing!"

Simsa was silent.

"My darling Paul," said the female voice, not even trying to conceal her love, "I'm so desperate that I went through my daughter's schoolbag to find your number in her record book. Now I'm phoning from a telephone booth so they can't listen in. Oh, Paul, Paul, give me your address and I'll come and give—"

added the female voice, not trying to conceal an infinite boldness,

"—myself to you!"

"My dear lady," said Simsa with a smile, so as not to upset her, "I apologize for disturbing you at this inconvenient hour, but yesterday's telegram from Professor Wolf informing you that the

32

skiing excursion has been extended, did not say everything."

"You're frightening me," said Mrs. Tachezy, rising from the settee where they had just taken a seat. "Mr. Simsa, has something happened to our—"

she asked pressing her right hand to her left breast,

"—Lizinka?"

"Heavens," said Simsa hastily, "no, our—"

he said, repeating the possessive pronoun, unconsciously taking possession of her at least verbally,

"—Lizinka is just fine. I assure you, dear lady, that the delay is merely to protect our institution."

His tone, and the snow that fell like a curtain behind the window, transforming the forenoon into twilight and creating the illusion that the whole world was as silent and innocent as the snowflakes, calmed her down. Before she returned to the settee, she took the fancy goblets from the china cabinet, along with the bottle of Courvoisier that nine months earlier had been brought by the man sitting beside her, his excellent build set off by his skiing outfit. It occurred to her that although they had opened the bottle for three birthdays and for New Year's, it was still not empty. That was a reflection of the extent of their social drinking. As she crossed her legs so as to display their classic lines—this time she congratulated herself for putting on only a particularly charming morning dress—she raised the cut-glass goblet, its every facet reflecting the snowflakes, and joined her guest in sipping the mellow liquid.

"Go on," she said, taking from the tiny pocket of her robe a cigarette case that appeared to be diamond-studded, although, like every gift from Doctor Tachezy, it was not the real thing, "Mr. Simsa."

"Yes," said Simsa, taking from the tiny pocket of his ski pants a massive lighter that appeared to be made of brass, although, like every Dupont lighter, it was made of solid gold, "my dear lady."

He recited the official report about the New Year's party in the mountains, as written in the first hour of the new year by Professor Wolf, and memorized by HIENS before dawn, while the others were either in a nervous or an alcoholic coma. Before the police were called, they had naturally rung up DOOR. As a result, just as the snowstorm had died down like an exhausted stallion, a special group from the capital arrived and took over the case. They were still in danger, though, because through DOOR, NESTOR had sent word that they remained personally responsible for the school's remaining "leakproof." The investigating officers helped. Even though it was perfectly clear to them that the deed had been done by the mad Masin, they detained all the people at the chalet. Only Associate Professor Simsa was taken away in the morning with apparent symptoms of hepatitis. What he did then, while the chalet was under quarantine, was to make lightning visits to the parents.

He kept all of New Year's Day for Richard's family. He didn't even get them to answer the door until just before noon, since they had come home

132

in the early-morning hours from the Butchers' New Year's Ball. Their reply to the terse statement that their son had tortured a young MD to death whereupon in all probability he had committed suicide, was typical.

"Shee-it!" said Richard's father. "The fucking new year is sure starting out great!"

"Well," said Richard's mother, "all that crap about grandsons is down the toilet."

Then she went to the kitchen to cook the traditional New Year's hog's-head soup, where she shed a few tears after all. Simsa remained with them until late afternoon, when he was certain that, from the viewpoint of the school, they were all right. He didn't like doing it, but he had to remind them that any indiscretion would be subject to strict reprisals. For example, the authorities had proof that most of the objects of value in their apartment had been obtained through illegal meat deals. Richard's father gave Simsa a look that was both reproachful and contemptuous, and said, aptly, "Cut the bullshit. Even if we were to rip you open ass-first, you still couldn't fart the boy back for us!"

He then visited the twins' dark-haired mother, who at last repaid him for accepting her son Peter at the school, and left the next morning, having combined business with pleasure. Simon's father was averse to any further difficulties, Frantisek's was no problem, being an employee of the corrections system, and Albert the orphan wasn't even on the list. He spent that night with the mother of the twins again, who repaid him for accepting her son Pavel at the school. Now he was at his last stop, sipping excellent cognac in a pleasant room still fragrant with evergreen. Outside it was snowing picturesquely, and he was speaking with an attractive woman in the prime of life. He would be able to report to DOOR that HIENS was still impenetrable. All the same, he felt uneasy.

How did it happen that, in a situation that bordered on the intimate, in the proximity of a woman who was well within his reach, he did not feel any excitement? As he spoke, he risked being labeled rude and alternated glances between Lucie's bare knees and her bare décolletage, imagining her in various obscene positions to get his organism functioning.

But she wasn't herself either. As soon as she determined that the events leading to his visit concerned her daughter only peripherally, she continued to display a polite interest but her thoughts were elsewhere. The misfortune of the youth—whom she permitted to take her daughter skating only to spite her husband—was overshadowed by her own tragedy, that of a woman whose inner fire had once upon a time been quenched by Doctor Tachezy. She now could add to her anger at him, which was about as helpful to her as an aspirin to a junkie, an anger of a higher order. It was a cathartic rage at herself, that in the past sixteen years before the visit of Simsa, the apartment with its comfortable settee where she spent most of her days alone, had been visited only by the postman and the plumber.

It was high time she put an end to that!

She did not fail to notice how during the conversation—which she had long since stopped following—Simsa glanced surreptitiously from her knees to her décolletage, and the idea that the cognac had brought to the surface was quickly ripening into action, urged on not only by the libido of a love-starved female, but also by the heart of a grateful mother. In addition to her yearning to fill the awful void inside her, she felt a moral obligation to give of her body to satiate this love-starved man who gave of his spirit to satiate her child.

But how to win a man like that? Sixteen years is just a flash in the life of a planet, but an eternity in the love life of a woman. She couldn't offer him the innocence she had once offered Oscar and Doctor Tachezy, nor did she have fame or money at her disposal. It depressed her to realize that other women, by their husbands' sides, had grown in sixteen years to become movie stars, academicians, Olympic athletes, prime ministers, and notorious terrorists. While her own daughter would, at the age of sixteen, be the first hangwoman in the world, all *she* could offer a lover, thanks to Doctor Tachezy, was marble cake. God, she sighed to herself, to what depths I've sunk! I, Lucie Alexander, the pride of my family, the gem of my class, the jewel of dancing school, and today I can't figure out how to offer myself to a hangman! She was startled to hear herself sharing her husband's prejudices. Her shame at that, and her desire to make it up to the teacher for the—albeit unvoiced—insult, suddenly showed her the way to seduce Simsa.

Meanwhile, Simsa had his hands full of his own troubles. Not even the most luxuriant erotic fantasies brought on the usual response. What's up? he wondered cynically. At that point Mrs. Tachezy leaned forward, as if to observe something down by her feet, and then she vanished. He stopped talking, a bit startled, and waited a moment. Then he cleared his throat. No response. He spoke her name, embarrassed. Finally he picked up the corner of the tablecloth and looked under the table. With her eyes shut, Lucie was lying there on her back, her left knee bent as if she were going somewhere, her right hand tucked into her décolletage as if she were looking for something.

Simsa had seen many people faint, but always at the worksite. It was one of the tricks commonly used by clients when he approached them with the "necktie," as Karli used to call the noose. When Simsa had been just a beginner, who viewed anyone with a high school diploma as God, he used to wonder that a doctor of philosophy or a lady minister couldn't think of something more original. He had learned from Wolf how to bring them around, by spraying them with the hose for flushing away feces, and when that didn't help, by slapping their face. Neither was suitable now. In his initial confusion, he wanted to telephone Doctor Tachezy, but he decided against it. He remembered him as a drunkard with a violent temper, God knows if he'd believe that Simsa had been there to discuss the school with her. Her appearance and her behavior indicated that she had plenty of lovers, and Simsa had no desire to be the one to catch her husband's furious revenge. So he acted on his own. He placed his arms under Lucie's knees and behind her shoulders, picked her up, and laid her on the settee between the window and the Christmas tree. To make sure that she was alive, he carefully extricated her hand from behind her neckline and plunged his own inside. He was delighted to feel her heart still beating. His brain regurgitated some old data: a faded health poster showing a lifeguard resuscitating a drowning man. Simsa leaned down on Lucie, placed his mouth on hers, and began to revive her by giving her the kiss of life.

All the while, of course, she had been fully conscious. Her instincts told her that if she couldn't offer a lover wealth, fame, or power, she could at least give him her helplessness, the opportunity to rescue her and bolster his ego. Watching his actions from behind her almost-closed eyelids, she had no doubt that he understood, and she was moved by the charm with which he initiated the love game. She was enchanted by the feigned indecision as he moved from her to the telephone and back, the pretended concern with which he placed her on the settee, the way he used the pretext of looking for a heartbeat to touch her breast. And when he kissed her with such ardor, she wound her arms around his neck and responded with equal ardor.

At first he was startled, but he relaxed immediately. He was much more at home with this. In fact, her brunette fragrance electrified him. His indisposition vanished.

"What," breathed Lucie, as he unbuttoned her robe with a deftness acquired from long years of undressing violently resisting clients, "should I call you?"

"Paul," he whispered, as his experienced fingers unhooked her brassiere.

"And you can," she said brazenly, as he adroitly removed her pantyhose, "call me Luce!"

She used the name that Oscar had coined, implying with the sound of its homonymous twin a libertine, Bohemian tone. Using it, she did away with the practical, down-to-earth Lucie, and irrevocably overstepped the shadow of her marriage.

Simsa felt very much at home. He tossed her pantyhose to the ceiling, ripped open the zipper on his ski pants, and overpowered her impatiently, while the flimsy fabric stopped at its zenith, uncrumpled, and slowly sank to the floor like the initial rocket in the fireworks of love. . . .

Doctor Tachezy couldn't believe his eyes. In the place that for sixteen years had been exclusively his was another man, acting very much at home. At that moment, the fellow became aware of his presence and turned his head.

"Hi," said

33

Mr. Alexander. "Are you surprised to see me?"

"Hi," Doctor Tachezy said. "I mean, good afternoon, yes, I mean no, I'm not."

He couldn't figure out just why his father-in-law should be visiting him at the Institute, for the first time ever. The only logical explanation, that he was bringing him Sturz's *Etymologicum Gudianum,* seemed fabulously improbable.

"I've come," said his father-in-law, turning the page of the newspaper where he had been working a crossword puzzle and opening it out to another page, "to ask you what this is supposed to mean."

In the middle of the page was a photograph of a couple on ice skates, so clear that even Doctor Tachezy recognized the girl as his daughter and her partner as Richard Masin.

"That," he said, "is Lizinka."

"And what," asked his father-in-law emphatically, "is *this?*" And the engineer pointed at the caption beneath the picture, that appeared to have nothing to do with the skating pair: NOT BY BUNS ALONE!

He proceeded to read aloud and at first Doctor Tachezy suspected him of having gone insane. The author of the article described his childhood in the epoch of social injustice, when as a baker's son he grew up in such misery that, as he wrote with bitter pride, his sole toys and playmates were rats. He went on to describe in detail his courageous participation in the revolutionary struggles of bakers, which gave birth to the epoch of social justice, opening perspectives for young bakers that he himself had never dreamed of. After an enumeration of the benefits gained in the field of baking, he finally got around to describing the experience that led him to write the article.

That was when Doctor Tachezy had to admit that his father-in-law had not gone mad.

Emphasizing that back-breaking work in bakeries had not allowed him

136

to take part in sports, which were the bailiwick of young aristocrats, the revolutionary pensioner wrote of his visit during the Christmas holidays to the skating rink with his granddaughter, who did own a pair of skates, thanks to the position of his son, secretary of the bakers' union. There he was witness to an extraordinary performance by two figure skaters, whom he determined to be—young bakers. He took their picture with a camera that he had received for merit from the union, and he was submitting the photograph as evidence that his tireless struggle had not been in vain: that it had given birth to a bright future, when bakers live not by buns alone, but skate around like young aristocrats.

"How do you intend to explain to me," said Mr. Alexander icily, "that you have managed to let them label my daughter's daughter an apprentice to a manual trade?"

Doctor Tachezy's eye traveled over the spines of the volumes that contained almost all the mysteries of human language, but he knew that they could not give him an answer. And yet, his scientific mind, accustomed to resolving philological equations with any number of variables, did not let him down. He found a solution as effective as it was simple. Without knowing it, he used a trick used by animal tamers to save themselves from wild beasts: turning the threatening one against another wild beast. It was not malice that guided him, but rather the hope that from the encounter of two, a third would emerge victorious: he himself, and his humanitarian ideals with him.

"Why don't you come," said Doctor Tachezy, astonished at his own wiliness and his courage at leaving during working hours, "to our place. Lucie will be pleased . . ."

Simsa was on the verge of coming, gasping at the liberating fall almost within reach which always constituted a release from his mortal bonds, when there was a mighty click in his brain, as if someone had flicked a switch, and he couldn't go on.

"Please, for God's sake, *please* . . ."

34

exclaimed Luce, just about to touch the shore where she had last set foot sixteen years before with the unscrupulous Oscar.

But Simsa had stopped everything, staring at an object that had been within the range of his vision the whole time, but that he had only just perceived in all its contexts: beneath the Christmas tree, apparently tossed there in the rapture of the prospect of Christmas holidays, lay Lizinka's school bag. Now he knew what it was that had irritated him so: just as a few grains of uranium beneath a marital bed can cause sterility for generations, as a bottleful of LSD in a city's water supply can drive its entire population mad, this worn and yet unique bit of leatherwork caused his magnificently disciplined and perfectly functioning persona to undergo a breakdown both physiological and moral.

It shocked him that he had carnally entered the selfsame womb from which had issued forth Lizinka's own unbesmirched body. If he had had Wolf's erudition, he might have relaxed in the realization that he was experiencing the opportunity to carry through the classical complex of Oedipus in a new form: he was engulfed by it, even if the mother was not his own. But all Simsa knew of antiquity was crucifixion, and so he had to bear another realization, one that weighed as heavy on him as a cross:

That he was in love with Lizinka Tachezy.

"Go on!" exclaimed Lucie. "Go on and come!"

"Excuse me," said Simsa. He rose, zipped up his fly, and, softly, the way he was accustomed to approaching the "waiting rooms" of clients, left the room and the apartment.

Emerging from the taxi he had ordered for the purpose of impressing his father-in-law, Doctor Tachezy was almost bowled over by the departing Simsa. The scholar found the man in the skiing outfit familiar, but he couldn't place him, particularly in association with the fancy sports car he climbed into. Doctor Tachezy gave the cabdriver a big tip, again for the benefit of his father-in-law, and held the doors for him: the house door, the apartment door, and the door to the living room . . .

When she heard the zip of the fly and the opening of the door, Luce thought that her lover had had to go to the bathroom. She was sure that he would take the opportunity to remove his clothing, so that they be separated only by bare skin. *Off with your clothes, lovely lady; only a nude body should approach another in a lovers' embrace!* she whispered the Arabic verse to herself excitedly. She left her eyes shut for fear that her blush at the sight of his naked body might disclose her inexperience. She wanted to appear dissipated, so that he could cast aside his inhibitions and quickly help her make up for what she had missed. When the doorknob clicked again, she quivered with the strength of her emotion and the proximity of bliss.

"Paul . . ." she called to him eagerly.

There was no response. She opened her eyes and thought she was dreaming. Her husband and father stood in the doorway in an astonishment that was almost infantile.

Absolute situations reveal the relativity of experience. If, in the course of sixteen years, she had experienced less than many another woman had crammed into a single day, now she crammed more thinking into a second than many another woman had into sixteen years. She immediately killed off the flighty Luce inside her and replaced her with the practical Mrs. Tachezy, feet on the ground. She was the only one who could save herself in the eyes of her husband and of her father, who might have forgiven her an infidelity that would count against the Tachezys, but never a scandal that would besmirch the name of Alexander. In a flash she analyzed the game and determined (1) that Associate Professor Simsa had the instinct of a cat that flees a house just before an earthquake strikes; (2) that he was a connoisseur of the female psyche and vanished to prevent her from being paralyzed by panic; and (3) that now it was up to her to instill into her own behavior a plausible explanation before the two men recovered sufficiently to think about it.

"Paul?" Doctor Tachezy echoed, but fortunately he was so fascinated by the alabaster of the beloved body, which in fact he had only seen once before by daylight, on a manicured lawn.

"Lucie?" said Mr. Alexander, who unfortunately came to his senses far more rapidly, being familiar with the alabaster from the days when he used to wipe its bottom.

By then she had already leaped from the settee, embraced her father with her left and her husband with her right arm, and, drawing each of them to one of her breasts, she burst into tears.

"Not the shawl!" she screamed, repeating it like a plea for mercy. "Not the shawl, no, no, not the shawl!"

When they had calmed her down with a tranquilizer and covered her up with a blanket, she related, in fits and starts, how she had fallen into some sort of fever, which turned into a phantasmagoric nightmare: she saw her husband and father approaching her, each holding one end of a shawl, about to strangle her. Finally she calmed down to the point where they could bring up the reason for her father's visit.

Frowning at both of them, Mr. Alexander labeled their decision catastrophic, and the fact that they had kept it from him he referred to as scandalous. Doctor Tachezy considered adding his voice to that of his father-in-law, and for the first time in a year felt his humor improve: because she could not reveal Lizinka's true field of study, she would be obliged to join the two of them in trying to find a solution.

Whereupon Lucie Tachezy decided that if her husband had invited her father to discuss the matter, she was finally in a position to reveal to her father, oath or no oath, what she had been obliged to conceal from him up to now. She described the fall of Lizinka's star until HIENS appeared as a salvation, where she had succeeded, in spite of her husband's opposition, in getting her daughter accepted. She described the program of the school and her daughter's chances.

Mr. Alexander looked as if he had fallen from one of his own bridges.

When Lucie finished talking, he left without a word for the bathroom.

Doctor Tachezy suddenly knew himself not to be the wretch that his wife took him for. At the moment of her defeat, however, he didn't want to be inconsiderate.

"Lucie," he said consolingly, "I don't think you need be so unhappy. For the rest of the school year I'll work with her, and meanwhile we'll look around and find—"

he added cheerfully

"—something else."

His father-in-law entered the room, wiping his hands with his handkerchief. He took off his wire-rimmed glasses, the ones he used to read with, and took a pair of heavy gold-rimmed ones out of their case, the ones he wore when he was communicating matters of principle.

"Never," he said, "have I interfered in your marriage, even when it was direly in need of interference, but this time I must make an exception and agree with—"

declared Mr. Alexander,

"—my daughter."

Doctor Tachezy stood there gaping. Lucie Tachezy suddenly realized that he was even more of an imbecile than she had taken him for. At this point of his debacle, however, she wanted to be merciful: she gave him a reassuring smile.

"If," continued the engineer, "I could turn back the hands of time, I would tell her too that it is better for a young, beautiful, and clever girl from a good family to be the first hangwoman than the last—"

he added with revulsion,

"—kitchenmaid!"

"Darling," pleaded Mrs. Tachezy, putting all her love and yearning into her voice, "stop torturing me and say something!"

"Madame," said

35

Simsa, finally interrupting his silence, "would you kindly tell your daughter to bring a toothbrush, we won't be back until—"

he added with a sudden inspiration,

"—Sunday."

He hung up, disconnected the telephone, and fell back onto the couch. The die was cast, but that did nothing to quell the excitement of his body or the debasement of his soul. He had never felt the latter before, and he was as shattered as a man who gets his first headache at a mature age. What, he asked himself, is the matter with me?

He focused his eyes on the opposite wall. It was white and devoid of pictures, and often served as a screen for the movies he used to show his brunettes. His favorites were Popeye cartoons and documentaries from all the world hockey championships. The former made him shed tears of laughter, the latter often made him lose his voice as he cheered. Now, when he was seeking a firm foothold in the tangle of his thoughts, some mysterious relay in his brain clicked, his eyes dropped, and the views of his spread thighs and the erect phallus recalled to his mind the rear sight and the bead of a pistol long lost. In his mind's eye, he could see the boy that had been Simsa, already a candidate for noncommissioned officers' school, dressed in a thin, light pair of fatigues, shivering on the back of an ancient truck that groaned and rattled through the icy tunnel of the night. That morning, snow had fallen and so had the government, and soldiers were expected to see to the functioning of various vital worksites threatened by strikes. Simsa's unit recognized its destination by smell before they could see it. The odor of soured blood and flesh long dead led them with precision to the slaughterhouse.

When they arrived in the slaughtering hall, they were welcomed by civilians in rubber coats of a variety of hues; their behavior indicated that they were special service officers. The thud of hooves and a furious bellowing sounded from outside. The animals hadn't been fed for three days. A man in beige rubber asked if anyone had ever done any slaughtering before. Silence. He asked if anyone would be interested in trying it. Simsa was the only one to raise a hand; he didn't even know why he did it: whenever the state addressed him, no matter how big the crowd, he always replied "Here!" His comrades were split up into teams that were to drive the live cattle in and drag the dead ones out. They were led by a civilian in green rubber; by then it was obvious that the colors revealed their concealed rank. In addition to the one in beige, a civilian in black rubber remained with Simsa, since there was no job left for him.

"So?" asked the beige one impatiently, "how about getting a move on?"

"There is," said Simsa, examining the slaughter stunner, "a problem."

"No time," said the beige one bluntly, "for problems!"

"Precisely!" said Simsa. "This plaything will just stun the beast, and then we've got to knock it off. How about lending me your pistol?"

"You intend," said the beige one, uncomprehending, "to *shoot* them?"

"We'll be working faster," said Simsa, "and they couldn't care less."

The beige rubber coat looked at the black one who, Simsa realized, was the boss of the outfit. He saw mistrust in the cold blue eyes. A boyish feeling of stubborn defiance came over him, the same defiance which had enabled him, a bastard, to face the world for the past sixteen years. The beige one produced a heavy 9-millimeter automatic from his shoulder holster and Simsa hurried to the stone-block platform at the end of the wooden guideway.

The wood and the concrete hall gave a frightening dimension to the roar of the first animal's hoofbeats. Simsa felt like turning on his heel and running; it sounded as if the slatwork tunnel would disgorge a bull that would trample him and his ridiculous little pistol into mincemeat. But he thought of the cold blue eyes, and he felt a youthful urge to live dangerously, the same sort of urge with which his contemporaries entered the gates of *corridas*. He spread his feet, placed the barrel of the automatic on his raised right forearm—he was left-handed—lined up the sights, and exhaled.

He was pleased that it was an ordinary calf that came charging out of the dark tunnel. Blinded by the lights, it tried to stop short. The large sacrificial platform, smoothed by generations, provided no friction for its hooves, and it slid up to Simsa on its backside. The terror that he read from close up through the sights was almost human. Simsa was not a delicate soul, he had encountered death before: at the orphanage it had suffocated his roommate with scarlet fever, at noncommissioned officers' school it had ripped to shreds an excellent instructor whose pet demonstration had been to pull the pin of a grenade, urinate on it, and only then to throw it. Never before, however, had he held death in his own two hands. . . .

The explosion almost deafened him, and the bullet ripped off a big ear that slapped down on the stone floor like a raw slab of steak. The calf was as startled as the marksman. It stood motionless, and the emptiness in its eyes grew even deeper. Simsa pulled the trigger again. This time the recoil pulled the barrel downward. The bullet tore off the animal's lower jaw. The pain jolted the animal onto its hind legs. It wanted to moo, but all that its now open throat permitted was a croak. Now Simsa was faced with a furious creature seeking revenge. It was then that his soul followed his body out of the short pants of a boy, and he felt a wild masculine hatred. So, he raged inwardly, you want to get me? *Tough shit for you!*

When the animal leaped, he leaped too, not sideways like a toreador but straight ahead like a bull. His hand with the pistol had so much strength in it that the thin cartilage between the calf's eyes gave way. He could see the barrel of the pistol slide into the calf's head like a monstrous thermometer, and he knew that he would in fact be trampled unless he did the only thing he could do, immediately. He did. The shot was muffled to inaudibility, but the visual effect was unreal. The previous shots had already shown him that the bullets had been specially prepared. The enclosed space of the animal's skull multiplied the effect. As he watched,

142

it seemed like a slow-motion scientific film: just above the barrel, a third eye opened in the middle of the forehead—a crater ejaculating a white mass. He was blinded by that cetaceous spout, and it was only by deduction that he realized that the dying beast had caught him with a flood of its own brain.

He heard footsteps, voices, an order, heavy breathing, the sound of dragging hide and the rush of flowing water. Before he wiped the viscous fluid out of his eyes with his sleeve, the dead body was gone; a classmate of his was washing the last bits of blood into the gutters, the clearing team was pulling a cart with the calf on it toward the freezers. He licked his lips. The disgusting taste of raw brain stayed on his tongue, but he didn't spit it out, he gritted his teeth. Hang on! he ordered himself with his newborn masculine obstinacy. The hall echoed again.

He needed two shots for the next calf, after the first one it fell on its side and kicked its hooves in the air. That one had been aimed at the heart, for the second he chose the head again. He only placed the barrel against the skin, but the ejaculation was repeated. Quick as a flash, he wiped off the gray jelly because a third animal was running out of the tunnel. He waited until it slid up to him, strode forward like a fencer, and when the barrel touched, he pulled the trigger. The calf went out like a light. He wiped the slimy stuff off again, jumped over the carcass, and bolted the door. It resounded again as the fourth body tumbled against it. The ring was cleared, but he remained motionless.

"What's the matter?" barked the beige coat.

"I'm out," he replied smartly, "of lead."

The man in beige pulled a spare clip from a holster under his rubber coat. When he swung his arm back to toss it up to Simsa, he was stopped by the hand of the chief, who added his own clip. That encouraged Simsa; he loaded the automatic and proceeded. With the second batch, his main intention was to do away with that nasty brain-spray. He pulled up the door and stood by it. When the calf emerged, hesitantly this time, lacking the momentum of a running start, he shot it in the ear. The bullet flew through the soft parts and slammed into the concrete somewhere; it had destroyed the calf's balance mechanism, and the beast, shaking its head and mooing mournfully, ran around in circles, their diameter indirectly proportional to its increasing speed. It took a while, Simsa had to keep jumping out of the way like a *bandillero,* before he could catch the nape of its neck with the pistol. Then he found that a shot in the nape showed up like a crimson button while the work of the bullet remained concealed behind the armor of the skull and the palisade of the teeth.

Now he knew, and he ordered them to release one calf after another. He began work on his technique. He stood directly by the gate, so that he might be able to reach the nape in a single bound, and fire. Four times it worked perfectly. He reloaded with the third clip and called for another six.

"Let's give 'em a chance!" he joked.

The cool blue eyes held unconcealed interest. Simsa wanted nothing more than to excite them to admiration. The sound of twenty-four hooves hit the eardrums so hard that most of the assistants covered up their ears. Simsa didn't notice. Leaning his right shoulder against the wooden passageway, he held his left hand with the automatic at eye level. He didn't consider the possibility of a miss. The eight deaths that he had dispensed with twelve shots, while seeking to establish a style of his own from his own inner resources, had steeled him. No longer was he a man with a pistol, but a man-pistol.

The lead calf, maddened by the hoofbeats and the mooing of the others, leaped out and past Simsa, so that it appeared he had shot too late. He was the only one who saw the crimson signal light up, and who knew that it was just dead meat sliding across the stone. By then he was firing again, and the second carcass was stopped only by the body of its predecessor. The third slid into them with such force that the first flew over the edge onto the floor of the hall like a bale of hay. The remaining three calves arranged themselves in a neat line. Nothing moved in the mass of flesh, skin, and horn.

The cool blue eyes grew warm with appreciation. And Simsa, whose only bond with mankind so far had been the law of subordination, suddenly felt a hitherto unknown liking for the man in the black rubber coat. Pity, he thought, that this is just a one-time encounter. Who knows, I might find in him— He stopped himself: his home was the state, and only an ingrate could ask for more. So he kept on shooting as long as there was anything to shoot, and then, come morning, he nearly froze on the back of the personnel carrier.

He didn't even have time to fall asleep on his cot when they were calling him up for a physical. A career soldier spends his whole life either harassing or being harassed; he didn't even object that he had just slaughtered two hundred head of cattle, that his left hand was numb and his left ear almost deaf. Beyond the gate stood a jeep with a canvas top. The driver indicated that he should sit in back. Once he had crept in and settled down sleepily, the door slammed shut with the echo of a tank hatch and he found himself in complete darkness. As the vehicle started up, he felt around and then he understood: from the hinged cuffs for hands, feet, and necks, he could tell that the canvas top concealed an armored cage for transporting prisoners. He wasn't afraid, though. With the radar of an individual who had been on his own since infancy, he could sense danger. He felt that the use of this vehicle was more a show of favor. Besides,

144

although the times were stormy, he couldn't imagine how anyone could have anything against a green kid who had knocked up a girl or two and knocked off a few calves. He yawned, found himself a comfortable spot between the leg irons and the neck irons, and went to sleep.

He was awakened by a sharp slap on the face, but that was only because the driver was afraid he had suffocated on the way. Simsa climbed out, did a few kneebends to wake himself up. Then he looked around. He was standing beneath the terrace of some mansion, its façade still pale in the spots where the letters HOTEL DIANA had recently been removed; from there he could see a meadow that led to the banks of a lake, where burned stones bordered the black circle of a dead (later he never confided to Wolf his reason for refusing to visit the place when he found out which site had been chosen as the executioners' recreation spot) campfire.

In the Stag Room—with walkie-talkies on the tables supported by antlers—the three men from the slaughterhouse sat waiting, now dressed in elegantly cut suits. The one who had worn the black rubber coat introduced himself as Colonel Artur, he referred to the beige one as Major Bodan and the green one as Captain Cyril. Simsa realized that the names were covers, and that the initial letters indicated their position in the hierarchy. Then the commander clarified things for him.

"It is clear," Colonel Artur began, "that the revolution has succeeded, but that does not mean our enemies have been defeated. True, we have a police force and courts, but there is nothing that guarantees their reliability: that is why the revolution must constitute another organ, a covert one. And that organ is SEAR.

"It represents," the Colonel continued, "the guarantee that even the most dangerous of reactionaries, those who pretend to be revolutionaries, will be brought to light. Of course, success is assured only if each and every member of the Secret Army of the Revolution adheres to its supreme code: the code of ALADAS. Here is a sample of the complexity of this service: secrecy is both vertical and horizontal. Orders and reports are submitted in whispers and in ciphers. And of course, the punishment for violating the code of Absolute Loyalty, Absolute Dependability, Absolute Secrecy is the absolute penalty.

"It follows," he concluded, "on the other hand, that members of SEAR, maintaining ALADAS, have extensive powers, since they are subordinate only to the supreme leaders of the state. If an action is based on the law of the revolution, a member need not answer to any other law, and he may punish reactionaries even on a preventive basis, with a guarantee of his own nonliability. The fact that Simsa is here is the result of his performance at the abattoir. His records from various institutions indicate that he is a disciplined person, and the deciding factor is the fact that he has no family. He has been reported to his former unit as having been the victim of a traffic accident, in order that he might begin a new life as a member of the big family of SEAR. Of course," the blue eyes smiled, "he can cease child-support payments to that clever little gypsy girl—and next time take care."

As he spoke, the shriek of a bird sounded, the call of hungry love. Simsa realized how much he had been missing during his solitary years. He suddenly felt a deep desire to spend his life near this wonderful man, surrounded by the wonderful outdoors. The bird began repeating its mating call, when the bell in the commander's hand pealed loudly. The door flew open and a blond youth, not much older than Simsa, stood at attention in the doorway.

"Sir!"

"Tell them," directed the Colonel softly, "to gag him!"

"Yes, sir!" whispered the blond youth and vanished.

"What do you have to say?" asked Colonel Artur.

Simsa stepped nearer so that he might fix in his mind the face of the man who had made him into a human being, and then, out of irrepressible pride, proud vanity, mean self-interest, or perhaps even for the basest of coin, he sold his own humanity. Was it possible, he wondered, that so much had happened in the mere two years that had followed? . . . With his left hand, he pressed the massive barrel of the automatic to the spot directly over the base of the nose, so that the track of the bullet sliced through the entire space in which that treacherous brain had woven its intrigues. He caught the encouraging glance of

36

Seven, and felt for the trigger.

Soon after his arrival at SEAR, numbers had replaced names. For a month or so, he was on the books as lance corporal Libor, then he became Thirty-seven. Colonel Artur, now known as One, informed his men briefly and gravely that vile traitors were trying to penetrate SEAR, which they rightly viewed as the most powerful shield of the revolution; for that reason, the powers-that-be had established the Secret Revolutionary Army Police—SRAP for short—for which One's unit had been singled out. It would appear, on the surface, to be under the command of SEAR, but in fact SRAP would be keeping SEAR under surveillance.

The numbers were supposed to intimidate the enemy—like the pressure gauge of an impersonal machine that cannot be affected by wiles or emotional appeals—but also to mobilize its own members—like the altimeter of their individual positions in the service. Given the quality of the personnel in the unit, the only way to improve one's position was by superb performance or tragic occurrence; during the first six months, Simsa rose only by a single rung after Thirteen accidently pulled the trigger at his own temple while showing a treacherous SEAR officer how to shoot himself. Simsa's advancement was hindered by the fact that the task of investigating unreliable members of SEAR was turned over to older members of the unit, who knew them personally and hence were better able to finger their weak points. Fortunately he was billeted in a garret room with the blond youth whom he had seen that first night in response to Colonel Artur's bell; then Sergeant Olda, now Thirty-one, a former actor, was just as anxious as Simsa. He came up with the idea that they not stay with only the recommended daily karate training, but that they improve their qualifications.

There were still a few clients, as they called those they interrogated, left in an isolated cellar of the mansion, third-rate schemers who were kept there only so that they should not reveal the secret of SEAR to the authorities, not to mention the secret of SRAP. To all intents and purposes, they were there for life. With the approval of One, who was obviously a fan of Simsa's ever since the slaughterhouse, the two young men began to make use of their free time. They would take one or another of the clients to the ceramic-tiled examining room, and ask him if he knew Franz More. When the client denied it, they started to work on him, and continued until he confessed. Thanks to a fortunate idea, they were soon as good as their older colleagues. They mastered the techniques of interrogation by means of light and noise, frequent awakenings, forced jogging, and even straitjackets; they mastered interrogation with water and electricity; and they did not overlook the possibilities afforded by teeth, nails, and eyelashes. Because they were working on their own, without advisers, they "discovered America" any number of times, but they also came up with some real novelties. Years later, Simsa was to make good use of them, when he would amaze Wolf during the planning sessions for the school at the Café Sparta. They enjoyed their work and Simsa regretted that he was no writer and was unable to adequately record the fantastic confessions that were the clients' outpourings; the joke was that the name of Franz More came from a play that Thirty-one knew. The high moral principles that they learned daily from their instructors naturally did not apply to the refuse of society; they continued to extract lies from those men, so that they might be prepared when they would receive orders to extract the truth.

He made a significant discovery while following a SEAR man who was following a national skiing champion who was suspiciously often frequenting the company of foreign champions. All winter long, the champion lived in the best hotel, and those who were following him naturally had to do likewise. When for the first time in his life Simsa lay down on a soft bed, his sensations were comparable to those of amatory bliss. If he had previously looked down his nose at luxury as reactionary, now he understood that the revolution offered its progeny everything—even luxury! When his friend Thirty-one arrived to spell him, it shook him. But he pulled himself together in a hurry and when reporting to One, he was ready to give the state and the revolution—in his mind, those two supreme authorities now merged into a single unit, as the Father and the Spirit in the minds of believers—both comfort and life.

As usual, One's statement was brief and astonishing: the brain of SRAP had succeeded in uncovering a conspiracy right in the heart of SEAR; because Simsa was not acquainted with any of those who had been arrested, and thus could not be influenced, he had been included among the interrogators at the Cenker, which is what they called the Central Bunker. When dismissing him, One addressed him as Twenty-nine. Simsa almost blacked out from his sudden leap into the twenties. It included a third-floor billet, and while they lacked baths, the rooms there were singles. He moved right away, while Thirty-one was still in the mountains. Having been promoted over his friend's head like that, he didn't want to irritate him further.

The next year remained in his memory as one long night, which was transformed into an endless day by the thousand-watt light bulbs in the Cenker. His questioning no longer referred to the unknown Franz More, but rather to well-known public figures who were still roaring in the voice of the revolution from public podiums, and the ones who answered him obediently, often after the first blow, were also revolutionaries, now tractable, but whose names had just the day before caused the blood in reactionary veins to run cold. Simsa contributed significantly to their ultimate mass confession to being foreign agents. After their execution, SEAR was secretly dissolved and replaced by SRAP. He learned of it when he was being congratulated on his seventh promotion in a single year; now he was Twenty-two.

That evening, a banquet was held to celebrate, in the midst of which he was interrupted by a youth who stuttered: "In the Stag Room—you're wanted by . . . One."

Simsa had to cover up a smile when he heard the holy respect with which the lad spoke the number. But when he marched into the Stag Room, chest out, he realized that his own respect had not diminished in the past twenty months. The whole top seven were there, including One's deputy Four, Two's deputy Five, and Three's deputy Six—each of them a terror to the reaction and the counterrevolution, as well as Seven, the administrator. They called him Ink and he was respected only when he went from room to room with an old-fashioned satchel and paid out to each one separately—for secrecy's sake—his salary, bonus, and remuneration. But there in the Stag Room, Simsa registered only One, and saluted.

"I, Twenty-two," he whispered according to regulations, "am present on your orders, One!"

"At ease," said One almost inaudibly, then: "Cancer is often speedier than the scalpel, and then there is nothing left for the scalpel than to be twice as quick as the cancer. We have received an anonymous but unfortunately well-informed report that one of our—I hesitate to refer to him any more as a man—was planning an assassination attempt for tonight. This fratricidal—"

continued One, and the fatigue crinkled in the corners of both his eyes,

"—murder, which was foiled only by swift action, indicates that the enemy has penetrated for the first time inside the structure of SRAP. Not only must this focus of counterrevolution be cauterized, but an investigation must be undertaken to determine whether or not it has spread. The seven of us have decided that this challenging task will be given to you."

It was only thanks to his trained ability to register automatically every bit of incoming data that Simsa was able afterward to recall the other parts of his instructions: that the patient be interrogated in the old cellar, in order that morale of SRAP not be disturbed; that no holds should be barred in the effort to make him admit who was to have been his victim and who had recruited him; that Simsa would need protection, and that he would be moved to the second floor, where he would have peace and quiet and a bathroom; and finally that the interrogations would be attended by observers in the persons of Six, Five and Four.

Evidence of the care with which the project had been planned was in the fact that Simsa's first *probod* (protective bodyguard) reported to him at the door of the Stag Room. The behemoth, whom he hadn't seen before, led him directly to his new room, where his things were waiting for him. He took his briefcase with all his own instruments—the examining rooms were equipped, but like the bricklayer and his trowel, he had become accustomed to his own tools—folded a clean pair of overalls into it, and went.

When he arrived down in the cellar, the client was already lying on the examining table (as an associate professor he would recall that excellent piece of equipment with nostalgia, but then where are the snows of yesteryear?) and the observers were sitting around it. As he fastened the red *toak* (which is what they called the torture cloak), he glanced at the client and his hand froze. The fellow was his only friend, formerly Sergeant Olda, later Thirty-one. What showed in his eyes was not the wiliness of an ambitious actor but rather a mute reproach.

Simsa's initial impulse was to exclaim, No, wait! This is a mistake! Everything I've learned that helped to get me to this table was learned right here, beside this . . . he's my blood bro—

That was when a shutter clicked in his brain as he recalled the words that Thirty-one used to say: that SRAP wasn't a girls' finishing school but a fighting unit, and that a few lives were an acceptable price to pay for all mankind to be happy.

His fingers buttoned up the last button on the toak—it all had happened so fast that it looked as if the button had just snagged—and Simsa was back in shape. He turned the cowardly look away with a contemptuous glance of his own. His eyes mounted the challenge: *Let's go, buddy—now you'll admit that you're Franz More himself!*

But it soon became apparent that the irresistible force had come up against the immovable object. SRAP had chosen its men well and trained them even better. Besides, the client knew the entire repertoire and was made of the kind of stuff that no one there had ever encountered. After twenty-four hours, Simsa could say that he had done everything humanly possible. The observers repeatedly broke tradition by going out to have a smoke in the corridor, to conceal their nausea. Alone, Simsa measured the depth of moral mire of the individual that he had at his already numb fingertips: the client must realize, from the degree of the interrogation, that he hadn't a smidgin of hope, even should he confess; if he was still opting for more pain rather than swift termination by means of a bullet to the head, which any *probod* would have granted him, it must have been to protect someone who would complete the dastardly deed, and perhaps prove that Simsa was a dilettante.

After a short break during which they all got a few winks of sleep while a physician put the client together as best he could, Simsa mobilized all his strength and experience. Twenty-four hours later, Olda lacked teeth, hair, fingernails, and nipples, but Simsa lacked—a confession. He knew it was now or never. And that was when his vivid imagination came to his rescue, as it would do not long afterward with the schnoose, and later still with his extraordinary invention. In sheer desperation, he borrowed the nutcracker that Six, a compulsive eater addicted to walnuts and other snacks, carried with him, and started on the client's genitals. So far Simsa had avoided that area, sensing somehow that this perfect work of nature would someday determine his own destiny. God, prayed the atheist Simsa silently—an indication of the gravity of the situation—if You're up there, help me! He had barely begun when a miracle happened. The client gave a hoarse croak, opened his lashless eyelids, and mumbled through toothless gums: "Twen . . . ty . . . feven!"

Then he passed out, and to all intents and purposes, Simsa did too. From a distance he could hear the enthusiastic praise, through a fog he

150

could feel his *probod* more carry than lead him to his bed, and then he fell deep into the soft darkness. When he awoke he was Twenty.

But that was just the beginning of his steep climb. Twenty-seven was on the table already. Unlike his reticent predecessor—whose unconsciousness, in spite of the best efforts of the physician, had resulted in his exitus—the cohort suffered verbal diarrhea. With a flood of promises, oaths, and, finally, macho though he was, with a veritable waterfall of tears, he tried to convince them that Thirty-one had framed him out of the desire to get back at him for having won a month's earnings from him gambling. It was as if Olda were the keystone which, removed, lets the whole wall fall down. After less than a single shift—granted, Simsa went right for the testicles—Twenty-seven admitted that he had been recruited by Thirty-eight, to do away with . . . unfortunately, he never got to say who was to have been done in, since at that point Simsa had crushed his left testicle. The right one went an hour later, in an attempt to use pain to awaken him from his coma so that he might finish what he started to say.

They arrested Thirty-eight right away, but they waited two days for Twenty-seven to terminate without regaining consciousness; it was after this experience that Simsa developed the ballbreaker, as he christened the new tool, which was in essence a nutcracker with a blocking mechanism. During the hiatus, he was once again received by One and promoted to Eighteen; the shadow of depression had vanished, and One radiated cool energy, the way he had that day at the slaughterhouse. He said that under the circumstances he was unable to grant him a well-deserved leave, but that he would like to make up for it by means of a little something that Simsa would find in his room.

It was profound gratitude he experienced for One that night, when he felt himself rising and falling with the extraordinary brunette whom he found, fragrant and naked, in his soft bed. He would never forget her, not only for the pointiest breasts he ever encountered, but mainly because she revealed to him undreamed-charms of lovemaking. When the next evening the *probod* called for him to accompany him downstairs, it was the first time ever that he hadn't felt like going to work. When he was leaving, however, she stood at perfect attention, her tits like a pair of lance tips, and reported to him as One hundred-and-three, detailed for his permanent service as his *perphyd* (personal physiological aide).

He lit into Thirty-eight with fresh energy. At the outset, all Simsa got was a tale of woe: the two in the morgue had laid it on him to get even with him for advancing faster than they had. He was a tenacious youth, but Simsa wasn't born yesterday, he had taken a huge stride, like a child in a drawing class that suddenly grasps perspective. He surprised the client by serving up his novelty—Four had named it the Tomato Crush when he was reporting on it enthusiastically to One—right off. In return, Thirty-eight surprised him by spilling his confession the moment the metal jaws chilled the delicate skin down there. He revealed that he had been recruited by Twenty-four and Twenty-three, to do away with Three. The effect of that revelation was tantamount to the explosion of a hand grenade.

In view of the alacrity of his confession, Thirty-eight survived the interrogation with only a few bits of cosmetically reparable damage, and he could take his place as a witness. When the two he had named accused him of being a SEAR agent out to discredit the sons of SRAP, and that he was trying to even the score with them for some girl or other who had put out for the two of them but not for him, Simsa decided to work on them together—and that was the genesis of the idea of double executioners. A single crushed nut was all it took for the owners of all four to start to sing: they admitted having recruited Thirty-eight, and added in a single breath that they themselves had been recruited by Fifteen and Fourteen to eliminate Two.

Of course, that was like the explosion of a mine, and it was no wonder that Three and Two turned up in the cellar personally. One wanted to be absolutely certain, because a unit that works in absolute secrecy can exist only under conditions of complete dependability. From that point forward, Simsa could no longer act with delicacy, and the nutcracker had an absolute ball: they revealed the full extent and the precise source of the threat.

In the course of their joint interrogation, the two last named admitted that they had been recruited above all to wipe out One. From their screams, the attentive listener could piece together the segments of a monstrous plan, cunning in its apparent impossibility: One was to have been stabbed to death in the Stag Room and his corpse sewed into a stuffed bear; the remaining members of the top seven were to have been accused of having kidnapped him and liquidated immediately thereafter by the main conspirators, who would then have taken over power: they were Thirteen, Twelve, Eleven, Ten, Nine, and Eight!

That was like the explosion of an incendiary bomb, and One himself turned up. In an atmosphere that was not far from hysterical, he retained a sense of matter-of-fact objectivity. First of all, he ordered them to bring all the seven who had confessed. No one dared voice any opposition, and so they even brought the two from cold storage. One didn't blink an eyelash. He ordered them to explain to him what ideal, reward, or person had led them to turn their backs on the ideals, rewards, and persons that had brought them to SRAP. What followed was like something out of a dream: except for the two frozen stiffs, they all swore that both the confessions and the accusations had been figments of their imaginations, and that they had invented the most impossible absurdities in order that

152

the commander himself notice, before they were crippled or killed, that they had fallen prey to a fiendish plot.

Simsa turned deadly pale. He, who in his entire life had done away with nothing but a few calves, was indirectly being called a sadist, out to eliminate his comrades! It was insulting, but it was also dangerous, in an atmosphere of suspicion where, as he had seen, all it took was a single word and a fellow was done for.

But once again, One did not disappoint him. He said in a dry tone that if everyone adhered to ALADAS the way Seventeen did—to add weight to his statement, he promoted Simsa on the spot—the shadow of treachery would never have fallen on SRAP. He declared that in this country, a man was innocent until proven guilty, and that the interrogator was under his own personal protection until interrogation. Whereupon he ordered that they be arrested or cremated respectively, and that refreshments be served before any new arrests were made.

The food was served on an improvised board made up of two of the examining tables put together lengthwise and covered with clean sheets. Years afterward, Simsa came across a reproduction in a magazine that reminded him of that meal: it was called "The Last Supper of the Lord." It recalled to him the sight of One, sitting under the surgical spotlight which surrounded him with a white aureole, breaking loaves of French bread into pieces and distributing them. It was a moment of perfect peace, but there was also an element of comic relief: in the middle of the feasting, Seven arrived, familiarly known as Ink, with his half-glasses and his little satchel, and asked them bleatingly if they would kindly go to their rooms to receive their remuneration, since today was the bookkeeping deadline.

"Fuck," said One informally, because aside from Simsa, they were among themselves, "off, chum—"

indicating that Seven take a seat,

"—we've got a deadline of our own to celebrate—half of the outfit's dead on the line!"

The cellar echoed with raucous laughter, for the last time. A moment later, all SRAP trembled on its very foundations. The door opened and the chief *probod* filled the doorway. He answered only to One, and there was amazement and anger in his face. He strode along the table, and with three swift blows to the backs of their necks with the edge of his hand, he stunned Six, Five, and Four. Then he placed three pieces of paper on the table before One.

The top paper was an order to the SRAP physician, to immediately inoculate rabbits number 38, 24, 23, 15, and 14; according to the code, that meant that the prisoners be immediately liquidated by injections. The five were of course the five crown witnesses!

153

The paper in the middle was Number Five's order to the captain of the guard to expedite the creampuffs; that was a coded statement of free passage for the hearse to the district crematory. On the bottom was another order, that pastry-cooks number 13, 12, 11, 10, 9, and 8 be allowed to leave with it. So the newly accused had fled in a panic, reportedly leaving in their rooms "half-consumed bottles and cigars and half-consummated wenches."

When they came to, Six, Five, and Four shouted in unison that the orders were forgeries and the signatures too. Whereupon One turned them over to Simsa. They responded after the fashion of those for whom other people's corpses are simply flattened wheat stalks, but who fall to pieces at the thought of their own death; when Six set eyes on the ball breaker, he lost control of his bowels. They tried to outconfess one another, until even Simsa began to feel sick. But at the same time, they begged that they be allowed to repeat their confessions to the powers-that-be. Their motivation was transparently clear: they would cast doubt on their own words by shameless contentions the way their accomplices had. Naturally, One turned them down flat.

Then he dismissed Simsa, and ordered Seven to confine everyone to quarters, to bring the candelabra, and to summon the doctor with his syringe; that could mean only one thing—trial and execution. As he was closing the door to the cellar, Simsa looked back to glimpse One taking his place between his two deputies as the tribunal.

He was so exhausted that he allowed his *perphyd* only to bathe him, and he fell asleep as soon as his body touched the sheets. He slept the sleep of the just, until the hand that had vainly been slapping his cheeks grasped his genitals.

"At ease," he called out, still half asleep. "Cone-tits, m'dear. . . !"

A moment later, because he had learned over the years to traverse the gap between sleeping and waking in a single bound, he was standing at attention beside his bed, having recognized Seven, and having realized that the comical administrator was filling One's orders that night.

"I, Seventeen," Simsa reported in a whisper, "am at your service, Seven!"

Then he thought he was still dreaming, when the skinny fellow with the silly spectacles pulled himself to attention too, and with his little satchel pressed tightly to his right thigh, exclaimed in an even quieter whisper, "I, Seven, am at your service, Two!"

And from the strictest of subaltern positions he began to relate the events of the previous evening to an astounded Simsa: Six, Five, and Four had tried to save their necks by revealing that the true heads of the conspiracy had been Three and Two. The latter two, before anyone could stop them, had shot the three informers literally to smithereens, which of course was as good as an admission of guilt. Fortunately they had emptied their clips, so that they could be disarmed, and One had seen no alternative but to shoot them on the spot himself and to request the powers-that-be for the loan of special commandos, for use in "disinfecting" SRAP, before the new blood of a fresh shift could rejuvenate it. One was at that very moment waiting at the reserve post, and was sending the car for his new second in command, "to bring," added Seven in less than military terms, "the second batch."

Simsa, a soldier to the marrow, oriented himself immediately.

"Hop to it, Seven!" he barked. "Move your ass!"

He was dressed in a flash and strode toward the door. Although he realized that this was no time for detail, he decided as he passed the bathroom to at least get his toothbrush. When he opened the door, he froze. A strange man sat on the edge of the tub, wearing a green beret, with camouflaged fatigues tucked into his high-laced, thick-soled boots; his sleeves were rolled up and he was holding a passive supine body under the surface of the water overflowing the bathtub. He recognized it by the conical breasts sticking out of the water like dual periscopes.

Had circumstances been different, he would have leaped at him. This time, however, his sixth sense told him that the fellow must have arrived with Seven, and must be carrying out the orders of One. It dawned on him, and he shuddered at the thought, that not so long ago he had been lying between the breasts of a viper. The fellow in green got up clumsily to salute him. The body immediately surfaced and it seemed that the water would carry it to Simsa's feet. He flinched and retreated a step; a chill went up his spine at the sight of that black triangle in which he was to have been torpedoed.

"Carry on!" he said brusquely and walked back out without his toothbrush.

In the hallway, he stumbled over the apelike body of his *probod*. Blood was streaming from a long slash on his throat. It had taken death to make him show his true colors: his face was in a hostile grimace and evil glared from his fogged eyes. Simsa was horrified. God, he thought, stepping over the body, how they hated us! And how close they came! He could tell that One had struck seconds before zero hour.

The car was standing at the spot where two years earlier, Simsa had first set foot on the property; One had inherited the huge limousine from the commander of SEAR, who in turn had accepted it as a bribe. The chief *probod* jumped out from behind the wheel and obsequiously opened the back door for him. Seven, with his eternal satchel, sat down in front. The car took off smoothly, only to brake sharply at the main gateway. Three more commandos stepped out into the spotlight: two were holding automatic rifles at ready, the third was aiming a pistol. Seven rolled down the window and took a paper out of his satchel. The one with the pistol folded up the paper and gave Seven a very respectful salute. The gate opened and the car sped through at full speed. As Simsa looked back, he barely glimpsed dozens of glowing cigarette ends along the outside wall, illuminating rosy faces under berets. He thought to himself, So this is how the Night of Long Knives looked. Except that this time they would slice an evil growth from the body of the motherland; he was proud to be one of the blades.

The limousine moved through the forest and continued through the apparently deserted space of the military zone. The soft sound of the engine, the constant velocity, and the vehicle's excellent suspension drew Simsa out of the hectic maelstrom inward to contemplation. Relaxing, he leaned back into the upholstery and gazed straight ahead, where between the two immobile heads he could watch the highway that appeared to be reeled in under the wheels. He was separated from the men in the front seat by bulletproof glass, and he recalled his first trip along the same highway, wedged between the fetters of the mobile cell. Then he had arrived a nobody, without a number, now he was leaving the number two man. The strange thing was that he didn't know where he was headed this time either. Although the times were even stormier, he was still unable to imagine, even after all he had been through, who would want to hurt a Two, who had not only contributed to the uncovering of plotters inside SEAR, but had himself been the person to uncover the even more treacherous members of SRAP. He yawned and dozed off. . . .

He was awakened by the sound of rhythmic blows. With his eyes still closed, he tried to figure out what it was. When he finally gave up and opened them a crack, he immediately opened them wide. He was sitting alone in the car, facing downhill on a slope that led down to a mixed forest—he was never to forget the sight of the conifers, reaching up against the moonlit sky like cardboard cutouts, and the deciduous trees like wire sculptures. The hillside resembled an upside-down soup spoon, its tip dropping off steeply to disclose the topographical situation: the forest grew all the way around the rim of a chasm that in the planet's volcanic infancy had spewed white-hot sperm. Deep below the cliff wall opposite was the black, oily gleam of a lake. Only one obstacle stood between the vehicle and the lake: a weeping willow, born of a seed blown there from who knows where, that was just being chopped down. The gnarled trunk fell with a swish to the edge of the cliff, bounced like an acrobat on a trampoline, and vanished by leaps beyond the edge of the spoon.

He knew that he ought to get himself out of this coffin, but he was incapable of motion. Terrified, he saw two figures; metal gleamed in one of their hands. *Betrayed!* was the only explanation that flashed through his

156

mind; he visualized himself bouncing like a rubber ball between the upholstery and the glass, while the car turned somersaults down to the water, and he felt a sharp pain in his testicles. He still had time to wonder why his testicles, since he had never suffered . . . and the thought was catapulted out of his mind by an even more horrible one: wasn't it the *ballbreaker* that the fellow was coming at him with?

The only thing that salvaged his prestige was the terror that paralyzed him. It made him appear icily cool when the chief *probod* opened the door respectfully, holding an ax along the seam of his trouser leg. Through the open door, Simsa could see Ink standing at attention. He could hear the croaking of frogs and smell the heavy odor of rotting vegetation. His organism caught like an engine that had been flooded, and his military reflexes clicked into place. He jumped out—he had to force his heavy legs to obey him—and he nodded to them, hiding his trembling hands in his pockets. He was still on his toes: for the world to return to its proper tracks, they still had to give him their report. He froze again when Seven opened his satchel and took a big pistol out of it—then handed it to him, butt first.

"Here, sir," Ink said solemnly. "Your weapon."

Simsa recognized it ht off. It was the 9-millimeter automatic with which he had felled a herd of veal. He understood that it took the place of a notification of promotion and that only now was he officially becoming Two. He had just enough time to weigh it in his palm with emotion, when it was covered with a sheet of paper.

"Here, sir," said Seven discreetly. "His confession."

A narrow cone of light fell onto the paper. The chief *probod* had flipped on a flashlight and was holding it accommodatingly over Simsa's shoulder. The further Simsa read, the more confused he became:

> The undersigned admits that, out of hatred for our people, he did treacherously liquidate the revolutionary organizations called SEAR and SRAP, and with them, dozens of the finest sons of our people. I am aware of the fact that the only penalty for this loathsome crime is death, and I pledge myself, until such time as the sentence should be carried out, to make good my guilt by means of exemplary service to our people.
>
> Signed
> JOSEF KAPUSTA

"Who," asked Simsa, uncomprehending, "is *that?*"

The light left the sheet of paper, slid like a will-o'-the-wisp across the carpet of rotting leaves, jumped over the rear bumper, and came to rest on the trunk. Seven moved as silently as the beam of light.

"Kapusta, Josef, now ready," he said, pressing the lock on the trunk, "for execution of sentence, Two!"

The lid flew up. The beam of light passed over the spare tire and the gas can and came to rest on what looked like a huge infant. It was a man, wrapped up in a camouflage tarp like a baby in a blanket, with a gag in his mouth instead of a pacifier. Simsa turned to stone.

The bundle that had arrived with him was formerly Colonel Artur, latterly One. His blue eyes gave off neither the much-touted coldness nor the much-feared wrath; they reflected nothing but a pitiful plea.

In his first shock, Simsa wanted to exclaim, Never! It's a plot! Everything that brought me all the way to the rank of Number Two I have from this very . . . he's my true fa—

Something clicked in his brain.

Simsa raised the pistol—it all happened so fast that it seemed like nothing but a moment of concentration—and he was back in shape again. He turned the murky dark look of the hunted beast away with his own coldly dark look of the victorious hunter. You, he thought, wanted to have a bigger head than all of us? OK, pops, I'll give your brain some room to expand!

He pressed the massive barrel of the pistol to the bridge of the nose and felt the splash of a warm whitish stuff on his face: the evil was flowing out of the rascal like steam. *My first!* he thought to himself. He licked his lips, so as to always remember this taste, too. It was milder, and above all more repulsive than the flavor of calves' brains, but no sooner had he swallowed then it seemed to him that, like in the fairy tale, he could understand the language of the animals and the birds. Thrilled, he took another taste. He was amazed to note a piquant, aromatic flavor melting on his tongue, one that he classified above all known delicacies. Then he heard the owls and the crickets and the frogs repeating in hundreds of voices: "Now you're One! Now you're One!"

If he had been a believer, he would have known that he was experiencing with his own senses what is known as transubstantiation. As a result, the smile that had been born in him two years earlier when he felled his first calf for mankind, now that he had rid mankind of his first vulture was released from the shell of his soul and broke all the way to his face. Simsa began to laugh.

He was still laughing when Seven slammed the trunk lid shut, the chief *probod* released the handbrake, and the car rolled down the hill like a giant horse that had been kicked in the belly; it groaned and reared up as it hit the stump of the willow, ripped it out of the ground, and rolled it ahead of itself to the edge of the spoon and tumbled into the depths of the lake. He laughed and laughed, and the little fans of wrinkles that were to be so characteristic of him crinkled the corners of his eyes. . . .

158

"Quit your whinnying," said the chief *probod,* "Simsa!"

He took the pistol out of Simsa's hand along with the paper and frisked him.

"How dare you—" Simsa raged, but then his voice and vision left him. Betrayed after all! he sighed to himself as a karate chop put him out like a light.

He was awakened by new sounds, but mainly by the fact that he was cold. He was lying on his stomach in wet leaves. Apparently he had been there for a long time; he was cold through and through and a light haze was rising over the forest opposite. He didn't move, he just opened his eyes. The hillside he was on was full of men in berets and camouflage fatigues. One fellow jumped out of a moving vehicle that kept on going until it disappeared in the depths along with a piece of hillside. Simsa was sure he recognized the "creampuff" hearse. He realized that they were in the process of liquidating, and he broke out in trickles of icy sweat. The instinct of self-preservation told him what to do: play dead. Perhaps they would just toss him down; he told himself feverishly that he was young and in good sha—

"Simsa!" ordered a piercing voice. "Attention."

His military instincts overcame even the instinct of self-preservation and snapped him to attention. Before him, on a folding chair, sat Seven, behind him the chief *probod,* both in commando uniforms. For a change the man who was standing held the satchel, while the one who was seated held the nutcracker. Simsa began to quiver. A fresh pain in his testicles almost bowled him over.

"As the commander," said Seven in a voice that was not in the least that of a bookkeeper, "of the newly formed Secret Revolutionary Army Guard, or SRAG, I want to commend you for your bravery in the liquidation of the criminal organization known as SRAP. Because you are among the minority of its personnel who are still usable, I ask you if you are prepared to serve our people—"

and it was no longer Seven speaking, but the new One, raising the nutcracker in a gesture that clearly indicated Simsa's job,

"—under me?"

"I am," whispered Simsa unhesitating, to drown out the increasingly brutal pain in his groin, "prepared!"

"You are speaking," barked the former chief *probod,* "to a general!"

"I am prepared," Simsa whispered again, "General, *sir!*"

"*Out loud!*" thundered the general, so loud that Simsa flinched. "A SRAGGER has nothing to be ashamed of!"

Simsa replied in the affirmative so loudly he startled himself.

"Give him," said the former Seven, "his confession, Colonel!"

The former chief *probod* reached into the satchel—it appeared that he was the Ink of SRAG—and handed Simsa another sheet of paper, along with the flashlight, so that he might light it himself. As Simsa read, things became clearer to him.

> The undersigned admits, that out of hatred for the revolutionary state, he did contribute significantly to the brutal liquidation of the revolutionary organization SRAP and personally liquidated its revolutionary commander. I am aware of the fact, that the only penalty for this loathsome crime is death, and I pledge myself, until such time as the sentence should be carried out, to make good my guilt by tireless service to the revolution.
>
> Signed
PAUL SIMSA

He finished reading, and with what was left of his strength—the pressure in his groin was becoming unbearable—he gaped at his own handwriting and recognized even the typical errors in punctuation. All of it, including the signature, looked so credible that he caught himself thinking back, to recall when he had written it. He could well imagine how convincing a court would find the confession. And the thread of his recognition picked up like beads the memory of the orders from Six, Five, and Four, as well as the "confession" by One: regretfully, he knew that there was no longer any question that the alleged authors of those documents, devoured by the flames of the crematory furnace or the predatory fish in the lake, had never written them. Atop that anonymous cliff, in a strictly watched spot that undoubtedly wasn't even on the maps, he finally arrived at the understanding that politics is nowhere near as straightforward, and that the state—even the revolutionary state!—is nowhere near as just as he had imagined. He would have very much liked to draw conclusions for his entire lifetime from this realization, but the paper in his hand gave off the smell of ruin. Why? he wanted to scream. Why me, of all people? He was on the verge of being overwhelmed by the pain, and he knew that it was the product of his fear.

The General rose, walked up to him, took the paper and tapped it with a fingernail.

"That is just in case," he said emphatically, "it might ever occur to you to turn—"

and there was a warning note in his voice,

"—tail on me."

The pressure in his genitals exceeded the threshold of tolerance. Simsa gave a loud groan. He cursed himself for being so blinded by love that he had pledged to spend this night without a woman if it couldn't be the one he longed for. My kingdom, his mind echoed with some famous quotation that he used to hear from Sergeant Olda, for a whore! But he was in such bad shape that he couldn't even find the strength to phone one. That was when another quote surfaced in his mind, one used by Wolf when they found themselves lacking one or another bit of equipment at some rural hangery: "Do it yourself!" With care and a little distaste, he took his defter left hand and grasped his organ, painful with desire, imagined the angelically pure and hence diabolically seductive body, and did

37

it himself.

He returned from the bathroom a new man. The destructive pressure was fading harmlessly away like a pulled tooth, and everything returned to its usual proportions. Lizinka was an inexperienced, though enchanting child, while he had, after all—he smiled—experienced a bit and—he grew grave—survived a bit, too.

Even SRAG. The political experience that crystallized in his mind the night that the flames and the water closed over SRAP was to protect him for good and ever from his noncritical naiveté. He put all his vitality into the service of a plan that, paradoxically, had been put in his mind by the man who warned him against it: a plan of how, without delay and without risk, to "turn tail." He had the good fortune of the chosen: the General himself gave in to the pressure of a highly placed friend and sent him out with the order to "temporarily fortify the ranks of the state execution squad," which was finding it difficult to contain the wave of mass political trials. Simsa didn't have long to wait for the first applause—he could still hear it today. His services were requested by the leonine master executioner for another round, and that decided it: the next wave washed both the Colonel and the General into the central execution grounds. When Simsa spied them through the peephole of the "waiting room," he feigned an attack of toothache. Wolf's jealousy had in the meantime turned to friendship, so that the older man went as far as to send him to his own dentist. She in turn determined an abcess of such great proportion that she extracted the tooth. While she was doing it, Simsa encountered another shock: he found that he was exceptionally sensitive to pain. Try as he might to control himself, his hands and feet tried to defend him with such a vehemence that she was on the verge of calling two attendants from the psychiatric department. At that point, a dark-haired technician returned from an extended lunch hour and as soon as she touched his hands, his pride did not allow him to move a muscle—perhaps that was when the idea of a hangwoman germinated in his mind! (Moved, the dentist suggested to her husband that he invite the sensitive lad for dinner, and when he did, Simsa was amazed to find the lady who served him boiled beef with dill sauce to be his dentist and his chief's wife; because she was as much a puritan as Wolf was, Simsa concealed his private life from her, and for years she tried to find him a bride; she use herself as a model for her choices, and he fled in desperation from all the flat-chested blondes she produced, which moved her too, but also pleased her, and so thanks to Simsa, her mind adjusted to her husband's admission but, regrettably, her body did not.) Swollen-faced, he hurried from the dentist's back to his worksite, which brought him a commendation and a bonus; he never told a soul that he had actually returned only to make sure that the SRAGGERs were truly done and finished. . . .

His satiated genitals had given way to his refreshed mind, and so Simsa could view the scene of Lizinka's forthcoming seduction from a distance. He saw three obstacles. The first was Wolf with his absolute morality, forbidding any extramarital relationships and categorically prohibiting promiscuity on the worksite, not to speak of anything happening between a pedagogue and his pupil. (And what about Mrs. Wolf? he suddenly thought; he decided to surprise her at work on Monday and make her an ally, even if it cost him his whole mouthful of teeth.) The second was Mrs. Tachezy, who interpreted that unfortunate coitus—interruptus at that—her own way, and would most probably stand opposed not only as a wounded mother, but also as a woman scorned. Finally, and worst of all, there was Doctor Tachezy, who was fixed in Simsa's memory as being orientally inscrutable, and who could unleash a veritable hell not only as a father deprived but also—should Lucie decide to take revenge on him by telling him—as a husband wronged. Yes, the only way to overcome these three obstacles led through a fourth—Simsa started to get excited again, and his brain had to work hard to convince his body that he was thinking of her now not as a man but as a tactician—obstacle, the hymen of his elected. As soon as it was penetrated—and he had both the strength and the desire to do it—as soon as the *causa belli,* as the Doctor would have said, was no longer an inviolable *virgo intacta,* as Wolf would have said, but a plain, ordinary gal who's lost her cherry, as he read in modern literature, the balance of power would shift unrecognizably. . . .

He moaned. Although he was lying motionless, his hands and feet outstretched as if he were about to be drawn and quartered, the image was so vivid and so inescapable that it materialized, erupting again from his groin in a flow of white lava that rained on his belly, his thighs, and his face for long seconds.

Simsa was so much a prisoner of his passion that he didn't even nod to the janitor, who angrily quit sweeping the hallway and fixed him with a stare, only to move swiftly out of his path when he noticed his expression; but it was again yearning and not dementedness that, after hours of torturous half-sleep, had tossed him up on the shore

of morning and slipped him behind the wheel of his sports car, to weave in and out through the sparse Saturday-morning traffic toward the gate to the slaughterhouse. It was at the foot of a statue of a calf, gazing credulously up at the statue of a butcher with a mallet, that he caught sight of a little figure, hopping up and down. The glow of her hair restored his judgment, and he recalled the first rule of the amatory chase: the more you want of her, the less you ask of her. He stamped on the brakes and screeched to a bravura halt right beside her.

"Good morning," he said as nonchalantly as he could, to conceal his excitement. "Are you cold?"

Lizinka was captivated by a strange phenomenon. Whenever she jumped up, it appeared that the butcher was swinging the mallet down. When she landed with her knees bent, it seemed that he was raising it. When she stood still, the butcher stood still too, and the calf had a glimmer of hope. In reply to his question, she shook her head.

The Associate Professor looked around as if he couldn't believe his eyes.

"Where is everyone?" he asked, convincingly feigning surprise.

Her reply was a shrug of her delicate shoulders.

"Damn," he swore with a credible degree of confusion, "could we have gotten our signals crossed, and the rendezvous was an hour ago?"

Making sure she didn't have time to think, he reached over, opened the door on the passenger's side, and said, in the voice of an irritated teacher, "Hurry up, so we can catch up with them!"

From then on, he remained silent, since any undue attentiveness might arouse her suspicions. At the ramp to the freeway, he pressed the button beside the cigarette lighter; using his well-developed peripheral vision— an executioner must be able to see around corners, he taught his pupils, because, like an animal tamer, he works with material that is totally lacking in morality and is capable of anything—he observed with some satisfaction how delighted she was with the mechanism that raised the canvas roof that had been folded down in the back; then he closed the little convertible up tight. The warm air flowing into the car seemed to bear with it an intimate atmosphere. He realized that it was the first time he was alone with her, within touching distance of her skin, in the enclosed vehicle which in fact was a small mobile bedroom. Yes, there was a button on the dashboard that tipped the backrests of the front seats to the level of the back seat, forming a bunk on which he had brought many a virgin to sexual life, when it hadn't seemed worth it to bring them to his apartment or drive them out to his cottage. Lizinka's pure and defenseless profile evoked in him such a fear of losing her that for a moment he was tempted to take the next off-ramp and do it to her in the nearest woods . . . Fool! he reproached himself, this isn't one of your black-haired Lolitas who get in the car without any panties on! That was also when he realized that the fragrance of lavender and wild thyme that he smelled so intensely could not be from the surrounding fields, which were only just being aroused by the rising sun—it's spring, he realized, so this is the way spring begins!—but from her body, as unacquainted with bottled perfumes as her spirit was unfamiliar with passion. No, he had no intention of taking her like one of the dime-a-dozen "nooklets," as he liked to call them, who disgusted him as soon as he had used them. He wanted to have her like a queen, on a four-poster, to the sound of roaring cannons and the cheers of a crowd.

They drove past fields and piles of gray, floury snow along country roads before they were sucked in with a series of swishes by the tunnel formed by a leafless but dense alleyway of trees. A gray-pink façade grew rapidly straight ahead of them. The logs of a bridge rattled under the car's wheels and they stopped in front of a castle that was the depository of the Oriental Museum. There wasn't a living soul in sight, and certainly not a busload of kids.

"How come?" wondered Simsa. He got out and looked around, trying to see where there might be a parking lot, when he realized that he had fallen victim to his own fiction. But all the more convincingly did he elaborate on it.

"I'll ask around," he said to the girl and started out to the door in the heavy, double-winged gate. In the kitchen, where he was led by the fragrance of baking goose, the castellan's wife told him exactly what he had told them earlier when he phoned in Wolf's name. When he came outside again, he had to take a deep breath of fresh air. Bursting with oxygen, he stopped in his tracks.

Lizinka was stretching. Her arms were pulled back and she was leaning backward so that her body lay like a taut bow against the backrest. The front of her cardigan fell open and the white T-shirt modeled breasts that confirmed all Simsa's expectations. He gasped at the unexpectedness and the severity with which his sex responded; the tight jeans didn't help to soothe the pain, either. Because the deserted countryside seemed to have thousands of eyes, and there was always the chance of somebody coming out of the castle, there was nothing he could do. To make matters worse, the girl opened her eyes and he could have sworn that they were laughing at him. He clenched his teeth, rammed his right fist in the pocket of his jeans so as to alleviate the pressure from the left, and strode toward the car.

Inflamed by the sharp pain, of an intensity that he hadn't experienced since one bitter night long ago, and by the hungry passion that was stretched to the breaking point by the bow that was her body, Simsa discarded all his strategy. And so he blurted out to her all the phrases he had so painfully invented the previous night, to be spaced gradually and inconspicuously over the course of the entire day, to direct her to his intended aim.

"They're not here," he spoke tersely, as if he were writing a telegram. "Chief had lumbago. Couldn't reach us. How about some lunch? I know a nice place here. And now what? How about an Irish coffee? I have a cottage nearby. I have an execution tomorrow. Want to do your midterm early? You can sleep over. Well—"

he asked her directly,

"—how about it?"

He was determined to carry her off by force if necessary, but he was praying that she say yes; her acquiescence would be as valuable as an engagement ring, because it would mean that she had taken co-responsibility. As she sat back down and clicked on the safety belt, her reply was not quite unequivocal, but he could interpret it any way he pleased.

From the outside, Simsa's cottage was no different from the others in the vicinity. A short distance away was an old prison where they scheduled executions when central operations was becoming overcrowded and the occupants there were falling victim to a dangerous neurosis. He had transformed the basement of his cottage into a hive where he formed and materialized his ideas, goaded on by the ambition to catch up with and—why not admit it—to overtake his mentor. The rest of the cottage he made into a reflection of his view of the good life: luxury, supplemented by top-notch functional technology.

Now, when the sound-sensitive device responded to the toot of his horn and opened the garage door, and the electric eye swung open the front door, he had something to brag about. He left the shutters closed because it was a sunny afternoon out, but he did start up his stereo—selecting a pleasing cassette that the Doctor had obtained for him from the confiscated recordings of a group jailed for decadent music—which in turn made the disco lights in the living room go on and the bar shelf tip open. Carrying a bottle of Irish whiskey, he led the girl past the dishwasher to the stove, complete with microwave oven, where he switched on the coffee grinder. While it was going, he showed her his own sculpture, which he referred to jokingly as The Monument to Contented Clients: from the very beginning, he had glued small pieces of every noose he had ever used; to save her the trouble of counting, Simsa boasted that there were ninety-eight of them.

"Unlike hockey," he grinned, "we don't count assists."

He took her to the lavatory, asked her to sit down, and enjoyed her amazement when the bowl began to give off a carillon tune, a Christmas gift from the Wolfs, at whose home he had first admired it. Then came Simsa's pride and joy—the basement. It contained a workshop that would have been the delight of any machinist, electrician, or cabinetmaker. And in the center, under a spotlight that sharply illuminated its streamlined design, stood the product of years of effort, an invention that truly deserved the adjective "revolutionary." The prototype had stood there for three years already, and was intended to stand there until Wolf left his post for a well-deserved rest. Simsa wished him a long and happy career, but he had to be prepared to become top authority in the field and at the school himself; for that reason he made sure that he had prepared an inauguration gift for his homeland, one of exceptional value: a hanging table.

He had not even showed it to Wolf yet. Since the demise of SRAG, Lizinka was the first person who revived in him the feeling of total self-confidence.

"It is," he told her now, and his own voice sounded strange to him in his excitement, "a well-known fact that an execution on a vertical hanging apparatus allows for all sorts of unfortunate surprises and undesirable effects. As long as he can feel the ground under his feet, the client tends to struggle for his or her life, irrespective of the fact that it already is the property of the state. A particularly strong neck can resist even the best noose and the most perfect jerk for as long as a number of minutes. Of course, all that is very visible, and the physiological effects intensify the feelings of animosity toward executioners.

"The hanging table," continued Simsa, placing on the table a life-size mannequin, "eliminates these problems. The client is brought in from the 'waiting room' all wrapped up, so that he hasn't got the slightest chance. And the execution itself in its cleanness resembles electrocution." He pressed a button.

Three pairs of steel semicircles tipped out along the two long sides of the table and joined with a click to form three hoops, tightly enclosing the doll's ankles, its waist, and its neck. Right after that, the table pulled apart so that the larger section holding the body jumped away from the smaller section containing the head. Although the gap formed was a mere

166

eight centimeters, the sudden jerk combined with the separation were clearly enough to break the neck.

"An error," continued Simsa, "is not apparent on the client, and the act can be repeated any number of times if needed. The neck-cuff also serves to silence the customer; urine and feces remain in the clothes in the horizontal position and do not disturb the dignity of the moment. One might," he added tremulously, because like every creator, he did not truly perceive his work until he saw it along with the viewer, "object that the table is not in keeping with the letter of the law, which calls specifically for hanging. Not so!" He pressed another button, and that said it all: the hoop around the neck was attached to a telescopic rod which emerged rapidly, raising the upper part of the body. It was no more than half a meter long, but even so, although half seated, the doll was quite clearly hanging by the neck, if only symbolically. The law had been fulfilled.

As he brought the table back to its original position, he watched the girl tensely. She finally tore her eyes away from the doll's neck, which had stretched to resemble that of a goose, and for the first time he read in her eyes an interest that distinctly exceeded the relationships of the school-room. He lost no time. He led her upstairs with the suggestion that she might take a bath on the way. He poured an abundance of a liquid into the current of water, so that the surface was covered by a foam of bubbles dense as whipped cream.

"It'll be like bathing under a feather quilt!" he declared with feigned joviality as she started undressing in the bathroom, "and I'll get you a cup of coffee!"

He was always very proud to be able to say that women came to him themselves, and he loathed the men who used alcohol or even drugs as substitutes for sex appeal. He used to make this specialty of his only when his partner's energies were flagging; he would dose them on the basis of their condition, and he himself would drink only caffeine-free coffee; he had stayed true to his athletic nature, remaining an amateur who frowned on any sort of doping. In order to avoid any mistakes, he used two antique grog glasses, one with the etched portrait of a youth wearing a feather in his cap, the other with a girl wearing a Renaissance headband. He took the latter and poured it two-thirds full of whiskey. He made an exception this time and served the Irish coffee right off the bat, so that Lizinka would lose her inhibitions more quickly.

"Here I come, ready or not," he warned hypocritically, walking into the bathroom. "I'll have a drink with you so you don't—"

He lost his tongue, like an art gallery guard who walks into a room expecting an ordinary portrait and finds a Renoir. The greenish tiles, which always formed a crude contrast to his ladies' raven-black hair, suddenly became velvet against which flowed a cascade of golden silk. Besides the hair, the only thing visible above the white muslin of the foam was the delicate little face, but the knowledge that all of her was within arm's reach, all of her and naked, aroused him to the extreme. Unfortunately he was still dressed in his traveling clothes, belted and zipped and snapped, and besides, in each hand he was holding a full glass. But before he handed her one of the glasses and stood the other on the sink, before he proceeded to take the glass away from the girl because he realized it would be an obstacle to his intentions, and before his finally empty hands succeeded in undoing the complicated horseshoe belt buckle, nature had jumped the gun. He nearly blushed as he felt the wetness hot on his thighs, but he acted quickly to avert an embarrassing situation.

"I'll make myself," he said, handing a glass into the foam where he thought her hand must be, "comfortable too—enjoy it while it's still hot!"

He took a navy-blue corduroy robe from a hook, stepped over the little pile of the girl's clothes on the floor, and as he left, he tossed her his characteristic smile, the one that her mother had wept over. He had no way of knowing that the insignificant—considering his potency—pollution had started a tectonic crack in his destiny of the sort that invisibly foretells seismic catastrophe.

Although he literally ripped the sticky jeans and underwear off his body, by the time he returned the girl had downed the contents of the glass. The whipped cream formed a filter that soaked up the taste of the whiskey, and in her innocence, she thought she was drinking Viennese coffee. When Simsa walked into the room, he was as startled as an art gallery guard who instead of a chaste Renoir finds a display of pornography. Lizinka no longer lay concealed by the fragrant blanket that filled the room with an audible rustle as the bubbles gave up their ghosts. The hot bath combined with the strong alcoholic beverage had made her uncomfortably warm, so she was stretching her arms and legs out of the water; the breasts that surfaced in the process surpassed Simsa's most optimistic fantasies.

And yet he felt a sense of disappointment. He had expected the girl to fight harder for her virginity, and he was willing to prolong the struggle in order that they might both have more powerful memories. But then, the innocence with which she was giving herself to him, not taking her grave yet unfocused eyes off him—all that made it up to him. Now he need not, dare not wait any longer! The gesture with which he pulled open the scarcely tied cord on his robe was almost ceremonial. Lizinka—

—observed them. Right beside Mr. Simsa stood a man, most likely his twin brother, because he looked so much like him, even down to the long navy blue robe. She tried to figure out which of them was Associate Professor Simsa, but the two of them moved in unison to untie the cords,

168

drop their robes, and then they were even more identical. As the two of them climbed in the bathtub, they slipped and fell on top of her. She had to laugh at how the tub was suddenly full of them, and how they both slipped and slid and had to keep grabbing hold of her. She felt uncomfortable not having her bra on: she was afraid that Mr. Simsa and his brother might be annoyed.

When Simsa finally dropped on the girl, his first impression was spoiled by a wave: his lips, open for a kiss, were flooded with the acrid taste of the bubbles. As he tried to expel them with his tongue, his knees were trying to separate the girl's legs; he decided he would take her right there in the bathtub so that she should not suffer too long; he knew from repeated past experiences that warm water eases defloration. Then he discovered that, decent girl that she was, she had worn the bottoms of a bikini bathing suit, with an elastic waistband and an interlocking clasp. (Why just the bottoms? he wondered; he had no way of knowing that it had been just out of absentmindedness.) But instead of concentrating on overwhelming her with tenderness, he now had to figure out how to work the unfamiliar clasp mechanism, and, what's worse, he had to do it blind. He did not become flustered, however; he knew how to concentrate, as in decisive situations, like putting the noose over a client's head while knocking his feet out from under him, and the center of the schnoose knot had to wind up in a spot the size of a penny just behind the ear. He finally succeeded in undoing the clasp; he slipped both hands flat under the fabric and deftly pulled it down over the pleasantly small and firm buttocks and the long, smooth legs. As he turned her, and himself along with her, over on one side to complete the act, he got another mouthful of bubbles, this time enough to make him gag. He responded reflexively, covering his mouth with his more dexterous left hand, the one holding the bikini.

The silly scuffling, with Lizinka sometimes on top and sometimes on the bottom—so much like the games she had played with her daddy in the pond—was such fun that she never even noticed when one of the gentlemen got out of the tub. For a while the water parted to show once Mr. Simsa, then his brother, but soon there was only one of them left, choking and retching and covering his mouth with a hanky that looked like the bikini she had worn. That made her giggle, all the more so when the one who was left began playing tummy-tummy with her. That used to be her very favorite game in the water, when she and her daddy used to hold each other around the neck and bump each other under the water. The loser was the one who moved aside. Lizinka held firm.

The water, the bubbles, and the cough had numbed Simsa's senses a bit and had certainly distracted him. But the girl's surrender seemed absolute and her cooperation so assiduous that there came a moment when he noticed that what had separated them had suddenly given way, and triumphantly he thought, Success! The blissful expression on her face indicated that it had actually been painless, and he increased his efforts so that he might bring her to orgasm the very first time around; true, it would contradict all his past experience, but then, wasn't every aspect of this relationship miraculous? What intrigued and surprised him more and more was an extraordinary incorporeal sensation in the area of contact. For the first time in his life during the act, he lacked the feeling of physicality, but instead felt a sort of ethereal boundlessness, like, he thought for an instant, an immaculate conception . . . ! He sent his left hand down to investigate.

He yanked it out of the water, as if it were about to be sliced off for bearing false witness. He confirmed with his right hand, although that destroyed their embrace entirely, the incredible truth: his sex was in a state poetically described by a certain statesman of world renown when at an advanced age his attention was called to his unzipped fly: he declared sadly, "A dead eagle won't fly out of the nest."

The amazed Simsa discovered that the whole time he and Lizinka had been playing harmlessly like brother and sister. . . .

With his left hand he took out the red-bound identity pass and displayed it at the gate.

"Hangman!" he announced himself with the common term, since he had never seen her here before. "Hurry up, woman, I don't have time!"

"I can't let you pass," said

39

the tubby guard, "I have no record of you here."

"Not even for tomorrow?" asked Simsa nervously. With his right hand he kept stroking Lizinka's fingers, trying to electrify her with his touch so that he not lose contact with her.

The pudgy female guard studied a sheet of paper.

"Tomorrow I've got you," she said, finally.

"So open up!"

"Not today," she declared, "not until tomorrow."

As she stood there, almost blocking the narrow doorway to the district prison, he examined her through the sliding window. She seemed held together only by the straps with the holstered pistol, with which she probably couldn't have hit the side of a barn, and he wanted to spit on her. But he knew her type: she'd slam the window shut and they could pound themselves silly. And he needed to get in at all costs. He glanced at his wrist. It was almost eleven.

"Don't be silly, my dear," he changed his tone, "tomorrow begins in an hour."

"Well, then," she said, "in the meantime you can go for a beer."

He thought fast, and his brain did not fail him.

"Who's in charge tonight?" he asked before she could slide the window shut.

"Are you kidding?" she asked importantly. "You know I can't tell you—"

"Lieutenant Hons?" he guessed, and immediately knew from the look in her eyes that it had been a lucky one. "I want to talk to him!" he added peremptorily.

She showed her distaste by slamming the window. Simsa used the moment to grab the girl and attach himself to her lips. It was unfortunately still the only thing he was capable of: he kissed her all the more passionately, the less desire his body felt, trying desperately not to let Lizinka notice until he could put into practice the radical, but, God willing, effective cure he had in mind.

What he was experiencing was like some endless bad dream. He had saved the day quite easily in the tub when he realized that fortunately the girl had taken the situation to be a form of foreplay, and expected nothing more at the moment. He thought he knew his body like the palm of his hand and was convinced that the momentary indisposition was probably caused by those stupid bubbles. And sure enough, when he dried her off to the tune of some sensuous joking and carried her to his bed, he was in fine fettle again—at least he was for a few seconds, but no sooner had he mounted her, he had to hurry to pretend that what he wanted more than anything in the world was to cover her entire body with kisses. Later on, he had a drink of the whiskey himself, but it just made him perceive his problem even more clearly, and the more actively he tried to pull himself together, the more his own body seemed to him like an alien instrument over which he had no control. He made one last despairing attempt later in the evening, when he carried her down to the basement in the hope that he would be aroused by the alabaster of her body against the dark-red formica top of the hanging table. Before it happened, though, Lizinka fell sound asleep.

That was the critical moment when he had to admit to himself it was not a matter of a temporary indisposition but a serious psychological block, brought about—he couldn't help but recall the January encounter with her mother—by Tachezy women. He had to break it, and he had to do it today! The idea that after all his efforts, the girl would awaken the next day still a virgin was so distasteful that it made his stomach turn. The drink he had had on an empty stomach made him retch again, and he was feeling worse and worse.

When he tried in vain to approach her on the hanging table as she slept—so demeaning it was, it brought tears to his eyes to see the utter limpness of his flesh, contrasting so brutally with the total mobilization of his feelings—he recalled a discussion between the Doctor and Wolf about an interrelationship between execution by hanging and sex. Wolf had related with a smile how he had once figured this out himself, basing his assumption on the fact that male clients ejaculate in what seems to be the body's last attempt to survive—to talk its way out of the clutches of some queers who were after it. That was when the Doctor commented mildly that the fact of an orgasm *"inter vitam et mortem"* didn't leave him cold. Simsa remembered it so vividly, because the Doctor, who had never before shown any sign of sexuality, had come out of his shell—perhaps as a result of a larger than usual dose of tequila with sangria—and had made the comment with a gentle smile that brought to his face a quality of timid boyishness.

"Why do you think that people come to watch you work? Violent death—"

he added philosophically,

"—is the sex of the timid."

Simsa searched in his memory for more fragments of that conversation, but all he could recall—it had all been Greek to him at the time—was the bare fact that observing a strangulation can evoke an erection in the observers, and can sometimes even replace a normal sex life. The fact that he had never observed it in himself could have been because he simply had no such concerns. All the more then did he fix his sights on that solution now, when he needed a mere stimulus, an arousal that would start him functioning again, like a shake to an alarm clock. And that was when he conceived his plan.

When he had gotten the girl back on her feet with a shower and dressed her back in her jeans and T shirt—sleepy as she was, she didn't notice that he purposely forgot her underwear—he had another shot of whiskey, for courage. As soon as they pulled out of the garage, he rolled down the windows and put the top down. Although it was the first night of spring—it's spring, he realized dejectedly. So this is the way spring begins—there was a frost in the air. It had transformed the cottages, the meadows, the groves and the river into a silver kingdom. The beauty of it escaped him, he just needed the cold to wake her up. Minutes later she began to show signs of life: she tried to curl up into a ball to avoid the icy wind. By the time they were pulling into the district capital, she had come to entirely, with a chattering of teeth, and like an animal sought warmth the only place it was available—from him. When he put the top back up, closed the car windows, and took his paraphernalia out of the trunk, he pulled his canvas jacket over her, tying up the hood like a mountain climber might, with just her eyes and nose showing. That way, the girl looked just like a clean and neat hangman's apprentice ought to look. Now, when he was breathing warmth into her with his kisses, he felt the flowing of blood in his groin and recalled hopefully Wolf's expression, *Ça ira!*

Instead of the sliding window, one wing of the big gate opened with a creak. Lieutenant Hons stood before them, a kindly looking fellow in his fifties who had started out as a poet and who still occasionally used rhymes when he talked; his very plumpness was evidence of the unhealthy effects of working in the field of corrections. Behind him stood the angry female guard.

"Paul, old pal!" said Hons, "welcome indeed—what can I do for you?"

Simsa dropped Lizinka's hand just in time. He had her ID ready along with his own.

"We've come," he said as nonchalantly as he could, "to set up shop."

"But," said the lieutenant, worried that he might have overlooked something, "you're not due to string him up till Monday, are you?"

"We've got to work on a new hold," said Simsa, preceding Lizinka through the gate as is customary for a master executioner, "so they'd have a bit of a change."

Hons laughed gratefully. He always enjoyed Simsa's quips. He gave a perfunctory glance to their papers, which had numbers instead of names on them anyway, and nodded to Lizinka, who was now carrying the suitcase—it was almost empty. They walked through corridors, cloisters and gardens, to what used to be a church, now containing storerooms, garages, a laundry, but also a "waiting room," a hangery, and a coffinary in the ancillary chapel; the entire prison used to be a convent, and even now they still had to refuse entry to crazy tourists from as far away as Australia, who were after a glimpse of the famous Immaculate Conception of St. Anne; unfortunately the Gothic master had painted her on the wall of the chapel.

While Lieutenant Hons kept running ahead of them to unlock the next barred door and then falling behind to lock it after them, Simsa convinced him that on the basis of foreign examples, they tested the psychological preparedness of clients by means of sort of a closed dress rehearsal. Psychologists felt that clients would be less nervous during the performance proper, and the execution would take place with greater dignity. The experienced Hons approved enthusiastically. He added that this fellow, now, Miller, was a real bundle of nerves, like most perverts; he kept crying for one or another of the little girls he had raped, he refused to eat, calling for the prison administration to "spend the money to buy something pretty for their little graves." Fate had brought Simsa the right man in a sex murderer; his self-confidence was returning fast.

They found Miller deep in sleep, so that they were able to tie his hands behind his back with no trouble; Simsa was pleased to note that all he needed to do was give a soft snap of his fingers and Lizinka handed him the leather thongs precisely the way they had taught her in school. At that point, Miller began to act up. He didn't struggle, but his wailing and calling for a priest were unpleasant in the extreme. Hons, who during real executions acted as a general lackey, was relieved to hear that they wouldn't be needing him tonight. When he and Simsa finally got Miller—a fellow in his thirties with the body of a Greek god but the clouded eyes and limp movements of a junkie—from his cell into the chapel, Hons was polite enough to ask if he might stay, but he was glad when Simsa delicately turned him down.

"Well, Paul, old pal," he said quickly, so Simsa wouldn't have time to change his mind, "I'll leave you here and turn the key, and when you're done, we'll have some tea."

The only door to the chapel fell shut behind him, and the special key turned twice in the lock from the outside. Simsa was on the threshold of his dream. The chapel was just as they had left it sometime in the fall, he could not even recall whom they had done then. Because cleanup was only done right before an execution, the overturned three-legged stool still lay beneath the hanging apparatus, but what was more important to him was the fact that the bench for witnesses was still there. Miller was still whining for spiritual consolation, unaware of the fact that the national flag on the wall concealed the immaculate Saint Anne; before he had left, Hons had followed routine and regulations and had tied him to a marble column at the foot of which was a painted white circle with the words CONDEMNED STANDS HERE; that was the place where the clients stood to hear their sentence read for the last time. So as not to have to bother Lizinka, Simsa went for the neck that was now the property of the state, gripped it in the vise of his right elbow, and untied him. After rotating him in the right direction with his knee, Simsa demonstrated his amazing strength by grasping him from behind by the crotch with his left hand and actually carrying him to the hanging apparatus. There he kicked aside the stool, which would not be needed tonight, and snapped his fingers a second time.

"The noose, love!" he added, not quite in keeping with routine and regulations, showing that the actual significance of the scene was not lost from his mind for an instant.

She was true to the reputation she had at school: the rope landed in his hand in precisely the right position. It had been tied back at the cottage with an exceptionally simple knot, because it was only supposed to choke

174

him a little, no more than a shirt collar a couple of sizes too small. He turned Miller loose for a fraction of a second while he bounced like a pivot man under a basket to flip the fixed loop onto the hook. Then, with his right arm, he took the murderer around the waist, lifted him up a bit, and, with his left, tossed the noose over Miller's head, and finally releasing him so that his bare feet—he had lost his slippers somewhere en route—stood on Simsa's shoe. The rope was almost stretched taut, but at that point was causing him no pain.

"Look, Miller," said Simsa evenly, without a trace of contempt or hostility, "you've got to admit that one rope for four little girls is not a lot. It's only fair that you have it a little slower."

He reached for the hem of the man's nightshirt and yanked it up over the pervert's chest, as if he were peeling a giant onion. He tied the gown to the rope overhead, so that the fellow was naked from the neck down, and what's more, he couldn't see out. Then Simsa grasped him around the waist again, pulled his foot out from under the man's bare soles, and said, "Hang loose!" He stood him carefully on tiptoe. As Simsa walked over to Lizinka, he gave a professional glance over his shoulder to confirm that strangulation would not occur even if he dropped to stand flat-footed. But the fellow was going to have his fill of subjective sensations, because that's what it was all about. In a few minutes, when Simsa cut him down, Miller would be given his choice: either to keep his trap shut and have it over with on Monday quickly and easily, or to rat on them, and then he could consider this to be a merciful example of things to come.

Miller began to wheeze under the nightshirt as he tried with all his might to balance on his toes, and Simsa lost no time. With a single motion, he unzipped the canvas jacket and ripped it off Lizinka. In a flash he pulled off her shirt and undid the button and zipper on her jeans. He left the rest to the girl and started on himself. Then he had to finish undressing her, because she was staring fascinated—after all, he realized, this was her first—at Miller. Staring at the blood-red heart, the cornflower-blue lungs, and other organs in a variety of color and line, she thought that there must be a color X-ray machine in the room; she had never seen tattooing before.

Even Simsa was fooled for a moment, when the tattooed heart began to pulsate, but it was an illusion caused by a general twitch. The muscular body suddenly broke into a sweat. Then Miller lost control of his bladder. Then, convinced that it was curtains for him, he quivered as his penis began to rise into an erection. The naked Simsa, pressed close to the naked Lizinka from ankles to forehead, didn't take his eyes off him, registering with relief that the pressure in his groin was increasing. Yes, no doubt about it, the problem was gone! Now—*right now*—he had to penetrate her and then quickly, off to the cottage, to repay them both for

175

all their trouble with a soft bed—and bliss. He grasped Lizinka with his strong arms and placed her on her back on the low bench. He opened her submissive legs, confirmed with a glance the readiness of his organ—like a blackjack, he thought to himself with pride—and was on the verge of entering her when he heard a sound that made his blood run cold.

A fart.

He spun around. Miller was not standing on his toes—or on the flats of his feet either. He was waving back and forth on his heels, his knees bent, because the entire weight of his body was on

40

his neck.

V

School was out Friday, June 20. On Saturday summer began, along with the "hell week" of preparing for the matriculation exams. Wolf decided to schedule the traditional week not only to bring HIENS closer to other secondary schools, but for far graver reasons. He wanted to have some time to rest, because after the death

41

of Associate Professor Simsa—they had pulled his car out of the lake under the dam on March 24, but the body apparently remained jammed against the grille of the turbines—he had been carrying the school curriculum for three months all by himself. He was pleased that the school had survived at all: as luck would have it, Miller's sentence was commuted on Sunday with an order that he undergo psychiatric treatment, and it took a lot of doing to prove that he had hanged himself alone; Simsa's accident made any investigation impossible, they couldn't identify his assistant from the description, and so only Hons was penalized by a cut in his bonus. Following the advice of the Doctor, Wolf did not try to get a replacement for Simsa, so as not to make waves; he did all the work himself, confident that after summer vacation he would have Albert as his assistant to help out.

But mainly, Wolf needed the time to put his private life in order before it got entirely out of hand. He had no doubt that Lizinka—unwittingly, of course—had been the cause of both crimes, and both suicides. While Masin had been distraught with adolescent hallucinations in which he saw himself as avenger of the honor of his sweetheart, which she fortunately never was, Simsa apparently had become the victim of his own sexual perversion, the desire to have a strangulation to accompany a defloration, which luckily never came to pass. Wolf felt a chill run up his spine at the thought that a lust-maddened swine like that, who had failed him disgracefully and almost destroyed his life's work, had, in his base rutting, sullied her virginal body and her innocent soul. Then he realized that he was thinking of Lizinka with emotion, while he had promised himself that he would be strictly rational in relation to her. It was high time!

A year earlier—it seemed to him that a quarter of a century had passed—his attitude toward Lizinka had been that of a teacher who deserved her ongoing respect, and that fateful week in March, when he was obliged to put some very delicate questions to her in the interest of the school, he had wanted nothing more than to have her see in him an elder brother and confide in him.

This inner process gradually began to surface. He stopped calling on her almost entirely, so that he should not tax her noble timidity, and he included her with increasing frequency in practical exercises, in order to keep her from constantly retreating into her secret world. All the while he tried inconspicuously to see to it that her name be drawn as seldom as possible as subject, because he was afraid that someone less skilled, for example Simon, might inadvertently hurt her. Of course, they noticed it, but only once was there any comment.

"Hey," Frantisek said to her one exceptionally hot day in May as they were returning exhausted from a parade, at the conclusion of which Wolf had solicitously offered her his arm, "when are we going to start calling you Mrs. Wolf?"

He yelped and bent over in agony.

"Terribly sorry," said Albert, examining his boot to see if he hadn't scuffed the iron tip.

That was the last time anyone had made any stupid jokes on the subject. For that matter, soon all of them were taking advantage of the situation, when for instance Saturday excursions gradually lost their scholastic rigidity and instead brought all of them moments of conviviality, inspired primarily by Wolf himself. Although he couldn't take

178

Simsa's place in physical education, he played so hard that he not only retained his authority, but even gained their boyish admiration—the supreme reward for every teacher.

At first he stayed close to Lizinka only to draw any further danger away from her, and hence away from the school. But during those weeks a network of bonds developed between Wolf and the girl.

Except for a brief period in his late adolescence, which every healthy lad goes through, Wolf had always taken his emotional life as seriously as his profession. The blow that knocked him out of his intended direction as a teacher and launched him into the orbit of an executioner was like an earthquake; he emerged from it without any relatives or friends. That is why he had attached himself body and soul to the person who found him in the worst of crises.

He met Margaret when, for the first time in his life, he got a toothache; it happened just when he was scheduled to do a foursome, it was before Simsa came into his life and he was just barely able to do the first two; the remaining duo were clergymen who had not had the chance to shed their fat in the few weeks in prison. He knew that he had a rough job ahead of him, and he could feel the pain shooting from his jaw all the way to his brain. For the first and only time in his life, he asked that they take the third, who was already at the gallows, and amuse him somehow while they drove him to the night emergency dental station. The dentist on duty was tall and slender, her gravity and demeanor reminding him of Greta Garbo. She found that for a man of thirty-three he had an exemplary mouthful of teeth, no irregularities, no caries, flawless; the pain was caused by the growth of a wisdom tooth, and all that he needed was a pill and some self-control. She gave him the former and wished him the latter with a mild, nostalgic smile that engraved itself on his retina and his heart.

He finished off that night's difficult shift—the third condemned man had in the meantime gone out of his mind, and because Wolf couldn't get hold of anyone who could authorize a postponement and they couldn't even tie him down or slip the noose over his head, he and Karli finally shoved him in a bathtub and they all sat on him—and then he showed up at the emergency station again, having first asked the medical examiner, who was certifying the four deaths by suffocation, how long a wisdom tooth takes to grow.

"Is it raining out there?" she asked in amazement when she saw his wet clothes; he hadn't bothered to change so that he could get back to her sooner.

He shook his head, not taking his eyes off her. It was just after midnight and the door to the waiting room kept opening and closing: it was rush hour at dental emergency.

"Still hurt?" she asked impatiently, and added contemptuously, "a big boy like you has to put up with it—the best I can do is kiss it and make it better," she joked.

"Splendid idea," said Wolf, stepping up to her, embracing her with his viselike arms and firmly pressing his lips against hers. He liked the fact that she stiffened and tensed against him. He realized that in spite of her attractiveness and her age—he guessed her to be twenty-seven and he guessed right—she possessed a strong sense of chastity that protected her from having affairs. (Too bad that he hadn't investigated the reason for it then—he'd have saved himself a lot of grief!) But he also liked the fact that when he let her go, she didn't behave like a hysterical prude.

"Are you crazy?" she asked disdainfully.

"No," he replied, "my name is Frederick Wolf."

"I know that from your dental chart," she said coldly. "And if you try that again, the police will know it too."

"I won't," he said with equal matter-of-factness, as if they were still chatting about teeth. "I only came to ask if you are single."

He noted that she glanced at the coatrack. Her black coat and her black hat were hanging there, but he didn't register them at the time. For that matter, her reply came quickly.

"Yes," she said stonily. "Anything else?"

"Yes," he said gently. "I'd like to keep you company."

"It seems to have escaped you that I am working."

"No," he said, "it shocked me. A woman like you ought to be smelling of Chanel this time of night—not of antiseptics. I wanted to make it up to you."

He really kept his hands to himself, and, having borrowed a spare white coat, spent the rest of her shift sitting in the second chair and entertaining her with clever observations and sparkling *bon mots* that revealed erudition, wit, and above all a decency that she had encountered in a man only once before in her life . . . When the last patient left, the sun was rising. All of a sudden she didn't want him to see the traces of fatigue in her face, and she turned off the lights. The gray light of dawn suddenly seemed to swallow up the whiteness of fabric, furniture, and walls. All that remained in an otherwise indefinite space was a tall and sturdy man in black. She was overcome by fear, not of him but of the feeling that this very moment signified the end of a life that on one hand hadn't been worth much, but had been completely her own, and the beginning of something unknown, in which she would have everything but also nothing.

"Well?" she laughed tensely, clinking her keys, "was there something else you wanted?"

"Yes," he said. "I want to marry you."

Once again she escaped inside the protective ring of sarcasm.

180

"How nice of you," she said. "You mean for the night, don't you?"

"I mean," replied Wolf, "until my wisdom tooth quits growing."

"You'd better be careful," she said. "Sometimes a wisdom tooth keeps growing all your life."

"Precisely," he said gravely, "what I had in mind."

Whenever they recalled it, Margaret Wolf would say, "You said that with such conviction that doubting you meant ruining a love that blesses only one woman in a million."

That was how she justified that she had stood motionless as he unbuttoned her white coat—during the summer she wore it over nothing but some translucent underthings—and submitted to his caresses, and that she finally—her modesty did not permit her to do any more—loosened his tie. Later on, she swore to him that she didn't know when and how he had taken her; she was brought back to her senses by her own hoarse cries of newfound bliss, coming in waves, until she found herself swept up on the crest of the ninth one, cast into the stratosphere and redeposited . . . in the dentist's chair. . . .

One morning, blushing and still awed, she whispered to him that she was going to have his baby, and he, in a swell of joy exclaimed that finally he would be giving life, where so far he had only taken it. She did not understand. And so he confided in her. She turned paper white and related somewhat incoherently to the horrified Wolf that the great love of her life, with whom she had lived for a year, for whom she had waited for three years during the war, and for whom she had worn mourning—Wolf had automatically assumed that the black she wore was a compensation for the white she had to wear as a dentist—for the five years preceding her wedding, had died at the hands of an executioner!

Margaret was a sensible woman, by then her love for Wolf was a stronger, and above all a truer love than the love she had felt for the fallen hero, and she agreed immediately that there was no comparing a mercenary who kills people on the orders of foreign soldiers, and a constitutionally established executioner who serves his homeland and progress. (Hearing that, Wolf knew that he would have to keep his real trauma a secret from her forever.) But something in her body or in her soul, independent of reason or will, decided that she would pay dearly for this love: in the morning she awoke having lost the fruit of her womb, and in the process, her fertility as well. It was a great tragedy for both of them, but they overcame it. Wolf got over it all the more easily in the knowledge that he had found in Margaret a perfect mistress, one who passionately sought out his vitality, an erudite partner capable of following his thought processes, and an understanding friend in personal depressions and professional difficulties.

He glanced at her photograph in the *fin-de siècle* frame inherited from his mother, the first thing he had placed on his desk in the Wolf's Den, as the kids called his office. She still wore the same short hairdo and the same sad yet sarcastic smile that she had the night he met her. No one would have guessed that she was over fifty; last summer at the beach she had been surrounded by swarms of handsome locals, who, judging by her hips, her breasts, her gait and her complexion, guessed her age at an active and functional forty, and this summer it would be . . . This summer?

Suddenly he was back with both feet in reality, victim of his conscience, a self-loathing comparable only to what he had felt at the time of his misstep. An instinct of self-preservation made him try to cover it up with an indefinite but all the more furious irritation with her. Why, he thought to himself, is she still an albatross around my neck? Why didn't she do away with herself when she discovered her sterility? Then he felt his stomach turn with disgust at himself. He had no right to think like that, not now that he had decided to put their relationship to the test.

As confirmation, he dialed his own phone number. Listening to it ring in his ear, he glanced at his watch: it was 3:05, high time. With his free hand he locked the cleared desk and with his eyes combed the room to make sure he hadn't forgotten something somewhere. Her soft alto surprised him.

"Mrs. Wolf speaking."

He almost hung up; he came to his senses just in time.

"It's Rick." He decided at the last moment to use the nickname that she had used for him through twenty-five sunny years. He regretted it immediately when her reaction showed that he had gotten her hopes up again.

"Yes," she said breathlessly, "yes, Rick?"

"I just wanted to ask how you are."

"Awful," she replied. "You want to do something about it?"

"You know," he said, "that I have to leave."

"You're going after all?" she asked, as if it were news.

"Margaret!"—he couldn't hide his annoyance—"how can you ask?"

"Sorry," she said. "Then why are you calling?"

For a moment he really didn't know. He felt uncomfortable.

"I simply wanted to know how you are . . ."

"Awful. Terrible. Couldn't be worse. Anything else you want to know?"

His annoyance returned, and then he was in control of himself again.

"No," he replied tersely, "but I do have some advice. I know that there are enough barbiturates in your night table to kill a horse. I wanted to show you that I am concerned about you, because the end of love doesn't

182

mean the end of decency for me, but you make it all easier for me this way."

"Frederi—" he heard, but by the time he registered it, he had already slammed down the phone. He discovered that he was trembling. That hadn't happened to him in thirty years. That was it: this was the moment of truth. If he picked up the phone when she called back now, he would never go anywhere! She had on her side almost ten thousand dusks and dawns of leaning over him to kiss away his pain, and of spreading herself beneath him to accept the flow of his passions, while the other one still remained, and might always be, nothing but a chimera.

Of course, he could have canceled the trip, but NESTOR's blessing for it had restored the school's good name, and above all, he was unwilling to dodge the problem and never know, for the rest of his life, how it would have turned out. But on the other hand, if he returned in three days with the girl unchanged in body and soul, then his marriage would be saved not by pity but by surviving under fire. Then the trip would be an episode that they would occasionally recall, he with nostalgia, Margaret with bitterness, until it dissipated behind the gentle breath of the old age they would share. His mind's eye painted a pastel picture reminiscent of illustrated magazines: Margaret and himself, in deck chairs on a luxury cruise ship, holding hands under the robes. The evening breeze cools the skin after a day in the tropical sun and a huge Caribbean moon rises from the sea. They look into each other's eyes and they read mutual love and gratitude . . .

The moon kept on rising, until what appeared over the horizon like a mirage was the pale but radiant face of Lizinka Tachezy. Wolf started, looked at his watch and rose quickly, picked up his suitcase, his coat and hat, and ran out the door. At that point he didn't register the fact that, unlike her as it was, Margaret had

42

not called him back.

"Miss, do you have anything to declare?" asked the customs officer.

"No," Wolf spoke for her automatically.

The customs officer, still in the thrall of Lizinka, noticed him. Wolf realized too late that this well-built glamor-boy considered himself irresistible.

"You her father?" he asked Wolf, still politely.

"No . . ." replied Wolf uncertainly, struck where he was the most vulnerable.

"Then mind your own business," he said disgustedly. "Show me your luggage!"

The mere idea of an excursion, of course, was not enough to satisfy the Doctor, and Wolf's elaboration on it was simple yet inspired as only his ideas could be: HIENS (0002) would send out its first study delegation; in order that it stay true to the principle of secrecy and yet get the most out of the trip scholastically, they would officially deliver a wreath in the memory of the victims of the extermination camp at Holzheim-Niehausen. Wolf justified his choice of a small and little-known facility as being inconspicuous; the true reason, however, was what made the plan a stroke of genius.

"Professor—" the Doctor addressed him with unaccustomed gravity when they met at an execution.

Wolf was dressed in his work clothes and he was a little nervous. His private difficulties were exacerbated by the fact that for the first time in years, he had to do a woman, and a well-known woman at that. Her name had appeared in newspapers throughout the world when she, a bus driver, had rammed a parade celebrating the anniversary of the revolution, from behind, and claimed to have done it intentionally so that she get the rope. The political aspect of the case was such that the state would have preferred to hospitalize her for life, but the psychiatrists had judged her completely sane, and this made work for Wolf that he wasn't the least bit crazy about, for the execution of a woman always revived public resentment against executions.

"If it were not," continued the Doctor, "for our long-standing friendship, I would have to refuse you my assistance, but my confidence in you has led me to support your theory that a successful study trip abroad would best serve to justify the existence of the school and fortify its prestige. The Investor, on the other hand, insists, and I can't deny that I share his opinion, because this time it's my—"

the Doctor gave an apologetic smile,

"—neck too, that the enterprise be entirely irreproachable, and that this be guaranteed in a totally convincing manner."

Wolf was startled—did he know something?

"Well," said Wolf thoughtfully, to convince the Doctor that he was in on the birth of an idea, "I had originally wanted to take Albert along, as the pupil at the top of the class, but the condition that you give me forces me to take the Tachezy girl instead. At worst, I'll gain the reputation of an old Don—"

and Wolf smiled back at him,

184

"—Juan who has lost his senses."

"Bravo!" said the Doctor, and Wolf was reassured that he truly hadn't the foggiest notion of his intentions.

By then Karli was bringing in the condemned woman, and Wolf had his hands full. She had lost her taste for the rope. He regretted, too late, that out of some sort of vanity, he had never taken a good look at Simsa's schnoose. He realized anew that his dislike for doing women was justified: any man who publicly breaks a woman's neck obviously feels uncomfortable about the whole thing. Fortunately, even his tangled personal dilemma had not disturbed his professional reflexes. When he snapped his fingers, Karli rammed a gag down her throat and a diaphragm up her vagina, although the former was done more deftly than the latter; Wolf insisted on it ever since one woman had been so frightened she started to menstruate, and now he refused to risk having it look as if he had stabbed her or something. Besides, there was a psychological trick in it that worked on this one too: startled that Karli was doing something unexpected to her under her linen shirt, for a moment she stopped trying to keep her head out of the way of Wolf's hand with the noose. Then he heard Karli's whistle, indicating that he was through down there, and the rest was smooth as silk. He pulled the knot tight to her neck, with his knee kicked her legs out from under her, and as she lost her balance, reached up and did his one-two jerk with such precision that it looked as if she had stumbled and he had reached out a gentlemanly hand to catch her. Then he hurried to finish his conversation with the Doctor, who of course was favorably inclined toward him after an execution like that.

The result was that now he was here at the frontier with this extraordinary girl, but—in view of the need for secrecy—without his special passport, so that he had to put up with the harassment of any two-bit skirt-chaser who happened along. Now the scoundrel was rooting in his suitcase like a wild boar, and Wolf couldn't help but look forward maliciously to their return trip. The officer who checked passports entered the compartment and jabbed an elbow into the customs officer's rib, an indication that the train was ready to depart. At that point, the youth spied the large, wheel-shaped package on the rack over Lizinka's head.

"Is that yours?" he asked suspiciously.

"Yes," Wolf spoke for her.

Although it could have been a tire filled with poppy seeds, used on one side of the border to make cakes and on the other to grow opium, the customs officer gave a salute.

"Bon voyage!" he wished the girl.

"Thanks very much," Wolf couldn't resist replying in a nasty tone.

And the youth, who saw him as a lecherous old artist taking his mistress across the border for an illicit shopping trip, couldn't help but look forward maliciously to their return trip. The doors slammed and the train started moving. . . .

The formalities at the other border were strictly formal, so that a few minutes later, Wolf and Lizinka sat down in the dining car. If he was obliged to travel like a common citizen, he had decided that he would take advantage of it: the foreign currency that he had obtained from a special fund, and the money he had purchased at a favorable rate through Albert from foreign students, was hidden behind the girl's décolletage.

"We'll see," he smiled when he sent her to the restroom to conceal the bills, "just how much sex appeal you have, Lizinka."

As for him, he knew: he caught himself formulating the mildly feebleminded wish that he'd like to be that roll of smuggled greenbacks, snuggled in the warm darkness there, with the beating of her heart sounding through the wall that was her skin. While outside, the last day of spring and the longest day of the year was postponing its demise, he was witty and attentive, charming as never before. It was to the credit of both of them that an unusual atmosphere developed in the dining car, when the ladies present felt a weakness for that elegant charmer, while the gentlemen were overcome with the yearning to kiss everything that unreal creature had, from the ankles up. Even the stewards felt it: because she shook her head over all the items on the wine and cocktail list, they got her a pitcher of fresh milk at the next station. Enveloped in her slender fingers, the glass looked like a fat candle, and Wolf felt more like a priest than a pedagogue, not to speak of lover-to-be and perhaps . . . he didn't finish the thought, so as not to jinx it.

The extraordinary state of his mind was confirmed when quite spontaneously he began to tell her about insects. When he glanced down at his fingers and saw the gold-lined iron band—he had picked it up from the safe deposit box early that morning—with its almost invisible inscription in German, I GAVE GOLD FOR IRON—HH, it seemed to him that all he had to do was give it a twist and he would find himself in the past, not the past of the loyal owner of this relic from World War I, but his own past, to which the study of entomology had been the bright prelude. And as he drew for her on the paper napkins the determining features of all four suborders according to the articulation of their limbs—Pentamera, Heteromera, Cryptopentamera, and Cryptotetramera, he was amazed how he could remember so much of it after such a long time—it pleased him to think that if worse came to worst, he could still be a science teacher. Then he noticed that the sketches of insects' legs revolted her, and he hurried to switch tracks.

His earlier twinge of superstition recalled a funny story about the executioner of Nuremberg, Franntz Schmidt, who was supposed to hang a

186

band of robbers. When he found out that there were thirteen of them, he insisted that they either turn one loose or catch another. Rather than risk accusations of being too soft, they came to the tavern to get him, saying that they had fourteen; the last one had put up a struggle, so they'd gagged him, they said. When he got home, Schmidt's wife asked him, "Well, how did you like him?" "Like who?" asked Schmidt. "Why, your future son-in-law," replied his wife. "He went to introduce himself to you. Didn't he ever get there?" Lizinka laughed. It encouraged him, and he proceeded to tell her some of the other hangman jokes that at one time he had collected enthusiastically for the Doctor. An executioner comes home from the village green where he was using the red-hot tongs on a harlot, and as he walks in the door, he gets a slap in the face. "If I ever," screams his wife, "hear about you pinching a woman's bottom again, I'm going to leave you!" Or: An executioner has a fellow on the rack, and he's working so hard the sweat is pouring off him, and the man begs and pleads, "Just a little bit more, chief, and I'll be rid of my backache."

Her laughter was like champagne, it dispelled the tension of the previous hours and the depression of the previous weeks. Nothing is happening, after all, he told himself, relieved. All I wanted was this state of harmless playfulness that clears my soul and dissipates the fatigue in my bones! It would be a shame, he thought, to pollute it with passions, and make the unique spiritual accord turn into a sexual struggle. He was overcome with the desire to tell Margaret. So he lit a cigar, the way he used to do after making love with her when their relationship was at a peak. And glancing at the old cartridge-case lighter that had brought him luck once before, he felt sure that now it would bring inner peace to all of them.

Before going to dinner, he had paid the porter for a first-class sleeping compartment. That was how he put into effect the nucleus of the idea which had evolved into the concept of the study trip, after he had spent weeks trying to figure out *where?* It had become his dream and Margaret's nightmare ever since the night when the monotonous sounds of train wheels in his mind began to accelerate like the sensuous rhythm of native drums, until finally he accepted their challenge. . . . He cast aside his inhibitions, covered her with his massive body, grasped her delicate breasts with his rough hands, penetrated first her mouth with his tongue and then the rest of her. He expected her to give a scream of pain, and was surprised that she moaned the very first time around, like an experienced lover. Then her body exploded toward him, and he in turn exploded with his seed. When he emerged from blissful semiconsciousness, he heard Margaret's voice.

"That wasn't me you were sleeping with, was it?"

"No," he admitted, "it wasn't you."

He almost prayed that she not ask any further, but unlike her as it was, she did.

"Do I know her?"

Later on, he often reproached himself for not saying that she didn't, he could actually have said it with a perfectly clear conscience, since Margaret and Lizinka had never met. But he wanted above all to be totally open with her, and to avoid all tricks and ploys: she did know about Lizinka. Later on, though, he also admitted to himself that he had in part been guided by the irrepressible need to talk about Lizinka with someone. Margaret was the secret sharer to whom he whispered even classified information, when he felt that he would choke on it; to her misfortune, she was also the only one to whom he could admit his feelings for Lizinka.

"Yes," he said. "The girl in my class."

She was silent for such a long time that he raised himself up on his elbow to see if she hadn't gone to sleep. She was quietly weeping.

"For God's sake," he exclaimed, "you mustn't! Yes, I admit that girl arouses feelings of tenderness in me, even passion, but she takes nothing that is yours—if anything, it seems to me that I've—"

he added contemplatively, wiping the corners of her eyes with the pillowcase,

"—expanded!"

"She's young," whispered Margaret, "and lovely and full of life. How long will you be able to put up with coming home from a blossoming meadow to an arid desert?"

He wanted to shout, Don't talk like that! but even with the lights low, her face without its makeup and her breasts without their padding were enough to convince him that there was some truth in what she was saying. He realized that her years with him had been hard on her, and he felt such a surge of pity that at that moment he loved her then as never before . . .

. . . and again now, in the corridor of the sleeping car, as he gazed through the half-open window at the retreating horizon, showing the last bright claw of fading spring. The pleasant mood at dinner had returned everything to its normal track. He thought of his wife, whom he sincerely loved, while in the compartment, long since sound asleep, lay his young student, of whom he was heartily fond, and whom he was thoroughly delighted to accompany on a study trip, but who could never replace Margaret.

He entered the compartment, checked to see—they hadn't discussed it, she had taken the lower berth, she probably never even noticed the upper—that she was curled up snug as a bug in a rug, but just to be on the safe side, he flicked off the light to change into his pyjamas, and he climbed into the upper berth to read. By the light of the little lamp, he opened the book he had picked up at the station. He soon discovered that *Execution Squad* by José Tomás Cabot was fiction, not fact, and he skimmed the story, stopping to read in detail only the conclusion, which described factually if a bit sentimentally an execution by firing squad, including the *coup de grace*. He decided to put the book on the list of supplementary literature at school, switched off the light, and fell asleep. . . .

Rather than carry around the unwieldy package that, thanks to Lizinka, had passed through customs unopened, the cabdriver waited with it in front of the hotel while the two of them freshened up. Wolf not only took two rooms, but he insisted that they be on different floors, which convinced the reception clerk that they were illicit lovers. When they returned to the cab, the driver had to ask passersby for directions. A young couple he stopped didn't know; an elderly pair didn't answer him. Finally he stopped at a café and came running out with the joyful exclamation, *"Il Paradiso!"*

The former extermination camp now served as a dormitory for Italian workers. On this Sunday morning, the residents were writing letters home to their wives or brushing their black suits. When they saw Lizinka, there was no end to the whistles, lip-smacking, exclamations, and obscene gestures. The package Wolf was carrying made seeing and walking a problem, so he gave a sigh of relief when they finally arrived at a walled courtyard concealing a building, and the sign MUSEUM. He had to lean hard on the bell before a disagreeable little old man opened the gate in the wall.

"What do you want?" he barked, looking at the package with piercing eyes.

"Good morning," said Wolf with barely a trace of an accent; his intonation was perhaps the only thing that indicated he might not be a native. He explained courteously that they wanted to lay this wreath on the altar of the martyrs, in the name of the bakers, young and old, of their homeland. He ripped open the wrapping paper. The Doctor had come up with a clever idea of how to wipe out any clues: the wreath was made of puff pastry, with almonds baked into it in the bilingual motto WE SHALL REMEMBER.

"No tours on Sundays!" the man snapped; not even the wreath broke through his hostility.

"Then we'll come tomorrow," said Wolf calmly but firmly. "Or some other time." His bluff was successful—his opponent showed his cards.

"We're closed for repairs," he said nervously. "No sense in waiting. You can leave the wreath here if you want, looks like it's not going to wilt."

Before he could stop them, Wolf slipped past him into the courtyard, with Lizinka on his heels. Behind the wall was a narrow path bordered with a wire fence, which—from the cracked insulators on it—used to be electrified. It seemed to Wolf that he could hear the barking and howling of dogs.

"Leave it here!" yelled the old man. "Do you hear? Put it down and get out!"

"Can't we," Wolf said, not taking his eyes off the man, "have a little talk?"

"I haven't got anything," shouted the man so loud his voice cracked, "to talk about!"

"Not even if there were something in it for you?" Wolf wanted to know.

"Clear out of here before I call the police! You're trespassing on private property! And take that stupid ersatz wreath with you, you damned reporter, you!"

"You might take a look," Wolf insisted, "at this little antique, perhaps you recognize it . . . that is, if your name is Adolf Hofbauer."

He twisted the iron ring with the gold lining off his finger and handed it to the man so that the initials were barely visible. The old man stared at the ring in fascination.

"It was my father's," he said duy. "Where did you say you're from?"

Wolf told him again.

"But that's where . . . that's where my brother . . ."

He stepped closer to Wolf and gave him a mighty slap on each side of his face. When Wolf raised his hands instinctively to protect himself, Hofbauer punched him in the stomach and knocked him down. Then he stepped over him and behind

43

the desk, took the cover off the typewriter, put a piece of paper into the roller, and sat back.

"Name!" he said almost inaudibly. "If you lie on that floor another second, I'll break both your legs."

Although a moment ago he had been certain that he would never be able to get up for the pain, now his muscles shot him up and almost to attention. He strained to keep his fingertips stretched tight along the seams of his trouser legs, but could still feel them trembling so hard that it carried over to the rest of his body.

"Frederick Wolf!" he exclaimed as loudly as he could; he knew that they liked that sort of thing.

The blond man behind the desk looked as if he had just come from a concert. Under the dark double-breasted suit shone a snow-white, starched shirt, with a handkerchief in the breast pocket to match; the overall impression was completed by a narrow dark necktie with white polka-dots.

"Ah," he said in mock surprise, "just a second!"

He shifted some of the folders on his desk and pulled one out.

"Wolf, the teacher?" he asked.

"Yes!" shouted Wolf.

"Ah," repeated the man, put the folder to one side, walked back around the desk and reached out a hand, "pleased to meet you—I am Commissar Fritz Hofbauer."

Looking at the hand that had knocked him down made the blood rush from Wolf's head; he was incapable of word or movement. He was taut as a string and the sweat from his fingers had already soaked through the fabric of his trousers.

"Ah," said the Commissar, "forgive me the overture. Just a little misunderstanding—they gave me the wrong order of appointments yesterday. I'm going to have to talk to them about that. Well?"

Wolf came to his senses and shook the hand.

"Take a seat," the Commissar said, leading him over to the little conference table. "You've got to understand, we also deal with traitors here, and we can't handle them with kid gloves. You're an intelligent man, we'll surely get along. Smoke?"

Wolf flinched when the hand moved quickly toward him again, but it was holding a case with cigarettes and cigars. He shook his head.

"But you do smoke, don't you, Mr. Wolf?"

Wolf blushed, as if he had been caught in a lie. "I don't . . . I mean I quit . . . my fiancée . . ."

"That takes a lot of willpower, doesn't it? Can you believe that I don't have that willpower?"

Wolf didn't know how to react to flattery. He gave his shoulders an uneasy shrug.

"You know what? Light one up with me so I don't feel uncomfortable."

The hand with the case appeared again. Wolf thought fast. What is it that would impress this fellow? Stubbornness or docility? Then he recalled an oath he had sworn not too long ago. Of course he must above all save face!

"No, I really . . ."

Snap. A lighter ignited in the man's other hand. Wolf quickly took a cigarette. It's dumb to argue over a silly cigarette, the fellow is trying to make it up to me, why not take advantage of it, thought Wolf. But how did they know he used to smoke and quit?

"Thanks."

"Don't mention it. You probably know why I asked you here?"

"No . . ."

It bothered him that he couldn't keep his fingers from perspiring. And yet he had counted on the possibility of something like this happening, indeed he had been asking for it when he had hit on his colleague, Latin teacher Vorel, to get him into the anti-Nazi resistance movement. For a long time, Vorel had maintained that he didn't know anything, but Wolf's will was indomitable. Once he had made contact, as if to make up for lost time, Wolf became one of the moving forces of the little group consisting of a number of teachers and doctors from the local high school and hospital. It had been one of them who was the original stimulus for his activity, having since early childhood accused Wolf of being selfish and weak; when Wolf had been invited to a strictly secret meeting of the leadership, to submit an extensive plan for a campaign against the occupying troops, he was able to look triumphantly into the face of—his own elder brother.

"I don't," the Commissar said, "intend to beat around the bush. We know everything. If I were to act according to regulations, your town would be left to all intents and purposes without an intelligentsia. But I am a lawyer and I believe in discussion. I have investigated the characteristics of various persons and I think that you're my man. Well?

"When I say discussion," continued Hofbauer, "I mean mutual, honorable openness. I repeat—we know everything, but as foreigners, we cannot judge who will be more and who less useful to your country in the years to come. There is a war on, and we cannot leave activity against us unpunished, but what we can do is apply exemplary punishment to the most extreme radicals, who would be dangerous to your people in times of peace as well. Thus the realists, beneficial to the nation in any age, will be spared. Well?"

"I really don't know," said Wolf bravely, true to the oath he had sworn earlier to Vorel, then to School Inspector Kroupa, who led the organization, and finally at home, where his excited, suspicious brother demanded it of him. "I have no interests except natural science . . ."

"That proves to me," said Commissar Hofbauer, "that you have a broad outlook. As a student of nature, you know that to survive, a specimen need not be moral, but he must be strong. I am strong. Frankly speaking, you are not my only candidate. I wouldn't be surprised if the other one had fewer scruples than you."

"But we really don't have anyone who . . ." said Wolf, fading.

The Commissar rose. Both his hands were free again, prepared for the next blow. "Three names," he said, "and you go home. Or else you go down to our cellar here. Well?"

192

Moments earlier, Wolf had been determined to lay down his life rather than betray even a single one of his fellow conspirators. But this was a new situation, one that had not been foreseen in the oath, summarized somewhere out of the line of fire. If it were just a matter of his own person, he would gladly allow himself to be beaten to death, but hadn't the Commissar said that he had someone else he could call on? Was there not a danger that the other would collapse under the first blow and turn all ten of them in and destroy the whole group? This way he could save seven members himself. He took the burden of the terrible responsibility on his own shoulders and even took the time to sort out the ones who could most readily be spared, either because they were single or old.

"Melk . . . Novatny . . . Ries."

They were the physical education teacher, the French teacher, and the janitor.

The Commissar jotted down the names. "Well," he joked without cracking a smile, "see how easy it is? Go on!"

Wolf objected. "You only wanted three!"

"That was then," said Hofbauer. "You can forget that now. I want the other threesome."

Even in his excitement, Wolf understood: they know about six! He felt a flash of burning hatred toward the unknown traitor who was sitting back drinking up his thirty pieces of silver, while he, Wolf, was fighting for individual lives. But it occurred to him that even in chess you can win on a check when you know how to sacrifice pieces. Physicians can get away with a lot, everyone needs their services.

"Doctor Veld," he said. "Doctor Kahn. Doctor Grob."

He was exhausted, but pleased that the nucleus of the group had been spared and could go right on working. The Commissar was still standing. He spoke in an austere tone.

"Listen, teacher—leave it to me to differentiate between radicals and realists. You name all the resistance workers, without exception, to prove to me that you're telling the truth. We know them all."

Wolf could hear a roar that sounded like a river overflowing its banks nearby. It was the blood rushing to his head. If they know everything, why should he play the hero?

"Well?" snapped Hofbauer.

"My colleague Vorel . . ." Wolf said then; he tried to make it sound dignified and above all final.

"Go on!"

A painful silence. But the whip of his voice did not even allow Wolf a respite.

"Go on!"

"School inspector Kroupa . . ."

And that was the final line which he had no intention of overstepping. He wanted to save his brother at any cost.

"Go on!"

"That's all, Commiss—"

"I have treated you," Hofbauer interrupted coldly, "decently in the conviction that you too are a decent man. This way you force me to use means with which you regrettably became acquainted when we first met."

"Commissar, my word of—"

"*Stand up,*" yelled the Commissar, "when you talk to me—and don't mumble!"

Standing at attention again, Wolf tried to control his wobbly legs.

"You think I'm a fool? You think I don't know who it is you've been covering up for the whole time? Except that I want to hear it from you—otherwise I'll do away with you in his place!"

Perhaps if his brother had given him more attention and confidence over the years, perhaps then Wolf would have been willing to sacrifice himself—but now? In a boundless second of anxiety he recalled all their conflicts, culminating most recently in the incredible accusation by his brother that Wolf's entering resistance work at this point was no more than an effort to assure his future at five minutes till zero hour. But that hadn't prevented that dear brother of his from dumping him, unprepared, into this hopeless situation. And particularly since it was clear that their idiotic, bumbling conspiracy wasn't worth beans anyway and the Commissar had them all pegged, was he supposed to stick his head in the noose too? Then who would take care of their younger sister? And what about Helen, his impractical girlfriend?

"*Well, how about it?*" shouted the Commissar.

"Wolf!" exclaimed Wolf.

Hofbauer was visibly startled. "Wolf?"

"Doctor Wolf, Jean Wolf—my brother. . . ."

"I always," said Hofbauer, "wanted to show my brother around here, he always tended to underestimate me a little. I don't deny that the slanderous newspaper article about my past, which they even reprinted in your country, complicated my life a little. On the other hand, it gave me hope that

44

Fritz might turn up after all; your telling me about his departure back then only confirms my belief that he has a practice somewhere in South America."

194

As they descended the spiral staircase, Adolf Hofbauer in the lead, followed by Wolf ahead of Lizinka, so that he might catch her if she should stumble, it seemed as if the sound of barking and howling was growing louder.

"I had to lie low," their guide confided, as if to explain his initial mistrust, "at the beginning, until passions died down a bit. But then my dear Trudi, may she rest in peace, said, 'Don't be crazy, Dolfi! You were just following orders—and besides, the whole town made a living off it!' It was the fashion back then to make museums out of the camps; they were run by former prisoners and they were crawling with survivors who were out for blood. We learned a lesson: we didn't let it out—"

added Adolf Hofbauer, unlocking the steel door,

"—of our hands."

Although he was a professional, Wolf could not suppress his excitement. Modern execution rooms had become old hat, and the medieval torture chambers where he took the kids on excursions seemed more like something out of a fairy tale. Whereas in this inconspicuous structure, his guide had done more clients in a few years than he and all his predecessors and all his pupils would in all their lifetimes. Without thinking, he reached for Lizinka's hand, as if to share his excitement with her. They both were shocked.

It seemed to them that they had walked into a hell. First a penetrating stink hit their noses, their ears were deafened by an unimaginable din, and from all directions they were surrounded by the open jaws of dogs, fortunately tied up with strong cables. Hofbauer's lips were still moving, until he realized that his visitors couldn't hear him. He pulled down a lever on an electrical panel by the door. The effect was fantastic: the light in the room dimmed for a moment and the racket immediately died down to a chorus of agonized whines. The light bulbs resumed their original glow, the lever was back in its original position. The concrete floor of the windowless room was covered with dozens of dogs of a variety of races; a few were turning around in circles as far as their cables would let them.

"Just so it not be left unused," said Hofbauer, "we've set this up here. Unclaimed strays are sold primarily for laboratories. Around paydays, the greasers upstairs buy two or three of the fatter ones for a barbecue. But aside from the dogs, everything is in its original condition, with the original electrical system that protected the staff from wards with aggressive tendencies."

"Wards," Wolf explained to Lizinka, "were something like clients. They were found guilty of suffering from an incurable disease."

"That," said Hofbauer appreciatively, "is very well put. Today people are again beginning to realize that euthanasia is not a crime, but rather an act of supreme social benefit. Morons and madmen of all sorts are dangerous even in the most peaceful of times. For that matter, fewer than half of our wards came from hospitals and nursing homes—mostly they came from jails and other camps. We treated them all equally speedily and painlessly. Down!"

That was addressed to a German shepherd that had recovered from the shock and had begun barking again; Hofbauer patted him fearlessly on the snout and led the guests to the door opposite, turning his rather birdlike profile toward them as they walked.

"The so-called museum is permanently closed for repairs because we don't need any snoopers around here. I act as its custodian only on the occasion of exceptional visits. I consider yours—"

he bowed,

"—such an exception."

He had already been told Wolf's profession, but now it seemed that his courtesy was aimed primarily at the girl. Wolf was pleased, if oddly uneasy. In the neighboring concrete crypt, Hofbauer explained to them the two methods of treatment that had been used here. Recumbent wards—the raving ones in straitjackets, the senile ones wrapped in canvas—were placed on a steel table; stepping on a foot pedal made three long needles emerge, at least one of which could penetrate the heart chamber. Walking wards had their "measurements taken." They were first weighed on a normal scale, to reassure them, and then they were stood with their backs to a movable measuring rule on a metal stand against the wall. A pistol with a silencer was mounted level with the back of the head.

Wolf wanted to ask what the six hooks were for, labeled I through VI and mounted in a row in the ceiling at the very edge of the side wall. They looked like one hanging apparatus beside another, particularly with the long bench, now hinged down parallel to the wall, but their placement would have been extremely inconvenient. But meanwhile, Hofbauer was voicing his regret that in the confusion of the surrender they had blown up the adjacent crematory. True, it had been a small one, with a capacity of only a hundred units a day, which is what the state plan called for, but its very inconspicuousness today would be good for his business and the town. This way they not only had to take every old geezer who wanted to be cremated to the district capital, but even every dog that died: the dogs get burned there in between ordinary funerals, and they charge an extraordinary fee for each of them.

As they talked, they walked outside, onto an overgrown lot with still visible concrete foundations. Now Hofbauer was turning to Lizinka with increasing frequency. Her concentrated attention seemed to inspire him to relate long-buried details. He recalled the legend of the simple attendant at the local hospital, whose father, Heini, had fallen as a military policeman in the first war, while his brother had been with the police safeguarding territory conquered in the second. It was this irresolute youth who first comprehended the significance of "compassionate death" as propagated by the new, resolute regime. Where reactionary and cowardly physicians failed, he stepped in: he called on the relatives of patients and explained the humanitarian nature of the campaign so convincingly that no one could refuse to sign the papers. After consulting with experts, he established methods of treatment and set to work. Each day he would produce only as many corpses as he had arranged to deliver to nearby crematories. In less than a month, though, a full two-thirds of the hospital was vacant—free to serve the wounded troops—and Adolf Hofbauer was famous. He was charged with the wholesale processing of the entire south of the country, and that was when his native town began to profit: local property owners got a good price for their property, local entrepreneurs handled the construction, local tradesmen saw to facilities while merchants and innkeepers ran booming businesses. Adolf Hofbauer was loved, too. The camp could not be compared with the giants that disposed of entire nations and races, true, but it did its job, and more: when the flow of the aged, the idiots, the consumptive, and the cancerous ones began to ebb, they were replaced by criminal recidivists. There may have been an error or two at that point, when the higher authorities tossed in a few political prisoners for good measure, but he bore no responsibility for that, mind you—he never even got on the list of war criminals and he was able to stay at home. Not even the criminal charges filed by a few survivors abroad—which was what inspired that unfortunate article in the press—could do much damage. If necessary, all of Holzheim-Niehausen would testify: Adolf Hofbauer was innocent. That was why he could look both backward and forward in time with a clear conscience and the unshakable faith that the history books had already been written.

The man, so small yet so great, had in the meantime taken Lizinka's arm and was speaking only to her. Wolf, a step behind them, was trying to listen with interest, but he was surprised to note that his mind was mostly occupied with Lizinka. The traveling suit she had changed into for the wreath-laying ceremony suddenly made her seem quite grown up. She was taller than Hofbauer, so that she looked as if she were leading him as she leaned her head in the direction of his voice. And yet they did not look foolish—indeed Wolf had to admire how the differences in age and height seemed to be wiped out by the apparent glow of mutual understanding. He imagined himself in Hofbauer's place, and was startled by the degree to which the image was improved. Good God, he sighed to himself, I want her. Then why did I write her off so quickly? Was it in fact only on account of Margaret? What if I just wasn't sure I could handle it? What if it was the first sign of old age?

It bothered him—for a good while he couldn't concentrate, and only nodded foggily to Hofbauer's offer to drive the two of them to the hotel to rest a while before his little *soirée* in their honor.

Back at the hotel, he led the girl to the elevator where a swarthy, Levantine elevator boy was bowing, released her arm, and handed her the key.

"I'm going to take a little walk," Wolf told her dryly, "you have a nap. I'll call you at half past seven, so you don't oversleep."

The stroll, followed by a long soak in a hot tub, calmed him. Feeling very good, he slipped into a clean white shirt that smelled of lavender. He thought of Margaret. I ought to call her, he thought. Do I still have the time? He was horrified—it was one minute to eight. In a frenzy, he dialed Lizinka's room. She didn't answer. It took him only a few seconds to slip into his tux and dress shoes; he tore into the hall, slamming the door behind him, and, running toward the elevator, checked to see if he had money and identification. The elevator arrived empty. His mind flashed with the thought, Good God, what if that swine . . . He remembered the elevator boy's lecherous grin. When the elevator door slid open on her floor, he ran out like a wild man. Had she escaped Simsa only to have this dirty Turk have his way with her? He knocked on the door, hard. No answer. He rattled the doorknob. It held fast. The desk clerk! The elevator door began to slide shut. He caught it just in the nick of time, levering open the doors with his powerful arms. He tore out of the elevator and stopped short in the lobby.

Lizinka, dressed in black satin, the halter top embracing her slender throat like a noose, was listening to time speaking. First came the pealing of the clock in the lobby, which was a trifle fast. Then the clock at the railway station, which was correct. Finally the clock in the church steeple, which was a bit slow. She looked at the delicate wristwatch from her grandmother that her mother had let her wear for the trip. It showed a quarter past eight. She decided that she must have missed them, and was about to return to her room. At that moment, Wolf reached her from the elevator and Hofbauer from the entrance. Each of them simply offered her an arm.

Hofbauer drove them to the castle brewery. If Wolf suspected him of having plebeian tastes when they entered the high, vaulted hall that seemed to multiply the clinking of beer steins and the songs of the drinkers, he was obliged to take it all back a moment later. One of the leather-aproned waiters opened a connecting door for them and they found themselves suddenly in another world: the castle chambers were a part of the brewery establishment. A table was set for them in the castle library. It was a rare Empire antique table with three sides, so that each person was seated between the other two. To complete the symmetry, there were three three-branched candelabra, three waiters in livery, and from behind a screen came the soft tones of a musical trio.

Lizinka clapped her hands with delight, and Hofbauer bowed; now in a tuxedo, he looked like an orchestra conductor.

The cuisine was in keeping with the ambience. Following icy caviar with lemon, which they washed down with a thimbleful of real Russian vodka, came the *sole Coquelin,* little turbans of sole enclosing a feather-light salmon foam. The wine was white Frankish Thüngersheimer-Johannisberg. The next course was *Canard rouennais aux oranges d'Espagne,* a delicately crusty little duck, garnished with slices of orange and filigree *pommes soufflées,* accompanied by Pommard 1955 from the cellars of the Marquis de Monteclain. The culinary concert was completed with a Bavarian *Crème Rothschild* with English whipped cream custard. The final note on the timpani was the popping cork of a dry Pommery.

Throughout the meal, father Heini's ring lay in a velvet case in the center of the table. Wolf couldn't shake the feeling that it had shrunk, somehow, until he finally attributed it to his eyesight. You're going to have to get yourself some glasses, he told himself, vain or not vain. Hofbauer continued the monologue started earlier in the day, this time on a more personal note. He related to Lizinka—he only glanced at Wolf during the initial toast—the love story of his life with Trudi, from their childhood to her death, all the more tragic in its banality: following a dog bite, she had died of rabies. He never found out which dog it was, so—he admitted that it was done in a swell of olympian rage—he fried them all in their electric collars. Because he related with equal openness Trudi's devoted assistance with his euthanasia project during the war, Wolf turned to him at one of the rare moments when none of the waiters was standing over them and asked if he weren't taking a bit of a chance.

"Why?" asked Hofbauer, but then, when he realized Wolf's apprehensions, he explained with a smile: "But these fellows all used to work for me!"

That was when Wolf noticed that both the waiters and the musicians were all his and Hofbauer's contemporaries. Eight old men, he scowled to himself, and a child.

Toward the end of the meal, Lizinka rose apologetically and the waiters immediately stood in a line that led her to the proper door. Hofbauer turned to Wolf.

"Tell me, Frederick," Hofbauer used the first name in what bordered on a pleading tone—"can I ask you quite frankly what there is between you and her?"

"Between us . . . ?" repeated Wolf, confused.

"If you love her," Hofbauer continued quickly, "forget this conversation. But if she is one of many, leave her here for me!"

"I b-beg your pardon . . . ?" stuttered Wolf.

"I'll marry her," said Hofbauer. "She has the same fire and ice in her that Trudi had. I know it so surely that I had my father's ring cut down to her size this afternoon. So tell me—can I give it to her as an engagement ring? If so, you'll leave with my car and you'll have open credit here until the day you die. *Well, how about it . . . ?"*

The words snapped like a whip over the broad chasm of the years—the identical ones spoken by the Commissar that had led Wolf to the only blunder he had ever made in his life. This time, however, it was not some country schoolteacher who was facing a Hofbauer, but a seasoned Chief Executioner, who may not have been able to compete with the man in the number of clients done, but who otherwise stood head and shoulders above him like Van Gogh over a hack painter of postcard scenes. Wolf didn't bat an eye as he heard himself reply: "Sorry—she is going to be my wife."

At that moment he knew for certain that he would use the same words and the same tone of voice the morning after next when he told Margaret.

The trio stopped halfway through a baroque piece and played the flourish of a fanfare. Lizinka was returning. One waiter closed the door, the second followed her in case she tripped, and the most impressive of the three held her chair. Both men rose. She thanked them by dropping her eyelids, so that she missed noticing the immense difference in the colors of their faces. Wolf, unaccustomed to lying, was red. Hofbauer, unaccustomed to losing, was waxy white. But he was not going to be satisfied with what he had heard.

"Miss"—he turned to Lizinka in an effort at polite nonchalance—"I've just been told something by my friend Wolf here that raises our simple meal to the level of a true celebration. May I congratulate you?"

Wolf felt himself on a second crossroads in his life, and, as fate would have it, once again with an opponent named Hofbauer. The man gazed at Lizinka until she realized that he was determined to wait for her reaction until dawn if need be. She smiled apologetically and—

—nodded. Of course, Wolf knew that she hadn't understood a single word this time, as she hadn't all day, which was something that had escaped the loquacious Hofbauer; all the same, he was indescribably grateful to his love.

"Wolf," said Hofbauer, "bygones are bygones. I tricked you, as befits my profession, but in exchange I saved your life. I'm

45

a soldier, but I'm not suicidal. The war is lost. Help me disappear and I'll see to it that your past disappears too."

The Commissar's formerly natty dark suit was rumpled, his usually snow-white shirt bore visible traces of having been used at least once previously. But Wolf was far from jubilant. This man, who for the first time had sought him out at home, creeping up the blacked-out stairway like a thief, was still the master of Wolf's fate, no matter that the battlefront had crested just outside the town: all Hofbauer had to do was leave behind a few documents with Wolf's signature in his office safe . . .

The situation was all the more depressing in that, try as he might, Wolf couldn't picture himself as having been an informer. He considered his betrayal to be an intellectual, rather than a moral failure. Commissar Fritz Hofbauer had basely tricked him. He had trapped an inexperienced teacher by casting suspicion on him, and in so doing had conveyed the impression that he knew everything. How horrified Wolf was when after ordering the arrests, the Commissar admitted to him that he had been bluffing from the outset: that he had never dreamed a resistance movement might exist in such a backwoods town, that they had actually brought Wolf to him by accident, and that he had intimidated Wolf as a matter of routine; if he had held out, Hofbauer told him cynically, he would have been sent home after one more slap in the face.

If it were not for that absurd coincidence, Wolf could have listened to the thunder of the cannons of liberation with the same euphoria as the rest of the town. Instead he was at his wits' end. He had succeeded in saving three of the group arrested by convincing Hofbauer that releasing him, Wolf, alone, would be too obvious. Unfortunately, he had been unable to save his brother. This time it was Hofbauer who convinced Wolf that releasing Jean would be much too obviously owing to Wolf's intervention. All the less was Wolf able to forgive the Commissar for having taken such blatant advantage of his decency. In the end, Wolf found himself suspect after all. Here and there his greetings were ignored; people would stop talking when he walked into the room. He would visit his sister, and she would start crying when he arrived and not stop until he left. The worst of all was Vorel, whom he had actually saved: when they met in the hall at school, Vorel would turn away and spit. It was with extreme reluctance that Wolf had to ask the Commissar to take some discreet action before that fellow did something stupid. Could he have known that Hofbauer would have Vorel shot too?

As a result of all these tragic misunderstandings, Wolf found himself unable to savor the delicious moment he had anticipated for years as a faithful patriot, a moment when the chandelier was being rocked by the pressure waves of nearby artillery, tinkling the end of oppression; he couldn't fool himself into believing that he would be able to prove his innocence to the rah-rah patriots hunting alleged collaborators. He was so shattered that he was torn between the decision to flee and the decision to turn on the gas. Now, however, the creator of his misfortune was standing before him. And the unexpected offer he was making struck a spark of hope.

Wolf worked out the entire complex plan as Hofbauer spoke. That night, Hofbauer waited for him obediently in the garden of his villa; in the meantime, Wolf had tossed a letter into the school mailbox in which he explained that the mistrust brought about by his thoroughness in his conspiratorial role was forcing him to prove his innocence by action. If he died in the effort, he wrote with some degree of bitterness, let his blood cleanse his memory. In the blue ray of a flashlight, he sat in Hofbauer's Mercedes and examined the papers that the Commissar had agreed to turn over to him when they parted: originals of the fateful documents, as well as copies of the order whereby Hofbauer called for the immediate arrest and trial of patriotic teachers Frederick Wolf and his betrothed, Helen Jarocov. How he yearned to warn her! He loved her all the more for being the only one to believe in his innocence, but warning her would endanger the whole operation, in which he was the tool of a higher, historical justice. He prayed that fate be merciful to her and the front move into town in time.

Hofbauer put the documents in his breast pocket. Then Wolf assured himself that they had a spare can of gasoline, and lay down on the back seat, his briefcase with the roll of electrical wire in it under his head. Hofbauer covered him up with a robe and a coat and drove through the cordon of military police that closed off the battlefront zone. Then Wolf got out, his briefcase under his arm, and from there on he rode in front, to give the Commissar an alibi should they encounter any patriots. Hofbauer placed his identification papers in Wolf's care, along with his father's ring, which might also betray him. And while entertaining Wolf with tales of his family in the idyllic Camp Holzheim-Niehausen, Hofbauer cold-bloodedly drove the car through the country that was verging on uprising, while beside him, Wolf was summoning the strength to kill.

The problem was not that the Commissar carried a weapon. No, Wolf was relying on the element of surprise; a professional who had beaten to death or sent innumerable people to their death would not feel he had anything to fear from a science teacher, particularly a milksop like Wolf. But Wolf, brought up in a family of scholars, was a humanist to the marrow of his bones; the idea that he would have to take the life of a fellow human being—albeit on the sacrosanct orders of his homeland and as revenge for the murder of his comrades—depressed him more now than his fear had earlier. He was terrified that at the key moment—planned for when they stopped to relieve themselves—his basic good-heartedness might take over; that he would not find the strength to stun Hofbauer, to

202

bind him for safety's sake with the wire, to shoot him with his own pistol, and to burn him in his car with all the papers.

Before they reached the forest where Wolf intended to do all this, they had to drive through the district capital. On the main square, their path was unexpectedly crossed by history. Suddenly they found themselves in something that was like a scene from a movie or a dream: they were driving at a snail's pace among a crowd of people waving old national flags and tearfully singing the national anthem, so overwhelmed with their first taste of freedom that they paid no attention to the Mercedes. Wolf knew, however, that they didn't have a chance, that all it would take would be the first shout and the mob would trample them, car and all. He glimpsed Hofbauer's uneasy face turned in his direction, but by then he had already figured out a new variation on his plan, checked off in his mind to make sure he had all the necessary props, and then he gave the first shout himself:

"He–e–elp!"

With all the weight of his robust body, he pinned the Commissar to the door, and when he succeeded in finding the handle, they both fell out under the feet of the crowd.

"Hold him!" bellowed Wolf, "he's one of them—a murderer!"

In a moment several men fell on top of Hofbauer so that Wolf himself had a hard time disentangling himself. Now he had to see to it that the captured man not be allowed to get a word in.

"Look out!" he kept yelling. "He has a gun!"

Several hands felt around Hofbauer's overcoat pockets, and when they found a malevolent-looking automatic, they were convinced. Meanwhile Wolf had run around the tangle of men to get to Hofbauer's head, and, disregarding the teeth snapping viciously at his fingers, he rammed his handkerchief between them.

"I'll shut your filthy mouth!" he screamed hysterically, turning to the crowd. "That's the mouth that sent our people to death! Look—"

it had worked—the enemy was snorting through his nose to get enough air to avoid suffocation. Wolf jumped up, opened the briefcase, and waved the wire over his head,

"—here's what he used to truss us like turkeys with—here, it's your turn now!"

and the men kneeling on top of Hofbauer lifted the squirming body so that Wolf could bind it with the wire. The danger of the situation obliged him to hurry and above all to keep accusing the Commissar of worse and worse crimes. When he finished tying the feet, the riskiest moment had arrived: he had to move over to the car for a few moments. But by then he could tell that at least one of his helpers was exhibiting signs of an activity comparable to his own; he was a strong youth with a low forehead and the broken nose of a boxer.

"Put him up someplace," Wolf ordered him, placing the remainder of the wire in his hand, "so everybody can see him for what he is—"

and he pulled the Commissar's police identification card out of his pocket like a trump.

"—*Hofbauer the Hangman!*"

He handed it to a woman standing beside him and pushed his way to the car for the gas can. It worked. The woman raised the card over her head. The hated symbol infuriated the mob, which had still been slightly uncomfortable with the struggle of seven against one, and aroused a thirst for blood. The strong fellow gave the wire a tug and dragged Hofbauer across the paving stones like a sack. Wolf hurried after them. He couldn't let up as long as there was any chance that someone might discover the papers in the breast pocket. The end of the wire flipped up over the heads of the crowd and hooked onto the arm of a streetlamp. A little gypsy boy shinnied up the post, made a loop, and tossed the rest of it back down. By the time Wolf got to the lamppost, several men were already pulling Hofbauer up feet first.

"Wait!" Wolf ordered. He opened the gas can and began to pour gasoline on the Commissar from head to foot, as if he were preparing a monstrous roast *flambé*. He saw the eyes, mad with fear, and from somewhere in the crowd he heard shouted words that mobilized him to a decisive encounter.

"He's nuts!" someone called out. "Prisoners belong before a judge— this is a lynching!"

"Who said that?" raged Wolf. The hand holding the almost empty can pointed toward the crowd, which retreated and fell silent. "This swine here killed my brother! Weren't you in on it with him? Come out—let me have a look at you!"

No one responded—no one dared.

"Heave—" started the boxer.

"—ho!" some of the others joined in.

The feet touched the lamp while the head nodded within arm's reach of the crowd. The hair, stuck together with gasoline, looked as if it were standing on end. Wolf dropped the gas can, stuck his hands in his pockets, and stopped cold. Later on he shivered at what would have happened in the woods: without matches, the best he could have done with the papers was to eat them up. Fortunately, here he was among people.

"Matches!" he called. "Give me some matches here!"

A trembling hand appeared with a lighter made out of a World War I cartridge case; no one showed up afterward to claim the antique, and

Wolf kept it as a talisman. He lit it and looked up. The staring eyes were no longer human. Still, he hesitated. But then he felt a surge of cold wrath, the wrath of the avenger of family, nation, countrymen. Not even the pitiful moan, like the whine of a dog, could stay his hand. He raised the little flame to the sticky hair.

The sound was like a huge gas oven whoofing into flame all at once. For a few seconds, the Commissar looked as if he had been melted into a chunk of dazzling glass. Then perhaps terror, perhaps the terrible pain, gave him the strength to spit out the gag. His wailing rose inarticulately up the scale to an incredible height until suddenly it broke. The sound was replaced by a horrid stench. Wolf perceived a funereal silence in the crowded square, interrupted only by a rustling crackle, as if someone were crumpling cellophane. The flame changed color, but that might have been an optical illusion, as the white face turned brown. The heat made the small body shrink even more, and it began to move, as the individual muscles contracted. Hofbauer looked like an acrobat going through his tricks. People in the crowd were fainting and vomiting. Finally an air pocket formed between the clothes and the body. The fabric began to disappear in smoke, and with it, Wolf's youthful error. . . .

When the flame went out and Wolf took a taste with interest, he had to admit he had never had anything like it on his tongue. That noble

46

cognac, warmed in a snifter, seemed to release its century-old fragrance and flavor. Now it was his turn to applaud. Even Lizinka's face was glowing blissfully. Adolf Hofbauer was finally back to normal, and gave a mild smile. When Wolf imagined how he himself would react to losing Lizinka, he could appreciate the man's self-control. Moreover, Wolf was truly grateful for having been forced by the man to overcome a dead spot in his life and to arrive at a decision that otherwise he wouldn't have dared to make, in spite of the directness of his nature. He wondered how to make it up to him.

"In better das," Adolf Hofbauer spoke, "we used to hold *soirées* for close friends right at the center. Trudi invented a delightful game that could only be played there." He went on to explain that after the war, they naturally had to change the rules, which spoiled it a little, but even so it remained an interesting game, and of course, he smiled, it was a game of chance. No, he reassured his colleague that he needn't fear being fleeced of his property or his love. All he was doing, he said, was to offer them an extraordinary experience, in the course of which they would drink a little more good champagne. They accepted.

Hofbauer drove them back himself again, and everything must have been ready in advance, because when he led them in—by the back way, through what had formerly been the crematory—into the treatment room, the others were waiting, dressed, waiters and musicians alike, in long white coats; the effect was oppressive. They sat down, Lizinka in the middle, along one side of the long steel table, facing the wall with the mysterious hooks. Now it was illuminated with two spotlights that revealed every irregularity; right under the hooks the wall was almost mirror-smooth, while farther down it was as full of rills and valleys as a map. On the left, Wolf noticed a silver bucket full of ice and a bottle of the golden Pommery, on the right a set of percussion instruments.

The cork popped and the wine relaxed him tremendously; it was as if a wall had moved inside him, shutting off a corner full of somber premonitions, and revealing bright loggia, flooded with sunny hopes. He gazed at Lizinka electrified, almost forgetting about the game, until the headwaiter placed a slate and chalk on the table before him, too.

"In his novel *Shadows in Paradise*," spoke Adolf Hofbauer, opening a book at a marker, "Erich Maria Remarque wrote the following, in chapter twenty-three: 'I was once again in the room where the crematory furnaces stood, with a lump in my throat, scarcely breathing, because they had just taken me down unconscious from the hook on the wall where they hanged the condemned; while the victims, their hands and feet bound, scraped at the wall, the murderers placed bets on which of them would stay alive the longest.' Those words—"

continued Adolf Hofbauer, returning the book to the headwaiter,

"—do not reflect any particular sympathy on the part of the author, but they certainly serve to establish our game in world literature, a game that its witty inventress aptly named *Lastlotto*. I need not add that Trudi was far from being the kind of person who would, God forbid, make anyone suffer. We chose the patients for the game of *Lastlotto* from among the totally demented. The aim is for the player to select in advance the one who will last the longest. As Remarque implied, that one wins too; Trudi insisted that the one who survived be sent back to the asylum under one pretext or another. Here's—"

he added quickly, because his voice was beginning to tremble,

"—to her memory."

They drank. The musicians and the waiters snapped to attention.

"Not only I, but also," continued Hofbauer, including with a solemn sweep of his hand all those present, "all my fellow workers took Trudi's death so hard that we haven't played the game since. Today's session, which breaks the seal of our mourning, has been made possible only by the presence of our dear—"

Hofbauer turned to Lizinka,

"—young guest, who reminds us so much of our commandress. I hope that our honored—"

Hofbauer turned to Wolf,

"—visitor will not misunderstand my intentions, and above all I am confident that you, our beloved—"

Hofbauer turned to the ceiling,

"—Trudi, will not deny us your blessing. Well!"

He snapped his fingers. The sextet of men marched with a military stride into the neighboring room full of dogs. The dogs must have been subdued by electrical shock again, because the only sound was a sporadic whine, and the ones that were now being led into the treatment room had their tails between their legs and their gait was unsteady. There were six of them, most of them huge animals: an Alsatian wolfhound, an Irish setter, a Saint Bernard, a Doberman pinscher, and a mastiff; the exception was a tall, slender greyhound. They had choke chains around their necks; the men in white were leading them by the fixed loops on their leashes.

"Now, when the boys," said Hofbauer, "introduce us to the specimens, the betting begins. Each of us will write down the number of the hook that holds his favorite. Then it is up to the genetic background of one or another of them. In honor of Trudi, the rule still holds that the last to survive is freed. I'll bet—"

continued Hofbauer, placing his fat billfold on the table,

"—all my cash against any amount or item you choose to bet, Wolf. As for our young friend, I can imagine no more valuable forfeit than her—"

he spoke merrily, but he could not conceal his excitement,

"—kiss. Well?"

After a while, Lizinka nodded without a word.

Without a word, Wolf placed his precious cigarette lighter on the table.

Without a word, Hofbauer snapped his fingers a second time.

At that point, the headwaiter took over the game.

"Let's go!" he said. "Go!"

The first man led the line with the wolfhound. Like jockeys showing off horses in the paddock, they walked around the table in a circle, so that the players could examine the animals from close up. Wolf was excited. He felt obligated to Hofbauer, but he had no intention of lending him Lizinka's lips. He evaluated the chances of the individual dogs, convinced that his years of experience must be valid here as well. He immediately eliminated the Saint Bernard and the greyhound: the former because his great weight would break his neck right off, the latter lost the advantage of his light weight because of his long, thin neck, perfect for strangulation. With the next round, he scratched the Doberman and the mastiff: more likely than not their smooth necks would speed up their choking. The hairy setter and the muscular wolfhound would have roughly an equal chance.

The showing was over, and Wolf was still undecided. The dogs sat in a line at the heels of the attendants, strangely tremulous. The headwaiter glanced down the row, and exclaimed like a croupier before the roulette wheel begins to turn, "Place your bets!"

From the corner of his eye, Wolf could see Lizinka and Hofbauer writing on their slates with chalk, covering their inscriptions with their hands; that simple schoolboy gesture seemed to wipe out the age difference for a while. Once again he looked toward the dogs. In the brief moment that he had looked away, the scene had changed considerably. Two of the men had raised the plank that was attached by hinges to the wall under the hooks, and fixed it there by throwing a bolt to form a bench onto which the six were lifting their dogs. Then they jumped up on the plank themselves and each placed the fixed loop of the leash over one of the hooks. When they jumped down, they hurried behind the table so as not to block the view.

"Place your bets!" reiterated the headwaiter, and that was the cue for the others to bet; the bets must have been agreed on in advance, because now papers and pencils appeared in their hands for only a few moments. The distracted Wolf had still not decided on his bet. He observed that two waiters who had already stuck the writing implements in their pockets returned to the wall opposite, spat on their hands, and shoved them under either end of the plank bench.

"Time is almost up!" called the headwaiter and he began to count down as if he were about to launch a rocket. "Ten, nine, eight . . ."

Hofbauer put down the slate, blank side up, and leaned forward impatiently.

"Seven, six, five . . ."

Lizinka only turned her slate around and remained motionless.

"Four, three . . ."

Wolf put down a Roman numeral one. It belonged to the wolfhound.

"Two, one—*rien ne va plus!*"

The traditional finish to betting was underscored by a crash: the two waiters had pulled out the bolts and the plank smashed down to hit the wall. A typical circus drumroll sounded; one of the musicians had sat down behind the drums. Six dangling dogs' bodies swung beside the wall. Except for the Saint Bernard, who had broken his neck with the initial fall as expected and removed himself from the game, the dogs were all still alive and struggling with all their might. The apparently useless placement of the hooks now proved to be purposeful: the dogs had at least a minuscule chance of trying to relieve the pressure on their throats. They appeared to realize it and began with incredible energy to lick the concrete wall with their tongues on top and to scratch it below with all four paws, which did have a certain effect. Wolf imagined how much more effective the struggle of the wards must have been when they had put all their conscious human effort into it. He was brought back to reality by a crash of the cymbals announcing the exitus of the greyhound. The game continued all the more suggestively in that the animals' throats were too choked to allow the passage of sound, and the accompaniment was a sensitive drum solo. When he looked at them through half-closed eyelids, it seemed that the animals were pumping pedals. Then one of the competitors appeared to give up, and another cymbal crash announced the elimination of the Doberman. The going was getting rough. Although the leashes, made of extra-thick rope, were only choking them gradually, the remaining three animals were obviously on their last legs, so to speak. For a while it appeared that the mastiff had the advantage, but then it pushed off too hard with one paw and found itself swinging around, its back to the wall. An expression that resembled human amazement appeared in its canine eyes. It went so far as to stick its tongue out at the audience, but by then it had quit kicking and the cymbal marked the end to its participation. If Wolf had started out by viewing the entire great *Lastlotto* game as a problematic affair, now he had to admit that it had captivated him; he would never release any of his clients for it—customs from a barbarous war did not belong in a civilized peace—but with dogs, the game had a rough-hewn charm and real suspense. He stored away the idea that he would have to discuss with the Doctor the possibility of its inclusion in the curriculum. But there wasn't time for contemplation, because at the wall, a fascinating finish was taking place in which the setter was apparently the weaker. The headwaiter had already taken his place beside the wolfhound with a long yataghan to cut him down. Wolf rose to his feet. He noticed that Hofbauer had risen too. The malicious thought that flashed through his mind was, He's bet on the setter! The wolfhound's claws caught on the wall with such vehemence that he began to climb it like a telegraph linesman. It was so convincing that even Wolf caught on too late to the wolfhound's error: the closer the dog's body got to horizontal, the tighter the noose around its neck was pulled. It gave up all at once. The heavy body slid down the wall like a sack of flour and the snap of its spinal column disclosed that, in spite of all its efforts, it had ended up like the Saint Bernard. The cymbal clashed for the last time. A moment later came the flash of a blade and the victorious setter slipped into the arms of two men in white, who gently put it on the floor and loosened the rope around its neck. The drummer honored the victor with a tremendous drumroll. Wolf sat down quickly. Hofbauer was already seated, coming to terms with yet another disappointment.

209

"Lady luck let me down," he said, turning up his slate with a Roman numeral one on it, "twice today. How about you, friend?"

Wolf showed him his Roman one.

"Could it be," asked Hofbauer tensely, "that we have no winner? That would mean we split the pot. Miss, your bet will decide it!"

She passed him her slate. The number on it was clearly the setter's two.

"Yes," said Hofbauer, touched, "yes, you are indeed the reincarnation of my Trudi! Well—"

he turned to Wolf,

"—today we both lose. Pity. I've always regretted every kiss that went—"

he joked, although he didn't feel particularly funny,

"—to waste."

Lizinka got up. Wolf and Hofbauer rose too, thinking that she was indicating the end of the evening. Instead, she walked over to the wall, and when the two men in white moved aside for her she knelt down beside the setter, bent her face down to it, and buried her face in its fur. It looked like a long kiss. No one moved: the girl in black between the two old men in white and the five hanged dogs appeared to all of them like a priestess partaking in a mysterious pagan ritual. Then the setter raised its head weakly and began to lick her hand.

On her way back, she walked behind both Wolf and Hofbauer, and the two slowly turned to follow her with their eyes. She stopped between them, gently took their two heads in her hands and moved them toward each other; then she kissed them too—the short Hofbauer on the forehead, the tall Wolf on the chin. It was such a perfect finish to an unforgettable evening that none of those present spoke a word. Hofbauer offered Lizinka his arm, and when she took Wolf's arm as well, they all walked outside into the first night of summer, which made its own contribution to the mood.

*

Hofbauer did not accompany them inside the hotel. When he closed the car door behind Lizinka, he kissed her hand and said firmly, "Good luck, miss. I will never forget you."

Then he shook Wolf's hand. "Be good to her," he said. "She deserves it."

"I'd be pleased," said Wolf quickly, "to give you something to remember us by—something I have carried with me for thirty years. You too deserve it."

He gave him his souvenir cigarette lighter. Hofbauer flicked it. It burst into a tiny flame. He watched it nostalgically. Either he didn't realize that

Wolf had in fact lost it in the game or else he realized all too well that Lizinka, and with her, Wolf, had won it back.

"Thanks," he said. "I'm not a smoker, as you might have noticed. But if my brother returns, I'll give it to him with your greetings. Goodbye."

The politeness of the night porter and the reception clerk implied that they had been informed by their daytime counterparts both of the interest shown by Hofbauer and the impression made by Lizinka. They both accompanied Wolf, who was carrying the sleeping girl in his arms, to the elevator, and the reception clerk went with them all the way to her door. Wolf shut the door with his foot and walked over to the turned-down bed. He placed the girl in black on the white linen, and then he realized that he had crossed the threshold of his dream. He was alone with her, in a foreign country, in a hotel room, where no one could disturb them. His heart began to pound.

He spoke to her in a whisper. She did not reply. He touched her. She did not move, only her eyelid gave a flutter, as if he had breathed on it. What if she isn't sleeping? he wondered, aroused. What is she is just waiting for me to do something? He knelt and bent down almost to her lips. He followed her breathing. She was breathing as quickly and inaudibly as a child; surprisingly, her breath did not smell of champagne and cognac, but rather of farm-fresh milk. Overcome with tenderness, he buried his face in the satin, as if it were about to be transformed into a freshly cut meadow. He was a bit startled at the fragrance of roses, but that was only his surprise at the scent of rose oil that her mother had armed her with. Without moving his head from the valley between two soft mounds that he recognized as breasts, he observed with every nerve in his body the resurrection of his manhood, artificially anesthetized for so long: from the depth of his mature body, as from the crater of a volcano, hot magma was slowly but palpably rising to the surface. Amazed, he perceived how his fingers, guided from some unknown switchboard, were struggling with the top button of the trousers of his tuxedo. When it wouldn't unbutton, the fingers ripped it off—

"Mr. Wolf," he heard, "I know what you are after. But if we are both to be satisfied, let us be frank with each other—otherwise you'll be lucky merely to end up in the hole. Nowadays people are hypersensitive and it might turn out to be a matter of your

47

neck.

The young but already somewhat obese attorney stepped out from behind the huge mahogany desk and sat down on the arm of the soft armchair where he had seated Wolf earlier. Wolf could smell a strong perfume.

"You informed on those people," said the attorney in a knowing tone, "didn't you—and he had the proof of it on him!"

"I've always," said Wolf weakly, "been an honorable man and a patriot."

"Yes," said the attorney mildly, "I do not doubt that for a moment. I just have to know if you are certain that in the course of your attack of righteous indignation and justified patriotism, all the evidence went up in smoke."

Wolf inhaled, exhaled, and then spoke.

"Yes!"

"Well, hurray!" said the defense attorney; his fixed gaze from close up disclosed a sympathy that brought Wolf a ray of hope again.

Inexperienced as he was, Wolf had chosen the attorney to defend him pretty much at random. Right after the war, after they found the order to execute Wolf and his sweetheart, Helen, everything had looked good. The fact that it had been carried out only on the unfortunate Jarocov girl was simply a tragic coincidence. But owing to a similar coincidence, it was the girl's father, of all the surviving members of her family, who blamed her death on Wolf. A third coincidence was that the father lived in an outlying district and so was not put off by fear of him.

Wolf's deed, soon the talk of the region, had produced an unexpected side effect: the less people believed in his innocence, the more afraid they were of him. Wolf had founded an organization of former resistance workers and devoted all his free time to it. As he rose in various offices, the number of critical voices decreased. Finally even the school principal had to bow out, and Wolf had seniority on the decimated high school faculty. The vacant slot of school inspector appealed to him. And that was when an unknown farmer stepped into his life—the man whose daughter had received from Wolf a roof over her head, board and bed in the hardest years.

"Unfortunately," the attorney interrupted him unexpectedly, "that girl wrote him just before the end that you were probably an informer and that she was afraid of you."

"Helen? That's impos . . ." mumbled Wolf; till then he had believed with all his heart that the charge was based on inconclusive word-of-mouth evidence.

"The letter," said the attorney, moving closer to him, "is in the hands of the District Prosecutor. It's considered key evidence."

"What should I do?" he whispered.

212

"Pay him a call," said the attorney, bending closer and smiling at him. "Unfortunately he has issued a warrant for you. But fortunately—"

he added with a conspiratorial smile,

"—the District Prosecutor is a close friend of mine."

Wolf knew that it was true as soon as he crossed the threshold of the Prosecutor's office. The corpulent young man behind the government-issue desk kept an official expression on his face only until his secretary had closed the door.

"Hi there, Mirda," he said to Wolf's attorney. "Did you get home all right?"

As if Wolf were not there, he put an arm around the attorney's shoulders and led him over to the window, carrying on a lively conversation about some party or other. Then he dropped his voice, and Wolf was certain that they were talking about him, when suddenly he noticed that the cheeks of his defense attorney had turned crimson. For a moment Wolf thought that the man had broken out in a rash, until he recognized it as a blush. He looked at them a bit more carefully, and what he saw made him shudder: *Why*, he thought, *they're a couple of fruits!* He had always felt uncomfortable around homosexuals. Determined to find himself a new defense attorney right away, now he looked without respect even at the Prosecutor, who finally took a seat behind the desk; yes, his perfume was the same.

"It looks pretty bad for you," the Prosecutor said icily, "Wolf. There's enough for three nooses."

The totally unexpected onslaught took Wolf's breath away as he realized that he had other things to worry about than people's sex lives. He mobilized all his strength and exclaimed, almost shouting: "You have no proof! A letter from some crazy woman—"

Senselessly, he stopped short when he was overtaken by the irrational fear that the girl's father could hear him.

"Now, now!" said the Prosecutor derisively, opening a file and removing from it a large glossy photograph.

Wolf barely recognized himself on it. His jacket was crumpled, his hair mussed, and his expression that of a hunted beast, in spite of the fact that he had just completed a successful hunt of his own: above him hung the flaming Commissar Hofbauer. Nausea overcame him.

"You aren't," the Prosecutor struck out ironically, "being a little too sure of yourself, are you? Have you forgotten that documents have copies?"

"But I never signed any copies!"

As he heard the words coming out of his mouth, he turned numb with the realization of what he was admitting. Then he noticed that the two men were smiling. He blinked in surprise and thought he was dreaming when he saw the Prosecutor distinctly wink back at him. He wasn't dreaming.

"All the better, my friend," he said. "At least it will remain between the three of us. The originals would suffice for a hanging, though."

"But the originals—" Wolf starte, but decided to stop right there.

"Haven't you," asked the Prosecutor, "ever heard of the work of forensic laboratories? If a burned paper stays in one piece, it's easy to read what it says."

Wolf felt faint again. He could feel himself falling down a long, smooth, black shaft into a windowless room, with tiled walls, floors, and ceilings.

"Your situation is hopeless, but," joshed the Prosecutor, "in no way serious. It is entirely up to you whether I give the ashes to the experts as evidence or to the wind, and without that evidence, the Jarocov girl's letter is legally irrelevant."

Even as he fell, Wolf pricked up his ears.

"Mirda," continued the Prosecutor, "happened to hear about a problem I have encountered and indicated that you might be able to help. In that case I would forget the entire affair. What do you say to that?"

"And just what did you have in mind?"

"You apparently," said the Prosecutor, examining the photochemical evidence of the moment when Wolf had turned Hofbauer into a torch, "have a talent that we are in dire need of at the moment. In our district alone, a dozen men are waiting for the noose and we are feeding them at the state's expense, while those jackasses at the ministry arrested—for collaboration—our one and only—"

he said bitterly,

"—hangman!"

Wolf yawned. He was tired, but otherwise pleasantly excited. From a distance, heavy doors slammed, as

48

the passport and customs control moved to the neighboring compartment. On this side of the border, they took their work all too lightly; they hadn't even verified Lizinka's identity and were satisfied with the ripple of hair flowing out from under the sheets to the compartment floor. Wolf saw it as confirmation of his theory that Capital Punishment is the bearing pillar of a state: once it is taken off the books, state power is like a mere movie set and can be overturned by the first windstorm. The sounds of the little railroad station were muted by the blanket of night. The clock on the platform said seven minutes to two.

The night was exceptionally clear; the sky looked like something out of a planetarium. He saw a star falling slowly, but before he could think of a wish to make, he realized that it was a satellite. It occurred to him that it was a shame it hadn't been a meteorite, but immediately he chastised himself, ashamed that his personal wishes should be purchased by a cosmic catastrophe. He tried to imagine what man would encounter in all that incomprehensible space, and felt a pang of regret that he wasn't twenty years old—that might improve his chances of living to see the first contact with sentient extraterrestrial beings; he had never stopped wondering whether there were executioners out there, too. But now was the first time he caught himself thinking that he hoped there weren't. Ever since he had been obliged, as a pedagogue, to form a unified picture of his profession, he realized how very little he really knew about the subject. He cringed at the thought that new subject matter might be added to the already inexhaustible amount. He set aside his meditation on science fiction and returned in his mind to the letter that he had found waiting for him that morning at the hotel reception desk:

DEAR BROTHER,

Please accept the above form of traditional address, as an expression of respect used among people who share a profession. I want to apologize to you if perhaps my unexpected (even to myself) burst of emotion caused you any complications, and above all I want to express to you my respect. In these times, when a crisis in values is once again opening the path to power for Jews, cripples, reds and terrorists, you are progressing modestly but consistently in the purgative effort, maintaining its continuity for better days. For that reason I feel that it is my duty to inform you of a secret meeting held in the year 1956 in Monte Carlo, to investigate the problematics of executioners in Western Europe, and in South, Central, and North America. In view of the tactical nonparticipation of countries in which Cap. Pun. has for the present been abolished, the delegates selected to represent the field were elected as follows:

1. André Obrecht, Paris, France (54)
2. Cpt. John Eric Etter, New York, USA (48)
3. Joseph Francell, Etter's precursor (58)
4. Paul McCarter, Michigan, USA (46)
5. Camille Branchaud, Quebec, Canada (55)
6. Fernando Gollatz, Madrid, Spain (64)

215

7. Juan Medano Arosta, Valparaiso, Chile (48)
and 8. (actually No. 1) Albert Pierrepoint, Great Britain (45)

who convened the symposium and presided over it. The first item
on the agenda was a few words in memory of those brothers who
have died since the establishment of initial contacts in the mid-
thirties, e.g., Josef Maciejewski of Poland (suicide by hanging);
Peter Kowacz of Hungary (suicide by a bullet in the mouth); John
Ellis of Great Britain (suicide by razor in his own hairdressing
salon, after mistaking a lady who happened in to get a wash-and-
set for a woman named Thomson whom he had just done);
Hussein Jassara of Bulgaria (ripped open with a knife on the
street); two "Messieurs de Paris," Anatole Daibler (heart attack
in the métro) and Henri Desfourneaux (heart attack in delirium);
etc. Special concern was voiced in response to the on-the-job
accident of brother "Hazel" Woods (39), well known for his work
in Nuremberg: while installing an electric chair at Eniwetok
(Pacific), the high humidity in the air caused the electrical charge
to leap the distance from the "hot seat," as they call the chair in
the USA, to the executioner. Discussing the problem of remuneration, the brothers discovered that all of them were obliged
to have second jobs to make a living; the company assembled was
shocked by the report that the brother in Cairo is obliged to sell
the garments of the executed to keep body and soul together. A
resolution was approved to call on governments to assure
brothers the status of civil service employees, at a level corre-
sponding at least with that of a department head; during periods
of the abolishment of Cap. Pun., lost wages should also be
guaranteed. The symposium proceeded in all correctness, which
was violated only by brother McCarter, who reproached brother
Etter for still using the electric chair rather than the more humane
gas chamber; brother Pierrepoint called them to order. Brother
Obrecht received a round of applause for his proposal that if their
resolutions were not fulfilled, all the member brothers call a
strike. He stated that he personally would disassemble the
guillotine in such a case, since *les bois de la justice* are by tradition
his own property. Specialized problems were discussed, e.g.,
when the brother from Madrid asked for advice on how to
mechanize the garotte, the manual operation of which at his age is
becoming physically exhausting. In conclusion, the brothers
decided that the symposium should be held once every ten years.
It has not been held since, however, due to the well-known
disease of social movements: instead of looking for support to

216

international solidarity, many have given preference to half-hearted compromises into which they entered on their own. Fortunately, the new generation, to which I am bold enough to feel an appurtenance since I remain young in spirit (and, unfortunately, young in heart as well!), has more progressive views. Because even the idea of a symposium seems a bit constricting to them, plans are being made for a conference next summer. I am one of the organizers and I hope to be able to find word of my own brother in the process. I hereby officially invite you to attend, and ask that you ensure the participation of other brothers who in your homeland are enriching the field with new practical experiences, while we here can only reminisce and theorize.

Au revoir, your

ADOLF HOFBAUER
Currently Town Knacker
Holzheim-Niehausen

PS: I enclose an envelope with the winnings that your lovely fiancée left in my car. AH

PPS: I hesitate to remind you that this letter is strictly confidential, but what to do: such hesitation was the cause of the disclosure of the detailed report of the 1956 symposium to the writer (!) John F. Mortimer, who published it in the book *The Hangman, or, Documents of Human Cruelty*. Although I trust you implicitly, it is better to be safe than sorry: I am writing this in an ink that will disappear by this afternoon. Bon voyage to you and to Her as well.

The mention of Lizinka pulled a switch in Wolf's mind; the train had now arrived at the border crossing station. He remembered that in a quarter of an hour they would cross the border and to all intents and purposes the excursion would be over, and the peaceful calm that began to fill him was that of a man who had won out over himself. The previous night, at the hotel, when his fingers had ripped the button from his fly, Wolf's better self had broken through—that fine, essentially lyrical soul which he was unable to assert in his work and which yearned all the more to emerge in his private life. No! After Masin and Simsa, Lizinka finally had the right to the kind of love that was in keeping with her youth and beauty: a love that tiptoes gently down the long path of tenderness before it arrives at the jungle of passion. The struggle between his body and soul wound up with the decision that made everything fall into place: he would talk it over with Margaret! A sensitive and intelligent woman, she had

217

always been the only one who understood him, and she would understand him now as well. He could almost hear the words with which she would release him, and he felt a flood of regretful gratitude, which also served to douse the electrical charge of his desire for the sleeping girl. He had left her and gone up to his room, showered, and slept the sleep of the just.

He didn't call her room until late; they had breakfasted in the hotel dining room, which was already set for luncheon. They used the time remaining before the departure of their train trying to spend their hard currency. Wolf set out with the not unconsiderable sum that Lizinka had smuggled out for him, while she had three times that amount, her winnings that she found in Hofbauer's envelope. The difference in their natures was apparent in the way they did their shopping. In the hundred and fifty minutes they had left, Wolf spent over two hours making his choice, and then he bought everything at once: for the Doctor he bought tequila and sangria, for Margaret an expensive gold wristwatch with a *fin-de-siècle* face tactfully reminiscent of her age; the back of the watch was engraved with the date of their first meeting and tomorrow's date, when they would separate forever—that way Wolf closed off all his avenues of retreat, so that he not fall victim to compassion.

Lizinka started shopping the moment she walked into the department store and didn't pause for a moment, calling attention to herself this time by more than her appearance. The closed-circuit TV cameras informed the store detectives, and they in turn informed the management. Soon a store employee turned up, and after him another one, to take her shopping bags and carry them behind her. She didn't shop specifically for her father, her mother, herself; she bought what appealed to her, believing that it would make everyone happy, so that now, in the compartment, when his eyes—deprived by the activity of his mind of the merciful respite of sleep—wandered from one to another of the girl's packages, Wolf thanked Providence that he had been permitted to experience the unsullied joy of this lovely youngster whose worry-free start in life was the result of his own efforts and favor. Inevitably, his own beginnings came to his mind.

He saw himself again in a cell in the state's main prison, a cell that had been set up as his dressing room that evening before his first execution, one that he had prepared for more like a schoolteacher than an executioner: he had studied the anatomy of the human neck and throat in a home medical guide, and knot-tying in a boy scout handbook. Just before midnight, he came up with a splendid idea born of desperation, an idea that the Prosecutor, who started up the ladder with him like playwright with an actor, approved with alacrity: Wolf was permitted to visit his predecessor, who was waiting for his trial under the very same roof. After they had drowned with cognac Karl Hus's fear that his hour

218

had struck, the former executioner began to recite, like the Lord's Prayer, detailed technical instructions that he maintained had been handed down from his famous ancestor. (His doing so incidentally guaranteed his yet-unborn son a spot in HIENS years later.) The main thing in the recitation was an old-fashioned, exceedingly complicated knot; Wolf had brought his rope along, and practiced tying it with Hus until they came running to tell Wolf it was time to dress up for the execution; following an old tradition (which was not abolished until the time of the mass trials, when cleaning establishments simply couldn't keep up with it), Wolf put on the black gown in which he had taken his degree. He thought he knew the knot by heart, but when he found himself face to face with the man who until recently had still been the country's supreme collaborator, he fell victim to a terrible case of stage fright. After Hus's habit, he was doing the hanging according to the old continental method, one that then already belonged nowhere except perhaps in old etchings, but ignorance is bliss, and so he stood—today it seemed like a bad joke—on one ladder leaning against a high gallows and the client stood on a second one. His helper, unearthed on the basis of the same old photograph, was Karli, whose experience in boxing and driving cars gave him even less background in the field. And so it happened that when Karli removed the second ladder before Wolf had a chance to pull the too-tight noose all the way over the man's head, it caught on the man's chin and across his temple. Wolf was startled, indeed he was horrified, to find that he was suddenly holding in his two hands a head that was oozing tears and saliva around the gag in its mouth, while beneath, the rest of the body was twitching spasmodically, with no support. Some impulse caused him to jerk the head abruptly to the right, whereupon he felt the client suddenly go limp. And that is how, in the course of his very first execution, Wolf's famous one-two jerk was born (of necessity—which he wisely kept to himself) and he remained true to it over the years. He knew from the Doctor that no one had ever succeeded in imitating it, although many people had tried. The one-two jerk, he was told (to his surprise—which he shrewdly did not show) was the only thing that could prevent the extrusion of the tongue, which otherwise would blossom out into a repulsive blue flower.

The memory made Wolf smile. He felt like an old actor who gets goosebumps whenever he recalls his first performance. And his smile turned to a chuckle when he imagined how the Doctor would look when during the masters exams he would see the second generation's one-two jerk. A brief whistle sounded from down the track and the train gave a gentle jolt. The clock on the platform began to move by, imperceptibly at first, and gradually faster and faster until it disappeared entirely.

The smile froze on his lips. Now there were only a few minutes left to the border. He felt it to the marrow of his bones, the realization that that

would mean the definitive end to the most beautiful dream of his life—
unfulfilled.

Everything after that, even though it would in the final analysis be the
prelude to permanent bliss, seemed to have the bitter taste and the dingy
color of everyday reality: the talk with Margaret, discussions about
property settlements, the paperwork surrounding the divorce and no less
of it surrounding the wedding. Dozens of unfeeling bureaucrats would be
investigating, weighing, measuring, and stripping with their eyes not only
Wolf and Margaret, but Lizinka too. Could she take it? Would it not sully
her pure soul with dust that would pollute that first embrace, which Wolf
craved like a hot cleansing bath? And would it be so cleansing that it was
worth shattering his whole life?

The simple smells of the railroad station and meadows were replaced by
the complex fragrance of the woods. The moss on the embankment was
within arm's reach. When he heard a little sigh, he looked outside for
some small animal before he understood and turned inside. He froze. The
train's prolonged halt had raised the temperature in the compartment by
several degrees and now sensors in the sleeping girl's body took over
automatically: her arms and legs gradually liberated themselves from the
sheet, finally pushing it off onto the floor. Lizinka was wearing what her
mother in her extraordinary frame of mind had bought both for herself
and the girl: panties and a bra made of a fabric so delicately knit that it
seemed to take on the color of her flesh; her nipples and the triangle
beneath her navel were as visible under the fabric as if they were obscured
only by a puff of mist. To all intents and purposes, the only thing that
covered her was her long blond hair. As she turned in her sleep and curled
up, the long strands of her hair found their own paths and flowed across
and between her shoulders, breasts, even her hips and thighs, so that she
looked like a fairy imprisoned by the spider king. The pale blue
hemisphere of the night light at ceiling level gave her the dimensions of a
materialized dream.

At that moment, Wolf, the man with the iron will, felt his penis coming
mightily and irrepressibly to life; it pushed against the front of his silk
pyjama pants, and it was only with a sudden bend from the waist that he
saved his favorite night attire from being perforated. But that movement
brought his head within the force field of that magnetically attractive
body, and his always reliable brain suddenly began to rotate about its own
axis.

God, he said to himself, why do I keep forcing myself into such
inhuman self-control? Whom was he trying to protect with his Old
Testament inhibitions? Was there another man on earth who would have
spent three days and three nights burning up of his own free will, only to
deny himself a bliss never experienced before and probably never to be

220

experienced again? Would Margaret be that considerate if an equally attractive young man were lying here, as if made to be loved by her? Hardly! Then why must he be the one to forever take upon himself the responsibility? How much longer must he sacrifice the joy of a living body on the altar of dead principles? Until he tells Margaret? Until she grants him a divorce? Until she finds another man? (She may well have one already. She doesn't have nearly as much self-control as he, hadn't he himself seen how easy she was to seduce?) Until he requests NESTOR's approval to marry a student? Until he gets it? Until, until, until . . . ! Until his still manly body hunches over under the weight of years? Until the hair on his head and elsewhere turns white? Until his teeth, as yet white and firm, turn yellow and loosen up in his gums? Until his as yet firm, tan skin turns spotted and moldy like a fungus? Until his organ, now tumescent with vitality, weakens to just hang there like a wilted tulip?

The breathing that came to his ears now was wheezing, feverishly irregular, all the more startling in that it was his own. Hypnotized, he stared at the girl. She had just rolled over from her right side to her back, her legs in an acute V, her feet still childlike, her thighs already womanly. His ears registered a tiny sound as the button of his pyjama pants gave way and this time ripped itself off, so hard that it rolled all the way to the door of the compartment. The penis, liberated, swung up out of its prison and took full control of Wolf, who flipped the lock on the compartment door and then ripped the misty panties off like a piece of tissue paper, turned the girl crosswise on the bunk and opened her—essentially still sleeping—thighs so that he could place himself properly. Then he cast aside what was left of his prejudices and inhibitions, covered her with his entire massive body, rested his mighty hands on her delicate breasts, penetrated her—finally awakened—lips with his tongue, and then mercilessly entered her, breaking through her hymen like a drum. Lizinka screamed.

Her scream blended with the whistle of the locomotive, shrilly announcing their crossing of the border, but Wolf would not have let her go even if she had aroused the entire train. He held her—he was enthralled by her attempts to squirm out from under him, as the young Margaret once had—between the levers of his hams and the vise of his arms, and with his reamer and his tongue penetrated over and over her virginal womb and her nearly virginal lips, with the intense sensation of being a pump, drawing from the depths a miraculous spring and bringing it to the surface.

Then she was joining him, picking up his rhythm and finally collaborating totally, until suddenly the two bodies working against each other became a single body, moving and panting toward a single end.

Then Wolf gave off a dark shout.

Then her body shot up to meet him.

Then he doused the flame in her with the stream of his seed.

Then Lizinka cried out a second time.

Then they heard a furious pounding and a voice, which had apparently been repeating over and over: "Customs check! Open up! Right now!"

Wolf came to earth in a flash. He registered the lock and the peremptory rattle of the door handle. It was apparently a matter of seconds before they would bring a passkey. He raised up on his elbows. Lizinka's eyes were demurely closed, but her expression seemed to imply a certain involvement. He looked below and was horrified. His organ looked like a murder weapon left sticking in a bloody wound. There was blood on his and her thighs too, running down in trickles onto the sheet, forming scarlet bridges over the black undergrowth. For the first time in years, his hands broke out in a sweat and the malevolent roar in his head grew stronger, until he realized that it was just the virginity tax a woman pays to nature, once and forever. Then he heard the sound of running feet.

Wolf knew for certain that they were bringing the passkey, but he also knew by then that the two of them had nothing to fear. He would pull on his pyjama pants in a flash—he had no idea when he had kicked them off, but he was sure they were unstained—and she would simply pretend that as she slept, she had received her monthly visit from . . . He moved to slip out of her. He almost cried out. His organ was held tight inside the girl as if in a vise. He tried once more, but

49

no go.

VI

WOLF WOULD REMEMBER MONDAY, JUNE 30, UNTIL THE DAY HE died. Ever since his student days when he had literally read his way through the municipal library and worn a hole in the floor of the second balconies at the theaters, Wolf had always disliked stories in which everything worked out in the last chapter or the last act, when everyone got married and lived happily ever after. Now he himself was destined to crown his work and his life in a single day. Ahead of him lay a superhuman effort, and he dared approach it only because he trusted in himself and those near to him. How grateful he was now for years of teaching when he had learned to relate to people from the start, and to gain their confidence. He congratulated himself on his decision to always remain by

50

Margaret's side, which assured him of her indispensable support in life's crises. As he kissed her now to thank her for breakfast—she had prepared

223

his "workday," more opulent version, corn flakes with milk, two five-minute eggs, toast and jam with a smoky English tea—he knew that he needn't worry about her.

"At exactly six o'clock," was all he said. "Be on time—they'll be there only because of us!"

"Don't worry, Rick," she nodded, giving him an extra kiss for luck.

Thanks, he thought as he walked down the stairs; she was his good old Margaret again, and he regretted that his inborn restraint kept him from telling her outright. But all the more did he want to arrange everything for her happiness.

Knowing that today even seconds counted, the bald-headed Karli was standing waiting, cap in hand, by the open rear door of the car.

"To the Reegie! On the double!"

"Yes, sir, Chief!" said Karli, turning on the siren that made all the neighbors believe they were with the traffic division. The small housing project, the nicest in the city because it was built by the best qualified inmates of prisons, was inhabited exclusively by employees of secret agencies, so that nobody bothered to check.

Wolf only went to the "Reegie," or the Regional Courthouse, when he needed to pick up a "voucher" (Simsa's euphemism for the release document the prisons needed in order to turn over their clients to them). Today his mission was a more banal one: he needed a duplicate of his marriage certificate; he probably mislaid or lost the original during a move.

"Where is the records section?" Wolf asked the porter. He had expected to find the records archives in the most inaccessible corner of the building, but he hadn't expected to have to go through all the basements. When he finally found the door, it was barred, with a shoebox lid wired onto it, on which was written: GONE TO THE DENTIST. He swore softly and glanced at his watch. Half past seven. He decided to return during his lunch break.

So he arrived at school earlier than he had expected, but he could just as well have come late: thanks to the kids' devotion, everything had been ready the previous evening. All he had to do was walk through all the areas and look forward to the fact that the morning and afternoon guests would all get to see it this way. The oral matriculation exams were to take place in the classroom. The six desks were pushed together to form a single one, three chairs at one end for the examiners, and all the way at the other end, a single chair for the pupil being tested. Frantisek's suggestion appealed to Wolf; he liked monumental architecture and he didn't realize that Frantisek was inspired by an ulterior motive: at that distance the examining commission might overlook a crib sheet. The seventh desk stood in the corner; they called it the "sweatbox," where the

224

pupil was to sit before he was called upon. The desk was brought back from the storage room where it had been relegated on January 4 so that the class might erase Richard Masin from its collective memory. Margaret's Sunday tablecloth was spread out over the teacher's desk. That was where Karli would place the sandwiches, beer, and something a bit stronger that he was to bring for the halftime.

The CLASEX and the MODEX rooms were locked; they had been set up the day before for the afternoon's masters exams, and Wolf was unwilling to risk that in the bustle something could be misplaced or even lost. The corridor was decorated to his satisfaction, to show the families and visitors that the kids lived the same kind of lives here the whole year as their contemporaries did elsewhere.

Now the kids were waiting for him in the improvised visitors' cloakroom. As agreed, all the boys were in dark trousers and Lizinka in a dark skirt, and all of them wore the same shirts—

—the girl still hadn't opened her eyes, but when he tried once again to free himself, she moaned. That was when he realized that under the circumstances, there was nothing he could do but embrace her tightly and close his eyes too. By using the underestimated trick of playing ostrich, he at least put the onus of embarrassment on the ones who broke into

51

the compartment. The commandos were led by the young customs officer, who had been nursing his anger at the old creep with the dyed hair whose swinish intentions he would have willingly sworn to in a court of law. He had finally decided Wolf was a fashion coiffeur or a headwaiter from a fancy hotel, but Lizinka was obviously not one of your high-class call girls. She was apparently with him in all respectability and credulity, as if she were traveling with a maiden aunt. The customs officer hardly got a wink of sleep, so hard were his fingers crossed that she be able to withstand the advances of the old billy goat. He had noticed that their visa was for three days, and he had volunteered for a double shift today in hopes of meeting her again. He had no intention of delaying things by checking their luggage; the scoundrel was certain to have hidden any contraband in her things. What he did intend to do was ask him if he was her grandpa; he had made a deal with the fellows in green who check passports that they would pull him off the train into the office for a while, so he could make a date with her, anywhere, anytime.

As he pounded on the door, he wasn't concerned with official interests, he was the eternal Montague whose Juliet was being ravished behind that door. And when they unlocked it for him, he pushed aside piles of parcels to reveal a picture the like of which he had never seen, not even in the most obscene of the porn magazines that he always confiscated here. The image was to burn itself into his brain: those defenseless knees, separated as if by a boulder by the huge naked ass. He leaped forward at its owner, forgetting the little wooden box of rubber stamps he was balancing on his belly. It crashed into splinters, and Wolf gave a yelp. Straining his buttocks to withstand the blows of the customs officer's fists, he responded by taking control, as best he could, of the situation.

"Call a doctor!" he roared in his deep voice.

They called one, their own physician, as soon as they had subdued the customs officer. When the physician arrived, they were just getting them off the train. Those thirty minutes were among the most agonizing in Wolf's life, and he had to admire Lizinka for the way she was able to appear unconcerned, even as they tried to move them into the train corridor. Because the two were still joined, they had to be carried on a single stretcher, which of course was too heavy for the two men who could fit into the compartment. The stretcher-bearers finally figured out a way: they slid them out onto the platform through the compartment window. In spite of the fact that Wolf and Lizinka were surrounded by people climbing over them and crawling under them, raising them and putting them down, trying to figure out the best way to do it, the position they were in gave the two of them an extraordinary sense of intimacy. When an onlooker finally got around to covering them, all they had at the station was a collection of national flags, and he at least selected a neutral one. Wolf regained some of his composure and kept whispering to Lizinka that everything was going to be all right.

He was not mistaken. The physician, who was also a veterinarian, immediately grasped the situation. He didn't bother to call an ambulance or a surgeon, but he asked them a few questions and then said with conviction, "Just be still a while. You'll come undone shortly."

He explained that he had often experienced this phenomenon—rare as it is among human beings—in most mammal species in the course of copulation. The engorgement of both sexual organs with blood—particularly if one had never been in use before and the other long in disuse—can cause the simultaneous spasmlike tightening of the vagina and the expansion of the glans. He illustrated the resulting effect by comparing it to a smoker trying to unscrew a hot pipe.

The physician helped the two of them to turn over on the stretcher—Lizinka was finally on top now; he had been raised up on his elbows the whole time so as not to weigh too heavily on her—and then Wolf said he had to make a long-distance call. For the second time in his life, he dared to disturb the Doctor at home, this time at three o'clock in the morning, with Lizinka obliged to hear every word. He decided to trust her: she hadn't been a child any more for over an hour now, and she was doing splendidly. He was not concerned with what he was going to say: he just played the agreed-upon role of satyr with a bit more vehemence.

"Locked together?" repeated the Doctor and his laughter sounded surprisingly alert for the hour. "Well, that's something you're going to have to demonstrate for me," he continued, reverting to the old code, "Mister Chairman."

And the angry young customs officer, who meanwhile had been maliciously making a list of all the merchandise obviously purchased without an import permit, was surprised when his supervisor came to take over and fired him on the spot for destroying a government-issue rubber stamp tray against the body of a government official. . . .

Wolf cast a quizzical look at the girl, with a touch of concern in it. She shook her head a little, and so, relieved, he could devote his attention to the entire

52

class.

Wolf was relatively pleased with their appearance, but he had mixed emotions about their chances at exam time. Their grades on the written exams that they had been given on Saturday by the respective NEXICOLs at the various vocational schools, now closed for the summer, differed radically. The only one to get an A in all four subjects was Albert. The median grades looked like this:

Pupil:	Anatomy	Psychology	Literature	Language
Kazik, Frantisek	A	B	C	D
Kral, Pavel	D	C	B	A
Kral, Peter	D	C	B	A
Tachezy, Lizinka	C	C	C	C

Simon Hus had three failing grades, and the NEXICOL from SSHIT had refused even to assign him a grade. Under "Comments," he wrote, "The student is familiar with every organ in the human body, but the expressions he uses for them would be more suitable for a knacker or a hangman"; the NEXICOL perceived it as a schoolboy prank in the worst taste. Wolf knew he could help Simon keep his head above water, since the determining grade was the one in the major subject. But his sense of fair play won out, along with the realistic thought that a pupil who failed at graduation exams would be less of an embarrassment to the school than one who failed on the job afterward. He decided to leave the whole thing up to fate and the commission for the orals.

As for Frantisek, Wolf felt certain that his glibness would save him. The twins' grades indicated that they had used the same trick that had apparently gotten them through grades one through nine: he guessed that the three better grades were the work of Pavel (or was it Peter? He knew for a fact that one of the pair *was* a shade brighter than the other), whereas the grades in anatomy, in which they were both weak, were probably the work of the other. Because they were expected always to work together, he would have been delighted if today the better one were to take both sets of exams, but with a glance at their slicked-down hair, clearly parted on opposite sides, he couldn't for the life of him imagine how they could pull it off. But all that was incidental: the one he was truly concerned about was Lizinka.

All day Sunday he fought off the temptation to make an exception and simply to give her the questions in advance. *That's hypocrisy!* the lover in him screamed at the pedagogue: *You can give her your seed, but not the questions?* The professor in him was unhappy because that would mean none of them could draw their questions by lot, which was to be Wolf's proof of how well prepared they were. Finally, thanks to the Doctor, he resolved the problem. With newly regained optimism, he now was able to give his love a reassuring glance and to wish them all luck.

A key rattled and a barred door squeaked. Wolf set out—everything was timed to the second—into the corridor to welcome the prison warden who was accompanying the two other members of the examining commission. The Doctor avoided his outstretched hand and indicated with a nod that his neighbor took precedence. The middle-aged man with curly black hair looked as if he had just walked out of the establishments of a first-class tailor and a first-class hairdresser. The impression was spoiled only by the feverishly red face and the black band on his lapel.

"Wolf—" said Wolf, introducing himself uneasily.

"But, Beda, we're old friends," said the man.

"Yes, of course . . ." said Wolf, as he always did in such situations.

"Don't tell a soul," laughed the guest. "It's a wig, silly!"

Wolf registered his perfume.

"You!" he said, astonished, "I thought—"

"Governments," replied the former Prosecutor, "come and go, but the hangman stays the same."

Wolf was amazed that the former Prosecutor (what was he now? He must have retired already!) looked so much better than the judge in the bus had.

"The other day," Wolf said, still unnerved, but then he corrected himself, "about three years ago, I ran into—"

"Willi!" the former Prosecutor finished his sentence for him. "Yes, and he just about died laughing when he told us how you almost gave him cigarette money!"

Wolf looked reproachfully at the Doctor, who smiled an apology. "Yes," the Doctor admitted, "I knew about it, but I didn't want to destroy your faith in the future."

"That's right!" said the former Prosecutor. "The future is here—and so are we. Incidentally, Willi sends his regrets. Today of all days he's stuck with the trial of those human rights characters. If only he could at least give them the noose, but it's always the same: 'Next time!'"

"And what about Mirda?" Wolf asked.

The reaction was unexpected: tears started to stream down the former Prosecutor's cheeks, forming little rills: the red of his face was not due to a fever, but to makeup; now the traces of plastic surgery showed through where the tears had washed it off.

"Our friend the Defense Attorney passed away," the Doctor explained softly.

Wolf now registered the black band.

"Damn prostate," said the former Prosecutor, "and all a person's plans and dreams are down the drain!"

He took out a handkerchief, wiped his face, and stared thoughtfully at the reddish smears on it. Wolf felt a pang of regret; it was as if the flame of the campfire had just gone out, the campfire where the three of them once spent the night in meaningful conversation.

"And what are you doing now . . ." he asked, to bridge the gap of silence. "What should I be calling you . . ."

"Call me," said the former Prosecutor sharply, "NESTOR if you want to! Where the hell is the little boy's room around here, so I can put myself back in some kind of shape?"

When the door to the lavatory fell shut behind him, the Doctor told the amazed Wolf, softly so that the warden, who was looking around curiously, not hear, "He's exaggerating. He's a deputy. But look out—he's even more difficult than he used to be, and he's lost his emotional bearings. . . ."

"Ready!" Albert exclaimed, standing at clear-eyed attention, his soldierly stance marred only by his

53

hump, facing the commission, waiting for the Doctor to approach him with the hat. It was a quarter past eleven, and Albert and Lizinka were the last to be examined. Wolf had planned the order on an almost scientific basis, considering all the ramifications. First to be examined were the average ones, so as not to upset the evaluation of the extremes: that was Frantisek and the twins. He had considered putting each of the twins in a different threesome, so that they'd have time to repart their hair, but finally he decided that after the break, it had to be the turn of the trio of Simon, Albert, and Lizinka. His reason was an important one.

First up, Frantisek reached into the Doctor's hat, its contents carefully checked by the former Prosecutor as chairman-elect of the examining commission, and drew out two different-colored bits of paper: after Friday's consultation, the Doctor and Wolf had written questions in CURCLASEX on the white papers, and in CURMODEX on the pink. On the white he drew the difficult question of cataloguing medieval penalties. As Wolf expected, Frantisek dived right into the water and swam off, disregarding all style, in the effort to keep afloat; he hadn't made himself a crib sheet on this. He was correct in stating that back then, the death penalty applied to practically everything, and so he had only the nuances left to list: for criminality, it was the noose or the wheel, dissidents were decapitated or sometimes drawn and quartered; "ladies' mischief," as he called it, was covered with water or earth; and finally, witches and fags went up in smoke. Frantisek had no way of knowing that with that last statement, he had lit a fire under his own feet.

Fortunately, the former Prosecutor did not want to lose face in front of Wolf; he simply asked the boy frostily to continue, but from then on, glibness was no help to Frantisek; he just barely remembered that execution by burial alive had been varied by introducing breathing and drinking tubes so that the victim could have a few more days to enjoy life. And so the Doctor, who automatically took over the role of chief examiner, had to remind him of a number of things, for instance that when an adulterous couple was apprehended *in flagranti,* the two were impaled in the coital position, or that counterfeiting was punished by slow boiling in oil.

On the pink paper, Frantisek drew gas, and he described quite well the procedure, from checking the insulation of the chamber, filling the containers with sulphuric acid and with pellets of hydrogen cyanide, the pulling of the lever that combines the substances beneath the chair to release the hydrocyanic gas which rises like steam, and, upon reaching the respiratory tract, causes a prolonged, fatal spasm.

"And the st—" the Doctor prompted him.

"And the stink," Frantisek misunderstood the cue, "is awful!"

"And the *stethoscope?*" the doctor finally said outright.

That registered another error, of course, and Frantisek came all too late with details about the attachment of the stethoscope to the client's chest and the cable which leads out to the medical examiner who determines the moment of death. The oversight disconcerted him so much that he confused the final phase with the opening of the chamber.

"And the stink is *awful*," the Doctor mimicked him, "but neither you nor any of the witnesses live to tell about it!"

"Frantisek's omission of how the toxic gas is exhausted from the chamber enabled the commission chairman to give him a D. Even though Wolf felt that this was a bit hard on the examinee, he decided to save his objections for more critical cases.

With his hair clearly parted on the right, Pavel Kral stepped forward and drew questions on the history of the guillotine and on electrocution. He spoke slowly, with hesitations, but he made a better impression on the commission. Without prompting, he picked up a piece of chalk and on the blackboard drew the basic principle of the first decapitator, the *Diele,* a mechanism used in the Germanic countries since the early Middle Ages. Resembling its French successor in spite of its essential primitiveness, the blade—as illustrated on altar paintings in Padua and Barcelona—was a sharp wooden board which the executioner often had to pound for some time with a heavy mallet before the head fell to the ground. That led him to the origin of the Italian *mannaia;* Pavel drew a second sketch, as it was immortalized by Lucas Cranach, which showed a rope-suspended ax dropping along wooden tracks, so the blow could more easily be repeated. These mechanisms, opined Pavel, must have been known to Doctor Guillotin when he strove to give the revolution equality of punishment. The problem was finally resolved technically by a German mechanic named Schmidt, who used to visit the home of master executioner Charles Sanson, where they would get together to play duets. The apparatus made its debut on April 21, 1792, and the honor was not given to a revolutionary, but, concluded Pavel, putting down the chalk, to a robber named Pelletier.

He fell silent. Only the experienced Wolf could tell how nervous he was, from the way he kept rubbing the fingers of his left hand together, although it was his right hand that was chalky.

"And," asked the Doctor innocently, "what do you know about a decapitation apparatus called the Louisette, which was put into operation the selfsame day? Yes, my young friend, the revolution gave wings to innumerable talents, and it was a certain Doctor Antoine Louis of Metz who advised Schmidt to include a 'lunette' to hold the neck, but also, and mainly, came up with the idea of a slanted blade, which clients can thank for the fact that, if the blade drops at all, the head will fall too. My reference—"

the Doctor noted pedantically,

"—is to several cases of failure of the release mechanism, the time-consuming repair of which gave the clients time to incite the witnesses against the executioners, until now there is always one henchman there holding a handax behind his back, so that in case of emergency the master executioner could lop the head off manually, like Friedrich Heer of Hamburg did to Josef Bender, who filched a pair of trousers from a freshly bombed store. But above all—"

he returned to the original topic,

"—Louis tested his device in the hospital of the home for the aged at Bicêtre, first on live sheep and then on corpses, children's corpses to start out with so as—to quote Barring—'to break the machine in carefully'; those present—to quote Kernshaw—'who were handed the separated heads for friendly evaluation, expressed discreet enthusiasm.' Louis's misfortune rested in the fact that he died a few months later, and with him the appellation 'Louisette,' because Guillotin remained in the public eye for twenty more years. Of course, as your exposition shows, the important thing was not the invention but its introduction into general use, and no one deserves more credit for that than—"

added the Doctor respectfully,

"—Joseph-Ignace Guillotin."

Pavel did rather well with electrocution. He described the attachment of the electrodes, including the slitting of the right trouser-leg, so often, as he said, overlooked; nor did he neglect to mention the "mask of mercy," ostensibly to protect the client from viewing the preparations, but in fact protecting the executioner from possibly being hypnotized by the client, as was the case with Robert Elliot, who stopped in the middle of buckling the straps, broke into a sweat, and was unable to continue until the prison warden slapped his face. Pavel also listed correctly the two opposing schools of thought, low voltage and high voltage. While the former—he wrote on the blackboard in tabular form—sends through the body

500 volts for 50 seconds
1000 volts for 8 seconds
500 volts for 50 seconds and

a final 2000 volts at the end, as a mercy shock, the latter begins at ten thousand volts and goes on up to thirty; that is the one popular in motion pictures and TV, because it dims the lights in the entire prison. The disadvantage of the former is the length of time it takes, which was discussed back in 1929, when Roy Paterson in Auburn doled out the power to Mary Farmer, Pavel related, charging her up like a battery, for almost an hour before she quit screeching. The advantage is, he continued, that even over such a duration, there are no physical traces except a deformed head, a facial grimace, and mild burns to the limbs. On

232

the other hand, Henry White of Ohio, who survived the initial ten thousand, was done in a flash when the voltage was tripled, but then he literally gave off a flame and the witnesses were passing out from the stench; moreover, the hysterical physician declared that, in violation of the sentence, White had not been electrocuted but that he had been roasted instead.

"Finished?" asked the Doctor when he fell silent.

Pavel nodded.

"You mentioned the problems," said the Doctor with an amiable smile, but Wolf was sure that he was setting up another trap, "of electrocution. Does that mean that it is not one hundred percent effective?"

"Oh, no sir," Pavel replied, confused, "no, it is!"

"And what," exclaimed the Doctor, "about Fred Phillips?"

Pavel was a living question mark. So much for your A, you poor kid, thought Wolf.

"That," said the Doctor emphatically, "is the precedent that every electrocutioner must bear in mind! After the physician pronounced him dead, Phillips' body was turned over to a Doctor Cornish, for scientific purposes. The latter concealed his intention of bringing the executed man back to life. He succeeded, and the resultant scandal wound up before a court, where the state of New York lost its appeal for a new execution. Phillips was permitted to travel to Mexico under an assumed name, where fortunately, out of sheer joy, he—"

the Doctor added, turning to Wolf for his confirmation,

"—drank himself to death."

Wolf was obliged to nod. Pavel was lucky to get a B.

All the more nervous was the Professor in his anticipation of the less talented twin. Instead, however, it was Karli who appeared in the doorway with a platter of sandwiches. He carried them over to the main desk with such self-assurance that Wolf allowed himself to be taken in.

"Gentlemen," he said with a bountiful wave of his hand, "there's a time to work and a time to eat!"

"Just a moment," objected the chairman. "Not till halftime. We've only had two so far!"

"Karli," exclaimed Wolf, "what's the matter with you?"

"They told me, 'Now!'" Karli defended himself.

"Who told you?" Wolf snapped.

"I don't know," replied Karli unhappily; he had problems with his memory.

"Leave it here and get lost!" ordered Wolf, "and send Peter Kral in."

Convinced that it made him less conspicuous, Karli backed out of the door. The second Kral walked in immediately afterward, his hair conspicuously parted on the left. To Wolf's dismay, he drew a question that would have been better for his brother: "Is the executioner a humanist?" To his surprise, the weaker of the Krals neither turned pale nor began to stutter, but instead, with no gross misstatements, proceeded to enumerate examples which Wolf had used throughout the year to fortify their pride in their profession.

He named Alessandro Bracco of Rome, who wept when ordered by the pope to use the horrible *"veglia"* against Renaissance beauty (Peter referred to her as Miss Italia) Beatrice Cenci, who had her father killed because he kept raping her: Alessandro hanged her naked by all four limbs over a column with a diamond tip; as her muscular strength waned, the diamond ripped open her lovely belly. Bracco wept again when he decapitated the innocent girl and the headless body squirmed in such spasms that, Peter related, her lovely breasts came uncovered. Overcome with sorrow, Bracco raised Beatrice's lesser half and called out, "Lo, the head of a Roman maiden, victim of her own beauty!"

"Do you know it in the original?" the Doctor interrupted him, but he hurried to recite it himself, accompanying his words with dramatic gestures: "*'Ecco, la testa di una donzella romana martire della sua belezza.'* But I only added that—"

he reassured the lad amiably,

"—for the sake of interest. Continue."

Peter continued in the same vein. He brought up master executioner Klaus of Bern, who couldn't bear watching when a crosswind blew the flames under Hans Jetzer, who was being burned at the stake, in such a manner that only his feet began to slowly char, and so Klaus smashed his head with a mallet, for which deed he was promptly fired, with the label of weakling. He recalled the eighteenth century philanthropist, Franz Joseph Wolmut of Salzburg, who by his courageous petitions to the archbishopric more than once succeeded in getting permission to decapitate petty thieves rather than hanging them; they made him godfather to their children, and thus he bears the lion's share of the credit for the success of one of the latter, the Reverend Mohr, author of the Christmas carol "Silent Night." Of contemporary figures, Peter named Jack Johnson of Chicago, who in 1965 made a courageous TV appearance—Wolf recalled regretfully how he and Simsa had envied him at the time—to debate with "cop-killer" Witherspoon. The latter successfully tried to arouse the sympathy of the viewers by claiming that he had killed the policeman in a fit of rage, whereas Johnson would be killing him in cold blood. "That," said Johnson calmly, "is my business!" and hundreds of thousands of Americans applauded.

"You've quoted," said the Doctor, "Bracco and Johnson. Do you know any more substantive quote? For example Des— Well . . . ?"

At least Peter didn't embarrass himself the way Frantisek had. He was silent.

"You mean," frowned the Doctor, you've never heard of Desfourneaux?"

"Henri," Peter rattled off promptly, intent on correcting a bad impression, "Desfourneaux, executioner, or Monsieur, of Paris and of all France, succeeded in doing a full 255 male and two female clients in the eleven years from his appointment in 1939."

"And do you know," asked the Doctor, "why?"

"No, sir . . ." admitted Peter.

"But you must know that," said the Doctor uncompromisingly, "because Desfourneaux's famous statement could come in very handy. After the war, they accused him of being the fair-haired boy of Nazi tribunals, and that he never should have allowed himself to be used for executing French patriots. 'I let the ax fall,' he replied to his critics, 'that is all; understanding is not the affair of—'"

added the Doctor, indicating with a nod to the chairman that he was through,

"'—an executioner!'"

"Now to CURMODEX," the chairman instructed Peter.

Peter had drawn execution by firing squad, and he made a short shrift of it. He described its wartime variations, both solo execution, where a squad shoots in the manner of "eye-heart," and the commander ends it with a shot to the nape, and mass execution, wherein the marked area is first scattered with machine gun fire and then with soil. He moved on to the civilian version, as practiced in some American states, and he described a system of closed cabins which are fired on after the volunteers—generally relatives of the victims or hunters—receive the order through their earphones. It is a common manner of execution, but from a professional viewpoint relatively uninteresting, he added; that is why it has become the domain of amateurs.

The practice of execution by shooting did not interest the Doctor, and so he did not ask any questions. Peter Kral bowed and walked out of the room; only then did Wolf notice that he had been rubbing the fingers of his left hand with relief, and that on his right he had obvious traces (but he was never at the blackboard!) of chalk. He realized then that by his entrance, Karli had covered up for a speedy reparting of hair and hence a switch of the two brothers. The former Prosecutor had already suggested that Peter get a B for his exam, and, pleased, Wolf agreed; after the break, the school would have to swallow a bitter pill.

Wolf's fears intensified when the chairman of the commission refused a drink—"Now I know," he explained tragically, "that one mustn't pros-

235

trate one's prostate!"—and the Doctor did not even allow himself to be tempted by his love for tequila, after Wolf, having intentionally delayed until now, finally presented him with the souvenirs from his excursion. So that poor Simon Hus could only pray for a miracle.

Wolf felt a faint glimmer of hope, when in CURCLASEX the boy drew the stake and in CURMODEX hanging, which they had covered the most extensively. As for the stake, DOOR's favorite, Romilda, would undoubtedly be brought up, the girl for whom he had learned the eighth-century Lombard love story by heart; for that reason Wolf had told it to the kids in detail. But even the slim vestige of intelligence with which he responded to the strongest impetus seemed to have deserted Simon now. To prove that the fault was in the student and not in the school, Wolf tried to prompt him himself. But it turned into a monologue, and when Simon finally let himself be heard for the first and last time, he gave himself the crowning blow.

"—and because," Wolf urged him, "she was driven to betrayal by her passion, they took the stake and impaled her . . . ? Her what . . . ?"

"Asshole!" exclaimed Simon. After that, he never said a word about hanging.

Wolf had not expected the explosion that followed Hus's departure. When it happened, he wished more than anything that he could have walked out of the room with him. But HIENS was his ship now, he had dreamed it up, he had sat it out in official waiting rooms and had sulked it out of destiny, and he couldn't leave the bridge just because a seaman had fallen overboard. He tried to defend Simon by recalling his famous ancestor and his mightily wronged father.

"Surely a certain," he added, "lack of intellect is balanced by other attributes. I am convinced that for example, a mass—"

he continued bravely, because he was stricken with shame,

"—execution would be something he would perform far better than others, and that would ensure his future in the countries of the Third World. Let's let him pass through to the masters exam—"

"Beda," the chairman said informally, "it is in keeping with your nobility of spirit that you refuse to let anyone down, but if we were to let him slip through, we'd be doing you a disservice: your first opponent to come along would find it easy to prove that his kind of executioner is a dime a dozen today, if only among the prison guards, and a state needn't waste funds on their education. No, Frederick! It is precisely because his name is Hus that he mustn't be allowed to shame himself or you. So—"

he added strictly, so as to save Wolf the need to make any further comment,

"—let's continue!"

236

Albert was next. He walked into the classroom, clicked his heels, and waited. The Doctor rose to hand him the hat.

"One moment!" the chairman broke in, "let him answer Hus's questions, at least we'll have some comparison!"

"Fine!" said the Doctor.

"Ready?" asked the chairman impatiently.

"Ready!" Albert exclaimed. And he told of the siege of Cividale del Friuli. The city had almost withstood the siege, but when Kakan, the king of the Avars, who had slaughtered the whole district, was inspecting the fortifications, he was spotted by Princess Romilda, and, as Albert described it, she fell prey to unbridled lust. She sent him a message that she would turn the city over to him if he would take her as his wife. The barbarian promised to do so, and when she had the gates thrown open, he ordered all the adult male Lombards killed and the women and children sold into slavery. No sooner had he kept his promise by making Romilda—as Albert spoke, Wolf had an intense flash of memory of the train compartment at night—his wife, he ordered twelve of his Avar warriors to ravish her, whereupon he had her—the person responsible for the massacre—publicly impaled on a stake, concluded Albert.

"Do you know," asked the Doctor, and Wolf quickly changed his train of thought, "what Kakan said?"

"He said," Albert replied, "'This is the husband you are worthy of!'"

"Do you by any chance know it in the original?" the Doctor asked slyly.

"'*Talem te dignum est maritum habere,*'" replied Albert, "is how Diakonus put it. The original in the Avar tongue has unfortunately not survived."

His knowing this was a put-down for the Doctor, and Wolf realized the Doctor would not forgive the boy until he had given him a hard time; his hopes fell.

"Was this," asked DOOR, concealing his irritation with a smile that was even more amiable, "the first execution by impalement in written history?"

"Only in Europe. One of the great stakers of history was Assurbanipal in the seventh century B.C., of whom it was said that he surrounded conquered cities with a fence comprised of impaled prisoners."

"How were they impaled?" inquired DOOR.

"As a rule, anally," replied Albert.

"You mean they just rammed it in?" asked the chairman with interest, revealing his ignorance.

"It depends. Nobody, if you'll excuse the expression, fucked around much with a captive. They took and slammed him down onto the stake and pulled him by the legs so he couldn't squirm loose."

237

"And otherwise?" asked the chairman, intrigued.

"Otherwise," replied Albert, "the condemned man knelt down and the greased stake was introduced about half a meter into the anus and only then was the whole thing stood up and left to gravity."

"And this was the way," said the Doctor, "they did Romilda, then!"

Look out! Wolf wanted to shout, but he needn't have worried.

"No," said Albert and his eyes, resembling those of a doe, fell directly on the Doctor. "Kakan ordered that Romilda be wedded to the stake."

"Meaning?" asked DOOR, no longer able to conceal his irritation.

"Via vagina," replied Albert tersely.

Wolf's anxiety began to dissolve; looking at the annoyed Doctor now gave him a strange feeling of pleasure.

"When," the Doctor did not give up, "was the beginning of the golden age of the stake in our historical times?"

"In the sixteenth century," Albert replied promptly. "The Turks used it so extensively that it was introduced in Europe so people would get used to the idea. It was most popular in Vienna."

"And when," asked the Doctor tirelessly, "did Europeans encounter it last?"

"In the year 1800," Albert replied without hesitation, "when young Suleiman-el-Halebi, murderer of Napoleon's best general, Kléber, was impaled before the entire French expeditionary corps in Egypt. For four hours he recited his surahs, even after the stake had emerged from behind his neck. Only after the departure of the Egyptian executioner did the French guard give the client a drink, so that he croaked right off, like anybody impaled would after taking a drink."

"Why is that?" asked the Doctor hypocritically.

"I don't know!" replied Albert so loudly that Wolf flinched.

"You don't know?" inquired the Doctor triumphantly.

"No, sir," replied Albert pleasantly, "not even the greatest expert on impalement, Siegmund Stiassny, has been able to answer that question."

Wolf's heart dropped back in place, although he was startled at the lad's playing with fire.

"Is there," the Doctor continued his onslaught, "any way to regulate the progress of the execution?"

"Yes, sir, there is," replied Albert. "If the end of the stake is rounded and dull, it does not wound any important organs in passing, and apparently forces aside the stomach, the liver, and the spleen, which increases the client's chances of living to see an amnesty. For that matter—"

Albert anticipated the Doctor's next query,

"—a rounded stake was sometimes stuck harmlessly up people's

238

behinds as a symbolic warning, or in special cases, they just used a fat beet root."

"Do you know," asked the Doctor, "what that is—"

"It is called Raphanidosis," replied Albert swiftly, confirming what Wolf already suspected: that he had been doing research outside of school.

"But," said the chairman tensely, "that needn't have been so unpleasant . . ."

Wolf realized that the former Prosecutor was seeking a replacement for his lost lover, and was worried that the unsuspecting Albert might say something unsuitable that could transform the commission chairman into his mortal enemy.

"No," replied Albert, "and the author of the most apt statement about execution by impalement was the brother of Louis XIV, famous as an expert on all types of love: 'Impalement on the stake is the punishment that ends the nastiest but begins the nicest!' "

The elegance of his reply disarmed even the Doctor. His silence indicated that they could proceed. They had agreed in advance that the one-two jerk not be tested during the matriculation exams—Wolf in all modesty insisted on that—nor the schnoose—the Doctor in all caution insisted on that, so as not to remind NESTOR unnecessarily of Simsa. The two methods, each of them a key aspect of the school's curriculum, would of course be demonstrated during the masters exams. The question in CURMODEX on hanging encompassed only classical techniques used for want of anything better and for a lack of communications—Wolf looked forward to the uproar that his report would cause at the upcoming world conference—in every country except this one, or as Simsa used to quip, "in what's left of the world." Albert began with the Scottish method, as prescribed by the grand old man of British executioners, John Ellis:

"The prerequisite," he said unhesitatingly, "is a good thick hempen rope about two inches thick, pulled tight so that the strangulation line runs round the neck to the nape. In a fall of two to six feet, the soft portions of the lower palate are violently driven up against the gullet and the upper palate. This prevents breathing through both nose and mouth, causing one to pop right off. Ellis was the one—"

he continued with an assurance that transformed the oral exam into a lecture,

"—who authored the preliminary 'test by sandbag,' for all practical purposes eliminating the risk that the rope might break under the weight of the body; its disadvantage is the weighing of the clients, which makes them nervous. The proponent of the English style was his son, Albert

Pierrepoint: the knot is placed so that the fall causes it to strike the head near the right jaw; the sharp movement causes the total deformation of the vertebrae in the neck, to such a degree that the method can be called more humane than—and here the son criticized the father—the Scottish one, which allows the rope to slide along the neck and cause long and torturous—"

he added with a bravado that transformed the lecture into a demonstration,

"—asphyxiation."

The three members of the commission thought that this Albert would not remain in the shadow of his namesake.

"Outstanding!" cried the chairman, for the first time revealing the grade he was giving the examined pupil. "And now call in the next one!"

As Albert left the room the Doctor went so far as to applaud him.

That applause, directed once again after so many years at a competitor, set Wolf back on his heels. He was glad that Albert was so beholden to him, but he decided not to let him out of his sight. It's a good thing, he thought, that the boy has that horrid hump on his . . . but then he felt a flood of shame, and his thought was stifled. Lizinka was standing in the doorway—

"Scandals won't solve anything," Wolf said firmly, looking at her mussed hair and her red eyes. He resisted feeling compassion, so that he might have the strength to carry it through to the end, and he repeated to himself that he had a damned good reason. When he had tried to phone her, while lying under

54

Lizinka and she had not answered, he succumbed to a bad conscience: instead of rushing to her aid—he thought of the barbiturates in her night table—he was lying there, essentially in comfort, with a lass who had given him a great deal, but in comparison to Margaret, hardly anything at all. Yet he was unable to force nature, nor could he—when the vise of love finally let go—give wings to the taxi driver who drove them home from the border. All he could do was to give him a juicy tip to obligate him to take the sleeping girl home, and to have himself driven home first. When he unlocked the door, it was just after six in the morning, and he was shocked.

Their apartment, always almost as sterile as a dentist's office, now bore all the signs of a vicious burglary or a police search. In the hallway he had to wade through piles of objects scattered across the thresholds of the kitchen, the living room, and the study. When he turned on the light—dawn was only just beginning to illuminate the apartment—he realized that he was treading on his own shoes tossed out of the closet, his own clothes ripped off clothes hangers, his shorts and shirts pulled out of dresser drawers and nastily rumpled, and on his own novels and even reference books swept out of the bookshelves. Almost in a trance, he worked his way to the bedroom door and when he opened it, he understood why even the most intelligent people become murderers, although they could easily deduce that they would end up in the hands of an executioner.

On the broad chaise longue, where for years he had made ardent love with Margaret and for years afterward had tenderly embraced her, a chaise unsullied by any mistress, lay his own wife, naked and intertwined with a skinny long-haired youth young enough to be her son, and, with a bit of goodwill, even her grandson. When she noticed her husband, she didn't show the slightest sign of surprise.

"Good morning," she said derisively. "Will you make us some coffee?"

His recollection of what followed was foggy. But he definitely remembered striking his wife for the first time in his life and dragging the punk by the hair to the living room door; when the kid's shouting got to be too much, Wolf picked up a pair of socks from the hall floor and rammed them into his mouth, all the while looking around wildly.

"Look in the hall closet," said Margaret, who hadn't even flinched after the blow, and who was leaning over to watch him from where she lay. "There is enough clothesline there to hang the whole house with. And yourself too, so nobody could screw it up later. The hangman—"

she laughed spitefully,

"—hanged himself!"

"He's all I want!" he shouted, "and you can bet your sweet behind that I'll get away with a suspended sentence!"

"Hardly." She was still laughing and he could see a trace of blood on her teeth. "I know how to pick my lover boys."

"In a minute he's going to be a lover girl!" shouted Wolf, breaking the neck off a wine bottle the two of them had apparently been drinking during their session; all he needed for a castration was a good-sized splinter.

"He is the only son," remarked Margaret sweetly, "of the Deputy Minister of Justice. He came to sign up for your school."

Wolf may have been willing to place his career and his freedom on the altar of personal honor, but now he realized once again that the school superseded him. It was a part of him and yet it was not his—as any great work did not belong to its creator. Margaret knew his Achilles' heel. He tossed aside the glass splinter, spat in Lover Boy's eye, and went to take a cold shower. When he returned, the boy was gone, but Margaret hadn't changed her shameless position.

"I thought," she said, "that you'd be moving out, so I got things ready for you."

"You might have asked me first," he said, "and saved yourself some effort."

"There, there," she said with feigned sympathy, "didn't that tramp give you any?"

"That tramp," he said, determined to repay her with brutal frankness, "is the woman I'm going to marry. And the one who's moving out is going to be you."

Although she had expected the first statement, and had paid him back in advance, she still felt a faint glimmer of hope that she was wronging him, that the whole marital crisis was the product of her overheated imagination. Now even that glimmer flickered out, extinguished entirely by his last statement, and she saw black. She picked up a second bottle that was lying on the chaise and threw it at him, hard. It missed him and smashed a lovely porcelain sculpture of a set of teeth that she had gotten from Wolf for her fiftieth birthday; the bottle remained intact.

"Scandals won't solve anything!" Wolf said firmly, grasping at one last opportunity to restore order to his and her lives. "I love her and I can't live without her, and I have a proposition. If you don't complicate the divorce, I'll see to it you get a studio apartment, where you can spend the rest of your life—"

he couldn't help but add bitterly,

"—playing around with your little boys."

For a while now he had had the impression that she was looking not only through him, but through the walls of the room; her eyes, bloodshot from lack of sleep and from the contact lenses she hadn't removed, released a flood of tears now, and her lips whispered, "Karl . . . "

At first he thought she was calling for her fledgling bed companion, and it galled him, but then he realized that for the second time since he had naively boasted of his profession, she was speaking the name of her hanged sweetheart. Even more than the first time, when their youth and their love promised to repay them a hundred times over for all their losses, it brought home to him his own mortality. He was so close to losing this person, the dearest and only one he ever had.

He leaned over her and began slowly, gravely, almost scientifically, with his dry lips to soak up one tear after another, finding a painful bliss in their saltiness, as if they were burning away his sins, and then he continued down her long throat, which he as a connoisseur had valued most of all, down her breasts, which were almost indiscernible but also

242

unchanged after a quarter of a century—and once again were all the rage—until he arrived at the base of her mound of Venus. He thought of the Deputy Minister's son, and it hurt, but it wasn't anger or wounded pride but rather a feeling of guilt, because after all, who is to blame when ripe fruit is stolen if not, he asked himself, the gardener?

Throughout his caressing, she hadn't moved, and perhaps it was her very lack of interest, combined with the painful recollection of how lustfully she had been humping and how hoarsely she had been urging on the influential stud who couldn't even appreciate it, that made him forget the psychic barrier that had long ago halted their marital relations, and made him simply enter her until she cried out the way she had that time in the dentist's chair and all the weight of the world fell from his shoulders as he made love to her the way he had in the dream when he had taken her for Lizinka, but this time consciously, for herself, and so he wasn't even surprised, though immensely pleased when, as they approached the pinnacle of the resurrection of their love, she moved away, straddled him and fell on him, while he shed all his psychological bonds and spilled up into her, exclaiming to her, as he had in the days when he had still called her his Roman lad, "Mark . . . Mark . . ."

and then, moist with sweat, holding each other in their arms until they caught their breath again, she spoke the words he had always dreamed about:

"Rick, I think that last time, you made me

55

a son."

Although he was always ready to intervene on their behalf or to arrange for contacts without which HIENS couldn't have been born or survived, the Doctor had resisted all invitations to visit the school in person. His position, the growing importance of which was confirmed by his important contacts, apparently made such demands on him that he sometimes even had difficulty getting away to witness executions, and once went so far as to request that they stretch out the initial phase of one execution in case he should be delayed; he barely made it, when Simsa—it was that far back—could no longer pretend, in view of his reputation, that the knot had gotten tangled. And so for a long time, Lizinka had just been a concept that he viewed abstractly; he would merely ask after her grades, so that he could keep NESTOR posted. After the business on the border, though, he began to display more interest in her.

"Congratulations," he said to Wolf when they met three days after the excursion. "I always was a fan of yours, and now I envy you besides."

He had made the usual lunch date with Wolf in a little tavern with cozy curtained booths. The intimate lighting made the place ideal for clandestine meetings of lovers, but its guests were exclusively men who resembled one another in dress, behavior, and even appearance, like husband and wife after years of marriage. A few steps away was the street where all the central bureaus of the public and the secret police were located. Although the guests were careful to pay no attention to anyone else, Wolf noted that as the Doctor passed them, they inadvertently sat a bit taller.

"That debasing scene?" asked Wolf, amazed.

"The vitality," the Doctor corrected him, "that permitted you to take any part in it, as a contemporary of yours I can appreciate it. But isn't there any danger of betrayal on the part of the—"

the Doctor asked, frankly disturbed,

"—the wench?"

"Danger?" Wolf was puzzled.

"What if you knocked her up? Or what if," asked the Doctor, upset by his own imagination, "she was knocked up already and she throws the blame on you? She's got plenty of witnesses!"

"And why," asked Wolf, astonished, "would she?"

"And why," retorted the Doctor, "wouldn't she? Aren't you the ideal match? She'd come out ahead, like an actress that marries a director. Do you know what has killed off the largest number of talents? Not wars, not even execution grounds, but beds. How many potential poets, how many scientists, indeed how many executioners have buried their talents between a pair of pretty thighs, only to discover one fine day, to their horror, that it is the trap of all traps, all the more monstrous in its velvet softness. You were really caught in the jaws of that trap, and if an hour later you were released, you can take it as the finger of Providence and avoid it forever. Or else you will soon discover that the velvet withers, but the cage remains, and you will be paying for a fleeting moment of pleasure with all you have, until the trap disintegrates with rust, except that will be too late—you'll be free but impoverished, materially and spiritually. And, Frederick—"

the Doctor addressed him by his first name for the first time in all those years,

"—wouldn't that be a waste?"

"But," Wolf objected, "I've been happily married for a quarter of a century."

"Happily?" asked the Doctor in surprise. "Then why are you tempting fate with some half-baked Lolita?"

"Have you ever," Wolf responded, "seen her, Doctor?"

In CURCLASEX, the question Lizinka got was the wheel, and for a few seconds, the blood drained out of Wolf's head. Has the man gone mad? he thought feverishly, or has he betrayed us? (For, after due consideration, the Doctor had decided to give Lizinka the questions himself.) Dissertations had been written about the wheel; the stake was a peripheral phenomenon by comparison. He was a trifle relieved when the Doctor, who otherwise had left the candidates to their verbal devices, pointed to the human skeleton in the corner of the classroom and told her, "Draw it on the board for us."

Lizinka wasn't much of an artist, but fortunately she wasn't being tested in her drawing skills. In a few minutes, she had come up with a figure remotely resembling a skeleton.

"Bravo," said the Doctor, and the grateful Wolf noted that he was boosting Lizinka's self-confidence and psychologically influencing the chairman in her favor. "And now, my dear, indicate with numbers one through nine the order in which you would break your client."

Wolf prayed that she would recall the failure of Richard Masin, which he had later made up for so childishly. When after a couple of hesitations—her hand guided the chalk in the air above the drawing as if it were a chessboard—she inscribed a one and a two on the shins, he began to breathe again. But when she finally put the number nine on the neck, he was overcome with weakness again: now what?

"Bravo," said the Doctor when her hand with the chalk dropped to her side, and her credulous gaze rested on him again, "very good!" He praised her performance at such length that on one hand he aroused the impression that she had resolved a profoundly tricky question and on the other he gave so much detail, from the number of spokes in the wheel, determined by the oldest law books from Friesland to be nine, only to be raised, with the gradually increasing solidity of human bones, to a full twelve, to the alternate *manière française,* where the bones were broken with an iron bar, all the way to the intensified version, when before the final blow the heart and genitals were excised from the living victim and stuffed in his mouth, as was done for example in 1692 to the Ritter Grandval for the unsuccessful—"Yes," nodded the Doctor, as if Lizinka had commented, "that was his mistake, if he had succeeded, he'd have gotten a medal!"—assassination attempt against William III of Orange, he gave so much detail that he practically exhausted the textbook.

Wolf, for years a teacher, recognized that he was witnessing a trick common among pedagogues when helping a favorite during an exam, while the commission perceived no more of it than the audience would during a magic act. The Doctor concluded quickly, and, covering his notebook with his hand, marked down her grade. When he met the chairman's quizzical look, he returned it coolly.

"No questions?" The former Prosecutor was surprised.

"Everything," the Doctor returned his surprise, "was said, wasn't it?"

The chairman, with his lack of knowledge, could not respond to that in any other way than by simply instructing the candidate, "All right, CURMODEX!"

The question called for Capital Punishment throughout the world, and Wolf prayed that Mrs. Tachezy had understood his gentle hint on Wednesday.

"While you have the chalk in your hand," the Doctor said with uncharacteristic sharpness, "write down the tables on the board, so it's clear, just the exceptions, first the nations where Capital Punishment—and don't you dare refer to it by the vulgar expression 'ceepee' or you'll make us drop your grade then and there—has for the present been abolished by the law, and second, a list of nations where it is in the statutes but is not used. As for the nations where executions do take place, just list their precise number so we don't spend the whole day here. All right now—go ahead!"

Unlike the chairman of the commission, who perceived the Doctor's businesslike tone as indicative of his attitude, Wolf knew that the question had been made as easy as possible for Lizinka to answer. Nonetheless, he watched anxiously as the lone figure stood before the blackboard, having already written down the headings, thinking hard, with the fingertips of her left hand pressed tight to her forehead. Lizinka

was observing the inside of her hand. On her index finger, her middle finger, her ring finger and her pinkie, she had all the nations in categories 1 and 2 written in indelible ink (fortunately there were not too many of them). The other nations were written on her palm, very small and squeezed together. Then she began to copy them swiftly and Wolf was distinctly relieved . . . until he gave an inward gasp. *Idiot!* Wolf thought in the Doctor's direction, for the first time in his life violating the rules of subordination. The moment he noticed the cardinal error, he realized that it was not the girl's fault: she was copying the United Nations statistics as they were listed in the texts, whereas the Doctor had (intentionally?) inverted the order! So that under the title 1, she listed Belgium, Luxembourg, and Nicaragua, which of course belong under 2, whereas under 2, she wrote Costa Rica, the Dominican Republic, Ecuador, Finland, Iceland, Colombia, the German Federal Republic, Austria, Sweden, Switzerland, Uruguay, and Venezuela, which of course belonged under 1. Then she turned around and looked at him, the way she had always done during classroom lessons.

He was unable to give her even the smallest indication of what had happened, and all the more feverishly did he wonder what he would do when the two of them tossed her out on her ear. The only thing that occurred to him in that split second was that the entire charade was a vote

246

of confidence on the part of the Doctor in himself and in the school in general.

To Wolf's amazement, the Doctor said, "Bravo!" and continued: "At first glance it is not a very happy balance sheet, but if we examine it more closely, we note that in many of the nations listed, no executioner is at least allowed to go hungry, and that the third and last group contains the largest and includes the most populous countries in the world. And now, write down and circle the number of nations in which a decent person can still feel secure, so that we can—"

added the Doctor, glancing at the chairman as if he were speaking for both of them,

"—go to lunch!"

Good God, Wolf wondered, could they have overlooked it? The chairman had the statistics right under his nose, but be that as it may, it was all Greek to him. But the Doctor? He could have recited that list in his sleep, backwards! The only explanation left was the one that occurred to Wolf during the oral in CURCLASEX: that he was helping Lizinka deliberately! That he was violating his iron principles, which was evidence of two interesting things: one, that he could get away with it, and, two, that he was willing to get away with it. Because of me? wondered Wolf suspiciously. He was forced to admit that it was rather because of her.

"Well, now, really!" came a sharp reprimand from the chairman, interrupting Wolf's thoughts, "you can't be serious, young lady!"

He looked up to find a catastrophe. Wolf's hint had gotten through to Mrs. Tachezy, but it had not occurred to Lizinka's mother to add up the number of countries that use Capital Punishment. Now Lizinka, her left hand back to her forehead, had been trying for the impossible. With the abbreviations dancing in front of her eyes, she strove to count them, and in the end she wasn't sure if she hadn't miscounted by ten. To be on the safe side, she subtracted ten and put the number 98 in a circle on the blackboard.

"The number of countries that exercise *ceepee,*" said the chairman maliciously, although he certainly hadn't known it before he read it on the documents before him, "is a *hundred and eighteen.* You may go."

Lizinka nodded and left the class, still holding the chalk.

And when the chairman suggested a D, Wolf moved to erase the blackboard rather than object, since he could well imagine the verdict if that misogynist had discovered the first mistake too.

"So far," the Doctor spoke up, leafing through his notebook as if he hadn't heard the chairman's suggestion, we have given an A, two Bs, a D, and we've flunked one. If we add a C, we'll have a model statistical curve. I know, you—"

the Doctor turned to Wolf,

"—are for a stricter grading, as a matter of principle, and it is thanks to that attitude that before our very eyes the field has taken a giant step into the next millennium, but perhaps if Mr. Wolf would let us—"

the Doctor turned to the chairman,

"—talk him into making an exception this time, and being a little softer, he might agree with us on giving Miss Tachezy a C."

"All right," mumbled Wolf; he would have preferred to sing it out. Now that the nervous tension was miraculously dissipating, he was glad it had all happened. By showing his willingness to risk his position and his school for her, he had put his feelings through the first real trial by fire, and he began to look forward madly to the evening and the dénouement of his extraordinary plan.

The former Prosecutor recorded a C for Lizinka, without noticing, manipulator that he was, that he himself had been splendidly manipulated. . . .

"Now, that does it!" raged Wolf. "I'm going upstairs and make a scene like you've never seen, anywhere!"

"Oh, please, sir," begged the

56

porter loyally, "he's sure to come back, Novak is like a clock—it's just those poor teeth of his!"

"That," Wolf growled, "is his problem! I'm busy this afternoon, and I need—"

From the porter's booth came the ring of the telephone; an apparatus almost as ancient as the courthouse building itself, it rang with a sound like an alarm clock.

"Hello? *Hello?* Mr. Novak!" the porter exclaimed in relief, "there's a gentleman here to see you."

"Novak," said Wolf in a masterful tone, having just torn the receiver from the porter's hand, "this is my second trip here today to pick up a duplicate of my marriage certificate. Do I have to go to the chairman of the court? I know him well!"

"It's my teeth," said the voice on the other end.

"I know my way around in dentistry too," Wolf interrupted, "and if you're not here this afternoon by the stroke of half past five, I will see to a state check of all your dental treatments over the last ten years. Understood?"

"But that's after office hours . . ." the voice objected mildly.

248

"You can bet your life," said Wolf categorically, "that if I don't find you here, you won't ever have another office hour as long as you live! All right?"

"Yes, sir," the voice broke, "if you please . . ."

By then, Wolf was on his way to his car. Where have I heard that voice before? he wondered, but he gave it up. The worst was still ahead of him. He was pleased not to have found Lizinka in tears after the orals, but rather playing their favorite game of Meat.

Simon was, traditionally, "It," but when they called the students into the classroom to read them the exam results, he wept so long and so loudly that they had to interrupt the ceremony and commiserate with him collectively. So it was not until Lizinka was departing with her classmates for their last lunch at GRECAN that Wolf found a chance to wordlessly telegraph his question again, a question that weighed heavily on his mind: she shook her head and he sent her a joyful and congratulatory look, indicating that he was crossing his fingers for her.

"I've got to drive to town and back," he said to the other members of the commission. "Can I give anyone a ride?"

"Thank you," said the Doctor, "you've had enough of us for a while. We'll go somewhere and get ourselves a rare steak and a glass of red wine, to get in the right frame of mind for the masters exams this afternoon."

"I ought to be thanking you!" whispered Wolf as they shook hands.

"Don't mention it," whispered the Doctor, giving him a conspiratorial wink; then he added with concern, "is everything arranged with the trunk?"

"It's all taken care of. Karli is reliable—he'll take it over in time!"

Now Wolf proceeded to repeat his instructions to his henchman as they approached the barred windows, and, showing their special permits, drove through the armored gates that opened and closed like an accordion.

"Yes, sir!" said Karli as he opened the door for Wolf.

Upstairs, everything was in order; the topics of the masters exams had been established in advance; this time it wasn't a matter of material that could be studied, memorized by rote, or cheated from a crib sheet; this time it was a question of skill. They had spent almost all of June polishing it up; now the set had been checked, the props laid out, the costumes put on, and only one thing was lacking: the audience.

Wolf had worked up the concept of the masters exams with Simsa, but paradoxically, it was Simsa's misfortune that gave them their real spark. On Monday morning, March 24, when Wolf had identified Simsa's sports car at the dam, he arrived profoundly depressed at the tavern where he had been hurriedly invited by the Doctor. The news he heard from the Doctor first evoked confusion, then annoyance, and finally—surprisingly—a creative spark. It dawned on him, in all detail, how to culminate the masters exams. A new era in the field could not be welcomed in with a better gala première. But back then, he couldn't have guessed in his wildest dreams that he would be linked with the heroine of this grand show not only by the thread of common interest or the cord of mutual sympathy, but by the strongest of cables.

Coincidence, the force that guides destinies and history, was also the author of the dramatic entanglement. The morning after their splendid reconciliation, Margaret came to him in tears and announced, in his idiom, that her red rider had come to her during the night. Wolf was as shattered as she. On the spur of the moment, he waved to a passing taxicab and in a few minutes was ringing at the Tachezys'. He assumed that the girl had told her parents everything, but he wasn't particularly concerned. Ironically, he saw as his advantage the same thing that Simsa had once assumed: that what was done couldn't be undone, and that he was no hit-and-run driver, but a serious man who accepts responsibility for his deeds.

The welcome he received from Lizinka's mother bordered on the ceremonious. For a while he felt that she was welcoming him as her future son-in-law, but soon he saw that she simply didn't know anything. He couldn't know that he had enchanted her on his first, and to date only, visit since the previous Easter. She had often thought of him, yes, even that silly infatuation for the superficial Simsa had been, she now realized, an unconscious effort to come closer to this charming fellow. Even now, her heart began to pound, and so, once again thanks to Wolf, the invisible stationmaster Destiny blew his invisible whistle, in spite of the fact that the new (yet old) bed of bliss, Oscar's couch, wasn't scheduled until the next afternoon.

"Professor," she breathed, regretting that she wasn't wearing her dress from France, or even her pretty robe, "have you come to see *me?*"

"I wouldn't have the audacity," he said, uneasy because he hadn't quite expected this approach, but possessing enough presence of mind to remove his hat with a sweeping gesture and kiss her hand, "without calling first, madame. Actually, I'm checking up on my students before examinations, and I wanted to make sure that our study trip didn't set your daughter back any."

As much as he believed fanatically in speaking the truth, he also recognized what he referred to as the "holy lie," when the truth would do more harm than good. That is why he used to do the essential preliminary examination of clients, referred to by Simsa as the "neck check," in a white coat, smelling of one of Margaret's antiseptics. If Lizinka, as a daughter, was being considerate of her parents, he couldn't stomp in and

250

announce, Hey, lady, I got a piece of your daughter! He couldn't abide grossness in his work, much less in life.

"Lizinka," said Mrs. Tachezy in a tragic tone, "is sick."

"Sick?"

"No reason to worry, Professor, just the usual—"

she continued, blushing at having to talk about it with him, of all people,

"—female things—our Lizinka still hasn't gotten used to it. But why don't you drop in to see her, she's flat on her back, poor thing."

Lizinka was reading *Helen's Babies,* nibbling from a plate of raisins and almonds. After every five pages she chewed up an almond. After every ten pages, she took a raisin, but she just sucked on it and chewed it up only with the next almond.

"Lizinka, look who's come to see you, well, finally—"

her mother hastened to add when she looked over the situation,

"—you're taking it a little easy. Up till now I couldn't tear her away from her textbooks and notes!"

The texts and notebook were on a small table by the window. The obvious fact that she hadn't touched them since she got home told Wolf more about her condition than a dozen physicians.

"If you don't mind"—he turned to her mother in the most matter-of-fact tone—"I'd like to see how she's doing, test her a little . . ."

"Oh, just help yourself," said Lucie with false sincerity. But she couldn't keep from adding, "Is our Lizinka having any problems?"

Her nervousness was understandable; it was her first opportunity to ask about her daughter's progress; HIENS reported to parents only in critical cases.

"Ou Lizinka," Wolf said, "is near the head of her class. All I am doing today is an ordinary consultation, the kind I have with all of them."

"Then," said Lucie, relieved, "I won't disturb you." As soon as the door closed behind her, he felt like ravishing the girl as he had on the train, kissing her cheeks, her eyes, her lips, and those nipples that had so captivated him two days earlier that he had fallen on them like a nursing infant. But he was prevented from doing so by *Helen's Babies,* the raisins, the almonds, and the possibility of Mrs. Tachezy's return.

"And," he asked with exaggerated volume, "how are we feeling before taking exams? And—"

he added in a fond whisper,

"—after making love . . . ?"

Her reply was a pained grimace.

"That's just fine," he gushed loudly, "that—"

he added in a consoling whisper,

"—only happens the first time . . . !"

To his surprise, she didn't seem consoled.

"Is something the matter?" he asked out loud with self-assurance. "What—"

he added in a nervous whisper,

"—is wrong? Where does it hurt?"

Using the spine of *Helen's Babies* as a pointer, she indicated the epicenter. It was not, however, at the spot the Doctor nostalgically referred to as "the trap," but directly under the saucer of goodies, in the geometrical center of her belly.

"Ah, then it really is only," he reassured himself softly, "your red rider?"

Her uncomprehending look reminded him that the girl couldn't possibly understand his chaste euphemism dating back to the days when he was as shy as she.

"I mean," he continued in a whisper, "just your period? Well, that's—"

he exclaimed jovially,

"—no problem!"

Her eyes told him that he was both right and wrong. It took a moment before he understood.

"Or not—" he whispered frantically, "you mean your red rider did *not* arrive?"

And when she nodded solemnly, he forgot all vigilance and decency.

"Did not arrive!" he thundered.

Once again he felt faint, but this time out of sheer joy. In need of air, he opened the door.

"Professor . . ." gasped Lucie, unable even to pretend that she had just been walking past.

He came to his senses. The premature joy that he had shared with Margaret had taught him a lesson. If it wasn't all a dream, his seed must have preceded the expected arrival of the red rider by mere hours, and the new life would be less than two days old.

"My mother did not arrive," he explained, inspired by the concept that occupied his mind right then. "I waited at the station, but maybe she'll be on the next train.

"Well, child," he exclaimed in the voice of an old schoolteacher, consuming Lizinka with the gaze of a young lover, "keep up the good work. My fingers are crossed. Have her—"

he turned to the mother with a subtle hint,

"—take a look at the map of Capital Punishment throughout the world!"

Then he hurried to contact the Doctor, and after him, Margaret, and—he admitted it—manipulated each of them to do what he wanted. He

252

didn't enjoy doing it, but then, had he not been obliged to give up his beloved insects to do what others required? Now let his own intellect make others do what *he* required!

Lucie picked up the hint, and after going through her daughter's textbooks and finding out what it was all about, she turned for help to her husband. As usual, he failed her: all he could suggest was that Lizinka simply memorize the lists.

"Have you gone crazy?" shouted the mother. "Your daughter is in there flat on her back with the cramps and you want her to memorize a hundred and thirty-three countries?"

She soon realized that it wasn't intentional sabotage on his part, that her husband really didn't know what else to suggest. In desperation, she called on Oscar again, he was home for a change, and alone at that. When she explained the problem, he suggested immediately that the girl write the lists of countries on the palm of her hand, in the form of the international abbreviations used on license plates. Not only that, he reached to the bookshelf over his couch for his autoclub atlas and looked up the abbreviations, whereupon he finally transported Lucie on that couch to the shore that she hadn't visited in sixteen years, after having been dropped just short of it six months before by the repulsive Simsa, who had met his just deserts. Oscar appeared to be sincerely captivated: in her little golden date book, he marked for her all the days when they could repeat—"That's great, honey," he smiled. "I'm jealous of the jerk," he added breathlessly, "who made you suffer like that!"—their journey. She admitted neither to him nor to herself that it could only be Doctor Tachezy; she responded with a guilty sigh, by means of which she fired him up so masterfully that he immediately set to sea with her again.

As she approached shore the second time, a strange thing happened: she caught herself squeezing her eyes shut so that she could imagine that the bliss she was experiencing was not brought on by the ordinary if pleasant wolf that was Ossi, but rather the mysterious and unique Wolf himself, whose first and second visit had awakened her from her long sleep. That was why two days later, on Saturday—she had been sitting chain-smoking as she waited tensely for Lizinka's return from the NEXICOL's exams, silently swearing that she would betray her husband three times that very same day with Oscar, for sitting there indifferently playing with his stamp collection—Wolf's arrival took her breath away.

"You want to see . . . but Lizinka isn't . . ." she stammered, and the blood rushed to her cheeks.

"No, madame," said he, sweeping his hat off and kissing her hand. "I particularly picked this time of day to find you alone."

"But my husband . . . unfortunately . . ." Lucie mumbled with difficulty; she was having trouble breathing and her breasts were heaving; for

253

the first time ever she did not wish she were wearing her dress from France or even her fancy robe, but rather that she were dressed in nothing but her skin; it occurred to her that she might very well risk it and sweep him right into the bedroom; she was absolutely certain that her husband would not get up from his stamps now.

"What I meant," Wolf hastened to clarify, "was the two of you!"

Even though she sobered up immediately and saw her previous idea as the product of an addled mind, it made her aware that from the first time she had set eyes on him, Wolf had become number one in her life. She listened to his voice as if from a distance, explaining in the living room, briefly and matter-of-factly, what he had been obliged to keep from both of them—he bowed apologetically first to one and then to the other—in the interest of the investigation.

On Saturday, March 22 of this year, in spite of express instructions to cancel a planned school excursion owing to the illness of the head of the school, former Associate Professor Simsa had lured their daughter to his cottage, which constituted the crime of kidnapping. There he had drugged her and tried to force her to his will, unsuccessfully, thanks to the girl's brave resistance—but all the same it constituted the crime of attempted rape. In order to weaken her resolve, Simsa proceeded to commit a judicial murder before her eyes and the only reason he finally failed to have his way with her was thanks to the prompt intervention of state officials.

Their splendid daughter, continued Wolf, had asked that her parents be spared in the investigation. Now, three months later, when it was obvious that the girl had survived the experience without ill effects, he, who next to her parents was the closest to her, had taken it upon himself to inform them and hear their response. In order to escape justice, the pervert had pretended to drown in an auto accident and was officially declared dead. Now that he had been captured, the state had no legal right to try him, and so it was decided to leave the culprit to the parents and the school.

As soon as she heard that Lizinka had emerged from the experience unscathed, Lucie feigned continued attention, but her whole mind was concentrated elsewhere; she was trying to communicate with the Professor with her eyes and failing miserably; for some incomprehensible reason, the Professor was waiting impatiently for her husband's response.

Doctor Tachezy rose and walked out into the hall without a word. He leaned one hand against the wall and for a while observed the painting of the winter landscape. He must have shifted it, because he suddenly noticed that the children were tobogganing uphill. He straightened the picture carefully and walked into the bathroom. There, he removed his jacket and hung it on an empty coathanger. He pulled his shirt off over his head, removed his wristwatch and placed it on the shelf underneath the medicine cabinet as he always did at bedtime. He wet his toothbrush and squeezed the last little bit of toothpaste onto it. When the minty foam tingled on his gums, he felt a pang of bad conscience: what would Lucie and Lizinka use for their teeth? That was when he remembered that it was three o'clock in the afternoon, and that the horror that he was trying to escape was not something he had seen on television but something that had actually happened to—

—his child. When he reappeared on the threshold of the living room, he was naked to the waist, with a mad-looking fluoridated foam at his mouth, but for the first time he spoke like a normal human being.

"And tell me," he asked hoarsely, "what the hell are you

57

executioners for?"

At a quarter to three, just before the warden arrived with the guests, Karli called from the gate for someone to come and give him a hand. Two carts came rolling in, pushed with the help of Frantisek and the twins. One of them contained a lidded basket that gave off the sounds of wild squealing and the other held a silent steamer trunk. They barely had time to lock them in the Wolf's Den when the sound of keys rattled in the barred door to HIENS.

The masters exams were conceived in such a manner as to satisfy the demands of experts—who would be there, probably still quite skeptical, to see if this new, coddled generation, contained at least a single talent worth hiring—and at the same time to capture the attention of laymen—this was to be the first time the kids' work was to be presented to the parents. Simsa had been better acquainted with modern tastes, and he had come up with the idea of a show in which the pupils would demonstrate their skill for the experts and acquaint the others, entertainingly and engagingly, with the glorious history, the workaday present, and the secure future of their new profession. When later, Wolf was putting the project together by himself, he abandoned Simsa's outmoded and vulgar music-hall theatricality and arrived at a serious celebration, one utilizing the techniques of the avant-garde stage and the modern showroom.

During the month of June, the pupils transformed the CLASEX into what Wolf called the Hall of Tradition, with displays of the broadest range of period execution and torture devices and equipment, some in the form of models and some rare originals that Wolf had obtained during the school year during excursions by bribing museum administrators. The black walls bore reproductions of etchings and paintings depicting the entire palette of classical executions, the gem of the collection being a twelve-part cycle of altar paintings entitled *The Torturing of the Martyrs*.

The MODEX in turn was freshly whitewashed, to document the immense progress that the executionary sciences had undergone thanks to modern technology and ideology. Wolf had named it the Hall of Open Doors, because it was possible to walk right into the cabin with the electric chair and into the gas chamber, where one could even sit down in the chair reserved for clients. The walls were decorated with large glossy color photographs of interesting executions from all over the world.

During the initial adaptations, the two rooms had been separated by sliding doors across the whole width of the room; now the doors were propped open, and for the first time, the two large chambers were transformed into a relatively spacious hall. The chairs were placed so that spectators could turn them at will, to follow the action at either end of the hall. In the center, where the two rooms joined, a circular area was reserved for an old discarded lamppost and beneath it, an ashcan that Karli had rounded up in some warehouse and had painted bottle green.

Finally, they had hung a sign reading VISITORS on the girls' washroom and on the boys', STUDENTS; because every square meter of the school was utilized, that was where the students were waiting until the guests settled down in the hall and left the corridor vacant to serve as a backstage area. Wolf's sense of order and innate good taste helped him to overcome the handicap of never having done any directing since his early days as a teacher. He had no illusions about being able to compete with professionals, but at least he wanted to save the audience from embarrassing moments such as those which occur when amateurs put on costumes, make up their faces, and prance about the stage to impress relatives and friends.

So the performers remained concealed, the corridor still echoed with the squeaking of shoes and the buzz of voices, and Wolf, intentionally maintaining just the right distance, neither standoffish nor pushy, was responding noncommittally to uneasy opening-night greetings. He noted with satisfaction that not a single one of the faces he had grown used to seeing over the decades at execution grounds all over the country was absent, and he was especially pleased, for the kids' sake, to notice a representative of the Third World, who was apparently visiting prisons here for schooling in penology. Most important to Wolf, however, was the presence of the Tachezys, who had received permission to have Mr. Alexander accompany them. Then the former Prosecutor and the Doctor separated from the crowd to wish him good luck and success in the name of them all, took their seats in the hall directly beside the lamppost, and

256

pulled out their notebooks for recording grades. A mass exodus from the corridor followed, so that the bell, set for 3:15, fell only on the ears of Wolf.

He leaned against the wall, shut his eyes, and took several deep breaths. Too bad, he thought with regret, that Margaret isn't here. In spite of all her reservations, she was always the one who gave him courage before tricky mass executions. But for good reason her entrance wasn't scheduled until six, and so he had to be his own moral support. He opened his eyes and did a few knee-bends, the way he always did before going to get a client or in the break between individual numbers. He put out his hand—it wasn't shaking. He took his pulse. It was normal. He knocked on the door to the boys' washroom and when they came out, exceptionally subdued, he wished them all good luck. Leaning over Lizinka's shoulder, he whispered in her ear:

"Arrived yet . . . ?"

She shook her head bashfully and followed the others toward the door to the CLASEX, even more ethereal and desirable in her majestic costume than ever before. And with all his intelligence and imagination, Wolf somehow could not adjust to the idea that striding with her might very well be his—

—son. He tore his eyes away from them, softly opened the door to the MODEX, and walked on tiptoe behind the last row of seats. The heavy curtain was still down and two of the four portable spotlights illuminated the practice scaffold on the back wall of the CLASEX. Freshly varnished, it appeared very true to life; the impression was fortified by a pile of dirt, a large caldron, and a thick stake. By then Albert, who functioned as stage manager as well as participant, had struck the gong, and at the intersection of the two light beams appeared—

—Lizinka. She was wearing her mother's wedding cape dyed red, and on her head, an effectively faked crown labeled HISTORY. In one hand she held a staff and in the other a little wicker suitcase, covered with circles indicating years instead of hotel stickers; the clever implication was that Dame History was traveling in time. Although the wicker was a bit out of keeping with the style, it was essential: the sound from the cassette recorder inside it had to be heard. Lizinka struck her staff on the floor and the suitcase began to recite Wolf's text in Albert's mild voice:

"I am History. I am both He and She; I both give seed and give birth. I crown the strong, I forget the weak, I punish the unworthy—and today, we shall hear more of that!"

Behind the scaffold, Albert struck the gong again, while on the tape, Albert changed his tone. In the introduction, Wolf wanted to establish the atmosphere of the passion play, and used the brisk poetry of melodrama.

257

Considering the fact that he was no poet, his lines nonetheless possessed some genuine merit:

> In the beginning, the tools of our trade
> Were the elements four, by the good Lord made:
> Water and earth and air and fire,
> Helped the first criminals to expire.
> But as humankind on its journey began,
> God saw the need for a right-hand man,
> And so the honor he did confer
> On henchman, axman, executioner!

Lizinka struck her staff on the floor and retreated into the half-light beside the podium, so as not to distract the audience. Why aren't they applauding? Wolf worried, but by then, Mrs. Tachezy had already given a spontaneous signal to those who were too shy to begin clapping. Applause early in a performance can have an electrifying effect, and that was what happened here. In the slow but distinct rhythm of the music that followed the verses—considering the fact that he was no musician, Wolf had made a surprisingly precise choice: the medieval atmosphere of the scene was complemented by the Wedding March from *Lohengrin*—Frantisek was climbing onto the scaffold dressed in black leotards as Master Franntzn, and behind him, in black leotards, henchmen Peter and Pavel, dragging a client in a rough linen shroud. It was Simon.

The program was inventively composed in such a manner that each pupil would do his own exam, and, in addition, take the role of his classmates' helper where the need arose. It was bad enough that they had had to eliminate the failed Simon's independent number and take the trouble to cut and splice the tape; having someone step in for Simon in the other numbers would have been a calamity: the unplanned changes and breaks would have deprived the composition of its tension and rhythm. Fortunately, before lunch the commission chairman had accepted the explanation, which even improved Simon's frame of mind. Simon felt himself catching a toehold, and he tried to get an even firmer grasp by the quality of his performance, all the more so since his old father was sitting in the front row, ignorant of the boy's failure earlier. Ham that he was, Simon rolled his eyes, gnashed his teeth, wheezed painfully, to the point where Wolf was afraid that he might go so far as to speak. Frantisek, however, knew it was a matter of his own passing or failing, and he took charge like an old stager.

When Simon opened his mouth, Frantisek snapped his fingers and below, Albert did a drumroll. It frightened Simon, and that was the point when Frantisek did the execution. He tripped him up and the pudgy lad fell over behind the pile of dirt, through into a padded pit, with such conviction that the audience gasped. While Simon, unharmed, crept back out unseen, Frantisek leaned over the pit and placed a thin tube where the onlookers would have expected Simon's mouth to be; Peter and Pavel spat on their hands and in a trice had spaded the dirt into the pit. They all took a swig from a wineskin that Master Franntzn offered around. Then Franntzn poured some wine down the tube, whereupon the Wedding March from *Lohengrin* sounded again, and from behind the scaffold, who should mount the stairs but—Simon. The applause was silenced by shushing from the more experienced theatergoers who realized that his reappearance merely indicated the end of scene one.

To the sound of another drumroll, Frantisek tossed a sack over Simon so deftly that the helpers had no trouble "drowning" him in the caldron. That too had an opening into the pit, and beside it a basin of water to splash, so the effect was perfect. After the three had taken another swig and Master Franntzn had poured a little off into the water, *Lohengrin* sounded for the third time and, like a flattened moon, Simon's ludicrous head rose once more over the steps. The applause lasted through to the next drumroll, when the twins joined forces to lift Simon, while Frantisek hoisted him directly over the vertical stake. When they dropped him and proceeded to give his legs a yank, the audience groaned, and when the point of the stake emerged behind Simon's neck, all the women covered their eyes. But then laughter shook the room, and when they peeked through their fingers, they saw Simon getting off the stake, which of course was collapsible, holding in his hand the point of the stake, which of course was extendable.

While the happy Frantisek, the worst behind him, was taking his bows, Wolf reflected regretfully that because of Simon, the Chinese torture had to be dropped; he had thought it up with Simon in mind, and he knew the boy would have passed. In a bald wig with only a pigtail of hair—the insignia of Asian executioners—Simon would have mounted the scaffold dressed in a kimono, where Albert would in the meantime have prepared the first *dujka* (since New Year's in the mountains, they had started calling all the practice dummies *dujkas),* hanging by a pigtail on a column with its feet just barely touching the scaffold, its Asiatically sallow belly bare. Then Albert would have lit the alcohol burner. Simon would have brought his own pincers, a meter-long pipe with one end welded shut and a cage with a rat.

The subject of the scene was to have been a typical Chinese penalty described by a European witness on July 22, 1920, in Canton. After Simon would have released the rat from the cage into the pipe and pressed the open end to the "belly," he would have grasped the pipe with the pincers and moved the burner so the flame heated up the closed end. An observer with any intelligence would deduce that the rat would have only one direction in which to go to escape the heat. To the sound of Oriental music—Wolf had aptly selected the melody of "In a Persian Market"—beneath the scaffold Albert was to have given off inhuman wails, but the main shock for the audience was to have come when the pipe was removed, in the form of brilliant realism: during rehearsal, it had only taken the rat a few minutes to chew its way through the *dujka's* belly, since it was made of a big slab of cheese.

But Wolf had to forgo all that and console himself with the knowledge that he still had the initial scene for next year. Now he was again enjoying the aspect of the enchanting Dame History, who had run through the corridor during the applause to the door to the MODEX, so that when she reappeared it was behind the back of the audience. Because the first two spotlights went out and the other two, aimed in the opposite direction, went on, the spectators had no problem orienting themselves and swiftly spun around in their chairs in expectation of further surprises. When the sound of shuffling feet and chairs died down, the tape recorder spoke again. Unfortunately, it had been impossible to cut out the first and the last line, which referred to the omitted scene, but Wolf hoped no one would notice.

> Chinese tortures were clever, it's true;
> But the Western mind was inventive too!
> Progressive refinements come to be;
> The offspring of technology.
> Before the engine run by steam
> Appeared the first beheading machine.
> Yet decapitation, as we shall see,
> Remained an art: voilà, scene three!"

Frantisek, who had taken over the gong, struck it at the precise moment of the last word, cleverly covering the omission of Simon's number. On the tape, Albert changed his tone of voice again: on th instructions of the director, he spoke with the disinterest of a newscaster;

"In 1938 in Vienna, murderess Marta Marek was sentenced to the supreme penalty. The sentence was more symbolic than anything else, since Austria hadn't executed a woman in thirty years. Dame History, however—"

on the tape, Albert paused while Lizinka struck the floor with her staff,

"—decided otherwise. After the *Anschluss* of Austria to Hitler's Germany, Vienna's *Gauleiter* ordered that the sentence be carried out. All the same, the family of the Reich's executioners was not enthusiastic:

260

the attractive red-haired, blue-eyed woman was a cripple in a wheel-chair."

The door to the corridor opened and the twins, with colored aprons over their leotards and peaked caps over their eyes, walked in pushing a wheelchair from the prison hospital. A wave of whispers washed through the audience: in the wheelchair, instead of an attractive woman, sat the hunchbacked Albert. Wolf could feel the air crackle with suspense.

"The man who was wheeled to the machine the day before the execution, in a chair as similar as possible to hers, was the famous Johann Baptist Reichart of Munich, who in his productive career had done three thousand one hundred and sixty-five clients. He was to perform his most famous execution at the close of—"

—the voice of Albert spoke while the body of Albert flew out of the wheelchair that Peter and Pavel unexpectedly tipped forward, and landed close to the practice guillotine. Albert leaped swiftly to his feet and in a moment was back in the wheelchair,

"—that very night. Again and again, he devotedly skinned his knees so that they could determine the exact spot to stop the chair and so they could polish up their dumping technique until—"

The "Blue Danube Waltz" sounded and Albert was tipped out of the chair, nearer and nearer, until finally he landed in place on the base of the guillotine.

"—until Johann Baptist Reichart—"

the invisible Albert described what the visible Albert was demonstrating,

"—made a chalk line on the floor and pronounced words that have gone down in history for their down-to-earth humanism."

The waltz died down and the live Albert-Reichart declaimed in a deep voice, "As she falls, grab her under the arms in time, so she doesn't break her nose and bleed all over the place!"

Frantisek gave a drumroll and Wolf could sense the spectators stop breathing.

Out of the spotlight where they had retreated for a moment, Peter and Pavel quickly placed a female *dujka* in the chair. It was dressed and made up meticulously on the basis of period police photos. Albert stepped up to the guillotine, and Wolf could tell that he too was excited now. The drumroll intensified. The twins pushed the wheelchair into the light and, precisely as rehearsed, they moved forward, flipped the chair forward at the chalk line, caught the falling *dujka* just over the base of the guillotine and placed its neck carefully in the lunette. With a single gesture, Reichart-Albert closed the lunette and pulled the lever. The heavy, slanted blade thundered against the base, the red-wigged head rolled into the basket, and the confetti with which the neck had been stuffed splashed upward in a splendidly effective shower of red.

The attentive audience grasped the change in genre. The smiles left their faces and it was obvious that the storm of applause was not just for Albert's performance—even the Doctor was clapping, which indicated a good chance of an A grade—but for the memory of the incomparable Reichart and also his statement, "There's no such thing as a client a hangman can't do." Wolf used the blackout, planned for a change of sets, to slip out into the corridor again; he wanted to be free to move about if there were any slipups. The difficulty of the performance increased from one scene to the next: if Frantisek's and Albert's jobs had been made easier by a willing classmate or a convenient mannequin, now the element of the irrational was entering upon the scene, precisely as it did in real life. It was time for the basket and the trunk.

Pavel and Peter tossed aside their aprons and caps, slipped jeans over their leotards and, trained by arduous rehearsals, hurried to the office; Wolf was amazed at how those two greenhorns, last year capable at best of skinning a dog alive, now were operating within a precise time schedule, using top-level technology—and they didn't even need him anymore . . . He was overwhelmed with a feeling of nostalgia, the same kind he was used to feeling when he thought of his age; then another blow of the staff to the floor of the hall sounded, and it was as if youth itself were calling to him.

So as not to disturb, he peered through a crack in the door and watched Dame History's next intermezzo. While Albert's snorts sounded from the boys' washroom (I'm really going to have to pull some strings and get them some proper showers), his voice sounded from the MODEX, once again in a declamatory tone:

> We see bright futures proudly beckon;
> The modern world will have to reckon
> With criminals' increasing numbers!
> *Woe betide them . . .*
> For we have Science on our side;
> The hiss of gas will stem the tide!
> Let them all beware, we say:
> The electric chair will make them pay!

With these inventive lines, the author gradually began to transform Dame History into an executioner, in order to lead smoothly into Lizinka's own masters exam.

But now, a brisk Dixieland tune swept the audience across the ocean and the suggestive rhythm relaxed them, as the director had intended. All

262

the more surprised and once again electrified were they when a terrible screaming filled the whole school: the twins had dragged in the basket, and, after removing the lid, they jumped on the "client."

Over the years, Wolf had arrived at the bitter realization that if there was a topic woefully neglected in art and journalism, be it out of squeamishness or a lack of information, it was that of execution. But even the few hundred mentions—a mere trifle when compared to the number of, say, acts of coitus described, although in the latter it is always a matter of identical motions—avoid the essential problem: the transportation of the client to the site. He used to complain to the Doctor that it was as if they assumed that after the sentence was pronounced, everyone simply rushes forward to stick his or her head in the noose. In reality, however, even the muscular Karli could display a collection of scars that he had as souvenirs of innumerable sets of teeth and nails, not to mention the number of bruises and bumps that time had healed, and the amounts of dried spittle. That was why the whole of January had been devoted to "Preparing the client," and Wolf wanted to demonstrate the result of this work convincingly. Using as a subject someone from the ranks of the students, no matter how much he would struggle, would have left the impression that it was all a prearranged game; the occupant of the trunk was being saved as the highlight of the evening. The idea that resolved the problem was a stroke of Wolf's genius.

A client of imposing proportions, guaranteed to captivate everyone with his struggle to stay alive, was obtained by Wolf for the price of the meat and two tickets to the masters exams from the man whose courtyard had been the scene of his first encounter with Richard Masin. The brother-in-law of the provincial prison's warden was intrigued by the idea, because success here would resolve his annual hog-slaughtering problem. At noon on examination day, he delivered his surplus swine, and the twins had before them their first live execution.

Although they had spent the entire month of June practicing on Karli, they discovered right off that tying up that patient, good-hearted man and tying up a panicky beast was as different as chalk is from cheese. The hog, up till then lazy and immobile, was now raging like an Arabian stallion, and the boys had their work cut out for them just to keep their faces out of the way of its flying hooves. The decisive moment finally came when Pavel caught the hog from behind in a double nelson and flipped it over onto its back; then Peter tied its hind legs and then its front legs so tightly that he had to loosen the knot for an instant so his brother could remove his hands. The whole time, the animal was giving off entirely unpiglike squeals; if you closed your eyes you would swear you were hearing an hysterical woman screaming for her life.

By the time the boys succeeded in pulling the black "pardon mask"

263

over the pig's head, so that the squealing continued only *con sordino,* they were covered with sweat, in spite of their excellent physical condition, so much so that even the spectators in the back rows could see it. As the spotlight-heated air grew intense with carbon dioxide, so did the sympathies of the audience. A second salvo of applause rewarded the brothers when they managed to drag the noisy lardball to the electric chair, and a third when they succeeded in strapping it in and attaching the electrodes to its bandy legs. The squealing fell silent when they closed the door. Each of the two masters candidates took his place on one side of the control panel.

Looking at the two of them, their hair parted on the left and on the right, trying inconspicuously to catch their breath, Wolf felt compelled to forgive them for all their innocent schoolboy pranks and deceptions; now, when there wasn't a comb in the world that could help them, they were demonstrating the knowledge they had gained, and were doing the school proud. They had to work with low voltages, which still *(Allons, enfants!* You're fighting for your successors, too) was all that HIENS was equipped with. Because of the layers of fat that protected this client better than the average one, and with a view to a desirable tempo for the performance, they had decided it would be better to make the discharges short but intense; the calculations were obtained by the Doctor from some secret computer, and now all they could do was hope that the programmer knew his business. Once again a drumroll sounded.

"Go!" ordered Pavel, and together the two boys pulled the lever up to 1000. Through the big round windows, there was an excellent view of how the first flow of current, referred to as a "blow," made the pig leap; it reminded one of familiar shots of astronauts training in high gravity, when the straps look as if they would burst. But all that happened was that the "pardon mask" loosened and slipped, and after the initial shock, Wolf realized that it was all for the good.

"*Go!*" exclaimed Peter this time, and the two of them grasped the lever fraternally and pushed it to 2000. The "hard blow" lasted only five seconds, but it was enough to make the pig lose all its bristles, as when a butcher scalds it with hot water. At the same time, its eyes literally dissolved, which was very effective without the mask.

"*Go!*" shouted Pavel again, and the lever was brought back down to 1000. After this "blow-up," the tension broke and the animal fell back in the chair; clearly visible were the spasms that passed through its body like waves on the sea. The pig was obviously unconscious and on its last legs.

"*Go!*" barked Peter for the last time, and the lever went up the scale to the maximum, which here was the peak input of an electrical heat-storage stove, 4000 watts. That was what is referred to as the "blow-out," a mercy charge, and the last violent twitch of the lightly browned body was no more than the motor response of the now-dead organism, which only idiots, raged Wolf silently, like the doctors Piedlievre and Fournier in their report to the French Academy could view as the "painful and barbarian inhumanity" of this most modern (what do they want? For the executioner to beat the client to death in his sleep?) of executions. The drumroll ended with a sharp tap of the sticks, and the light in the cabin went out.

There was a storm of applause, joined for the first time by the commission chairman. Wolf breathed a sigh of relief; it seemed that they had finally broken through. Then the lights in the hall dimmed, to facilitate another change of scene, and he realized that now everything was at stake: year zero of the school was about to conclude, and it was the turn of—

—Lizinka. After a few seconds, when the tension in the hall had also peaked, Albert's voice sounded, this time into the darkness:

> Without the stake, the garotte, bullets, gas,
> Our modern world would never have come to pass;
> And now the fates have cleverly assigned
> *The world's first*

Suddenly the spotlights went ı. They were all directed at the lamppost. Under it, on the ashcan, stood Lizinka. She tossed her crown away gracefully in the direction of the gas chamber and dropped the cape from her shoulders. She stood there in the uniform shirt and skirt like the embodiment of emancipated woman, and Albert's voice was like a fanfare:

> —*hangwoman* to aid mankind.
> May she travel with us out to blood-red Mars,
> Svelte as the gallows, chaste as the stars;
> May the grateful planets obey her stern behest,
> For *strangulare humanum est!*

With the last words came the notes of a stirring march, and, in time with the music, an honor guard of four marched into the MODEX from the corridor; under a triumphal arch made of rope, held up on either side by the twins, Albert and Frantisek were pushing a cart with a massive trunk on it. The kids had also succeeded in effecting a quick change, so that their entrance resembled a holiday parade of citizens on a float.

To the sound of rhythmic applause, they marched in place for a while, until Albert gave the signal and they went through the motions that they had rehearsed to precision: Albert himself switched off the tape recorder

265

and a dramatic silence filled the room; the twins placed the trunk on the floor and, after Frantisek and Albert had unlocked the two locks in unison, tipped it over. Doctor Tachezy, sitting uneasily in the front row, clenched his delicate hands into fists: tumbling out of the trunk, curled into a ball, came

58

Simsa.

"But how," asked Wolf in amazement when the Doctor had described in detail the Simsa-Lizinka adventure, from their rendezvous under the statue of the butcher and calf all the way to Lieutenant Hons's return to the erstwhile chapel with a cup of tea, "do you know all this?"

"Why, from Simsa," replied the Doctor.

"But he . . ." Wolf stammered; an hour before, he had seen a crane pull the sports car from the depths, its open doors spewing rivulets of water and white fish bellies.

The Doctor took out his billfold and with it, a photograph. He put the picture on the table in the restaurant booth and took a sip of his wine, not taking his eyes off Wolf. The Polaroid color snapshot showed a man who was indubitably Associate Professor Simsa, a bit shaken but very much alive, smiling into the lens. Under his chin, a bit stiffly, apparently on the instructions of the photographer, he was holding a newspaper, folded so today's date was visible. Wolf realized that the previous morning, when the waters behind the dam were supposed to have closed over Simsa forever, the type for that newspaper hadn't even been set yet.

"But how . . ." Wolf began again, and the Doctor stopped torturing him. He explained that the Associate Professor had appealed to him for help, quite correctly, the previous evening, and that he in turn had succeeded in getting hold of the right people in time. That was why the incident had not gone beyond the doors of the prison. But all the same the Doctor was scandalized. Alerted by the old Masin case, a closer look was taken at HIENS, to determine if someone hostile to the school was enrolled there. Certain documents compromising to Simsa had turned up in the investigation.

"But where . . ." Wolf wanted to ask, but the Doctor was ahead of him.

"He is awaiting sentence," he explained.

"What sentence?" Wolf was finally able to complete a question.

"The supreme one. He has enough for three nooses. Right now he's in some fancy detaining area for the ones who have been checked off, the ones who have officially been buried but who might come in handy someday, and Simsa . . . God knows I was—"

the Doctor sighed,

"—I was fond of him, but all the angrier at his deception, has a mighty big debt to pay. Since he betrayed the school as its first Associate Professor, let him serve it well as its first—"

the Doctor proposed, and Wolf knew then how it applied to the girl,

"—client!"

Simsa was "bagged," as they called it at the hunting lodge, on the morning of the last day in June, as he emerged from the toilet, still dressed in government-issue pyjamas. But the pursuit had, in fact, begun that first Sunday in spring when, after a friendly scolding, they suddenly took away his car keys with the explanation that they were going to detain him for a while, to prepare him for a special mission. Thanks to the Doctor, he felt better; he wanted nothing more—certain that his inexplicable impotence was cured for good—than to embrace Lizinka, and so he objected. But the man who until that moment had had nothing but a pleasant smile for him suddenly turned cold and placed before him a sheet of paper. The old ink had faded a little but it still served to convey Simsa's "confession" that he had liquidated the revolutionary organization along with its commander.

"*. . . and I pledge myself,*" he read with the sensation that he was playing a role in a bad mystery thriller, "*until such time as the sentence should be carried out, to make good my guilt by tireless service to the revolution.*"

He was annoyed that they were now presenting this idiotic IOU, signed when he was a youthful nonentity, to a mature specialist who long since had even improved his punctuation, and when they brought him—this time by helicopter—to the familiar hunting lodge, he felt a twinge of the old pain in his groin. But he soon determined that the place had become a deluxe repository for prominent people prior to important missions.

When, on the way from the toilet, they ordered him to climb inside the steamer trunk, just as he was, so that they could smuggle him into a psychiatric clinic for high state officials, he objected that he hadn't an inkling of what he was to do there. Further instructions, he was told tersely, would be passed on to him upon his arrival by someone whom he knew. Instincts from his stint in the secret army were still intact: he clicked his bare heels and curled up so they could close the lid.

The trunk was a tight fit and poorly ventilated. From the bumping and the noises, Simsa guessed that they were transporting him on the back of a truck, and he tried to view his situation in a more favorable light: he recalled how he had emerged from a mobile cell to a dizzying climb in rank. That reminded him of another trunk, the trunk of the limousine, and the fate of its occupant, and he once again felt uneasy. It didn't help that soon he was drenched with sweat, and after an hour, that he could feel every bone in his body. He was relieved when they unloaded the trunk and carried it somewhere, and then wheeled it somewhere on something with rubber wheels. Unfortunately, when the trunk was set down, it was not opened by anyone he knew, or by anyone he didn't know either. Simsa was doomed to an interminable wait. He was depressed most of all by the fact that the whole time, he hadn't heard a single human voice, and even now, all he could hear was a strange grunting sound, like a pig.

As he had so often in the past, he tried to fall into an unconcerned sleep, but this time it didn't work; he wasn't a young man any more, or a secret soldier; he had plenty to lose and plenty to fear. Fear . . . ? He sniffed the air and was horrified: the odor of his perspiration, sweetened for years with deodorants from abroad, had a sharp and sour edge to it. It was a familiar smell and at first he thought with disgust of urinals, until he realized with dismay that this was exactly the way nine out of ten of his clients start to smell as soon as they set eyes on the gallows, as if they were already beginning to decay from the inside out.

From nearby, he heard the unmistakable squealing of a pig. He felt a panic fear that soon he would be shaken out of the trunk into the maw of a planked corridor echoing with the hoofbeats of the herd, and he, scraping his elbows on the planks, would run for his life until the tunnel disgorged him onto a stone slab, where a cold circle of steel would be pressed to his forehead. He could visualize how, three fingers above the root of his nose, a huge Cyclopean eye was opening, spraying a warm gel—and his stomach flipped over. Once again he mobilized himself, he began to breathe deeply and in fact succeeded in arresting the nausea. The realization that he would not have to start his new mission by having to clean up his own vomit struck him as such an important victory that he was overcome with a sense of euphoria. Then the trunk was moved.

"Ça ira!" he exclaimed to himself to bolster his courage, a motto he had learned from his mentor, and it was as if it had miraculously opened the locks: the trunk lid flew open and he fell out onto the floor.

The fear he had experienced, the nausea he had overcome, the weakness of his senses and his muscles along with the misleading programming he had received made him feel mentally as if he were dreaming and physically as if he were in free-fall. After hours of darkness, the spotlights blinded him and he recognized neither the room nor the faces around him. But all the same, he was the focus of the action.

"Hep!" exclaimed Albert into the deathly silence; they had taken over

268

the monosyllable they had recently heard used by circus acrobats. The twins raised Simsa to the height of their shoulders.

"Hep!" shouted Frantisek, taking the coil of rope and tossing it over the cast-iron arm of the lamppost—they had adopted the method from photos of the streets of Teheran, which showed public executions being conducted using stout poles fitted out with ropes and pulleys. They didn't, however, want to look like copycats, and so they took over only the general method, while the old-fashioned lamppost was supposed to lend ambience to the scene with an image reminiscent of antique prints.

"Hep!" yelled the twins now, bending Simsa's head forward like an angry bull's. Albert's fingers caught the end of the rope as it fell and began to flutter. In a flash, Simsa's neck was encircled by a schnoose that under other circumstances would have had him bursting with pride as a teacher or with envy as a colleague. The foursome was working like a perfect team now, and without exchanging a word, they knew that success was at hand, and that they could transform it into a triumph.

The premonitions of a loving mother are nothing compared to those of a good pedagogue: Wolf realized their intention even before they did, and froze. Hanging a client, a professional at that, albeit a prepared one, without tying his hands was so presumptuous, indeed so brash, that it was challenging the gods. It was an iron-clad rule that the instinct of self-preservation acts faster than the best noose or grip. He was petrified by the image of Simsa coming to his senses, reaching for the lamppost, and pulling himself up with one hand while he loosened the knot with the other, and jumping down in their midst. What then? All right, they could take him! And then? The gas chamber was still no more than a model, the electric chair was occupied by the pig, the guillotine by the mannequin, the shooting range downstairs was not yet completed, and the thread on the garotte was stripped. True, Simsa was not under the jurisdiction of the law and they could do anything they pleased with him, say, decapitate him on the block, but what would their colleagues say to that? That after a year of study, the kids had studied themselves all the way to the Dark Ages? Why are those kids taking (and why am I standing here like an imbecile, when even the greatest maestros do not hesitate to tap the orchestra to a halt in midsymphony?) such chances? *Think!* he wanted to exclaim to them, but they were ahead of him.

"*Hep!*" called Albert, Frantisek, Peter, and Pavel in unison. The first two put all their weight on the end of the rope that was touching the ground and gave it a steady pull while the other two released their burden and joined them. Simsa, his feet crossed under him like a Buddha, was raised over their heads. Precisely as planned, they had knocked the wind and the voice out of him, but that was all. His arms shot upward when all

269

of a sudden his protruding eyes glimpsed at close range—someone known to me, he rejoiced, will give me further instructions—the beloved face of—

—Lizinka. In his fading, deranged consciousness, he was seized by the conviction that he was finally awakening from a horrible dream to a lovely reality. He could hear the sound of rushing water and suddenly knew that he had fallen asleep in the bathtub at his cottage, lulled by the warm water and the girl's body awaiting him. The thought made him drop his hands, which sought the hardness of his erect penis. He had to smile at the dream of his former impotence. He grasped her delicate breasts, but that was another, and the final, dream, because—

—Lizinka, standing on the ashcan, took his chin in her left hand and the nape of his neck in her right, to carry out a one-two jerk that was right out of the

59

textbook.

"Well, if that doesn't take the cake!" Wolf exclaimed angrily, although he knew it wasn't really the porter's fault. His ears were still ringing with the frenetic applause and the calls of "Bravo!", his palms were still tingling from the congratulatory handshakes, and his heart was overflowing with new sensations. When, in addition to the Doctor, even the commission chairman had risen with all the rest to applaud the author-Professor up onto the stage, Wolf felt a surge of pride that had nothing to do with brash conceit, but was rather the justified—and sometimes the only—reward of great men; this, he now knew, was the joy Michelangelo must have felt when he lopped the last bit of stone from his David, or Nobel at the sight of his laboratory in ruins, aware that he had invented dynamite and could establish the great prize. It was no exaggeration, and everyone who came forward to congratulate him said that this thirtieth of June was the zero hour of a new cultural epoch. And as for his pupils, he felt an extraordinary emotion toward them.

When suddenly—Wolf was particularly touched that Simon was among them—they flocked around him and unexpectedly—the Doctor was just apologizing that his duties did not permit him to stay and celebrate and the former Prosecutor jokingly maintained that he was responsible for Wolf's triumph, because, as he now admitted, the ashes of the lynched Hofbauer had revealed nothing incriminating—began tossing him up to the ceiling, so that in passing Simsa's face, he could rejoice at how a clean

270

one-two jerk really does keep the swollen tongue behind the teeth, and forget about conflicts and grades, petty pranks and painful disappointments. He was being tossed and caught by the hands of honest and decent youngsters who for a whole year had confidently placed themselves in his hands like obedient and sensitive instruments without which he would never have been able to perform his great composition. He felt a surge of regret that he would have to part with them, except of course for Lizinka and Albert, and he decided then and there that he would think up a way—attestations or recertifications—not to lose touch with them entirely. Or class reunions—he visualized a parade of past graduates, headed by himself and these pioneers.

"C'était très intéressant et très joli!" a Third World delegate complimented him, confirming Wolf's past hopes by explaining that in his *"patrie"* they still used the primitive method of sending the condemned *"primitivement"* into the jungle, to be devoured by *"quelqu' animal,"* and *"sans contrôle"* at that. "After what I have seen today," he switched into English, "I will suggest to my uncle the president that we introduce hanging." His native land, he continued, was still not prosperous enough to be able to invite consultants with such a "master's know-how," and he stuck out his tongue and placed both index fingers on it, apparently the supreme compliment, but perhaps, he continued, this "splendid idea" would be helpful. Then, in his excitement, he proceeded to switch from one language to another, including his native tongue, suggesting that his *"patrie"* would deliver "bananas and coconuts" in exchange for *"urdli manghi penghe,"* a term he seemed unable to translate; he kept pointing to the finished Simsa until finally he climbed up on the ashcan and touched the tip of his finger to the schnoose. The idea of exporting tied schnooses intrigued Wolf, and NESTOR's deputy promised to follow through on it; indeed, why not, when it meant rare exotic fruit in exchange for a mere idea and a piece of rope.

Wolf would have liked to share his impressions with one of the Tachezys, but he couldn't see Doctor Tachezy anywhere, and the girl was surrounded by her mother, her grandfather, and almost all the guests of honor; amid the general enthusiasm, the commission chairman would not dare deny her an A, which meant that he recognized her as the queen of the exams. When even the foreigner asked if "that hanggirl" were single, Wolf felt a surge of jealousy and desire so strong that he had half a mind to rip her out of their grasp and lock himself in his office with her. He rejected the impulse as undignified and besides, they had made precise plans and he had first to resolve his other major problem. So at least he consoled himself with the thought that soon he would be able to describe his victory in detail to Margaret. But he was blocked for the third time by the sign, GONE TO DENTIST.

271

For a while he stared at it incredulously. Then he ran back through the labyrinth to the courthouse lobby and, contrary to his habit, he began to yell at the porter, who could not help him.

Instead, the man tried to calm Wolf down, saying, "Even Novak's wife has been looking for him!" But that interested Wolf even less.

He realized that it was hopelessly after office hours so that there wasn't anyone who could help him. Not having that stupid piece of paper in his hand threatened to destroy his complex timetable and with it to disrupt a number of human destinies. Just when his impotence, exacerbated by the fact that he had come to it from the height of omnipotence, threatened to bring tears to his eyes, the door from the street opened and in walked the Doctor. His flushed cheeks and rapid breathing indicated his haste. Wolf felt a surge of relief, but before he could speak, the porter began.

"Novak!" he exclaimed, passing on all the abuse that Wolf had heaped on him, "Where the devil have you been all day? The gentleman here—"

he continued, pointing with exaggerated respect to Wolf,

"—has been looking for you since this morning!"

Good heavens, thought Wolf, this fellow has gone mad! He turned to the porter, saying with heartfelt awe, "Listen, that's . . ."

"Yes, I know," the porter nodded respectfully, "that's Novak. The gentleman here—"

he turned back to the Doctor,

"—was on the verge of going to complain to the Chairman, and if it hadn't been for me . . ."

Before Wolf could get a word in to rebuke the porter in stronger terms, the Doctor spoke.

"Thank you very much," he said so abjectly as to almost sound servile, "Mr. Tuma. My upper plate broke in two and they had to make a new mold, don't worry—"

he turned to Wolf so urgently as to almost sound desperate,

"—sir, I'll help you right away, kindly follow me!"

He took Wolf's arm and politely steered him forward to the stairs to the basement. They walked through the labyrinth in silence. It was not until the Doctor had unlocked the grating, removed the shoebox lid with its sign, and guided his guest into a sort of rotunda with tunnels of shelving radiating from it in all directions, that he gave him an exhausted look and spoke.

"May I," he asked, "help you?"

"We've lost," mumbled Wolf, "our marriage certificate . . ."

"Ah," said the Doctor, "why didn't you say something? I'd have . . . but you can make it anyway, you aren't due for twelve minutes yet, are you? Kindly take a seat."

272

Removing his jacket, he indicated the only chair in the room, a sign that whoever worked there did not encourage long visits. Wolf stared at the shirt with the patched elbows. Then the Doctor took a cotton working smock from a nail on the wall and with an apologetic smile disappeared down one of the tunnels.

Wolf sat up and started to look around with urgency, in the effort to find some explanation. Nothing in this room differentiated it from dozens of others: shelves, filing cabinets, ladders, walls, and linoleum-covered floors. Only one item indicated a clue to the personality of its occupant: almost hidden between two stacks of papers on the desk was the photograph of a woman. The frame was decorative, made of hammered copper; the woman had a peevish, disagreeable expression. Wolf felt as if his head were a glass of tea, leaves and all, that had just been stirred: innumerable particles were floating about, but would not coagulate into a coherent idea.

"Is your wife's name Margaret?"

Wolf jumped when the Doctor spoke from beside him.

"Yes."

"Here," said the Doctor, handing him a yellowed document, "is the original, which shouldn't leave the office, but we don't have time to copy it, so take it, just kindly be sure to return it."

"Yes," said Wolf, and then he forced himself to add, "thanks . . ."

"I," said the Doctor—and Wolf grasped for the saving thought that this might be the Doctor's exact double—"thank you again, the success was yours, but perhaps I can justify my delay by reporting that the response was even more significant than you know. HIENS—"

the Doctor continued, confirming once and for all his identity,

"—won out completely, and the rewards won't be long in arriving. But please, I'd like to use the remaining—"

—he looked again at his watch,

"—seven minutes for myself. Yes, my name is Novak and I never got a doctoral degree. Nonetheless, the fact that I let them call me Doctor is not to further my career, but rather for a worthy cause. While you were predestined to be a teacher, fate made me into a weakling, forever ill and teased by my peers and ridiculed by insensitive parents, which inspired in me the burning desire to become an executioner. Yes—"

he nodded, registering Wolf's amazement,

"—I wanted nothing more than to be able, with my own two hands and with impunity, to kill them all, and my toy chest concealed playthings that would have given my parents a heart attack had they ever bothered to examine them: from a primitive thumbscrew to a relatively sophisticated model of a guillotine capable of slicing a pencil in two; my childish frustrations deserted me along with my adolescence, but the era of war crimes, though it didn't affect me the way it did—"

remarked the Doctor, interrupting Wolf's wondering about how he should address him now,

"—you, made me spend all the time I could spare from my studies and my love life researching the supreme penalty and becoming its staunch proponent, I said love life—well, I encountered love early on when I fled to the arms of a woman considerably older than myself for the protection and tenderness which I was denied by my parents. That and her—"

the Doctor lowered his voice as this intimate passage filled him with discomfort,

"—mature passion made me emotionally and physically dependent on her, something that might be condemned by some young fool but not by a man of your experience. At the outset it seemed to be a good thing that my wife, yes, she married me the day I came of age, so that I might not, as she said, be at the mercy of the elements, well, my wife was a clerk in the judiciary administration. I heard from her that they were looking for someone to replace old Hus and volunteered at once, but she declared that I wasn't going to put my good name in jeopardy unless the rewards were considerably higher. In vain did I object that it wasn't all that good a name—she was bluffing, she had read somewhere that the executioner has the right of the last night with beautiful clients—and what had to happen happened, the state, which never likes to pay, decided to resolve the problem another way. I never finished my studies—she was afraid that I might fall for some scheming coed, and when they refused to let her into the lecture hall with me because she had no student ID and she looked too old, she accused the coeds of being whores and took me home with her once and for good. I'm not—"

the Doctor hurried to add, raising both hands, palms out,

"—complaining, I'm just taking the opportunity to make a friend outside of my incognito status. And so I wound up here, without any skills, which for some reason seems to satisfy my wife to this day. The first years passed and then one day the Regional Prosecutor called me after he'd lost a classified file. I put it together for him out of the archives here and in exchange obtained admission to an execution, that was the time you were doing the blind man, remember—"

the Doctor asked urgently, and Wolf, though he couldn't recall a thing, nodded eagerly, admitting to himself that the Doctor would have had the same magical effect on him even if he were in charge of the toilets,

"—him? Under the gallows, with a finger to your lips to ensure our silence, you assured him that he had been pardoned and that you were just taking his measure for—"

the Doctor mimicked Wolf's long-forgotten gestures, and Wolf recollected his early efforts at a psychological approach to his clients,

"—a suit. It gave me an idea: the next time the prosecutor, who would have been lost without me, had to give me three and then five and later on even more admission chits, which I in turn secretly offered to other gentlemen who wanted something from the files, and gradually built up my reputation as a man with influential contacts and perhaps two occupations. The stormy era turned into a huge merry-go-round, so that when you were doing the Regional Prosecutor, I was there again, except that I got my admission chit from his deputy who used to get his from me, and when the third round passed through your hands, I was simply the Doctor and no one knew about this hole any more, while my wife to this day knows nothing—"

he laughed and Wolf had to admit that he would never cease to be amazed by this man,

"—about the Doctor. Think what you will of me, but I have punished her this way for all she deserves. She does not know and will never know that her little gray mouse is in fact an *éminence grise,* with the power to influence the highest decision-making in spheres of life and—"

the Doctor slammed his round little fist onto the desk until even the framed photograph jumped,

"—death! I make no bones about its being at least in part the result of the times, when the most delicate instructions are given orally since no one is willing someday to bear the responsibility for them or to let himself be spat upon in history books. But above all it was thanks to my own strategies and cleverness, God, and—"

now the Doctor addressed him with uncharacteristic bathos,

"—you, Frederick, are my witnesses that I never took advantage of it for my own person, but rather in the interest of all men of good will who are protected by Capital Punishment from extinction, so I leave it to you whether the man called the Doctor, extensively feared but to you no longer an enigma, should continue to exist, or whether the only one to survive should be the harmless but totally useless—"

he concluded with an unexpected question mark,

"—Novak?"

"And why, then, do you keep her picture here?"

"Because," replied Novak, "she comes in here to check up on me, and also because I use my imagination to transpose her into the execution that I have just witnessed, so that now, after your masters exams, I'll have the blissful pleasure of imagining that harpie being buried alive, drowned in a sack, impaled on a stake, decapitated, roasted like a hog, and on top of it all, hanged like a used rubber from a lamppost. What—"

he exclaimed and, enthralled by the thought, he clapped his hands together,

"—a joy!"

Meanwhile, outside in the corridor, there was a sound that Wolf identified by associating two bits of data.

"The porter," he said quickly, "mentioned something about her having been looking for you . . ."

"When?" The Doctor was aghast. "Why didn't you . . ."

From outside, the doorknob was turned briskly and the door was more forced in than opened.

"Good evening," both men said to her impersonally. . . .

"The plaintiff," the woman intoned, "realized that her jealousy was unfounded, since throughout the marriage the defendant had conducted himself both in the home and in his job in an exemplary manner. Nonetheless, she remained jealous, and when the defendant reproached her, she denied him his rights in the marital bed, out of wounded pride, which led to the further alienation of the two parties. Even though the parties displayed good intentions, reconciliation did not occur and at this time, the relationship has deteriorated to the point where the plaintiff and the defendant no longer have any emotional bond between them. Because this marriage has thus ceased to fulfill its social function since they are unable to consummate it with offspring, this court declares the marriage of

60

Margaret and Frederick Wolf null and void—"

recited the female judge, laying the paper down,

"—by virtue of divorce. The decree will be sent to you in duplicate, to what address?"

"I beg your pardon?" Wolf asked, confused.

"Where," the judge asked, this time with a noticeable lack of formality, "do we send the papers?"

"Why," Wolf said, "to our place . . . !"

"I just thought I'd ask," the judge said amiably, starting to unbutton her robe, "since you just got divorced."

"Oh!" Wolf saw what she meant. "I forgot. Well, send it—"

he came to his senses, but he repeated uneasily,

"—to our place anyway, we'll both be staying there . . ."

"Whatever you say."

276

As Wolf, depressed, had run up the stairs from the basement, he had paused on the last step to gaze with admiration toward the courtroom door. As they had planned, Margaret Wolf had come here dressed for the evening's program; she wore a long, sheer dress with spectacular pleated sleeves that opened out like a fan when she raised her arms; it contrasted sharply with her short hair, bleached white on Wolf's request. Although she had never set eyes on Lizinka, some sort of intuition made Margaret stress each detail that differentiated her from the girl, even transforming her years into an asset.

Wolf felt a twinge of pain that less than a week ago, this noble beauty—he clenched his teeth with rage—was being humped by a young snot who probably had never done anything but masturbate before. Once again he felt a surge of desire so intense that he was tempted to take Margaret in his arms and possess her right there on the stairs, and then to drag her away, as far as possible from that door behind which their kinship would be dissolved by a simple sheet of paper. He had to remind himself in all haste that he had insured himself fully against just that loss, and that this crisis was in fact the living water that was reviving—in the final week of their marriage, they had made love every day—their half-dead love.

"We thank you very much," said Wolf after signing his name below Margaret's. They had plenty to be thankful for: the judicial act that the Doctor had arranged, and through which, by an irony of fate, the Doctor's own secret had been uncovered, had taken place at Wolf's convenience, and on the spot, without delays.

"Don't mention it," said the judge, wrapping her robe in a plastic bag from which she had taken a bathing suit.

"Here," said Wolf, handing her an envelope. "Buy yourself an ice cream cone!" His jest concealed some irritation—after all, he had sworn to eliminate corruption, and besides, nobody ever gave *him* a tip. But on the other hand, he could not refuse to honor the Doctor's suggestion, since the "clever little judge" whom the Doctor had recruited for the proceedings had had to make a special trip into town from her vacation cottage.

But the judge refused to accept the money.

"That's all right," she said to his surprise, "it wasn't any bother."

"Oh, but you had to make," he objected politely, "a special trip to town."

"Well then," she replied quickly, as if she had learned it by heart, "if-you-really-insist, my-boyfriend-has-a-bright-little-brother, maybe-you-could-give-him-a-chance?"

"How do you . . ." Wolf gasped and corrected himself, "what are you talking about?"

"Oh, I'm sorry, I forgot," said the judge uneasily, and now, when she looked like an embarrassed schoolgirl, Wolf fleetingly registered surprise that anyone so young could be on the bench, "to introduce myself. My name is Zelenka."

"Pleased to meet you," he said, perturbed. "But that doesn't explain—"

"Willi," she interrupted him, "Zelenka is my father. He would have taken your case himself but he was busy today with those so-called dissidents!"

A picture surfaced in Wolf's mind: the miserable old man in the crowded bus, lisping his boasts about his daughter's finally getting "into univerfity." Then he heard the voice of the Doctor: "When she's told, she'll start distributing long sentences and nooses . . ." He turned to her with new interest: in any case she had done the divorce like a trooper.

"Oh, that's right, Suzanne," he said, "now I remember. Here, write down the boy's name and address for me. . . ."

"My dear Professor," she said, tremulous at her mission and at his proximity, "allow me once again, now that we are alone, to congratulate you with all my heart on your life's success, and to thank you for the care you have devoted to our

61

children!"

Lucie Tachezy had been charged by the rest of the parents with the task of delivering the speech, since it was her idea in the first place. The idea of establishing contact with Wolf in this unusual manner, allowing herself to gaze long and directly into his eyes, and to transmit along with the innocent words her own intimate message, was one that had occurred to her right after Wolf's departure on Saturday. She suffered a bit of a shock when Doctor Tachezy, whose opinion she had asked just as a formality, had sat right down to compose the speech for her; she had to go to all the trouble of evoking a new conflict to make him retreat again into the bathroom so she could get out that night to see Oscar. Once there, she unsettled Ossi by insisting that he turn off all his sexy lights, which deprived his lustful eyes of considerable pleasure; imagine his dismay if he had only known that in his irresistible embrace, she was surrendering her body to Wolf! Sunday morning she found the text of the speech on the threshold of the bedroom, along with the coffee. . . .

From the beginning, it had been planned to hold the graduation party in the school proper, and NESTOR's original objections had been countered by Wolf with the contention that it was supremely important that the parents get a taste of the school's atmosphere, and besides, if they were all going to get drunk, that it would be better behind locked and barred doors. Later on, it was specifically determined what each family would bring to drink and to eat. No one could have guessed that a simple oversight, the kind that as a rule turns into a calamity, would instead present them with an unexpected feast.

When the delighted spectators finally left—after Wolf's departure, Albert had taken over the role of host, confirming his rapidly growing authority—and the kids were washing up and changing while the parents joined Karli in setting up the refreshments and getting acquainted, they all smelled a delicious, familiar fragrance. Looking for its source, Karli opened the door to the chamber with the electric chair—and rushed for the fire extinguisher.

Peter and Pavel had worked so hard at getting the electrocution right that they could even have brought it off without any current. But as it was, in the intoxication of the applause—which can upset even an experienced matador, much less a beginner—they had neglected at the conclusion of their piece to pull the rheostat down to zero. The lever was left at about a hundred and eighty, and the pig was left to roast. After Albert confirmed that no one was in any danger of being burned as long as they didn't touch the skin, they began basting the animal to make the roast juicier, and under the chair, they stood all the metal vessels that went with the guillotine—the students used to call them head-catchers—to collect the drippings.

The festive board—in addition to the school, there were Mr. and Mrs. Hus, Frantisek's parents, the Tachezys and Mr. Alexander, the mother of the twins and their two fathers—was the product of the ingenuity of the kids: they took the long, horizontal torture rack from the CLASEX and laid the two sections of the school blackboard on top of it, using as a tablecloth the black fabric they had used in January when they were practicing covering a classical scaffold. For the present, only two people were seated there—an old man a young woman. Hus senior, who long since had been obliged to come to terms with the loss of his beloved vocation, was now shattered by the failure of his only son, Simon, and it was all the harder for him since the lad had been conceived with considerable difficulty after Hus's release from prison, in the last-ditch effort to ensure that the famous line of the Masters of the Blade of Justice did not die out; he would have liked to go home, but he thought that perhaps by his presence he might induce them to allow his son to be retested.

Lizinka had on the satanic satin she had worn on the escapade with Wolf, and was seated beside Mr. Hus, observing Associate Professor

279

Simsa who—since Wolf's abrupt departure for the courthouse had made them forget to ask for instructions—had been left hanging from the lamppost; they had just fastened the rope to the ashcan so that he not fall and hurt himself. Simsa's right eye protruded as if he were giving her a comical grimace; his left was almost shut as if he were giving her a coquettish wink. The index finger of his left hand was raised as if he were threatening her; his right hand was closed tight. His limbs and his face were a dirty white except for a dark circle where his legs met. After a while, Lizinka knew Simsa by heart, but she kept on studying him; she was going over her exam again in an effort to ignore the sizzling roast and the tempting delicacies: she was hungry as a horse.

Frantisek, who had been posted at the entrance, came running in from the corridor. "He's coming!" he shouted.

In a flash, the kids set up a double file to lead Wolf from the door to the parents, and at the end stood the trembling Lucie. Wolf, anxiously observing the response—after all, it was the first time Margaret had seen the place—crossed their plans by first going to his office. Margaret wanted to fix her face, and he wanted to do something that both prudence and his sense of fair play told him he must: for the third time he dialed the number that had always made his fingers tremble. As before, all he heard was a series of rings.

As soon as they had found themselves, happily divorced, sitting—he hadn't used the official car so as not to subject Margaret to Karli, who, as Simsa used to say, smacked of the cemetery—in a taxicab, holding hands the way Wolf liked, because that way some of her calmness entered him and tamed his own energy, he returned in his thoughts to the dismal crypt where the court documents lay moldering. He still felt the wave of bitterness that had welled up during the conversation until he was overwhelmed by the female behemoth. Although the man with the patched elbows had until that moment been the only person in the country he had feared, Wolf did not feel relieved; on the contrary, he felt like a sensitive child when he sees through a keyhole that the presents under the Christmas tree weren't brought by Santa Claus but by his father, in a sweaty undershirt, ill-tempered and cursing. The existence of the enigmatic Doctor made him feel that the forces of progress, which he had aided in a modest way by the exercise of his vocation, resembled Greek tragedies, which, seen in perspective, turn out to be puppet shows, with the jesting gods pulling the strings. Wolf had believed that there was, over him, the political Mount Olympus of his country, and above that, a sort of super Olympus that calmly surveyed, over the mountains of excrement exuded daily by the human race and through the fog of lies promulgated by a continually renewed class of criminal elitists dedicated to hoodwinking and exploiting humanity, a distant promised land in which man would

280

cease to be—and this expression always set Wolf back on his heels—a wolf toward his fellow man. Now he had to try to come to grips with the idea that perhaps the mass trials and the subsequent rehabilitations of those convicted, followed by the rehabilitations of their judges, were not a part of a brilliant if impenetrable plan, but only the wild skidding and maelstroms of an epoch directed by everyone and no one, so that it was entirely possible that the ones to have the last laugh would be those who had been done, and that even executioners might be abandoned in the *oubliettes* of history—or even end on the gallows. No, it was not for himself that Wolf felt fear, but for his school, and above all, now, for his son as well! Yes, the very one who would receive his body from Lizinka and from Wolf, his soul, he was the one who stood to lose the most if the Doctor were to be destroyed . . .

His morose reflections were broken off by an idea so surprising that Wolf dug his fingernails into Margaret's hand. She winced, but she immediately regained control, accustomed as she was to having patients bite her hand. But why in fact *should* the Doctor be destroyed? The only one who had unmasked him, as a result of an absurd coincidence, was he, Wolf! But *was* he in fact the only one? Could there have been other such coincidences, but those who had unearthed the secret had arrived at the same decision: the mighty Doctor must nt be allowed to fall on account of the mousy Novak? And had he really unmasked him? What if the Doctor had taken on the guise of Novak in order that he might be all the more the Doctor! Wolf tried that bit of nonsense on for size and decided that with a little effort it could be a workable hypothesis, particularly if he were to aid it himself . . .

"Yes . . ." said the familiar voice at the other end, but today it sounded palpably exhausted.

"This is the Chairman," Wolf said as usual. He was afraid that the man on the other end might ruin things, and so he continued with even greater servility than usual. "May I speak to you for a moment?"

"But of course . . ." the voice grew uncertain.

Wolf had always visualized him living in a modern apartment, with an austere study resembling a telecommunications center; suddenly he could picture a middle-class apartment, musty-smelling and stuffed with bric-a-brac, the telephone on a shelf next to the front hall closet so the user could squeeze in among the overcoats for privacy. He swallowed his discomfort and did not change the tone of his voice.

"Doctor," he said in a manner both obsequious and categorical, "you are urgently needed at the school. May I send a car for you?"

Wolf had always thought that the Doctor was transported by a special unit that had at its disposal countless vehicles of a variety of makes, with interchangeable license plates, cars which could easily be transformed—

he had seen the Doctor riding in them a number of times—into taxis. Now he realized that they had in fact been real taxis, and that he had sometimes even taken the bus.

"Car?" countered the Doctor, sounding uneasy, as if he knew exactly what Wolf was thinking.

"My JANT," Wolf hastened to add, to convince him that it hadn't so much as occurred to him, "is on his way down, he could be there before yours could."

There was silence at the other end of the line. Novak, don't drop the ball now, Wolf pleaded silently.

"One moment, please!" said the voice, adding, as he always did, "let me check my calendar."

Wolf was relieved, even though he guessed now that the calendar was and always had been the Doctor's wife. He heard a knock. "Yes," he said into the receiver, before realizing that it had been at his office door.

Karli entered and clicked his heels. With a sharp gesture, Wolf signaled him to be silent.

"Are you still there?" asked the Doctor sharply.

"Y–yes . . ." stammered Wolf, surprised.

"I'll be at the usual place in half an hour. Goodbye."

Wolf formulated his orders slowly and carefully and as usual, had Karli repeat them three times over.

"Yes, sir, chief," Karli said. Then his brain, dulled by countless knockouts, performed an unexpected feat when after so many other stimuli it recalled the message he had arrived with, albeit in a simplified form: "They're waiting for you—the pig and ASP and all of them!"

He ran out. Wolf had not understood him, and had not even tried. He was thinking over what had just happened and in his mind, he exclaimed, *Novak est mort, vive le Docteur!*

A moment later, Lucie Tachezy forgot her carefully memorized speech; try as she might, her mind would not serve her, and she was glad that she could dredge up enough words to get out of it without any major embarrassment.

"And we wish you health and wealth and," she concluded vaguely, "a speedy recovery . . . !"

Lucie yearned to find out who that chic-looking woman with Wolf was: the romantic dress and the white hair seemed to place her in that category of women who from childhood have tried to look older, to emphasize their animal vitality. Her curiosity would have to wait a while because Wolf, after shaking hands with Albert, was exchanging words with one family after another. His companion, whom he introduced with such decorum that Lucie could not even read his lips, gave each of the parents and pupils a charming smile, but then she stepped back as if she were mute. In fact, however, Margaret was observing

Lizinka. First of all, she congratulated herself on her own appearance and above all on having accepted Wolf's offer: only now did she realize how generous it really was. After seeing that gentle loveliness, marred only, as she now knew, by a single, well-concealed laceration, she wondered that she still—yes, again—got to sleep with Wolf. The girl appealed to Margaret so much that she had difficulty suppressing the impulse to walk right up to her and touch—she could almost hear the fiery hiss—the materialized sunshine that was her hair. But soon I'll be able—she was startled to realize—even to brush it. Why, I'll even be able—she let her imagination wander—to bathe her and—she pictured the broad, sunken bathtub that used to serve her and Wolf more often than their bed—perhaps even to bathe with her! And what if—she smiled for the first time since the arrival of her red rider—I really am a Roman lad . . . ?

Wolf first chatted briefly with Hus and his wife. On the wings of success, he promised them that he would try to get the commission to retest the boy in September. In exchange, Hus senior promised to coach his son all summer and, if he failed again, to sign him up as an apprentice butcher.

The exchange with the mother and fathers of the twins was all compliments. Wolf praised the boys and the family praised the school. And he heard what he had expected to hear: the two men, each of whom had recently been promoted, foresaw that in their new bailiwick the number of maximum sentences would show a marked increase. "And why," said the judge, and the prosecutor nodded, "should such a large district wait until someone from the capital finds the time?"

"Why not," asked the prosecutor, to the nod of the judge, "have district executioners who are familiar with local traditions and respect local customs?" The plural indicated that he meant the twins. The satisfaction that filled Wolf, rather than fear for his livelihood, proved to him that he had become a teacher, heart and soul.

The meeting with Frantisek's parents was the heartiest of all. He had not been a disappointment, but he hadn't been all that successful either, and his father had arranged in advance that the boy get the choice post of librarian in the prison where he worked. And whenever Wolf came to the prison for an execution, he would have a helper on the spot. That gave Wolf the idea that he might place future graduates this way for a start, before the export trade got under way. As was their custom from their worksites, they exchanged a few crude (the father) and a few delicate (the Professor) jokes, the mother invited the Wolfs to the prison ball, and they parted friends.

Lucie's nervousness turned into dismay when she began collecting her family and couldn't find her husband. Doctor Tachezy was close by, though: he was in the gas chamber with the door shut, and as he observed the action in the room—it resembled a silent film—he sat thinking. He responded immediately to his father-in-law's first call and joined his family in time.

"And to you, my dear lady," Wolf said to Lucie when he raised his lips from her hand, "I want to express my thanks in a number of areas, but let me start by thanking you for your kind words, which I appre—"

he interrupted himself apologetically in midword,

"—I haven't introduced my . . . actually, if I'm to adhere to etiquette, I ought to say, I haven't introduced you—"

he turned from Lucie to Margaret and his heart pounded as he realized the moment of truth had come, all the more dangerous in that it was based on a lie, albeit a holy one, after he had proven to Lizinka on Tuesday and the next morning to Margaret that he was unable to live without the one or the other, he had concentrated his entire intellect on the problem, and now he would see if he had truly found the answer to the question, to what woman would his new wife and his new mother-in-law be willing to relinquish some of their claims on him,

"—to my mother."

"How do you do—I am Mrs. Wolf," said Margaret Wolf, revealing her beautiful teeth that had never needed a dentist, "but my friends all call me Margaret and I am certain that—"

she spoke directly to Lucie, as she reached out her hand with majestic nonchalance to the two men to kiss,

"—we shall be friends, since what we have in common is the people who are the dearest to us!"

All it took was those few moments for Lucie to decide that the infantile dress, the hair color that best conceals gray, and the teeth, obviously of foreign manufacture, placed this woman in the category of those who for years had been trying to look younger to escape the approach of old age. Moved, she stepped forward and embraced Margaret. The flat chest that she encountered confirmed for her that this would-be Garbo was—her emotion changed to triumph—just an old lady. She decided immediately to become her friend, because that would best open the door to him.

Wolf was relieved. He had penetrated the Tachezys' last bastion, where everything would be decided man to man. With the certainty that Margaret was covering his back and attending to the mother, he sallied forth to take on the father.

"Professor," Mr. Alexander spoke up unexpectedly, in words that he had been rehearsing ever since the previous day when to his amazement and joy, his daughter had delivered Wolf's greetings with the invitation for this evening, "I've decided—"

he continued, opening an old engineering tool case and removing a large package from it,

"—to bring you something, a small but valuable token of my gratitude, since you have done more for my grand-daughter than many—"

he concluded disdainfully, with no effort to conceal which one he was talking about,

"—a relative, and for that I must thank you very much indeed."

While Wolf, uncomprehending, was removing the decorative gift wrapping, wondering feverishly how to get out of this blind alley, Doctor Tachezy was as certain as a prophet of what was inside. And yet, it took his breath away all the same when after more than sixteen years, he once again set eyes on the treasure for which he had been willing to make the greatest sacrifice in his life, and which had eluded him like a mirage: the Leipzig edition of Sturz's Wolfenbüttel manuscript, popularly known as *Etymologicum Gudianum*. He was on the verge of grabbing the folio and fleeing with his prize to a desert island, because he knew that he wouldn't ever be bored with it, not until the day he died, but then he realized that he was separated from the wide, wide word by a series of barred doors. He hung his head.

On Friday, Wolf had taken a note from the Doctor and paid a visit to the Computer Technology Center; this innocent title concealed the police data bank. The data on the Tachezys now proved invaluable. Capricious as life sometimes is, he would unfortunately have to insult the donor, but there was no time for regrets: the priorities were clear.

"I am," he said to Lizinka's grandfather, "deeply obliged to you, and I shall always consider it an honor that you thought of me, but because today I shall be depriving you of another—"

he continued, taking one step forward and another to the side, so that he ended up fortuitously beside Lizinka and placed his free hand on her shoulder like a proud pedagogue,

"—priceless possession, I hope I am acting entirely in keeping with your intentions—"

he explained, gazing with all sincerity into the gold-rimmed spectacles,

"—Mr. Alexander, if I place this one into the worthy hands of someone more competent; I am referring to—"

he added, handing the book to Doctor Tachezy,

"—your son-in-law."

Alexander looked as if he were on the verge of exploding—something that Wolf knew he had to prevent at all costs. Catching a supportive glance from Margaret, he drew Lizinka close like a fast friend. Then he braced himself and took his *salto mortale*.

"For that matter," he said, "my dear Mrs. Tachezy, Mr. Alexander, and Doctor Tachezy, your joy at Lizinka's success is not to be your only joy today. Perhaps it might have been more seemly to make the announcement in your home or in a fancy restaurant, but I think that there is no better place to settle a covenant than on a victorious battlefield, and so I make bold to declare, here and now, that I love—"

Wolf spoke intensely but softly, so as not to attract attention outside their immediate circle, ostensibly holding a simple friendly exchange a few steps away from Simsa, whose corpse had been rotated by a gust of warm air until it seemed as if he were spying on them,

"—Lizinka and Lizinka loves me, and so, dear parents and—"

he turned to Mr. Alexander, whom he needed to appease,

"Grandpapa and you, my dear—"

he turned to Margaret, whom he wanted to assure that the inner intensity of his feelings was unchanged, even though the external form was changing,

"—mama, we beg you to give us your blessing."

A heavy silence followed. Finally Mrs. Tachezy spoke.

"But," she said, forgetting that moments ago she had been dreaming of Wolf's embrace; as her viewpoint changed from that of a yearning woman to that of a decisive mother, she now saw a man who was well preserved but all the same, politely stated, of a considerable age, perhaps, she suddenly suspected, even older than her own father, "that's impossible!"

Even stronger than her reasons for not wanting him as a son-in-law came the urge to have him as a lover, and that prevented her from firing at him from the most effective guns, indeed, from firing at him at all! She resorted to a stratagem. If there was anything of which Lucie was absolutely convinced, it was the position that Doctor Tachezy would take in this matter, and she decided to put him in the front lines.

"Emil"—she turned to him in a tone that placed all the responsibility on his shoulders—"you decide."

In all of what was now almost seventeen years, Doctor Tachezy reflected, he had done nothing to improve the life of his beloved wife or to equip his adored daughter for her future. Now a man had turned up who would do it for him. This man, thought Doctor Tachezy, gazing at Simsa's corpse, had equipped Lizinka for her future in a single year to the point where she was able to settle accounts with a brutal pervert with her own delicate hands. This man had succeeded with a few words in making the mirage of the Sturz folio materialize in his own hands, and the father-in-law hadn't dared to say a word. Doctor Tachezy had no illusions that Wolf was guided by any fondness for him. But all the more did he realize that if at the critical moment he were to be instrumental in the consummation of the union, finally he too would be able to cull the fruit that he could place at the feet of his wife. A glance at the silent Simsa and it was as though he heard the bell and knew for whom it tolls; for bus drivers who shortchanged him, fish vendors who handed him carefully wrapped pipe instead of fresh pike, waiters who brought porridge instead of pork sausage, and, above all, for all those Oscars who had for seventeen years been trying to seduce his wife. They all marched before his eyes, and each of them was done with a different technique, but with an end as final as Simsa's. And he hadn't had to do a thing but point a finger at them for *his people, his family,* which was finally being raised from the misery into which it had been cast by three generations of bookworms, up past the millers, higher, past the engineers, all the way up to people like Wolf, who represented the sum total of the highest achievements of human thought and deed. . . . "The executioner," the quotation came to his mind, "requires a special designation in the family of man. Remove this incomprehensible element from the world, and in a moment order becomes chaos, thrones collapse, society vanishes." And then came the piteous voice of his wife, appealing to him for the first time ever for a final decision. Doctor Tachezy rose to the challenge. He stepped toward his daughter and her suitor, placed one hand—without relaxing his hold on the Sturz, for safety's sake—on each of their shoulders, as if to close an emotional circle, and embraced them.

"Be," he said simply, "happy."

The applause that followed was not for them, but for the Doctor, entering the CLASEX followed by Karli. Wolf was certain that thanks to the father's unexpected maneuver, his and Lizinka's ship had narrowly averted collision with two torpedos, and he wanted to decide the battle before the mother and the father-in-law had time to reload.

"Thank you, thank you," he addressed the two of them. "One moment."

So saying, he moved to meet the Doctor, retaining his hold on Lizinka's hand so that he drew her with him. Even now, he was applying the basic injunction from the chapter on "Preparing a Client"—under no circumstances pause in the task until the client is done!

"Doctor!" he exclaimed, "thank you for coming. I am preparing to conclude the school year, but the youngsters, the parents, and I simply cannot go our separate ways without your blessing, which is why we were bold enough to disturb the obviously pressing work of the man who is responsible for the launching of our—"

concluded Wolf, just as he and Lizinka, who had graciously taken the guest's other arm, brought the Doctor to the head of the table,

"—school! We hereby," he spoke as if he were on a podium, but without addressing those present, so as to avert any other prospective speeches, "conclude our first and unprecedented school year—an experiment and yet the first serious step on the path of life for you, its first students, and also a severe test for you, the first parents, since you too were tested, a test of your—"

he continued, gazing emphatically at Mrs. Tachezy,

"—civic maturity. Thanks to you, all those who will follow, and let me tell you that the applicants who are beating—"

he continued, gazing reproachfully at Margaret,

"—down our doors, will be spared a great deal of the fumbling and the errors that accompany anything new. That does not mean, of course, that we intend to walk the well-trodden path year after year, oh, no! I and my—"

he continued, gazing confidently at Albert and Karli,

"—fellow workers will do everything in our power to see to it that HIENS continues in its development toward ever higher—"

he continued, gazing challengingly at the Doctor,

"—institutions of education, so that ever new opportunities might be opened to our field of endeavor by the merging of the oldest of traditions with the most progressive—"

he continued, once again striving for Mr. Alexander's favor,

"—technology, and I can take this opportunity to announce in all pride that at our school, a machine has come into existence which for the first time mechanizes the most extensively used means of execution, and will soon save the efforts of executioners—"

and Wolf clapped his hands and Karli went behind the gas chamber and wheeled out an oblong rectangular object on wheels, covered with a canvas tarp,

"—the world over. On Friday it was finally patented and now for the first time I can—"

and Wolf clapped again and Karli pulled the tarp from the white table, with its dark-red linoleum top,

"—present it to the public and reveal that it has been named after its inventors—"

and Wolf glanced eagerly at Lizinka, for whom he had prepared this surprise as a reward for passing her exams and as a foretaste of all the gifts he would shower on her when she gave him a son,

"—WOTAN, or—"

modestly, Wolf quoted the clever suggestion of the Doctor, who deemed it immoral that Simsa's name might wind up in the textbooks, and on the other hand considered it only fitting that the scoundrel's would-be victim and her future husband be named as his heirs—a suggestion that made Wolf decide to offer the Doctor one-third of the profits,

"WOlf–TAchezy Neckbreaker, a hanging machine that is suitable, by dimension and design, even for use on a—"

288

joked Wolf in earnest,

"—spaceship; and now let me return from outer space to matters closer to ourselves, I would like to join our dear Lizinka Tachezy, who today became the first hangwoman of the world literally by a—"

Wolf's little joke was modified by his serious tone,

"—breast, since the world press reports that in Singapore, twenty-year-old Anita Chuan is expected to rise to the same office there, and to share with you the joy we feel since her and my families have given their blessings to our—"

Wolf had to raise his voice, because by then as planned, Margaret had already begun to applaud, to carry the others along,

"—betrothal."

Margaret's applause seemed to open wide the floodgates of approval; what followed was an ovation.

Wolf walked over to the only two who were silent and sullen. First he grasped Mr. Alexander's hand and shook it so adroitly that the father-in-law seemed to be cooperating. Then he turned to Lucie and kissed her so competently that not only did she seem to be kissing him back, but indeed, she was. He then cut the kiss short, and with the exquisite timing of a politician embraced Doctor Tachezy, whereupon he touched glasses with the Doctor, implying with a glance that this was a special day, one on which rank could be ignored. The Doctor understood.

They heard singing. Albert had sounded the note and the youngsters started in with a song that the future Assistant—and surely soon to become Associate—Professor had secretly been teaching them since early June, when he had, inspired by the poetic creativity of his mentor, added a verse to the classical lyrics.

> *Gaudeamus igitur,*
> *juvenes dum sumus!*

Wolf embraced his love so firmly that his huge hand quite encompassed the small breast. He felt the nipple stiffen. At the same time, he caught Margaret's benevolent and warmly approving gaze. *Darling,* his eyes telegraphed back, *thank you, and I won't forget you either!* He became rather excited by the thought that someday when Lizinka would be away on a business trip, or overcome by her red rider, or giving birth to his son, he would once again make love to the slim, cool body of his Roman lad.

> *Gaudeamus igitur,*
> *juvenes dum sumus . . .*

repeated the youngsters. And what, Wolf suddenly thought, if some hot summer evening, when all three of them were home in next to nothing, what if he were to succumb to a wave of emotion, of passion, and embrace them both? As soon as he had Lizinka not only before God and the world, but also before the law, as soon as she was completely at home with him, the reasons for the holy lie would vanish! And then why couldn't the two women who love him make love to him together?

Nestor, Doctor, HIENS and Prow,
Executioners are we now!

sang the youngsters. And Wolf noticed that Lucie Tachezy's lips were still half open, the way his tongue had left them, and the look in her half-closed eyes wasn't revulsion but desire. Good heavens, he said to himself, that one loves me too! For the first time he realized how frustrated this sensual woman must be beside the ascetic Doctor Tachezy, and from his groin came a flash to his brain, like a neon sign at the gates of Paradise, depicting a magical triangle of (1) the womanly charms of Lucie, (2) the boyish comeliness of Margaret, and above them (3) Lizinka's girlish beauty, and in its geometrical center Wolf himself, voicing the astonished—because he knew the positive answer—question of *Why not all three?*

Vos habe-ebi-it huuu-uu-mus! . . .

Simon was vomiting in the washroom for the third time—they had decided to leave it to him and had hung a sign labeled SIMON on the door. His father had fallen into a wheezing sleep on the bed of the guillotine after they had cleared away the remains of the female *dujka,* because at this time of

62

night, the prison was locked, as they had all been warned beforehand. There were less than three hours left till five o'clock. When Wolf, overheated from dancing with the lovely—she had forgotten her other worries when she found twice in succession that her future son-in-law could carry her over to that longed-for shore even on the dance floor—Lucie, opened the curtains and the window, he not only saw a strip of pale sky over the opposite wing, with several of its windows also illuminated (the lights were always on when the "waiting rooms" were occupied; that was where Albert would be making his debut next week) but he also heard the first twitter of the dawn concert. In spite of the fact that he had drunk an incredible amount of champagne, or perhaps precisely for that reason, his head was as light as a circus balloon and his thoughts as transparent. He looked around.

He had to smile as Karli, who had scarcely moved away from the electric chair all evening, took his skinning knife and sliced off yet another piece of dripping pork, with the look of a person who knows his eyes are a great deal larger than his stomach. Wolf's satisfied gaze moved on to the youngsters and from one of them to another, as they played—without Simon but with their parents—a game of Meat. Before him was a brand-new generation, without prejudices, without respect, and without senti-mentality—and hence also without the doubts and reservations that had so complicated his life. To them, the strife that existed between generations, ideologies, political systems, and world powers appeared like the raging of bubbles in a glass of champagne; for them, not just their class exercises, but all of life was a game, one big game of Meat, in which the only rule was to stay in the game.

He was pleased to observe Mr. Alexander carefully reassembling the garotte, after he had disassembled it piece by piece to get at the stripped screw, and he was even more pleased to see Doctor Tachezy holding a tray with the nuts and bolts for him; the truce between the two men seemed to be the sort that is not far from peace. With mild embarrass-ment, Wolf looked toward the scaffold where two heads leaned close together, the white head and the dark one of the two women at the base of his triangle. Their harmony indicated that his geometry was developing reassuringly; all the same, though, for the last few hours he had been unable to shake the feeling that Margaret harbored an emotion stronger than friendship toward the dark one and toward—twice he caught her stroking Lizinka with the same tenderness with which she used to caress his body in the days of the bathtub—the golden one; it was as if she had broken through some sort of barrier and liberated herself not only from a legal bond, but also from the constraints of not just his but even of her own personality. A light flickered on in his mind: I hope she doesn't lure those two away . . . He laughed at the lengths to which his pleasantly fatigued imagination was taking him. But where is . . . ? He rubbed his eyes and then, through the veil of cigarette smoke, he saw his

Lizinka. She was leaning against the WOTAN and staring at Simsa. Wolf wanted to reassure her of his presence and to feel the warmth of hers. He walked over to her, sat down on the end of the mechanism, and

291

put his arm (poor Masin, you never had a chance!) around her shoulders. Without waiting for his question, she shook her head.

On a sudden impulse he looked at his watch and was astonished to find that it was just three minutes short of a quarter to three. Exactly one week before, the tiny explosion of a pyjama button had launched a new epoch in his life. He no longer doubted that with his very first salvo he had succeeded in shooting down that damned red rider, the cause of problems in one marriage already, and in establishing that droplet of hope that was now growing as an embryo which on the first (he could forecast it to the minute) day of spring would emerge as a great little man to whom he would turn over all his memories and dreams, his work and his plans. He had to hold himself in check so as not to kiss her then and there; instead, he lay back on the dark-red surface of the WOTAN and, when she turned around in surprise, he suggested, half joking, half serious, "Lock me in!"

He had kept her after school several times to teach her how to operate the WOTAN, until he was sure that during the demonstration he planned for the opening ceremony of the second year—good heavens, tomorrow I have to get together with Albert and start on the entrance exams—of the school, there would be no doubt as to her coauthorship. He was all the more taken aback when under him

63

the table separated in two; tired as she was, she had absentmindedly pressed the wrong button. He watched her guilty (she is still a child after all, he smiled) expression as she corrected her error: the two sections snapped together, only to impale his coat collar (she pinned me like a butterfly!). The second time she made no mistake, and three steel (they ought to be white, black, and gold) bands circled his ankles, his waist, and his neck.

They were surprised by another salvo of applause, this time more like the beating of the wings (everyone was tired by then) of a bird, but all the more sincere. Before they knew it, they were surrounded by all the others, in fond appreciation of Lizinka's performance. The girl, unaware that she was the center of attention, stood with her hand on the control panel of the WOTAN, her eyes fixed once more on Simsa. She was radiant.

"Lizinka," said Wolf, mildly envious of the attention she was giving a scoundrel who didn't deserve it, and especially not from her, "say something!"

"He never," said Lizinka proudly, "so much as

64

farted."